T0326299

GETTING LUCKY

When they finished eating, Tawny cleared their plates and loaded them into the dishwasher. "Want coffee?" she asked.

"Sure." Truth was he wanted an excuse to hang out.

While she prepared the coffeemaker, he got up and moved behind her.

"I have store-bought cookies for dessert if you're interest—"

Before she could say more, he spun her around and boxed her in against the counter. "This is what I'm interested in." Then he laid his lips on her mouth and kissed her.

Slow at first. But when she kissed him back, he moved over her with the urgency of a man who had been dreaming about this for weeks. Raiding her mouth with his tongue. She tasted so good, like red wine and heaven. And the way she clung to him made him so hard he feared he'd burst the seams in his fly. So he pressed into her more, hoping for sweet relief. His hands inched under her sweater, finding soft skin.

She pulled at his shirt, untucking it from his waist, and laid her hands against his bare abs, making him hiss in a breath.

Never once did she stop kissing him . . .

Books by Stacy Finz

GOING HOME

FINDING HOPE

SECOND CHANCES

STARTING OVER

GETTING LUCKY

Published by Kensington Publishing Corporation

Getting Lucky

Stacy Finz

LYRICAL SHINE
Kensington Publishing Corp.
www.kensingtonbooks.com

LYRICAL SHINE BOOKS are published by

Kensington Publishing Corp.
119 West 40th Street
New York, NY 10018

All Kensington titles, imprints, and distributed lines are available at special quantity discounts for bulk purchases for sales promotion, premiums, fund-raising, educational, or institutional use.

Special book excerpts or customized printings can also be created to fit specific needs. For details, write or phone the office of the Kensington Sales Manager: Kensington Publishing Corp., 119 West 40th Street, New York, NY 10018. Attn. Sales Department. Phone: 1-800-221-2647.

Lyrical Press logo Reg. U.S. Pat. & TM Off.

First Electronic Edition: November 2015
eISBN-13: 978-1-61650-921-7
eISBN-10: 1-61650-921-X

First Print Edition: November 2015
ISBN-13: 978-1-61650-922-4
ISBN-10: 1-61650-922-8

Printed in the United States of America

To my sister, Laura Finz.

ACKNOWLEDGMENTS

A special thanks to my agent, Melissa Jeglinski of the Knight Agency, for helping me bring the best out in Lucky.

Thanks to Steve Simoneau for providing food inspiration.

Thanks to my beta readers: Jaxon Van Derbeken, Wendy Miller, and, as always, my family.

And to everyone who made this book happen: editor John Scognamiglio, production editor Rebecca Cremonese, and all the other folks at Kensington Publishing who worked tirelessly on the entire series. Thank you.

Chapter 1

"Come back here!" Lucky propped up on both elbows and watched Raylene shimmy into her denim skirt. "What's the rush?"

"I promised my parents I'd be back in time for dinner."

Lucky reached over and grabbed his watch off the nightstand. "It's still early."

"I have to shower and change," she said, pulling a minuscule tank top over her head.

"Shower here." *With me.*

Raylene scanned the single-wide trailer, and Lucky could've sworn she grimaced. Granted, it wasn't fancy—a tin can, really, with a few pieces of shabby furniture Lucky had rummaged from some of the outbuildings on his property. But he got the bed new and the place was clean. And temporary. Pretty soon his construction crew would finish converting one of the bunkhouses into his office and private quarters.

"It's best if I get home before anyone sees me in this." Raylene looked down at the miniskirt that barely covered the dental floss she called underwear and pulled on her cowboy boots.

The slutty getup might've gotten him off with the buckle bunnies he typically consorted with, but not Raylene. On her it didn't sit right with him. It made her seem cheap.

"Don't you think it's time to take us public?" Lucky swung his legs over the side of the bed, found his Levi's on the floor, and shoved them on, buttoning the fly. Next, he tugged on his ropers.

"We've been over this, Lucky."

"Yeah, well, I'm tired of all this sneaking around." He'd loved the woman since middle school, and was getting weary of the clandestine bootie calls. Sometime soon he'd like to take her on an actual date.

"I don't want Butch to find out while we're still hashing out the settlement. Besides, there's my father and your mother to consider."

Neither would be happy that Lucky and Raylene were seeing each other. A lot of bad blood between the two families.

Raylene pushed Lucky back onto the bed and straddled his lap with her long, tanned legs. "Try to be patient, baby. For me." She pouted prettily and then kissed him until he was snaking his hands under her top, reaching for the good stuff. "I've gotta go, Lucky."

"Ten more minutes." He moaned, hard as rock.

"Uh-uh. Daddy'll be home soon."

"For Christ's sake, Raylene, you're twenty-eight years old. A grown woman."

"You know how he is."

Yeah, Lucky knew Raylene's old man. A prick and a bigot. "Then go now. Because in another minute I'll have you on your back."

She giggled, reminding Lucky of their teens, when she used to flirt with him mercilessly. Of course, then she'd been dating Zachary Baze, captain of the football team.

"When's the divorce final?" he asked as she wiggled off of him.

"I'm not sure. Butch is being difficult."

"What the hell does he have to be difficult about? He was screwing your best friend."

She put her finger over his mouth. "Shush. I don't want to talk about it."

"Well, I don't like it, Raylene." He wagged his hands between the two of them. "Going behind everyone's back . . . It feels slimy."

"What do you want me to do, Lucky? Divorces take time. Colorado isn't California."

Lucky didn't know anything about the legalities of divorce in either state, but for the life of him he didn't understand what the holdup was. Raylene and Butch had been legally separated for months now. "I want this to be good between us. I want it to be right."

She bent down and kissed him again. "It is good between us. And nothing has ever felt more right."

"Yeah?" He stood up and wrapped her in his arms. "God, I love you, Raylene."

"I love you too. But if I don't get home . . ."

"Go then," he said, patting her bottom. "When can I see you again?"

"Mama and I are taking a shopping trip to San Francisco this weekend. As soon as I get back."

"While you're there, get some clothes that cover you," he said, staring at her ass—the same bubble butt that had filled those itty-bitty uniforms she'd worn while cheering for Nugget High. She bent over, letting her denim skirt ride up, giving him more than just a view of her behind.

He dove for her, but Raylene darted away, laughing.

"They've got a name for girls like you."

"Oh yeah, what's that?" Raylene rucked up her tank top, making a big show of fondling the double D's Butch had bought her. Apparently, the man hadn't thought his wife's natural breasts were big enough. Lucky had liked them just fine.

"I'm going now," Raylene said, putting on one last peep show of her nether regions before racing out the door of the single-wide.

A couple of ranch hands were sitting on the fence, taking a break. Lucky shot them a dirty look when they gaped at Raylene like she was a hooker.

"Call me when you get back, you hear?" he shouted. Raylene hopped up into her truck and peeled off.

The girl had gone a little wild, but Lucky chalked it up to Butch keeping her on a string. She just needed a good man to give her the proper love and respect she deserved.

Lucky's phone vibrated inside his back pocket. Fishing it out, he checked the display and answered when he saw it was his agent.

"Hey, Pete."

"How's the cowboy camp shaping up?"

"It's coming along. I'd hoped to have it up and running by now. But we've run into a few glitches. Nothing insurmountable, though." After ten years on the road, living out of hotels, Lucky had purchased the property with plans to come home and settle here. As fate would have it, Raylene had come home too.

"That's good," Pete said. "Hey, I just wanted to give you a heads-up. A reporter for *Sports Illustrated* is interested in doing a profile on you before the world finals. I know you said you want to lie low for a while to recoup from that fall you took in Billings and to focus on your new business. But this sounds like a great opportunity."

Lucky scratched his head. "Maybe I could give him an hour over the phone." Not too many pro bull riders made it into the pages of *Sports Illustrated.*

"That's the thing. He heard about your cowboy camp and how you're raising rodeo stock up there in the California Sierras, and wants to come up and spend some time with you. He seems to think this new enterprise of yours is a good hook for his story."

"First of all, it's the Sierra. Singular. It means mountain range in Spanish." People were always getting it wrong. "How long would he need? Because, Pete, it's September. I was supposed to open a few months ago. If I want to get this camp off the ground, I don't have a lot of time for schmoozing with a reporter."

"I know. But, hey, being featured in *Sports Illustrated* . . . you can't get better publicity than that."

True that. "Yeah. All right. When does he want to come?"

"I'll check with him and get back to you. Is there a place for him to stay or should I tell him to book a room in Reno?"

"We've got a five-star inn in downtown Nugget. The Lumber Baron. Besides, Reno is a good forty-five-minute drive."

"Let me get a pen. I want to write that down." In the background, Lucky could hear Pete digging through things. "What's the hotel called again?"

"The Lumber Baron. Hold a sec and I'll get you a contact." Lucky searched his phone and ticked off the bed-and-breakfast's number to Pete.

"Great. I'll let him know and will talk to you soon." Pete ended the call.

Lucky needed the distraction of a reporter like he needed a hole in the head. Ordinarily, he never shied away from the press, loving the attention. But he was way behind schedule. Once the snow came—which could be any day now—it would slow construction. The bunkhouses still needed to be winterized and as it turned out, the lodge, which he'd originally thought to be in good shape, needed all kinds of electrical work. Then there was the fact that most city folk didn't want to ride, rope, or wrestle steers in the freezing cold. Lucky hoped to attract Silicon Valley executives interested in using the ranch for corporate team building.

At least in future winters he and the owners of the Lumber Baron planned to team up on various ventures. The inn's event planner,

Samantha Dunsbury—now Breyer—wanted to rent out Lucky's cowboy camp for weddings and other functions where the guests could indulge in their warped vision of ranch life—hayrides and barn dances. It wasn't exactly the rough-and-tumble cowboy camp he'd envisioned, but it would help pay some of the overhead on the ranch. Right now it was paid for with Lucky's winnings from professional bull riding. But at twenty-nine, this would be his last year.

He wasn't getting those ninety- and ninety-five-point rides like he used to. Not with the bulls getting tougher every year. Not when he had a couple of inches of height and thirty to forty pounds on the average bull rider. He'd never been built right for the sport, but he'd had youth and vigor on his side. Now there were younger and stronger contenders.

Lucky planned on the cowboy camp being his next chapter. That and raising prime rodeo stock. So far, though, bull riding, despite the broken bones and bruises, was still paying the bills. He gazed across the ranch, a defunct camp used by church organizations, clubs, and schools for retreats. The place was still in a shambles and nowhere close to welcoming guests.

But when he finally got the cowboy camp off the ground, a *Sports Illustrated* story would be good for business. Pete was right. Lucky couldn't buy better advertising than that.

On his way to the lodge, a massive stack-stone and timber-log building that would serve as the camp's combination mess hall and cantina, an old Jeep Cherokee crawled down his road. He didn't recognize it as belonging to one of his workers. Then again, there were so many of them swarming the place, who could keep their vehicles straight?

Lucky stood to the side of the single-wide, out of sight, shielding his eyes from the sun, as a woman climbed out of the driver's seat. She headed to the trailer door and knocked. He continued to watch her, debating whether to see what she wanted or to scoot on up to the lodge. Occasionally, overzealous fans—usually women—showed up on his doorstep uninvited. Crazy as it was, just being on ESPN was enough to bring all kinds out of the woodwork.

Today, he wasn't in the mood to send one of them packing. But the lady didn't strike him as a groupie. Her clothes were too conservative, for one thing: a skirt that hit midcalf and a nice blouse. It was her boots, though, that caught his attention. Even from yards away he could tell they were quality. Not gaudy, but definitely expensive. And a good chance, custom-made. Not what you would expect from someone driving a beater car.

His curiosity got the better of him and he made his presence known. "Can I help you?"

She jerked up, like he'd caught her off guard, then just stood there staring up at him.

Finally, he stuck out his hand. "Lucky Rodriguez. Were you looking for me?"

The woman shuffled her feet in the dirt and cleared her throat. "You don't remember me, do you?"

"No, ma'am. Should I?"

She didn't say anything, just let her eyes drop to those elegant boots of hers. "Donna Thurston said you lived here now."

He nodded. It wasn't a secret that he'd purchased the old Roland camp and had moved back to Nugget, even if Donna was the biggest mouth in town.

"Could we go inside?" she asked.

Lucky hesitated, but the woman didn't look particularly threatening. Hell, soaking wet she couldn't weigh more than a hundred twenty pounds. There was something desperate about her though, like maybe she was looking for work. "Yeah, come on in."

The door to his bedroom was open and the bed showed signs of his and Raylene's recent lovemaking. He motioned to a ratty plaid couch and the woman took a seat while he chose the chair across from her.

"How can I help you, Miss . . . ?"

"Tawny."

Something about her rang a vague bell with him. But after a few seconds of searching his brain, Lucky couldn't place the name.

She stared down at her hands, which were locked together like a fist.

"Would you like a drink?" Lucky asked.

"Water would be nice."

He got up, hunted through his cupboards for a decent glass, filled it from the tap, and brought it to her.

"Thanks." When she looked up he noticed that her eyes were green. They too sparked an elusive memory, but he still couldn't quite pinpoint it.

She was pretty enough that if they'd crossed paths he would've remembered. The boots too. On closer inspection, Lucky thought they were some of the finest leatherwork he'd ever seen. Lots of hand-tooled flowers and a monogram. As a world-champion bull rider, Lucky knew good boots when he saw them. And those must've cost a boatload. Strange, because she gave off the vibe that she was down on her luck. Sad. And tired.

"So what can I do for you, Miss Tawny?"

"Just Tawny," she said. "Tawny's my first name."

Didn't tawny mean orange or brown? The thought popped into his head that her name should've been Jade, and again he got the distinct impression that he knew her from somewhere. He watched, waiting for her to state her business, then grew impatient when she just sat there.

"You looking for work, Tawny?"

She jerked her head in surprise. "No. Why would you think that?"

Clearly, he'd insulted her, though he didn't know why. Nothing shameful about needing work. Until Lucky had made it big riding the rodeo circuit, he took any job that came his way, to put food on the table. His mother's wages working at the Rock and River Ranch had never been enough.

"Unless you're looking for rodeo stock, I can't imagine what else I could do for you," he said.

"My daughter needs a stem cell transplant," she blurted. "I need your stem cells."

Lucky registered surprise. That was a new one.

As a high-profile athlete, he'd been asked for a good many things. Autographs, pictures, bull-riding lessons, and yes, even bodily fluids. But never once had anyone requested his cells. The woman was clearly a nut job. He rose from his chair, walked to the door, and held it open for her.

He wanted to tell her to have Donna lose his address, but tried to remain as polite as possible. "I think you've got the wrong cowboy, ma'am."

She didn't budge. "I'll go to your mother then."

"My mother? What does she have to do with this?" Where the hell did this broad get off?

"Katie has acute myeloid leukemia," Tawny said, and her bottom lip trembled. "The chemotherapy didn't work. The radiation didn't work and the cancer is back. You're my only hope."

Lucky stood by the door, wondering if she was just trying to scam him for money. She certainly wouldn't be the first. But his earlier assessment that she was crazy seemed more on the mark.

"How's that?" he asked, unable to help himself.

"Your HLA antigens have the best chance of matching Katie's."

Oh yeah, she was *loco* all right, and he'd just been beamed into an episode of *Star Trek*. "Katie's your daughter?"

"Yes." Tawny sniffled, and Lucky went into the bathroom and grabbed her a roll of toilet paper. It probably wasn't smart turning his back on her, but the woman was crying.

He shouldn't, but asked anyway. "How old is she?"

"Nine." Tawny locked eyes with him long and hard, like the kid's age should've meant something to him. It was slightly unnerving, because when she did that she looked saner than shit.

"And you think I might have these special . . . What did you call them?"

"HLA antigens."

"Right," he said. "And that would be . . . uh . . . because I ride bulls for a living?"

"No." She stood up. "That would be because you're her father."

Chapter 2

"What the hell are you talking about?" Lucky said, but Tawny could see the wheels in his head turning and sudden recognition blazing in his eyes. "Thelma Wade? You're Thelma Wade. But you don't look like Thelma Wade."

That's because as far as Tawny was concerned, Thelma Wade didn't exist. That girl had been puny, plain, painfully shy, and madly in love with Lucky Rodriguez, who'd obviously forgotten her existence the minute after he'd slept with her.

"For the sake of my business, I changed my name to Tawny."

"What's your business—shaking down wealthy bull riders?"

"I don't want your money. I want your stem cells."

"Fine, give me proof that the girl is mine and we'll work something out," Lucky said, but clearly thought she was either mentally ill or a con artist.

Tawny supposed her delivery could've been better—like perhaps she should've eased into telling him he had a daughter with a life-threatening disease, instead of dumping it on him like a ton of bricks. But he'd ruffled her.

At least he'd finally realized who she was and couldn't dismiss her out of hand. Though it had certainly taken him long enough to remember her. Sure, she didn't remotely resemble the seventeen-year-old girl Lucky had left in Nugget. But come on!

Tawny grabbed her phone out of her handbag and cued up a picture of Katie to show him.

"Nope," Lucky said, blocking her. "This ain't my first time to this particular rodeo, Thelma . . . Tawny, or whatever you go by now. You know how many women have tried to jack me up like this? So I don't want to see any photographs. All I want is a paternity test. Have your lawyer talk to mine."

He went into the kitchenette, pulled a pen out of a drawer, scribbled something on a piece of paper, and handed it to her. "Here's his contact info. I'd appreciate if you go through him for now."

"Look, we don't have to tell anyone." She didn't have time to take offense at his insinuation that she was a liar and a grifter. Her daughter's life depended on him. "If you're a match, the entire procedure shouldn't take too long."

"So you're telling me that our one and only night together produced a baby and that you waited until I came back to Nugget—until the child is nine and has cancer—to tell me all this? It's hard to swallow."

Tawny blinked back tears. "If you'd bothered to take my calls, you would've known about Katie."

"What calls? I never got any calls from you."

"I left messages and I emailed the address on your website. You never got back to me."

"Thelma, my mother lives in the same goddamned town as you. Did it ever occur to you that I didn't get any of those messages and that she was a direct pipeline to me?" His voice trembled with anger and Tawny backed away from him, although he made a good case.

"Given the reasons why you fled Nugget, I figured it was best not to tell anyone, especially your mother." She'd done it for him. Because her stupid teenage heart had convinced her that she was in love with the cowboy and she hadn't wanted to ruin his life.

"Do me a favor, Thelma. Call my lawyer." And with that he ushered her out of his trailer.

Fine. Tawny would do just that. She'd even hire her own attorney if that's what it would take to get Lucky on board. Anything for her daughter. She might feel guilty for springing Katie and the leukemia on him the way she had, but that wouldn't stop her from doing what she needed to do.

Yes, perhaps she should've tried harder to reach Lucky nine years ago. But at the time she'd done what she thought best. Especially since Lucky had left town under a cloud, and she knew if she told him about Katie he'd come home—even if it meant facing scandal. And possibly criminal charges. Because the old Lucky Rodriguez wasn't a man to shirk his responsibilities. Growing up, she'd worshipped the boy who'd worked any odd job he could find to make ends meet. But away from Nugget, he'd made something of himself. Lucky was the most famous person to ever come from their little ranching and railroad town.

So even when Katie got sick and Tawny was drowning in debt from putting her business on hold during long stays at the Ronald McDonald House while Katie got treatment at Stanford, she'd never asked Lucky for help.

But this was different. Lucky was the best and possibly the only chance Katie had to eliminate the cancer. Since chemotherapy and radiation failed, Katie needed the cancer cells in her bone marrow replaced with healthy ones. Siblings were typically the best candidates for a transplant, but Katie didn't have any. Biological parents were second on the list, yet Tawny hadn't been a match. There weren't enough proteins on the surface of her cells that corresponded with Katie's.

If it turned out that Lucky didn't have enough matching proteins, the doctors would have to look at other relatives and even strangers, decreasing the chances for a successful transplant. That's why Lucky was so critical.

Tawny headed back to town and swung by the Nugget Market to pick up a pint of ice cream for Katie. The girl barely ate anymore. Ethel, who owned the grocery store with her husband, Stu, stood behind the cash register.

"How you doing, Tawny? How's that girl of yours?"

"Feeling better." Tawny gave a wan smile and paid for the French vanilla, Katie's favorite.

Ethel bagged the ice cream and said, "If there is anything you need, you let us know, you hear?"

"Thank you, Ethel."

The town had been good to her. First when her father had suffered from emphysema and she'd had to drop out of high school to take care of him. And later with Katie.

Tawny still remembered coming home from the hospital after giving birth, and finding a giant gift basket of baby clothes and boxes of diapers on her doorstep. Later she'd learned that Donna Thurston, owner of the Bun Boy drive-through, had organized the gift.

With her father gone, it was just her and Katie now. At least the house where she grew up was paid for. It wasn't much, just a two-bedroom, one-bath Craftsman in a modest part of town, but it was sufficient. And the old detached garage in the back served as a perfect studio for her business. Before her father had died, as sick as he was, he'd managed to install a heating system in the space for Tawny so she could work well into the night, even in winter.

She pulled into her driveway alongside a truck she didn't recognize. Maybe the babysitter's boyfriend was home, visiting from the University of Nevada.

But when she walked into the house, Tawny found Colin Burke on his back, under her kitchen sink. The furniture maker was also Nugget's resident handyman.

"Hey," he said, tightening a pipe with a wrench. "Harlee mentioned that your garbage disposal wasn't working."

"Not for a long time," she said. "I kept meaning to call you, but money's been tight."

"Yeah, well, this one's on the house. I fixed your tub, too. That leak must've cost you a fortune in water bills."

"Thank you, Colin. I'll pay you as soon as I can."

"No worries." He got up and collected his tools. "The *Nugget Tribune* is making my wife a fortune."

Tawny laughed. Harlee had recently taken over the struggling newspaper, turning it into a successful news website. Still, Tawny doubted that the website was making anything near a fortune. "I really appreciate it."

Katie came in. "Hi, Mommy."

"How you feeling, baby?" Out of habit, Tawny felt her head. Cool to the touch, thank God. "Could you put this ice cream in the freezer for me?"

Colin grabbed up his tool chest and headed for the door. "Next time you need a home repair, call me. Financially, things are good for Harlee and me. I like to pay it forward when I can."

Her throat clogged, so she just nodded. After Colin left, Tawny paid the babysitter and made alphabet soup for Katie. They ate together at the small table in the kitchen nook. The same place Tawny used to study for the GED to get her high school credential. Someday she'd like to go to college. But with Katie, and trying to keep her business on track, school would have to take a backseat.

After dinner, Tawny got the scrap of paper with Lucky's lawyer's contact information out of her purse. She knew the 415 area code was San Francisco. It was too late to call now. First thing in the morning, she told herself. She didn't know the law regarding transplants and biological fathers, but she would move heaven and earth to get Lucky tested to see if he was a match.

If worse came to worst she would appeal to Cecilia. The woman would likely be angry that Tawny had kept her granddaughter from her all these years. But she'd make Lucky do the right thing. Everyone in Nugget knew that Lucky doted on his mother and that Cecilia Rodriguez had raised him on her own. Just like Tawny had done with Katie.

She hoped it wouldn't come to that. The last thing Tawny wanted to do was make trouble and put her daughter in the middle of it. Tawny just wanted Katie's health back and to live her life in the same quiet obscurity she had for the last twenty-eight years.

Lucky didn't know what to believe. Thelma Wade's transplant story was so far-fetched that it might actually be true. But a daughter? They'd only been together one time. It was the night after everything had gone sideways with Raylene Rosser at the Rock and River Ranch, which her parents owned. Lucky had spent much of the evening getting drunk at the crappy little park near Thelma's house and wound up having sex with her behind the swing set in the wee hours of the morning. Afterward, he blew out of town, hoping that with him gone, the dust would settle between his mom and the Rossers. She needed her job at their ranch. Badly.

The thing about Thelma was she never would've struck him as a gold digger. As a girl, she'd barely said boo to anyone in middle school. In fact, by the time high school rolled around, Thelma had disappeared. She'd dropped out because of family problems.

The truth was no one noticed her even when she was in school, so no one had missed her when she was gone. That night in the park had been a mistake, and he'd forgotten the whole incident until today. Until she'd shown up on his property.

Tawny? What the hell kind of name was that anyway? It sounded like something a stripper would call herself. She had said something about changing it for business. Maybe little Thelma Wade was an exotic dancer now. And a bloodsucking hustler.

As he pulled up in front of his mother's house, a Nugget police SUV backed out of her driveway and turned around in the cul-de-sac. He didn't bother to lock his truck, just jumped out and dashed for the back door.

Lucky burst inside to find his mother washing dishes in her stainless steel farm sink. "What's wrong?"

"Nothing, *mijo*. Why should anything be wrong?"

"I just saw a cop leave your house."

"That was Detective Stryker on his dinner break."

"He comes over here for dinner?"

"Sometimes." She looked at him. "Do you have a problem with that?"

"No." Maybe. Lucky wasn't sure how he felt about it.

His whole life Cecilia had been single. Except for his father, who'd taken off as soon as Lucky was born, he couldn't recall his mother ever dating. Weird, because at forty-eight she was still a beautiful, outgoing woman. What was odder, though, was the fact that Jake Stryker was having dinner with his mother and it hadn't gotten back to Lucky. In Nugget, people's love lives, or lack thereof, may as well have been splashed across a billboard. People here liked to gossip. That's why he wanted to come clean about him and Raylene, since their relationship would leak out anyway. And the conjecture about why he'd left all those years ago would start all over again. Nothing he could do about that.

"Are you hungry?" Cecilia asked.

"I could eat." He smelled pot roast.

Sure enough, she ladled him a large portion of beef and potatoes from the pot on her stove. As long as Lucky could remember, there had always been something good simmering in that pot.

"What are you doing?" Lucky watched her chop vegetables.

"Making you a salad to go with it. You need greens." She put a bowl and a bottle of dressing in front of him on the big center island.

"Thanks, Ma. So Jake Stryker, huh?" He was still digesting that piece of news.

"We're friends. Don't make more of it than it is. How's progress on the cowboy camp?"

Lucky let out a long sigh. "Slow, if you want to know the truth. I wanted to be up and running by June, and here it is September. And now some writer from *Sports Illustrated* is coming up to interview me. It seems like every time I turn around there's a new distraction to keep me from my goal." Like today. "And in December I'll have to leave for Vegas." For the Professional Bull Riders Inc. Built Ford Tough World Finals.

"*Ay Dios mio*, you're getting too old to be banged around like that." He knew she was talking about the concussion he'd suffered in Billings. Between the head injury and the cracked ribs, he'd been slow to recover.

"It'll probably be my last world championship for the PBR. I'd like to go out a winner."

"You are a winner." She kissed him on the cheek. "You don't need another one of those buckles to prove anything."

"No, but another one would go a long way to putting my cowboy camp on the map. Not to mention that the money would help pay the bills."

Cecilia creased her brows. "Are you having money troubles?"

He laughed. "Nope. Not even close. But you can never have too much green."

"I think you feel that way because you grew up poor. But if you ever need money, Lucky, I could sell the house."

Lucky eyed the grand kitchen. He'd bought her the rancher because her whole life she'd worked hard, taking other people's orders in order to care for him. Now it was her turn to be taken care of. "Don't be crazy, Ma. I have enough for a lifetime." He pulled her in for a hug. "The pot roast is good."

"I'm glad you like it." She sat next to him.

"Did you know that Thelma Wade changed her name to Tawny?" Lucky tried to sound casual.

"Of course. She did it when she opened her boot business."

"Boot business?"

"You don't know? She makes beautiful custom cowboy boots. A lot of celebrities wear them, even rodeo stars. I would've thought you knew."

Well, that explained Tawny's fancy boots, the ones Lucky had so admired. But it didn't explain why she was driving a piece-of-crap Jeep from the 1990s. "I ran into her today and got the impression she wasn't doing too well." God, he hated lying to his mother.

"Her little girl is very sick. Leukemia."

Shit!

"She has a kid, huh? I hadn't heard she was married."

"She's not. I don't believe Katie's father is in the picture."

"You know the guy?"

"No. That's always been a bit of a mystery, but no one's business but Tawny's."

"You've met the little girl, though?" Lucky asked.

"Maybe once or twice. They spend a lot of time in the Bay Area for Katie's treatments. I didn't know you and Tawny were back in touch. What a crush she had on you when you two were little. Used to follow you around like a lamb. Such a nice girl, and you barely gave her the time of day," Cecilia chided. Lucky knew the subtext, though. *You were too busy getting into trouble with Raylene Rosser.*

"We just happened to run into each other. I barely recognized her, though," he said as calmly as he could, but was starting to panic. What if the kid really was his? "I've gotta get going, Ma."

"You just got here," Cecilia said, and took his empty plate to the sink.

"I know, but I thought I'd stop by McCreedy Ranch before it gets dark and check out some stock Clay wants to unload." Okay, he'd say a few Hail Marys.

"All right. Will I see you tomorrow?"

"Yeah," he said. "I'll be over."

On his way out he tried to remember where Tawny lived. It had been ten years, yet he found her tiny bungalow with little effort. He still knew the town like he did the back of a bull.

He parked across the street and sat behind the wheel, feeling edgy about going in. About seeing the little girl who may or may not be his. *Nine goddamn years.* Finally, he climbed Tawny's porch stairs and rang the bell. He could hear movement inside and a few seconds later a young girl opened the door.

"Hello." She looked up at him with big brown eyes. Eyes too large for her pale, gaunt face.

Lucky studied her. "You must be Katie."

"Mm-hmm. Who are you?"

"A friend of your mom's. She home?"

"Yes. Would you like to come in?"

Tawny needed to talk to the kid about inviting strangers into their home. "Sure."

He crossed the threshold and gazed around the front room. There was an unfinished puzzle on the coffee table and the TV was on. The furniture, a set of mismatched chairs and a couch, looked pretty lived-in. Tawny came out of one of the side doors in sweats, her head wrapped in a towel.

"Hey." He bobbed his chin at her.

She quickly turned to Katie. "Go brush your teeth and get ready for bed, baby."

Curious about him, the girl seemed reluctant to go. Tawny gave her a look—the kind Cecilia used to give Lucky when she meant business—and the kid scampered off.

"What are you doing here?"

"I can't tell if she looks like me."

"Shush." Tawny grabbed his arm and pulled him out of the house. "I don't want her to hear you."

"Why?"

She glared at him like he was a fool. "Why do you think?"

"Beats the hell out of me. Unless you're lying."

She gave him another venomous glare. "Did you just come over here to tell me what a liar I am?"

Lucky blew out a breath. "I came over because I wanted to see Katie for myself. How long has she been sick?"

"She was diagnosed when she was five."

"It's bad, isn't it?" The girl looked so ashen that it broke his heart. No little kid should have to go through that.

Tawny nodded, and Lucky could tell that she was trying to keep it together. Even if it turned out that the woman was the world's biggest liar, Tawny was looking out for her daughter, like any good mother would do. His heart broke a little for her, too.

"Why didn't you try to get ahold of me when she was diagnosed?" Lucky asked.

"I figured you weren't interested in returning my phone calls when I was pregnant; why would you suddenly call me back five years later?"

"Tawny, I never got your messages. If I'd known that I got you in trouble, I would've done the right thing."

"You didn't get me in trouble. You got me pregnant. And until now, I didn't need you."

"Did it ever occur to you that I deserved to know that I had a child, whether you needed me or not? Did it ever occur to you that Katie deserved her father? What have you told her?"

"Look, I don't have time to do this now. Katie's waiting for me." He stabbed his finger at her. "You better make time to do this. You dropped a goddamn bomb on me today."

"Does that mean you're willing to help?"

He paced the porch. "That's the thing, Tawny. I would've helped whether she was my daughter or not. Because that's what people do. But out of the blue you tell me I have a kid after all these years . . . that's she's sick and needs this stem cell transplant. It's . . . I'm just reeling a little here."

She swallowed hard. "I know. It's a lot to take in. But I don't want to do this with Katie here."

"Then I suggest you show up at my place tomorrow and explain. Merely leaving a couple of lousy messages for a guy who's supposedly the father of your child doesn't cut it, Tawny. You should've done more."

"I had my reasons."

"Well, I'd like to hear them. Tomorrow."

She gave him a faint nod and slipped back inside.

Chapter 3

Tawny examined her latest project with a discerning eye. Each attraction on the boots' California vintage-style map—the Golden Gate Bridge had been particularly demanding—she'd carved by hand. Samantha Dunsbury, who'd recently married Nate Breyer, co-owner of the local Lumber Baron Inn, had chosen the design. Apparently, the Connecticut transplant wanted to show off her Golden State spirit.

The boots were black leather and the maps—yellow overlays with orange, blue, and tan icons—reminded Tawny of one of those kitschy "Greetings from California" postcards. Tawny had never done anything like the boots and couldn't stop admiring each hand-tooled detail. Grapes and oranges in the center of the map to denote California's rich agricultural heritage. The Hollywood sign to mark Los Angeles. A surfer for San Diego. Redwood trees covered the northern tip of the map. The Lumber Baron, a symbol of Nugget, sat close to the Nevada border. And a burst of orange poppies, California's official flower, decorated each boot's toe.

The boots were showstoppers, and Sam was paying beaucoup bucks. Tawny desperately needed the cash. From consultation to completion it typically took five months to make a pair of custom boots, especially ones this detailed. She usually worked on several pairs at once and had a few pat styles that were big sellers that she could knock out quickly. Still, it wasn't like she raked it in. But her clients paid top dollar and were extremely loyal.

For a special customer like Clay McCreedy's new wife, Emily, Tawny had worked day and night to make sure her boots were done in time for her wedding. She owed it to Clay's dad, the late Tip Mc-Creedy. He'd been Tawny's first customer and had kicked off her career. The influential rancher had worn her boots to every cattle auction and rodeo in the West.

And thank goodness her boots had become so in demand that her clients were willing to wait. Because over the last four years, they'd done a lot of waiting. Katie's medical issues had to come first, including long hospital stays in Palo Alto.

Unfortunately, the work gaps created a cash flow problem. Not to mention that as a self-employed single mom her health insurance costs were astronomical. And of course there were out-of-pocket expenses. Insurance didn't cover everything.

Katie stuck her head inside Tawny's studio. "Mommy, the Marcums are here."

"Okay. Coming. You dressed warm enough?" Although they were experiencing one of Northern California's famous Indian summers, the afternoons could get nippy, especially in the high desert.

"Yeah. I'm bringing my jacket."

Tawny made her way around her cutting table and leather samples to greet the Marcums. The couple had been an enormous help to Tawny, including Katie in their family activities on weekends and on various school nights so she could work.

"You've got your boots on." Tawny had made them for Katie after her last radiation treatment. Pink with silver hearts.

"Yep," Katie said. She'd tucked her skinny jeans into them and looked so beautiful and grown-up that Tawny couldn't resist snapping a picture with her phone.

She followed her daughter out to the backyard and unlatched the side gate. "You have everything?"

Katie nodded and Tawny watched her climb into the Marcums' minivan.

"Thanks for taking her." Tawny leaned against the passenger-side window and peered inside to make sure Katie had buckled up.

"It's our pleasure," Cindy Marcum said. "We'll probably grab dinner after the movie if that's okay?"

"Sure. You have my cell phone number, right?"

"I do," Cindy said, well aware of Katie's medical condition. "Don't worry, I'll text you a couple of times from Reno."

"Thank you." Cindy's husband backed the van out and Tawny waved goodbye.

She watched them drive away, then went inside to change, settling on a pair of jeans with bling on the back pockets and a Western blouse she'd scooped up on sale at the Farm Supply store. She finished off the outfit with one of her hand-tooled belts and red boots. For some reason she wanted Lucky to see her at her best. The man had only gotten better with age, and at eighteen he'd been damned fine to begin with.

She'd worshipped him all through adolescence, even though he hadn't known she was alive. He was too busy chasing after Raylene Rosser, the meanest girl in town. But like the rest of Nugget, Lucky had only seen Raylene's sweet façade. The girl voted most likely to be a beauty queen and have her own morning talk show. Kelly Ripa II.

Tawny had seen Raylene bopping around Nugget in her new Ford F-150. Word on the street was that her husband, a wealthy Denver cattleman, had dumped her for her best friend and she'd come home to lick her wounds. Tawny thought there was probably more to the story.

In the bathroom she fixed her hair, put on a little makeup, and headed for her truck. She didn't have Lucky's phone number, but the sooner they dealt with each other, the sooner he could be tested to see if he'd be a good donor match for Katie.

No one was more surprised than she when he'd bought the old Roland summer camp with plans to turn it into a dude ranch. After what had happened ten years ago, she never thought he'd come back. At least not for good. But Cecilia was here. Everyone knew that Lucky had bought his mother that big house on Mule Deer Lane.

Tawny looked at her gas gauge and, as usual, it was almost on empty. Before hopping on the highway, she cruised into the Nugget Gas and Go to fill up. Griffin Parks was in one of the bays with his head under a hood, but came over to the pumps.

"Hey," he said. "I've been meaning to drop by. When's a good time? I want a pair of boots."

Ever since Katie's leukemia had come back, a lot of the townsfolk had been buying boots. They knew she wouldn't take charity. Instead, they came to her studio to purchase seconds and samples.

"Really?" Her lips curved up in a suspicious grin, having never seen him in any footwear other than motorcycle boots. He was definitely more James Dean than John Wayne.

He smiled back, and Lordy, the man was good-looking—and rich as a king. The summer before last, he'd come into Nugget and bought the Gas and Go and Sierra Heights, a bankrupt gated community on the outskirts of town. But you'd never know it. Griffin was salt of the earth and worked as hard as everyone else did in Nugget. If it hadn't been a known fact that he pined after the police chief's sister, she might've been tempted to go after him. Although Tawny had never been any good in the love department. Too shy to flirt and too busy to date.

That's okay. All she needed was Katie.

"Yeah, really," he said. "I think I'd rock a pair of shit-kickers."

He'd rock anything. "Then come over anytime. I'm sure there are a couple of pairs that have your name on them."

"How's Katie?"

"She's doing okay." And hopefully would be healthy soon if Lucky turned out to be a match.

"You need anything, you let me know. I'm serious, Tawny."

She had to turn away before he saw her mist up, but managed to choke out a thank-you. Tawny didn't know how it was in other places; Nugget was the only place she'd ever lived. But people here overflowed with kindness.

With her tank full, she headed toward the old camp. She'd forgotten how beautiful the drive was. Although Lucky's property was only a few miles from town, the landscape changed here from deep forest to rolling hills. Cattle country. In the winter, when the fields were blanketed with snow, ranchers trucked their herds to the Central Valley or to warmer climates in Nevada. But now the land was dotted with Angus and Herefords and breeds Tawny didn't even know the names of.

When she got to Lucky's, the place was alive with construction workers. Hammering, sawing, lots of sweaty men eyeing her inquisitively. Surprised they worked on Saturdays, she nodded at a few in greeting and made her way to Lucky's single-wide. No one answered, and after standing there a while, wondering whether she should go in search of him or go home, a guy wearing a tool belt and goggles took pity on her and directed her to the lodge. That's where she found a shirtless Lucky swinging a hammer. His arms were ropey with muscle and his shoulders had doubled in width since he was a teen. It was strange seeing him again after all these years, no longer a boy but a man. Then again, he'd never been like the other boys. There had always been a maturity about Lucky that had separated him from the pack. She had a fleeting memory of him picking her for his partner in a silly square-dance class, when no one else would.

"Thelma's got more hair on her arms than Grendel," one of the boys had announced to the entire sixth-grade class. They'd just gotten done reading the *Story of Beowulf,* and the kid's pronouncement sent a chorus of laughter through the room, sealing Tawny's rep as class loser.

But then Lucky had squinted at the little jerk as if to say *I'll be kicking your ass later,* brushed past him, and offered Tawny his arm. That's when Lucky Rodriguez had first become her hero.

She took in a deep breath, walked a few more steps into the room, and made her presence known. Lucky stopped hammering and gave her a long perusal.

"We should go someplace more private—and quieter," he said as power tools screeched.

"What are you doing with this place?" she asked, taking a turn around the room and staring up at the open-beam ceilings and the gigantic fireplace. "It's nice."

"It'll double as a cantina for the cowboy camp and a banquet hall for events." He seemed anxious to get to their business, but she was curious about the place. For years it had been vacant, the owners deciding that it was more lucrative to lease the land to neighboring ranches as grazing pasture than to run retreats.

She supposed Lucky's bull-riding celebrity status would attract a wealthier clientele than church and school groups.

Lucky grabbed his T-shirt off a sawhorse, pulled it over his head, and led her to another outbuilding. Reaching in his pocket for a key, he unlocked the door and let them inside.

"What's this?" she asked.

"When it's done it'll be my office and apartment. Where's Katie?"

"She went to the movies with a friend." Tawny glanced at her phone to make sure she had enough bars in case Cindy tried to call.

"In her condition, is that okay?"

"As long as she stays warm and isn't out for too long. She wants to be like all the other kids and I want things to be as normal for her as possible until we find a donor." Between the chemo and radiation, Katie had missed out on enough of her childhood already.

There was no furniture in the room, so Lucky motioned for her to take a seat on one of the staircase steps. "After I left you last night I did a little research on the Internet. We can get a paternity test in Quincy. I just need a swab from the inside of Katie's cheek."

Tawny nodded. She already knew that.

Lucky joined her on the staircase. "Why didn't you try harder to get ahold of me, Tawny? Why didn't you go to my mother?"

She sat there quiet for a few seconds, then said, "I didn't want to make trouble for you, Lucky. After what happened at the Rossers' I didn't think it would help your situation for people to know that you got me pregnant that night."

Lucky blew out a sigh. "I suspect not. But you should've looked out for yourself. And from what I can tell, you could've used my help over the years."

"I didn't need your stem cells until now. Katie went into remission after the chemo. We were fine until two months ago. That's when the cancer came back. The doctors thought radiation might work. It didn't."

"I'm sorry." He started to reach for her hand and seemed to think better of it. "I wish I had known. I could've been there for her. And from the looks of things, you could've used my money and my support."

"I don't need your money. I have a thriving business."

Lucky cocked his brows. "Your car and house tell a different story."

"There was a time, Lucky Rodriguez, when my car and house would've been more than you could've dreamed of."

He flinched. "That may have been true once upon a time, but not anymore. Okay, assume for the sake of argument that you didn't need me. Did it ever occur to you that you were depriving me of a daughter, or your daughter of a father? And how about my mother of a grandchild?"

Tawny sighed. "You think your mother would've celebrated the news that on the same day you were accused of raping the richest girl in town, you knocked up poor Thelma Wade? That sure would've helped the Rodriguez reputation, don't you think?"

"You know damn well I didn't rape Raylene."

"I know it, you know it, Raylene knows it, but what about the rest of the town if the mighty Rossers had decided to press charges? Or run your mother out of Nugget? And don't think for one minute if they'd known about you and me that night, they wouldn't have done it just to be vindictive. Because those people are mean as snakes." And what about Katie having to live down the allegations that her father was a rapist?

"Raylene would've told the truth," he said.

"Yeah, because she was so good at standing up for you at the time." And if Raylene had known that Lucky was screwing around with Tawny, she would've called for a lynch mob just out of jealousy.

"She was a kid, Tawny. Afraid of her abusive old man."

That girl wasn't afraid of anyone, but far be it from Tawny to tell him. Clearly Lucky still had a soft spot for the viper.

"Maybe I was wrong, Lucky. Maybe I should've tried harder to tell you. But I was eighteen at the time and scared to death."

"What's your excuse for when you were twenty, twenty-five, or twenty-eight . . . while your daughter was sick?"

He wasn't going to let her off that easy, and Tawny probably deserved his anger. But she'd done what she thought he would've wanted. Kept her mouth shut.

"What did you tell Katie . . . about her father?" Lucky asked.

"The truth. That he didn't know about her and that I couldn't find him." At least half of it was accurate.

"And she's okay with that?"

"She's nine, Lucky. The last four years of her life she's had bigger things to think about."

"If that paternity test comes back positive . . . so help me. My old man ran out on my mother and me. I won't be that man. I won't be him, Tawny. I'll want a part in Katie's life. A big part."

Tawny closed her eyes. For so long it had been just the two of them. Katie was all Tawny had in the world. But if Lucky was the solution to getting her daughter's health back, she'd gladly pay the piper. Even if it meant sharing the most important person in her life with the man who could do the most damage to her heart.

Jake Stryker hung a U-turn on Main Street and flashed his lights. Twenty-one years with LAPD and he'd been reduced to issuing traffic citations. He laughed at the absurdity of it. But honestly, life had never been better. No smog, no traffic, no pissed-off ex-wives showing up on his doorstep, and no homicide scenes so bad that they drove him to the bottom of a bottle.

He had a good job working for the Nugget Police Department and an even better boss. Rhys Shepard might be twenty years his junior, but the kid had a good head on his shoulders, treated Jake with respect, and was fair. And fun. The three-man department—four if you counted Connie, their dispatcher—played basketball together, took turns buying lunch, and laughed a lot. In a town like Nugget the crime wasn't bad enough to make you lose your sense of humor. And that's what Jake had been looking for when he'd been hired on to the small-town police force. That and being able to move full-time into his vacation cabin, where a river full of fresh fish and mountains covered in endless hiking trails were always at his disposal.

Yep, he was living the dream, he thought as he pulled a brand-new Ram Laramie to the side of the road for doing thirty-five in a twenty-five-mile-per-hour business zone. As Jake approached the vehicle it only took him a few moments to realize that the driver was Cecilia's boy. Lucky unrolled his window and handed Jake his license.

"New truck?" Jake asked, and Lucky nodded. "You have trouble reading the speedometer?"

"No, sir. I guess I'm still getting used to the pedals."

Jake laughed. The kid was a smart-ass, but he could appreciate a bit of flippancy every now and again. "You on your way to your mother's?"

"Yes, sir. I hear you've been hanging out there a fair amount yourself."

"That a problem for you?" Jake asked, peering at Lucky over his sunglasses.

"I'm not sure yet. What exactly are your intentions?"

Fair question. "Your mother is a lovely woman. We're getting to know each other. It's all very respectful, Lucky."

Lucky didn't say anything, just held eye contact with Jake.

"How's the cowboy camp coming along?" Jake asked, looking for some neutral ground. "I hear you've got a crew up there today. Even working Saturdays, huh?"

"Yep. You giving me a ticket?"

"Nope. Just a warning this time. For the future, this is a twenty-five-mile-per-hour zone."

"Sorry," Lucky said, and then out of the blue, "You got kids?"

"Five." Jake grinned. "All daughters. Sometimes they come up on weekends. You'll have to meet 'em one day."

"How old?"

"Sixteen, eighteen, twenty, twenty-one, and twenty-four. The oldest, Sarah, is in her second year of law school and Janny graduated from UCSB in June."

"Wow," Lucky said. "You close with them?"

"Those girls are my life. Tara, the baby, loves horses. Maybe the next time she's up, I'll bring her over to your place."

"Yeah. Sure."

Jake tapped the roof of Lucky's truck. "All right then, take it easy in the city limits, you hear? And tell your mother hello for me."

Lucky started his engine and nosed out onto Main. He was a good son, Jake thought. Cecilia had raised him right. She was a fine woman and Jake enjoyed spending time with her. More than he ever thought possible, given his track record. There was a time when he'd played around and had lost three wives in the process. He figured it was a cop's life. It took him a while to grasp that no, it was a lonely life.

He started back for the station when Connie came over the radio.

"Jake, we've got a 10-42 at the Wade place."

"I'm on my way."

It took him less than eight minutes to get there and maneuver around the ambulance blocking the narrow street. He didn't bother knocking, just let himself in the house, where he found two paramedics standing over Katie Wade, who was lying on the couch.

Tawny came up to Jake. "I think I might've overreacted. She was at the movies earlier and ate too much junk food. I freaked out when she started vomiting. I'm sorry."

"No worries." He put his arm around her. "Better to be safe." Jake nudged his head at one of the medics. "How's she doing?"

"No fever, no headaches, no shortness of breath. It's up to you, Tawny. You want us to take her in?"

"I don't know what to do," she said, and took Katie's hand.

"I'm okay, Mommy. Really, I feel fine." Katie sat up. "I don't want to go to the hospital."

Katie looked okay to Jake. Pale, but he'd seen her worse. The poor kid. "We could monitor the situation," he told Tawny, and turned to the little girl. "And if you feel the slightest bit sick, you'll tell your mom, won't you, Katie Bug?"

"I will, I promise."

Jake looked at Tawny.

"All right," she agreed, and the paramedics nodded.

"We're right down the street if you need us," one of them said as he packed up to leave and carted his equipment out to the ambulance.

"I feel stupid," Tawny told Jake.

"This is what we're here for, Tawny. Nothing to feel stupid about." Jake squeezed her shoulder and kept his eye on Katie, who'd gotten up to turn on the TV. He intended to observe her for a bit, even if she appeared to be fine. Well, as fine as a little girl with leukemia could be. "Hey, while I'm here I sure wouldn't mind taking a look at some of those boots you've got. You want to help me pick some out, Katie?"

Tawny's daughter took Jake by the hand and walked him out to the studio, Tawny on their heels. Katie had plenty of pep in her step, nothing to indicate that she needed emergency care.

"Which ones do you like?" Katie asked Jake as he wandered Tawny's studio, perusing racks of boots. All kinds of boots—everything from classic cowhide to exotic skins.

"Whoo-wee. I like them all. You got any in an eleven, Tawny?"

"You like the skins?" She pulled down a couple of pairs from the shelf.

"I love the skins." He took the black ostrich ones and sat on a bench to try them on.

"I like those," Katie said, and her face seemed to take on a little color, which was good.

"Wow, they're comfortable." He got up and walked across the room. It was as if they were molded to his feet. "What, someone forget to pick these up?"

"No," Tawny said, and smiled. "I was experimenting with the leather, which came from a different vendor than I typically use. I can sell them to you for a hundred bucks."

Jake looked at her. "I'd be lucky to get a pair of boots like this for six hundred."

"I'm having a special."

"What you're doing is handing over the store." He knew she was giving him preferential treatment. Over the last year he'd been the one to respond to most of the Katie calls. Knowing that Tawny was on her own, he'd become particularly paternal toward her. "You take a check?"

"Mm-hmm. I know where you work."

"Walk me out to my rig, Katie Bug." He wore the boots as they went to get his checkbook. Maybe he'd come back and get Cecilia a pair. When he found out her size.

"They're looking good, Jake." Katie gave the boots a sideways glance.

Jake chuckled. "Maybe when you grow up, you ought to go into sales." When they got back inside the studio, he wrote Tawny a hefty amount. It wasn't charity. Ordinarily a man on a cop's salary could only dream of owning a pair of Tawny Wade boots. He was damned happy to have them.

"Thank you," Tawny said. "And Jake, thanks for taking such good care of us."

"Just doing my job. How you feeling now, Katie?"

"I feel good." The kid threw up her arms like she didn't get what all the fuss was about. A little charmer, that girl.

"I'm heading back to the station," Jake said. "But you don't hesitate to hit 911 if something comes up, you hear?"

"Believe you me, I won't," Tawny said.

Chapter 4

After dinner the following evening, Lucky came over. Tawny was in her studio working on Sam's boots when Katie came barreling in.

"That man from the other day is here again," she said. "He brought me this." Katie held up a doll.

Katie had long ago traded in dolls for computer games, but Tawny had to admit that the gesture was impossibly sweet. She couldn't picture big, bad, bull-riding Lucky walking through the doll aisle of a toy store, but it warmed her heart that he had. And made Tawny feel a pang of guilt for leaving Lucky out of Katie's life for so long. Hey, she'd done what she thought was best for everyone at the time.

"Did you say thank you?" Tawny asked her daughter.

"Of course." Because of the leukemia, Katie got lots of gifts. Donna and some of the other townswomen would show up with stuffed animals, slippers, and pajamas. Maddy Shepard, the police chief's wife and co-owner of the Lumber Baron Inn, often brought her DVDs. Clay McCreedy got Katie her first bike, said it was too small for Cody, but it looked brand-new to Tawny. And pink. "He's still here, though."

"Oh?" Tawny absently patted her hair. "Why didn't you send him in?"

"I will," Katie said, and skipped off.

A few moments later, Lucky's large frame filled her workshop. "So this is where you make the boots, huh?" He had on faded jeans, a denim shirt, and a pair of ropers.

She looked down at his boots and feigned outrage. "Ariats?"

His lips tilted up. "They're a sponsor. I get 'em for free. Besides, yours are too pretty for what I do." He gazed around her shop. "Wow. You made all these?"

"Yep. And a lot more." Inexplicably, she wanted him to know her accomplishments, and pointed to the binders that held pictures of her work. Boots she'd made for the likes of Merle Haggard, Chris Isaak, Madison Bumgarner, and Tom Hanks.

He popped one out and thumbed through the pages. "Hot damn, these are some fine boots. How much does a pair like this go for?" Lucky held up a picture of a pair she'd made for a Napa vintner, featuring dozens of hand-tooled grapes.

"Three thousand," she said, and he whistled.

He strolled around the room, taking in the cutting tables and her industrial sewing machines. "How come you're not rich?"

"It took me seven months to make that vintner his boots. Everything is done by hand and I only use top-of-the-line materials." She paused. "And with Katie's illness, the business has had a lot of fits and starts. I can't work a lot of the time."

"What do you do with all these?" He pointed at the rows of boots that lined the walls of her studio.

"I sell them."

"Where are the twelves?"

"Over there." She showed him a rack by the door, and he made a beeline for it.

She heard him take in a breath and watched as he removed the one pair of boots she didn't want him to see. Tawny kicked herself for leaving them out.

"I want these," he said, and started to try them on.

"They're not for sale," Tawny protested, walked over to him, and tried to pull them away.

"Everything is for sale. Name your price. I've gotta have these."

She should've been thrilled. Instead, she felt incredibly uncomfortable. Embarrassed, to tell the truth. "Seriously, Lucky, they're not for sale."

"Why the hell not? These boots were meant for me." With his finger, he outlined the inlay silhouettes of a bull rider, the Sierra looming in the background. "It's like you had me in mind when you made them."

She turned away so he wouldn't see her face. "They're someone else's." There were a lot of bull riders in Nugget. Feather River College had one of the top rodeo teams in the West Coast region. So what if they weren't world champions like Lucky? "He's already paid in full and owns the design. I'm sure you can find another pair you like as much. Or you could always commission your own design."

"Who purchased these?" Lucky wanted to know. "I'll buy them off him. Any price."

"I'll ask him if he wants to sell them to you, Lucky. But I wouldn't count on it." She faced him now. "I'm guessing you didn't come over here to buy boots. What's up?"

"I came to bring Katie the doll. And I brought a paternity kit. It's in my truck."

"Okay," she said. "I suppose you want to do the swab yourself to make sure it's on the up-and-up."

"The thought had crossed my mind, not that I don't trust you." He flashed a factitious smile.

"How about I do it while you watch? That way I can tell her it's another one of her medical tests." Katie had had so many over the last four years she wouldn't know the difference.

"That works. Should I go get the kit?"

Tawny looked at the time. "Her show's on right now. It'll be over in twenty minutes. Then she'll get ready for bed. I'll do it then, if you don't mind?"

"Nope." He wandered around her studio a little more. "Did this used to be a garage?"

"Yeah. My dad used to fix his clients' clocks in here. In winter he'd bring in a space heater. Before he died, he installed forced-air heating for me."

"I hadn't heard that he died. I'm sorry, Tawny."

"Thank you. I'm glad he's no longer suffering."

"You didn't really have any help with Katie, then, did you?"

"He died when she was two. But while he was alive he did what he could."

Lucky sat in the chair Tawny used to trace clients' feet. "Didn't he want to know who Katie's father was?"

Tawny hesitated, not wanting to rehash the past. It was done. "I told him he was a ranch hand passing through. That I didn't know anything about him."

"Jeez. Was he angry?"

"He wasn't happy. But eventually he came to accept my pregnancy and felt blessed to have Katie."

"My mother could've helped you, you know? . . . I would've come back."

"We've been over this, Lucky. I can't change the past." She put away her supplies and cleaned the table where she'd been working. "Why'd you come back anyway? You could've opened your dude ranch anywhere."

"It's a cowboy camp," he muttered, and Tawny stifled a laugh.

The whole town joked that Lucky Rodriguez thought a cowboy camp sounded more manly than a dude ranch. Supposedly, according to rumor, he hoped to attract corporations looking to team build. Sam told Tawny that Lucky had also worked out a deal with the Lumber Baron to hold country weddings and events on the property. Once he got it fixed up the way he wanted, Tawny thought the place would be beautiful for parties. Especially the lodge. The little she'd seen of the building had impressed her.

"It's my hometown," he continued. "Why wouldn't I come back? Plus, my mother lives here."

Tawny shrugged. "I just thought that with the Rosser ordeal, you'd want to put this place in your rearview mirror forever." That night, Lucky had confided the whole thing to her. Not because they were close, but because she was there. Convenient. The incident had shaken him. Although he hadn't admitted as much, she knew he'd been afraid of being arrested . . . of his mother losing her job.

"Nah." He waved her off. "Water under the bridge."

Water under the bridge. Even though it had happened a decade ago, it was more than water under the bridge. At least to Tawny. The worst part in her mind was that Raylene hadn't protected Lucky. If Raylene had spoken up, Lucky wouldn't have had to slink out of town the way he had.

She wanted to ask him if there was someone special in his life now, but held her tongue, not wanting to give him the impression that she was interested. Because she wasn't. Even if he did look like God's gift to women with those broad shoulders, big brown eyes, sexy five o'clock shadow, and enough cowboy charm to fill the Grand Canyon. Lucky Rodriguez had always been her girlhood fantasy. Back then, just a smile from him could make the sun come out on a rainy day. But she'd never been in his league and never would be—especially now that he was a famous athlete.

"How does Katie do in school?" he asked, making it transparent that he'd come for more than his requisite paternity test. Lucky was obviously burning with curiosity about Katie.

"Good, when she's able to go. I thought about holding her back a year because she missed so much, but her teachers thought she'd be able to handle the fourth grade."

"The fourth grade, huh?" He grinned. "She's a pretty little girl. Looks a lot like you."

"Hopefully not the way I looked in the fourth grade."

Lucky laughed. "Damn, you were scrawny." Tawny was surprised that he even remembered.

Lucky grew somber. "What if I'm not a match for the cell transplant?"

She let out a sigh, a sigh that said *I can't bear to think about that.* "We'll cross that bridge when we get to it."

He nodded, presumably getting the fact that she had to focus on the positive. If she didn't, she'd go crazy.

"You think she liked the doll?" Lucky asked. "I didn't know what to get her."

"I'm sure she loved it. It was nice of you."

"When she finds out the truth, will she think I'm a louse?"

"No," Tawny said. This time the guilt was more than a pang. "That distinction will be reserved for me." She glanced at her watch again. "I should get back inside."

"I'll get the kit." Lucky made for the door. "I want to get the results back as soon as possible."

A week later Lucky got the call. He phoned Tawny, who raced over to the ranch for an impromptu meeting.

"When will we tell her?" He sat on the new retaining wall, watching Tawny swing her legs back and forth. He figured she was nervous. She had nice legs, he'd give her that.

Except for the green cat-eyes, Tawny no longer resembled the Thelma Wade he remembered. Still on the petite side, her body had filled out in all the right places. The woman had breasts now and a curvy bottom. Her hair, once a drab bowl cut, was long and shiny brown.

He wondered if she had a man in her life. The idea of another guy playing daddy to his daughter sat wrong with him. But that was all about to change. Rodriguezes stuck together. Nothing was more important than family. And Katie was his child. His responsibility.

Tawny tilted her head back. "I don't know, Lucky. Maybe we should wait until you're sure you want to embrace fatherhood. Katie's a real-life person with feelings. You could hurt her."

The idea that he would hurt his own flesh and blood made him simmer with resentment. "Hurt her? You think I'd run out on my own daughter? I already told you I won't repeat the sins of my father. I don't want to put this off. It's bad enough it's been nine years."

She narrowed those green eyes at him. "You didn't even believe me at first. And now you're all gung ho to be a father?"

"Look," he said, scrubbing a hand underneath his cowboy hat. "I might've come off like a jerk, but women have tried to trick me before using the pregnancy card. I'm sorry if I offended you. You'll just have to trust me that I want to do the right thing here. A little girl needs a father as much as she does a mother."

His phone rang and Lucky tugged it out of his pocket, checking the display. "Shoot, I have to take this." He hopped off the wall and walked a couple of feet away. "Hey, Pete . . . Yeah, I'm still into it, but I've got a few complications. Give me a day or two to get back to you. We'll work something out, don't worry."

When he ended the call, Tawny asked, "Who's Pete?"

"My agent." He leaned against the wall. "I'd like to tell Katie today. As it is I've been sitting on pins and needles, waiting for the paternity test to come back. I feel like I've been lying to my mom by keeping it from her." And Raylene. Explaining this to her wasn't going to be easy.

"I think we should do the tissue test first, see if you're a match for the transplant."

"We'll do that, Tawny, just as fast as we can make the appointment. But I don't want to wait any longer to publicly claim my daughter. So I suggest that if you've got people to tell, you get to telling them, because by tomorrow the news will be all over town."

Probably sooner than that, and he didn't want Cecilia and Raylene hearing it through Nugget's famous gossip grapevine.

"This has to be done with kid gloves." Tawny's bottom lip quivered. The woman was a piece of work. She'd come to him, pleading for help. And now that he was officially stepping in, she wanted full control. "Katie has had enough upheaval in her life. I don't want to spring you on her. *Hey, here's your long-lost father.*"

"I hate to say it, but maybe you should've thought of that nine years ago." Lucky crouched down in front of Tawny, hoping to get through to her. "You've got to understand where I'm coming from. A man doesn't let his kid grow up without her father."

Only a pathetic coward did that. Just ask Lucky's father. Correction: Lucky's sperm donor. Because he'd never been more than that. As good a mother as Cecilia was, it had left a hole in Lucky, not knowing the man who had given him life.

Tawny clasped her hands together and in a low voice said, "It's just been the two of us for so long."

"You'll have to make room for me too," he told Tawny. "You owe me that, and frankly you owe our daughter that."

Tawny let out a resigned breath. "Just be kind, Lucky. Try to remember that she's a little girl and all this new information is bound to be very confusing to her."

Lucky got it. The last thing he wanted to do was make Katie's life any more difficult. "Should we tell her together?"

"I think I should do it alone and give her a few hours to digest the news before you come over and talk to her."

"Yeah, all right. That sounds reasonable." His phone rang again. When Lucky saw the caller's number he started to stuff the cell back in his pocket. "Sorry."

"You may as well take it," Tawny insisted.

"It can wait." But a few minutes after his phone stopped ringing, it started up again.

"Sounds important," Tawny said.

Lucky caved and answered it. "Hey, baby, can I call you back? I'm right in the middle of something."

"Is everything all right?" Raylene asked.

"Yeah, yeah, I'll tell you later. You talk to your lawyer?"

"Yes," she said. "He's trying to expedite things with Butch."

"That's good. I want to hear all about it, but this is a really bad time . . . Give me an hour or so."

"Okay," she said. "Love you."

"Me too." Lucky clicked off and slid the phone back inside his pocket.

Tawny lifted a brow. "Girlfriend?"

He may as well tell her the truth. It was bound to come out anyway. And something told him that Tawny had never liked Raylene much, especially after what he'd told her about that night at the Rock and River.

Most of the town had only seen what they wanted in Raylene. The girl who'd sold the most magazine subscriptions to raise money for Nugget Elementary. The girl who'd won the 4-H round-robin for best showmanship at the county fair every year. The girl with the brightest hair, the whitest teeth, and the nicest clothes. The girl who every other girl in Nugget should emulate.

To someone like Thelma Wade, whose pants never quite hit the tops of her shoes and who'd never won anything, Raylene must've been the Antichrist. But then no one knew the real Raylene like Lucky. She could be spoiled, self-centered, and vindictive, but mostly she was damaged, scarred, and lonely. A little girl who had no one until she had Lucky. And together they had everything.

"Yep," he said. "Actually it was Raylene."

Tawny balked. "You can't be serious? You're seeing Raylene Rosser?"

"Yeah. We've been keeping it on the down low."

"I bet you have," she said, her voice filled with sarcasm. "It's not every day a man dates the woman who accused him of rape."

"Ah, would you give it a rest with that already? It was a long time ago. And it was Raylene's old man who accused me of rape. Not Raylene."

"Whatever you say." She shook her head and swiped her purse off the ground. "I've got to get going."

"What do you mean, you've got to get going? We haven't finished with the game plan yet."

"I'll tell Katie when I get home. You can come over any time after five. But I'll tell you right now, Lucky, I don't want Raylene Rosser in my daughter's life. Katie's got enough problems."

Lucky pinched the bridge of his nose. "Come on, Tawny. I realize that this is new territory—for both of us. But try to be reasonable here. Raylene and I are together. She's a huge part of my life."

"I don't care who's in your life or who you date. It could be Attila the Hun for all I care. Just don't bring any psychos around my daughter."

"You mean our daughter," Lucky threw back at Tawny as she walked to her Jeep. He caught up with her and grabbed her arm. "Hold up a second. For the sake of Katie, you think we could try to get along?"

That seemed to register with her because she deflated in front of him. "You're right. I'll see you after five then."

"Yep, I'll be there."

Lucky got into his own truck and followed Tawny down the long drive to the highway. He wanted his mama to hear about Katie from him, before word got out. He thought about bringing his bull-riding helmet, but then Cecilia would just aim for his chest.

Jake Stryker's police rig was in his mother's driveway again. Lucky didn't know how he felt about the guy, but he wished Jake wasn't there right now. Inside the house, he caught the two of them in the kitchen in a lip-lock, like friggin' teenagers.

"You guys mind?"

"Maybe that'll teach you to knock next time." Cecilia smiled at her son but quickly pulled away from Jake. "Are you hungry?"

"Nah," Lucky said, and Cecilia felt his head to see if he had a fever.

Deciding three was a crowd, he excused himself to watch TV in the family room. He wasn't good company anyway. Flipping through the channels on the flat-screen, Lucky kicked off his boots. It would be nice when the workers finally finished his apartment and he could move out of the skanky trailer. Get some furniture like this, Lucky thought, stretching out on his mother's big velvety sofa. In the kitchen, he could hear his mom saying goodbye to Jake. A few minutes later she came in and scooted next to him on the couch.

"I was thinking of making coffee," she said. "Would you like some?"

"Sure, if you're making it anyway."

She padded off and Lucky heard the grinder going. He got up and followed after her.

"I've gotta talk to you, Ma."

Cecilia stopped reaching for the mugs. "What's wrong, Lucky?" He motioned for her to take a seat at the kitchen island. "I have a daughter. She's nine and Tawny Wade's her mother."

"Katie?" Cecilia sat there, clearly dumbfounded, her face a giant question mark. "How did this happen?"

He hitched his shoulders. "The usual way."

"You two were never an item. You were always chasing after Raylene." She said Raylene's name like it was an obscenity. "Explain yourself, *mijo*. Why am I just finding out about this now?" As he expected, she was angry. And disappointed. Cecilia didn't raise a son to bring a baby into the world and turn his back on her.

"Because I'm just finding out about it now."

"I don't understand."

"Do the math, Ma. It happened the night of the fight at the Rossers. I left the next day. Tawny says she left messages for me, but I never got them."

"Why didn't she come to me?" Cecilia asked. "Katie is my grandchild."

"The night we were together, I told her about what had happened with Raylene. She was afraid that if people knew I was Katie's father . . . it would look bad. It would give credence to all the nasty things Ray Rosser said about me. She thought she was doing the right thing . . . for me . . . for you."

"*Ay Dios mio!* How did you find out?"

"Tawny told me and we did a paternity test. She needs a stem cell transplant for Katie, and since I'm her biological father, Tawny's hoping I'm a match."

"I want my granddaughter," Cecilia said. "All these years she's been living right under my nose."

"I know, and I'm working on it, Mama."

"What do you mean, you're working on it?" Cecilia shot him a defiant glare. "All these years . . . Tawny should've come to me. I'm angry with her, Lucky. She had no right."

He put up his hands. "Ah, for Christ's sake—"

"Do not take the Lord's name in vain in this house."

"I'm sorry. But cut her a break, Ma. She's had a lot on her plate and did the best that she could."

"I would think you should be upset about this. Katie's very sick . . ." She stopped herself, but Lucky knew the implication. He'd looked up acute myeloid leukemia on the Internet.

Cancer of the blood and bone marrow was no joke. From everything Lucky had read, Katie could be living on borrowed time.

Chapter 5

About midnight, Jake pulled into the Gas and Go to fill his tank and his coffee thermos. Wyatt had taken the weekend off, leaving Jake and Rhys to cover his graveyard shifts. Dinner at Cecilia's had been tasty, as usual, but he could use a little caffeine to get him to morning. And the Gas and Go was the only business still open this time of night.

The community was divided on an around-the-clock filling station. Some liked the convenience; others thought it was bringing too many big rigs in off the interstate.

Jake was in the first camp. The town, mostly filled with ranchers and railroad workers, rolled up early. At least at the Gas and Go, Jake could still get a soda and a pack of those mini powdered-sugar doughnuts he liked after ten p.m.

So far, the truckers who came through only stayed long enough to use the john, fuel up, and buy a soft drink. Other than their diesel fumes and loud engines, they were nothing to complain about. A few times in winter, when the pass got snowed in, Rhys had let them park their rigs in the lot behind the police station. On the really cold nights, a few bunked at the Lumber Baron instead of their sleepers.

Tonight it was quiet, though. Just Jake and the silvery moon. He topped off his tank and left his truck at the pumps while he went inside. Griffin manned the cash register.

"What are you doing here so late?" Jake asked him, filling his thermos at the coffee counter.

"My night guy called in sick."

"That's too bad."

Griffin shrugged. "I don't mind doing it every now and again. Tonight's slow anyway. You filling in for Wyatt?"

"Yep."

"Can you believe Darla talked him into going to a spa? Last I heard they were getting one of those his-and-hers seaweed wraps."

"Doesn't sound so bad to me," Jake said.

"I guess the whole thing's free. Darla used to work with the spa owner in a salon in Sacramento. The woman wants her to carry some of her spa products at the barber shop."

"It might go over pretty well with the ladies in Nugget. Truth be told, I never thought those expensive shampoos Darla carries would sell in a town like this. But according to Owen, it's a license to print money."

"The old coot was supposed to hang out with me and play a little pinochle to while away the hours."

The barber and his cadre of old-timers, known around town as the Nugget Mafia, had taken a shine to Griffin and were always making themselves at home in the gas station. Jake supposed that now that Darla, Owen's daughter, had taken over the barbershop they had nowhere to congregate. "You have to get yourself some age-appropriate friends," Jake said.

"Yeah, I know." Griffin grinned. "Yesterday I had to show him how to stream movies on his new flat-screen. The guy wanted to know where the rabbit ears were."

Jake started to ask Griffin about Sierra Heights, the white-elephant gated community the gas station owner had purchased from bankrupt developers, but someone blew the horn from a Ford F-150, indicating that Jake should move his SUV. There were a number of available nozzles on the other side of the gas pump.

Griffin looked outside. "Who the hell is that?"

A blonde—in the tightest jeans Jake had ever seen, a Western blouse that was open to her belly button, a lacy black bra, and a straw cowboy hat—came busting through the door. "Would you mind moving your car."

It was more of a demand than a request, and Jake wondered if she'd missed the large Nugget PD logo on the side of his rig. Not that he was one of those cops who used the color of authority as an excuse to be inconsiderate. But other than him and Lindsay Lohan, the large service station was empty.

The woman looked Griffin up and down like he was a lollipop and turned her attention to Jake. "Who you looking at?"

That's when Jake smelled the booze. And people thought vodka was odorless. "Have you been drinking, ma'am?"

"No. Have you?" She stuck out her chest, and Jake didn't know if the gesture was meant to be belligerent or provocative. What he did know was she wasn't getting behind the wheel anytime soon. "Don't you touch me!"

Jake hadn't so much as breathed on her, but the gal was sloppy. "Ma'am, I'm gonna need to see your license."

"Uh . . . I don't think so."

More than a decade in LAPD's robbery-homicide division and now he was mopping up drunks at the Gas and Go. "If you want to drive away, you'll have to take a sobriety test, and I'm afraid that starts with you giving me your license."

"Do you know who I am?" She jabbed her finger at his badge.

"More important, do you know who you are?" Jake said, and heard Griffin in the background choking on a laugh.

"I'm calling my father," she said, and tottered backward on her high-heeled boots. "In case you didn't know, he's Ray Rosser of the Rock and River Ranch."

Jake knew who Ray Rosser was. Unlike Clay McCreedy, whose cattle ranch abutted Rosser's, the guy was a dickhead redneck of the first degree. Cecilia had worked twenty years at the Rock and River and had plenty of stories to tell. Jake figured Lindsay here must be the infamous Raylene. From what he'd heard from Cecilia, the girl was bad news.

"I think that's a good idea," Jake told her. "That way he can drive you home and you can sleep it off."

She dumped her purse on the floor, looking for her cell phone. She fished it out of a pile of makeup and tampons, made a big show of pounding in a number, then staggered off to a private corner of the store.

In a low voice, Griffin told Jake, "And I thought I'd die of boredom tonight. So that's Raylene Rosser?"

"I suppose so," Jake said.

"I've been hearing about her, but this is the first time I've seen her in the flesh." Griffin rolled his finger to his head, making the cuckoo sign.

Except for the black makeup around her eyes that reminded Jake of a raccoon, Raylene Rosser was a sexy woman, he'd give her that.

There was a time when he went in for the tarted-up types—drunk or not. He could see why Lucky would be attracted to her. Cecilia had told Jake that she was afraid her son was seeing Raylene on the sly, knowing that his mother wouldn't approve. Supposedly the boy had been hooked on the girl since grade school.

"Looks like I'll be blocking your pump a little longer," Jake said. "But I can't risk her driving away."

"No problem." Griffin looked out the window. "It's not like they're lining up. Besides, the other side is available. I don't know why she didn't just take that side in the first place and pull the hose around to her tank. Or back in."

Because she's loaded, Jake wanted to say, but refrained, trying to maintain his professionalism. Here in close-knit Nugget that was sometimes difficult to do. Everyone was up in everyone else's grill. It was the culture of the town and one of the reasons Jake liked it so much. People looked out for one another.

Jake checked the back of the store for Raylene. As soon as she'd gotten off the phone, he'd spied her perusing the magazine rack as if she didn't have a care in the world. Now she sat in a heap on the floor, crying.

Ah, Jesus.

"You okay, Ms. Rosser?" He strode to the back of the store, hoping her ride would come soon. He still had to drive through the backcountry while he was on patrol. And frankly, he didn't need this crap.

"Do I look okay?" she slurred, putting her face in her hands. "I'm disgusting. I bet you would be shocked to know that there was a time when people thought I'd make something of myself . . . something really good, like a movie star or a veterinarian." She let out a bitter laugh. "Instead, I'm a loser."

"Nah, you've just had too much to drink," Jake said. "It'll all look better in the morning."

"I doubt it. But th-th-thank you." She sobbed uncontrollably, and suddenly Jake felt sorry for her. Not only had she done a one-eighty, but black mascara ran down her face, making her look pitiful—and a little crazy. "My husband, Butch, had an affair on me with my best friend, Barb.

"*Butch and Barb . . . Barb and Butch*," she mimicked to herself. "My father actually thinks I should take him back. He doesn't think I can do better."

Philandering was a sticky subject for Jake. He definitely wasn't worthy to give advice on the topic. Fortunately, Lucky came through the door and Jake didn't have to respond. Lucky bobbed his head at Griff and headed straight to Raylene.

He acknowledged Jake with a similar nudge of his chin. To Raylene, he said, "Give me your goddamn keys."

Jake watched Lucky march out the door and move Raylene's truck to the street. When he came back in, he muttered that he was sorry for any inconvenience.

"You got here fast," Jake said. The old Roland camp was a ways out of town.

"I stayed the night at my mother's." Lucky scowled, and stuffed the contents of Raylene's purse back into her bag. Then he pulled Raylene up by the elbow. "We'll get out of your hair now."

Jake saw them get into Lucky's Ram and drive away. It looked like Cecilia had been right. No other reason Raylene would make Lucky her get-out-of-jail-free card unless they were seeing each other, which left Jake in an awkward position. Did he tell Cecilia or not? Because his guess was that there was no way Lucky would be telling her.

Ah, family drama. With three divorces under his belt, Jake had had enough to last a lifetime. It looked like he was in for some more.

"What the hell is with you, Raylene?" The woman smelled like a distillery and looked like a prostitute.

"Lucky"—she nuzzled her head underneath his neck—"I love you so much."

Lucky pushed her away. "I need to drive. You coming home with me, or am I taking you to the Rock and River?"

She let out a high-pitched giggle and hicuped. "I don't think that's a good idea."

"Because you're tanked or because you're with me?"

"I'm not so very drunk," she said, and Lucky rolled his eyes. "Daddy doesn't like you."

"Well, I don't like your daddy." In fact, Lucky hated his guts. "So I guess I'm taking you home. My home."

"I don't like your trailer," Raylene whined.

"I don't really care, Raylene." Because right now, he didn't like her. He had enough problems: his daughter's illness, his mother's disappointment, and Tawny's reluctance to let him be a full-fledged father to Katie. He sure the hell didn't need his girlfriend going out on the town, drunk as a skunk, dressed like a pole dancer.

"Why are you being so mean to me?" Lucky could see her pouting as the moonlight filtered into the cab of his truck. "You're acting like Butch. He treated me worse than a dog."

"Where have you been all night?" He couldn't stand the thought of her driving drunk.

"Reno, with my girlfriends. God, Lucky, you act like I'm not allowed to have any fun. You don't know what it was like being married to Butch."

"Can we not talk about Butch for once?" Lucky pulled to the side of the road and slammed on his brakes. "You drive back from Reno like this?"

"No, Hannah drove." Hopefully, Hannah had been sober. "Then why were you at the Nugget Gas and Go?"

"We met in the square and went in Hannah's car. When she dropped me off, I didn't have enough gas to get back to the Rock and River. Why are you interrogating me? What are you, jealous?"

"No, Raylene. I don't want you killing someone, or yourself. Jesus, you're twenty-eight and you're acting like you're in high school." He eyed her trashy getup and frowned.

"I'm probably having a midlife crisis after Butch," she said, and Lucky could hear remorse in her voice. And maybe shame.

Still, he was unable to let it go. "You're lucky Jake didn't arrest you for DUI, Raylene. I know you're going through a rough patch, but you've got to pull it together, baby. Okay?"

"Okay," she said, sounding so sad that it made him sorry for yelling at her. "Lucky, you ever wonder what would've happened if we'd gotten married?"

Lucky closed his eyes. *Every damn day.* "Yeah," he said softly.

"Remember that time in ninth grade when we planned to run away to Los Angeles together?" She laid her head on his shoulder.

He grinned in the darkness. "I remember."

"We had it all worked out. We'd save up and get an apartment and look for jobs. Me as an actress, you as a stunt man."

"We sure were idiots back then." Lucky chuckled.

"No, we weren't. We just had big dreams." She let out a long sigh. "At least one of us made them come true."

The cab of his truck got quiet. He supposed Raylene had never realized her dreams. Unless you counted marrying Butch and working in an accounting office, she hadn't accomplished any of the things they used to talk about. Raising horses had been one of them. Raylene had concocted this fantasy about buying a ranch in Wyoming, training wild horses, and winning the Extreme Mustang Makeover. They used to lie for hours underneath the giant redwood near her barn, planning their lives together. Man, he used to love to listen to her talk.

"Lucky?"

"Hmm?"

"That night you left, I wanted to die."

Then why didn't you tell the truth? "It was a long time ago, Raylene." He kissed her. "Let's go home now."

Tomorrow, he'd break the news to her about Katie. That wouldn't be pretty, but Raylene needed to hear the truth. Tawny had already told Katie but had put Lucky off for another day. Katie hadn't been feeling well enough for his visit, or so Tawny had claimed. He'd stayed at his mom's house, hoping Tawny might change her mind.

Today, he was going over there come hell or high water. But in the meantime, Raylene needed to know before the news spread through Nugget like a brush fire.

In the morning he made coffee and waited for Raylene to wake up. By now, her parents had probably put out a missing person alert—and Jake had probably told his mother about the scene Raylene had made at the Gas and Go and how Lucky had been the one to pick her up. He dragged his hand through his hair. Hell, they were both nearly thirty and still worried about the wrath of their parents. Kind of pathetic. He wondered if Katie would be the same when she grew up.

A kid. Holy hell, he had a kid. The idea of it still blew his mind. Sometime soon he wanted to go through his ma's old pictures and see if there was a family resemblance. He wanted Katie to look at the photos too. It was important to him that she know where she came from. There was so much to learn about her. What kinds of foods she liked, how she felt about animals, the activities she enjoyed. Like did she have a favorite sport? And then he thought about the leukemia. And it kicked him in the gut like a sucker punch.

He needed to talk to Pete about the cancer. The agent had good contacts. Lucky shot him off an email and went into the bedroom to rouse Raylene. The woman burned daylight.

"Hey, Ray, time to get up, baby."

She sat up, took his coffee mug, and sipped a few times. "You kicking me out?"

"No, but I've got things to do. And we need to talk."

"At least let me brush my teeth." She scooted out of the bed with just her birthday suit on and went into the bathroom. Lucky thought she looked good. Toned and tanned. He just wished she'd cover it up for the rest of the world.

A short time later she came out wearing his shirt. "What do we need to talk about?"

"I've got a daughter, Raylene."

She laughed, looked at him, and stopped. "You're not joking, are you?"

"Nope."

"Is that what one of your buckle bunnies is claiming? You should just ignore it. She's probably trying to get money out of you."

"It's not like that, Raylene. She's here. In Nugget. My daughter's nine."

Her face went white. "What are you talking about?"

"Thelma Wade. She goes by Tawny now. Her daughter, Katie."

"Thelma Wade? The girl who looked like a skinny boy with a bowl haircut and had the really weird green eyes? The one who dropped out of high school?" She scrutinized him like she still thought it might be a joke. "You had sex with Thelma Wade?"

"That's how babies are made, Raylene."

Raylene got to her feet. "Were you sleeping with her while you were sleeping with me?"

"You mean while you were sleeping with me behind Zach's back."

"Oh my God." Raylene started throwing on her clothes from the night before. "You were so jealous of Zach and me that you screwed Thelma Wade? What, you couldn't do better?"

Okay, now she was just being spiteful. The fact was, half of Raylene's popular girlfriends had thrown themselves at him, but none of them had been as nice to him as little Thelma Wade. He'd hooked up with her on the worst night of his life and she'd talked him off the ledge and helped him plan his exit strategy. That night, the woman had been his guardian angel.

"Raylene, when the hell you planning to graduate from high school? It's been a freaking decade. Grow up already! I just found out that I have a daughter and somehow you've made it all about you."

"What did you expect, Lucky? I loved you and you cheated on me."

"Cheated on you? We weren't even together. Your father made sure of that."

It started the summer of his twelfth birthday. Lucky began accompanying his mother to the Rock and River Ranch. Ray immediately put him to work cleaning tack. Five dollars a saddle and two dollars a bridle. If Lucky worked hard and fast he could earn thirty to forty bucks in a day. That's how he and Raylene came to be.

One sweltering July morning she snuck into the barn while he hefted Ray's show saddle onto a sawhorse. Without speaking a word, Raylene started removing the saddle's buckles and stirrups.

"I've got that," Lucky protested loudly. "What are you doing?"

She put her finger to her lips and in a low voice so no one would hear, she said, "I'm helping you. You could do twice as much tack with four hands instead of two."

At first, he bristled at her effort. It seemed dishonest that she would do half the work and he'd get all the money. And somewhere at the back of his mind he knew Ray wouldn't like it. This was not a job for the daughter of the manor.

But in the end, having her company won out. Soaping tack was a tedious chore, and Raylene entertained him with a steady stream of chatter. He'd never known a girl who could talk so much. And boy, was she pretty. All bright eyed and rosy skinned, with budding breasts. He could look at her for hours and never get bored.

It was in those days that Lucky started noticing things about Raylene that weren't right. Bruises. Puffy eyes from crying. And how nervous she acted whenever her father's name came up. Sometimes they'd ride together and Raylene would tell him things. Bad things.

For as long as Lucky could remember, he'd been a protector. And Raylene reminded him of the baby sparrow he'd rescued the summer before. The bird had fallen from its nest and had been rejected by its mother. Grace at Nugget Farm Supply helped him build a new nest out of a box and straw and told him how to feed the hatchling with an eyedropper. That's what he wanted to do for Raylene. He construed a plan to smuggle her out of the Rock and River to live with him and Cecilia, so he could take care of her.

"He'd find me," Raylene said. "And then he'd fire your mom and you would have to move away and I would lose you forever."

Ray Rosser didn't have to go to the trouble. He made sure to keep them apart by merely asserting his power. In the beginning, his efforts to tear them from each other only made them closer. He and Raylene would sneak around after school—first at the park and later at the rodeo grounds on the high school campus. Eventually they gave each other their virginity in Lucky's bedroom while Cecilia was at work. But Raylene's overwhelming need to please her father ultimately won out. Publicly, she dated the boys Ray deemed acceptable. And eventually married the man Ray handpicked for her. Butch.

"All right, all right." Raylene put her hand on Lucky's chest, pulling him from the past. "Let's not fight. Just pay her off, Lucky, and make her sign something to go away."

He jerked his head back. "Katie is my daughter, my responsibility. I'm gonna cowboy up."

"What about us?" Raylene huffed.

He'd known the news about Katie would upset her. Despite all Raylene had going for her, she'd always been insecure. Always afraid she wouldn't be enough. Ray Rosser had made sure to make her that way.

"Raylene," he said, "it is what it is. Could you please try to be understanding? We've both got baggage." He looked at her pointedly.

She leaned against him and inched her hands up his shirt. "You're right. And it was a long time ago. We're together now and that's what matters. What's she . . . Katie . . . like?"

"She's sick with cancer."

Raylene's eyes grew large. "Will she be okay?"

"We don't know. She needs a transplant." And Lucky went on to explain Katie's leukemia to Raylene.

"How awful," she said. "Thelma must be devastated. My heart goes out to her—the poor woman. Is she still as unattractive as she used to be?"

Yeah, Lucky thought, *a real bow-wow.*

* * *

Katie tried on her fourth outfit. Tawny didn't know where she'd gotten such a vain daughter, but apparently it was of the utmost importance that Katie look her best for her new father.

"Stick with the jeans and the heart sweater." Tawny sat on Katie's twin bed and watched the fashion show proceed. "Honey, he'll be here in a few minutes and you still have to put away all these clothes."

"I don't like these pants," Katie said, staring over her shoulder in the full-length mirror on the back of her door.

"Why? They look great." They were jeans, for goodness' sake.

"They make my butt look bad."

"They do not. Now stop obsessing. You look beautiful."

"I'm changing back into the pink pants with the stars on the back pockets."

Tawny tried to stay patient, knowing how big a deal this must be for Katie. "Okay, but you better get the show on the road."

Katie tugged on the pink pants, gave herself one last assessing look in the mirror. "Now I have to change my sweater. The hearts don't go with the stars."

Tawny had to keep from groaning. "How about the long-sleeved white top with the ruffle down the front?" The days were getting cooler as September slipped into October, and Katie was so susceptible to getting colds. Tawny wanted to keep her warm.

By some divine miracle Katie took Tawny's advice and pulled the white shirt over her head, dashed into the bathroom to brush her hair and back into the room to hang up the pants and shirts strewn across the bed.

"Do you think he'll like me?" Katie asked as she propped Lucky's doll against the row of pillows on her bed.

"He already likes you."

"How do you know?"

"Because how could anyone resist you."

Katie rolled her eyes heavenward as if to say *You only think that because you're my mom.* Together, they heard the knock and Katie quickly checked herself in the mirror while Tawny answered the door.

There, in a black Stetson, black jeans, and a pair of black snakeskin cowboy boots, Lucky stood, holding a big bunch of gerbera daisies. Katie had gotten lots of flowers during her many hospital stays, but Tawny would always think of these as her daughter's first bouquet, and felt her eyes mist.

"Come in," she told Lucky, and whispered, "Katie's nervous."

"Me too," he said, but looked calm as an August weather forecast. She figured when you rode two-thousand-pound bucking bulls in front of large crowds, you didn't let people see you sweat.

Katie emerged from her bedroom. She was too old to hide behind her mother's legs like she used to do at four, but Tawny knew she wanted to.

"I made lunch," Tawny said to ease the tension. "I thought we could sit and you two could get to know each other."

"Sounds like a good idea," Lucky said, and handed Katie the flowers. "These are for you."

For the next two hours they talked, looked at Katie's baby pictures, and Tawny watched Lucky Rodriguez wrap her daughter's heart around his pinky. She supposed it shouldn't have come as a surprise, since fifteen years ago he'd done the same with her heart.

"Should I call you Lucky or Daddy?" Katie asked, beaming at him across the table.

"You should call me Daddy." Lucky beamed right back, clearly as smitten with Katie as she was with him.

And in that moment, Tawny knew, regardless of her ambivalence over the situation, Lucky was in their lives now—at least Katie's.

She got up to clear the table while Katie and Lucky went into the living room to watch TV. As she loaded the dishwasher, Lucky came up behind her.

"You think we could talk outside for a few minutes?"

"Sure," she said. "Let's go inside my studio." Tawny told Katie where they'd be and led Lucky through the kitchen door and backyard. In the studio, she flipped on the heat, motioned for Lucky to take a seat on one of the try-on benches, and sat across from him. "What's up?"

"I think it went well, don't you?"

"Yes. She likes you. Please don't disappoint her."

"Tawny, one of the things you and I have to get straight is that I'm dependable. You're the one who decided to keep me out of Katie's life. So stop acting like I'll turn tail. What I came out to talk about is Katie's health. I called my agent and he's hunting down the best leukemia docs in the—"

Tawny cut him off. "How very nice of you and him, since Katie's oncologist and hematologist are some of the world's leading experts. Do you think I'm a country bumpkin, who can't take proper care of my daughter?"

"Ah, for Christ's sake, don't go getting coiled up like a rattlesnake, Tawny. All I'm saying is that you're no longer on your own. I'm here to help take the load off."

She put her face in her hands. "I know, I know. It's just that I've been doing it her whole life, Lucky, and I don't want to be second-guessed."

He pulled the bench close enough to hers so that they were touching knees. "I get it. That's not what I'm doing. I swear. But from here on out, I'm your hazer."

She smiled at him, knowing that *hazer* was a rodeo term for a steer wrestler's right-hand man—the rider who bookends the animal while it's running pell-mell across the arena, so the bulldogger can wrestle it to the ground.

"Seriously, Tawny, I've got a lot of time to make up for. And that's gonna start with back child support."

"You're not still mad?" She couldn't believe what an about-face he'd done.

"Hell yeah, I'm mad. Don't mistake this"—he waved his hand between them—"for me forgiving you. I'll probably never forgive your halfhearted effort to reach me. And my mother . . . you're on her shit list. I think the only other people on that list are my deadbeat dad and Ray Rosser."

And Raylene, if Cecilia was smart. How could Lucky possibly see that woman after all she'd done to him? Tawny tried to squeeze the picture of Raylene with Lucky out of her head. His personal life wasn't any of her concern.

"But for the sake of Katie, we need to move on," Lucky continued. "We need to get her healthy. I'm waiting for Pete to get back to me on specialists—"

"I already booked an appointment for next week," she interrupted. "Her doctors are at Stanford. It's just a simple blood test, so they'll arrange to have it done somewhere near here. I trust her doctors implicitly."

"All right." He nodded. "She looks good today, not as pale as the last time I saw her."

"Today's been a good day. Tomorrow might not be. We never know."

"Jeez." Lucky took off his cowboy hat and finger-combed his hair. "Poor kid."

"She's tough." Tawny presumed she got that from her father. The man was nothing if not resilient. He'd helped support his mother as a teenager, working more jobs than Tawny could count. Flipping burgers at the Bun Boy, riding fences for the late Tip Mc-Creedy, and wrangling at any ranch that would hire him. She used to watch him at the local junior rodeo. Even then, as a gangly young boy, he could make it to the eight-second bell on the back of a bull.

His only downfall had been Raylene Rosser. Apparently she still was.

"I want to take her to my mom's," Lucky said.

"It's late, Lucky. This has been enough for one day."

"I didn't mean now. But in the next couple of days. Tawny, my mother wants to meet her granddaughter."

Cecilia had already met Katie. Even if it was only a few times— Tawny had made sure to keep it that way. Lucky's mother had helped organize meal drives when they'd come home from the hospital. She and the Baker's Dozen, the local cooking club, had kept Tawny and Katie in soups, frozen casseroles, and covered dishes for weeks.

Cecilia Rodriguez was a kind woman, and Tawny had done wrong by her. But she'd only had the Rodriguezes' best interests at heart. There was no doubt in her mind that Cecilia would be a doting grandmother. Tawny should've been happy about that. Instead, she felt terribly alone.

"All right. We'll work something out," Tawny said, resigned.

"You too," Lucky said, and smirked. "You've gotta face her sometime."

Tawny didn't know why she did it, but blurted, "Will you be bringing Raylene?"

He shot her a look. "No, Raylene won't be coming. Not this time."

Tawny inferred that he meant Raylene would in the future—after the dust settled with Tawny. Great.

"You think you two could learn to coexist?" he asked, turning up the charm. "You know how it is with Raylene and me. It's always been volatile, but, Tawny, I've loved her for what seems like my whole life and we finally have a chance to be together."

"As I said before, Lucky, I don't care who you have in your life, but I'm very protective of my . . . our daughter."

"Raylene's going through some bad times right now, and it's messing with her judgment. But she's a good person."

Messing with her judgment? Tawny didn't know what Lucky was talking about, but she suspected it couldn't be good. When it came to Raylene Rosser, it never was.

"Anyway," he went on to say, "I'm sure there's a man in your life. Katie probably knows him better than she knows me." Since his daughter didn't know him at all.

Tawny didn't respond. The truth was she didn't want Lucky to know that there was no one in her life. There hadn't been in some time.

"Mommy?" Katie came into the studio. "Can I have a bowl of ice cream?"

Tawny looked at one of the clocks on the wall. "Not before dinner, baby."

"But we just had lunch."

"No ice cream between meals."

"But—"

"No buts, Katie. If you want a snack there's fruit or carrots in the refrigerator."

"Is Daddy staying for dinner?"

Both of them looked at Lucky. Katie more expectantly than Tawny, who could use a little space from Lucky and all his testosterone.

"Nah," Lucky said. "I've got to get back to the ranch, honey. But I'll be back tomorrow."

Fantastic, Tawny thought. *Now he's a permanent fixture.*

"Okay," Katie said, and wandered back to the house.

"Boy, no ice cream. What a hard-ass."

She started to berate him for not knowing anything about good parenting, but saw him grinning and stopped herself.

"I'd like us to go to my mother's tomorrow for dinner." When Tawny didn't respond, he said, "Come on, Tawny. You can't keep putting it off."

"All right. As long as Katie is feeling okay."

"I'll call you in the morning. You ever talk to your customer about those boots?"

At first Tawny didn't know what he was talking about. Then it came back to her. Yeah, those boots. "Not yet. Things have been a little crazy."

"Okay. Just don't forget. I want 'em."

Time to change the subject. "How's the cowboy camp coming?"

He hitched his shoulders. "Slow. Everything seems to take twice as long as it should. And I'm going to the world finals in December."

Making it to the world finals for a bull rider was like making it to the Super Bowl. Only the best of the best qualified. The winner was awarded a million-dollar bonus. Although Lucky had won three years in a row, this would be his chance to be the longest-reigning world champ in the history of the PBR. The whole town was talking about it.

"I'm sorry it's taking so long," she said. "But it'll happen."

"I'd just like to get out of that goddamned trailer. Instead of the apartment, now I'm thinking I need a house."

Yeah, Tawny thought, *for Katie and Raylene Rosser. Wouldn't that be cozy?*

Chapter 6

Cecilia checked her roast and Lucky checked his watch.

"They should be here any minute, Ma."

"I know. I hope Katie likes rosemary potatoes." She bustled around the kitchen like a chicken with its head cut off. "Make sure the table looks nice, *mijo*."

"She's nine, Mama. She doesn't care about place settings."

"Of course not, but I want everything to look nice for her first dinner with her *abuela*."

"Be nice to Tawny, okay?" Lucky said, and went off to check the silly place settings.

He'd been at his mother's for about an hour, and so far no mention of Raylene's drunken outburst at the Gas and Go and how Lucky had been the one to bail her out. That either meant Jake hadn't told his mother or Cecilia was too caught up in her first dinner with Katie to bring it up. Lucky bet that topic would eventually raise its ugly head. Half of Nugget probably knew, since Griffin Parks had witnessed the whole thing.

At least Raylene had been in a good mood today. She'd come over this morning, looking sweet and repentant, wanting sex and coffee, and he'd been more than happy to give her both. After weeks of sneaking around like schoolkids, she'd finally decided it was time to take their relationship public. Apparently she didn't want to be upstaged by a nine-year-old. It looked like Lucky would be front-page Nugget news for the foreseeable future.

"Lucky?" his mother called from the kitchen. "How does it look?"

"Beautiful. Smells good, too." He whiffed in the mouthwatering aromas coming from her stove.

God, his mama could cook. For twenty years she'd kept house for Raylene and her family at the Rock and River. Now he made sure she only kept her own. As far as Lucky was concerned, Cecilia Rodriguez should spend the rest of her days doing whatever made her happy. Cooking for her friends and family, volunteering at her church, working on her needlepoint, and maybe dating Jake Stryker. Lucky hadn't made his mind up about that one. Without a doubt his mother should have a man in her life. Lucky just didn't know if Jake was the right one.

From what he'd heard from Owen, the biggest mouth in Nugget next to Donna Thurston, Jake had been divorced three times. Not exactly a ringing endorsement of the man. But Jake sure seemed to make his mama happy. Ever since she'd met him at Clay McCreedy and Emily Matthews's wedding, Lucky had never seen her smile so much.

The doorbell rang and Cecilia came out from the kitchen. "Should I get it or should you?"

Lucky's lips quirked. He'd never seen his mother this fussy. "I'll get it, Ma."

He swung open the door to find both females dressed in their Sunday best. Katie had on a pink polka-dot dress—he was getting to think that pink was her favorite color—and little shoes covered in silver sparkles. But it was Tawny who made him do a double take. She looked like a freakin' runway model in a figure-hugging green sweater-dress that matched her eyes. Her hair had been pulled up, with little wisps around her face. Lucky had to turn away for fear of staring.

He just wasn't used to seeing her looking like this. Elegant, he guessed was the best way to describe it. Since he'd come back into contact with her, she'd always been casual, with her hair down and her boots on.

"Hey. Come on in." He picked up Katie and spun her around. His daughter. Just hearing her giggle, knowing that she was part of him, gave him the oddest sensation. A combination of warmth and fierce protectiveness.

"Hello, Katie." Cecilia held her arms wide and Katie tentatively moved into them.

"Hi, Ms. Rodriguez."

"*Abuela*," Cecilia said. "That's *grandma* in Spanish."

Katie looked over at her mother and Tawny gave her an imperceptible nod.

"Hi, *Abuela*."

"Good pronunciation," Cecilia said, and hugged Katie a little closer. "You hungry?"

"Yes, ma'am."

"I have so many good things for you to eat."

"She's been cooking all day," Lucky said.

"Thank you for having us, Ms. Rodriguez," Tawny said, handing Cecilia a bottle of wine and a bouquet of flowers. In return, Cecilia gave Tawny a weak smile and Lucky knew they were in for a long evening.

As they followed Cecilia and Katie into the kitchen, Lucky whispered, "Compliment her house and food a lot. That'll butter her up."

"You have a lovely home, Ms. Rodriguez," Tawny called to Cecilia's back, and Lucky smothered a grin.

"Thank you. Lucky bought it for me."

"He's a good son," Tawny said, and Lucky gave Tawny a thumbs-up. She shook her head and smiled.

On the kitchen counter, Cecilia had put out appetizers. *Queso fundido*, a cheese dip, served with chips and veggies, stuff Lucky's mother thought a kid would like. And from the looks of Katie dredging chips through the sauce, Cecilia had succeeded.

"I'm glad she's eating," Tawny said. "Lately the only thing she's interested in is sweets."

"That's because you're not feeding her the right things," Cecilia said, and Lucky saw Tawny bristle.

"Ma," he admonished.

"I just mean you have to be clever." She turned to Katie. "Try it with some celery sticks, *mija*." And Katie dutifully obliged.

"Would you like to see the rest of the home, Tawny?" Cecilia asked, and Tawny responded that she would love to.

Lucky decided it was safer to stay in the kitchen with Katie, and helped himself to some of the *fundido*. "Save room for the main course, kiddo." He gave Katie a gentle noogie on the top of her head.

When Cecilia and Tawny rejoined them, Lucky could feel the tension, thick as California's tule fog. He wondered if Katie noticed it too. Hell, the two women didn't have to get along. It's not like Tawny was his wife. Just the mother of his daughter, who she'd kept from him for nine years.

"We ready for dinner?" Lucky asked, hoping to lighten the mood in the room. "Katie and I are starved." He winked at his daughter, who seemed to bask in his attention.

"I was just showing Tawny Katie's room," Cecilia said.

"Oh?" Lucky wasn't aware that Katie had her own room. Out of the three guest rooms in the house, even he didn't have one specifically designated for him. But now he understood why Tawny appeared riled. His mother was moving in too fast, basically pissing on Tawny's territory. Not Cecilia's typical style. The woman was goodness personified, but don't ever come between her and her family. Just ask the Rossers.

Lucky glanced over at Tawny, who flashed him a tight smile. He tried to convey commiseration, but truly, who could blame Cecilia for trying to make up for lost time? In the end, it was Katie who made the peace by launching into a story about the new boots Tawny was working on for her.

"I designed them," Katie said, and proceeded to describe the boots in great detail. Sage with yellow butterflies and fringe.

"They sound beautiful, *mija.*"

When they finally sat to eat in the dining room, the mood had been dialed down to a low simmer. Katie continued to jabber away and Lucky kept his head down in case the dishes started flying.

"Ms. Rodriguez, everything is delicious," Tawny said, and Lucky had to give it to her. Tawny had class. And the kind of manners Lucky's mother usually liked.

"I was thinking," Cecilia said, passing Katie more of the potatoes while directing her words at Tawny, "that I could watch Katie after school, while you're working in your studio."

Tawny coughed and Lucky said, "Now's not a good time for this, Ma."

"A few days a week might be okay," Tawny said. "It would actually be quite helpful. Thank you for offering, Ms. Rodriguez."

Cecilia shot Lucky a victorious look. He had to say that Tawny's easy consent had floored him. But he knew Tawny was trying for Katie's sake. For her part, the kid seemed ecstatic, having already made mention of the large flat-screen TV in the front room. Nugget

Elementary was just walking distance away and close to a park with a public pool.

"Jake's daughters are coming up next month," Cecilia said. "I thought it would be nice if we could all have dinner together."

"I don't know. I'll have to see where I'm at as far as the cowboy camp and . . ." He trailed off, not knowing whether he should talk about the transplant in front of Katie. And quite frankly, he didn't know how tight he wanted to get with Jake and his family.

"Detective Stryker, from the Nugget Police Department?" Tawny asked, and when Cecilia nodded, she said, "I didn't know you were seeing Jake."

"I'll come," Katie burst in.

"Katie loves Jake," Tawny said in a teasing voice.

"Well, of course you'll come." Cecilia smiled at Katie

"You've somehow managed to evade the Nugget gossip mill, because I've not heard this news," Tawny told Cecilia. "He's such a great guy."

If Jake weren't in his late fifties, Lucky would think Tawny had her eye on him.

"We're friends," Cecilia said.

Yeah, friends with benefits. Just the thought made Lucky shudder.

"And you, Tawny? Are you seeing anyone?" Cecilia asked, and Lucky waited for her answer.

"Not right now, no," Tawny said, and Lucky wondered why not.

The table got quiet while they finished their meals, and afterward Tawny helped Cecilia clear the table while Lucky and Katie went outside to catch the last of daylight on the porch swing.

"Is this a Colin swing?" Katie asked.

"As a matter of fact, it is." Lucky had seen the local furniture builder's work and had snapped up a few pieces for his mother's yard. Then he'd commissioned Colin to build the farm tables and benches for the lodge at the cowboy camp. "How do you know Colin?"

"He's married to Harlee and sometimes comes over to fix things."

"What kinds of things?" Lucky was curious.

"A leak in the tub and our garbage disposal. He's nice."

"As nice as Jake?" Lucky winked.

"No one is as nice as Jake." It was cute how her whole face lit up when she talked. He'd noticed it when she'd described her boots. A little theatrical. Tawny had never been like that as a kid, at least as far as he could remember. She'd always seemed timid. Except for that time in the park.

"What about me?" he asked her.

"I don't know you," she said, and then got embarrassed, like maybe she shouldn't have said it.

"I know, honey. I'm real sorry about that. More than you'll ever know. But we're gonna fix it."

A week later, Lucky went in for his blood test. Tawny didn't know how she'd have the patience to wait for the results. Tonight, especially, she found herself at loose ends. Reluctantly, she'd let Cecilia take Katie for the night. Her daughter's first sleepover. Tawny had made sure to give Cecilia all her emergency numbers, with the assurance that Cecilia would check in with her before Katie went to bed.

As far as work, Tawny had finished Sam's boots and was too beat to start another pair. Harlee had called earlier and asked Tawny if she wanted to join her and a few friends at the Ponderosa. The old bowling alley and dive bar had been renovated by two women from the Bay Area and was now as nice as anything you'd see in Reno. Without the slot machines and craps tables, of course. So Tawny did the rare thing and accepted the invitation. She'd only known Harlee a short time. They'd met because the *Nugget Tribune* owner had done an article about Tawny's boot-making business. The story had actually gotten Tawny a few customers, and she'd instantly bonded with the live-wire reporter, who now sent her husband over every time the Wade house needed a quick repair.

She did a final check in Katie's full-length mirror and decided she looked presentable for polite company. Wherever Tawny went, she tried to wear a pair of her own boots. She liked to show them off. And tonight was no different. This time, she chose one of her vintage designs—a pair with black vamps, beige uppers, and overlay and inlay hearts and scrolls. She wore them with a short denim dress and an old Nudie's of Hollywood jacket she'd bought in a thrift store. The shopkeeper had sworn that it used to belong to Gram Parsons.

By the time she got to the Ponderosa it was already hopping. Harlee waved at her from the back of the restaurant, where she, Sam, and Owen's daughter, Darla, had commandeered a corner table.

"Nice boots," the police chief, Rhys Shepard, called from the bar where he was having drinks with his brother-in-law and Clay Mc-Creedy. The men beckoned her over.

"Thanks," she told Rhys.

"I saw Jake's pair and have been meaning to come over. You got anything left for someone with big-ass feet?"

"Sure I do."

"How long until my custom pair is done?" Clay wanted to know.

"I just finished Sam's. You're the next one up."

The girls were waving wildly from the back. Tawny nudged her chin at them. "I'd better get back there."

She said goodbye to the men and made her way to Harlee's corner.

"About time," Harlee said.

"Sorry. I kept getting waylaid."

"Because you look so cute," Darla said. Darla was Nugget's resident hair stylist. "But it's time for a cut, girl."

"I know," Tawny said. "I've just been so busy." And broke. "I'll make an appointment on Monday."

Sam waved to her from the other side of the table.

"Hey," Tawny said. "If I'd known you were coming tonight, I would've brought your boots. They're done."

"Yay!" Sam clapped her hands. "I can't wait to see them."

"Come by tomorrow and pick them up. I should be in my studio all day."

"I have an event to oversee at the Lumber Baron in the morning. But I'll come over after that."

"You've been holding out on us." Harlee pulled her into a chair, grabbed a clean glass from the center of the table, and poured her a margarita. "Lucky Rodriguez, huh?" She mouthed *Oh my God.*

"Yeah." Tawny huffed out a breath. Clearly word was out. "It was a long time ago. Well, obviously nine years and nine months ago."

"And you never told anyone?" Darla asked.

"It's complicated, but no."

"It's because of Raylene Rosser, isn't it?" Darla asked.

Harlee and Darla had no qualms asking the most personal of questions. Of course, it was Harlee's job. In Darla's case, she took after her father. The old barber had no boundaries. But Tawny didn't mind. The women meant no harm and had been better to her than most of the girls she'd grown up with. Although Owen had been here as long as Tawny could remember, Darla had grown up in Sacramento with her mom. Harlee had recently moved to Nugget from San Francisco, where she'd been a big-time reporter for the *Call*. Sam, who was more reserved, probably due to her Connecticut society upbringing, had only lived here nine months.

"Raylene was part of it." Tawny didn't want to get into the details. "But it's all good now." At least it would be if Lucky was a match.

"How's Cecilia taking it?" Darla asked.

"Uh, we're tiptoeing around each other. But she's crazy about Katie."

"Uh, duh. Who wouldn't be? The girl is so cute, right? And Cecilia is so nice. She'll get over it."

Tawny sincerely hoped so. She liked Cecilia, always had, and didn't want to be on her shit list.

"What about Lucky?" Harlee passed her the chips and salsa. "Is there a chance that you two might start where you left off?"

Tawny laughed because she and Lucky's start amounted to a quickie behind the Taylor Park swing set. "Nooooo. There's absolutely nothing there. He's with Raylene."

"That explains why last week he was the one to fetch her drunken ass from the Gas and Go in the wee hours of the morning," Darla said. "Griffin saw the whole thing."

Aha. So that's where Lucky's poor judgment comment had come from. "How drunk was Raylene?" Tawny asked.

"According to Griffin, drunk enough to pull the do-you-know-who-I-am card with Detective Stryker," Darla said, and Sam burst out laughing. "Griffin said it was kind of sad, because afterward she fell apart. Just sat on the floor and bawled her head off about her ex leaving her for her best friend."

"Okay," Harlee said, "I've only met her once, but I don't get what Lucky sees in her. Granted, she's very pretty, but she sort of struck me as a narcissist."

"Something about her, I guess." Tawny shrugged. "But as long as I can remember, Lucky has been in love with her. I mean the guy literally carried her book bag in the eighth grade. By the ninth grade he beat up anyone who looked at her sideways. Perhaps part of the appeal was that she was forbidden fruit. Old man Rosser wouldn't let his little princess date the help's illegitimate son, so they carried on in secret. It was very Romeo and Juliet." And kind of pathetic if you asked Tawny. But she'd give Lucky credit for his loyalty. Even after all these years.

"So how did you guys get together?" Leave it to Darla.

"Let's just say I was his revenge sex."

"Was it because of whatever happened at the Rock and River Ranch the night Lucky left Nugget?" Darla persisted.

Technically it was the morning after, but Tawny didn't contradict. The whole town knew that something bad had happened at the Rock and River that night. Something so bad that Lucky had hauled ass out of Nugget without so much as a backward glance. There were all kinds of rumors, including that Lucky had shot and killed a ranch hand for trying to get in Raylene's pants. But few knew the true story.

"I can't say," Tawny told Darla. "I'm sworn to secrecy. Plus, I don't want any of it getting back to Katie."

That stopped the questions, and the group went on to discuss Griffin's love life at length.

"He's dating," Darla said. "But he's still hung up on Lina, who pretty much lives in San Francisco full-time now while she's going to school."

"Who's he dating?" Sam asked. "Maybe Tawny should go for him."

The last thing she needed was another man who was in love with someone else. She'd done that with Lucky and it had crushed her. Although she'd just been a kid, he'd been her first love . . . her first everything. Tawny thought that she and Lucky were a lot alike. He'd never been able to get over Raylene and she'd never been able to get over him. Pitiful. And definitely time to move on.

"All I know is that she's a real estate agent—someone showing homes at Sierra Heights," Darla said. "He hasn't brought her around yet. But we're getting a group together for bowling and hopefully he'll bring her to that. You want to come too, Tawny?"

Darla and Harlee regularly organized bowling outings at the Ponderosa. They started doing it back when they were single, inviting all the other single young folks in town. Since then, Harlee had gotten married to Colin and Darla was engaged to Wyatt Lambert, a police officer with the Nugget PD. Now it seemed that even Griffin was hooked up. Other than Connie, the police dispatcher, Tawny would be the only single person there.

"I'll have to see what's going on," Tawny said. Life was pretty much on hold until they knew whether Lucky was a match for Katie.

Harlee put her hand on Tawny's arm. "I know you're waiting to get Lucky's results back. If he's not a match, I want you to know that Colin and I plan to be tested."

"Nate and me as well," Sam chimed in.

"Uh, I'm totally in, too," Darla said. "And you can count on Wyatt."

Tawny's throat clogged. "I don't know what to say. You guys blow me away. The next logical person would be Cecilia, since she's a blood relation. But if she's not a match, I will take you all up on your generous offers."

"Of course," Harlee said. "You can include just about everyone in town. We'd do anything for Katie."

"Thank you." It came out like a whisper, because Tawny was too choked up to talk.

"Hey"—Darla motioned to the other side of the room—"look who just walked in the door."

Raylene Rosser and her girlfriends made their way across the floor. Hannah, Debbie, Shelly—Tawny remembered them all from middle school. Not the nicest bunch. Although they seemed to be more toxic when Raylene was around. Of course they were all adults now. Debbie and Shelly lived over a few towns in Clio and were married with children. Hannah, divorced, lived and owned a gift shop in Glory Junction, thirty minutes away.

Tawny knew she'd been spotted by the group when the women huddled together and Raylene's head popped up to stare directly at Tawny. Raylene did a double take, her face going pale, as she quickly turned away.

Tawny had to give it to Raylene, she looked good. Her hair was longer and blonder than when she'd left Nugget, and either she'd filled out in the chest department or had had a boob job. Either way, men seemed to be enjoying her new look from the way they were gawking at her. Although they always had. Raylene just exuded that all-American cheerleader look. Perky and doe eyed.

"According to Griffin, she looked really trashy the night she came into the Gas and Go, smashed," Darla whispered. Why she whispered, Tawny didn't know, since you could barely hear over the jukebox anyway. "Supposedly she had the girls completely on display. Nothing but a black lace bra."

Tonight, Raylene dressed like the rest of the women in the Ponderosa. Jeans, sweaters, and Western boots.

"Perhaps we should go over and introduce ourselves," Sam suggested. "I feel like we're being judgmental. And snotty."

"I've already met her," Harlee said. "She came into the *Tribune* office to buy a want ad. The Rock and River is looking for ranch hands."

"Well, I feel like I should at least say hi," Sam said. "Anyone coming with me?"

"I'll go," Darla said.

When they both looked at Tawny, she shook her head. "I've known her my entire life."

Sam and Darla walked over to Raylene's table while Harlee poured Tawny and herself another margarita.

She held up the pitcher. "I'm gonna refill this at the bar. Be right back." Tawny tried to give her money, but Harlee wouldn't take it. "You can get the next one."

Right after Harlee left, Sam and Darla returned to the table and grabbed their seats.

"FYI," Darla said, "she's a bitch."

"Darla!" Sam reprimanded.

"What? I'm just being honest. All she did was bad-mouth Nugget—she called it *Deliverance*—as if she'd grown up in Denver instead of here. And, Tawny, she does not like you."

"The feeling is mutual." Tawny laughed.

"I think she feels threatened by you. She kept saying—"

"Darla, let it go," Sam said.

Tawny didn't need to hear. It was probably the same crap Raylene used to say when they were teenagers, when she'd called Tawny ugly, poor white trash, and a slew of other unoriginal names. The most clever one being hermaphrodite. Tawny had always wondered where Raylene had learned such a big word.

Tawny thought that after ten years of living in a metropolitan city and going through a nasty divorce, Raylene would've grown up a little. But when Tawny's cell phone pinged with a text message from Cecilia, she didn't give Raylene Rosser a second thought. Tawny had real problems.

Chapter 7

Lucky paced his mother's living room. "You sure we shouldn't take her to the hospital?"

"Yes," Tawny said. "The fever is mild and at the hospital there's always risk of Katie getting an infection. I'll just watch her tonight and if necessary take her to Stanford tomorrow." Tawny turned to Cecilia. "Thanks for texting me."

"The poor baby wanted her mother," Cecilia said, and Lucky had never seen his own mother look so worried. Well, maybe once before.

"You okay, Mama?"

"Of course. I'm just worried for Katie."

"So she always gets these fevers?" Lucky asked.

"It's a common symptom with AML," Tawny said. "That and rashes, bruising, and sometimes bluish-green lumps around her eyes."

"*Pobrecita*." Cecilia dabbed her eyes. "I hope you don't mind, but I also called Jake. I panicked because she was completely fine when she went to bed and then suddenly she was burning up."

As if on cue, Lucky heard a door slam outside and a few seconds later Cecilia ushered Jake into the house.

He gave Cecilia a hug. "I was on duty when you called, but Rhys agreed to fill in."

"Thank you." Cecilia burrowed in closer to the detective.

"We're okay." Tawny gave him a wan smile. "The fever is down now and Katie's sleeping."

"I'll make you a bed, *mija*."

Lucky was surprised that his mother had used the endearment on Tawny.

"I'll just sleep with Katie," Tawny said.

Cecilia took Jake into the kitchen to fix him a snack. Lucky eyed Tawny's outfit.

"Were you out?"

"Just at the Ponderosa with a few friends."

"You see Raylene there? She was going with Hannah."

"Yeah," was all Tawny said, and Lucky suspected Raylene got the surprise of her life when she got a load of Tawny.

Every time he saw her, he couldn't believe how beautiful she'd become. Despite a rather long awkward phase, he'd always thought Tawny was cute in a tomboy sort of way. Back then, she'd been all bones and sharp angles. Now, she looked like freaking Angelina Jolie. And he liked the Western getup she had on. It was real sexy, without being slutty.

"You make those boots?" He toed her foot with the point of his Ariat.

"I did."

"Nice."

"Thanks," she said. "You think your mother has a nightshirt or something I can borrow to sleep in?"

"If she doesn't, I probably do." He got up, went to one of the guest rooms, and rummaged through his spare stuff. When he came back, he held up a brand-new toothbrush and a National Finals Rodeo shirt. "Will this work?"

"That's great," she said, and took both items.

The shirt would probably swallow her up, but Lucky kind of wished he could see her in it. Funny, because he'd spent most of the day seeing Raylene in nothing. Things were going well between the two of them. Tomorrow he'd hoped to introduce her to Katie. But with Katie being sick, he wanted to wait.

"You hungry?" he asked her.

"No. You?"

He shook his head, tossed her a throw blanket, and sat on the couch next to her. "What friends?"

"Huh?"

"I was just curious about who you hang out with. When we were kids, you didn't seem to have too many friends."

"I was busy taking care of my dad. And later Katie. But recently I've been socializing with a few of the women who are newer to Nugget. Harlee Roberts, Sam Dunsbury Breyer, and Darla, Owen's daughter. Remember her? She used to come around to visit her dad when we were growing up."

"A little bit, I guess. How come you're not dating anyone?"

She let out a breath. "Between being a single mom to a daughter with AML and running my own business, I don't have a lot of time. Before Katie got sick I was seeing a park ranger. For a while there we were pretty serious."

"What happened?"

"Katie and I were spending a lot of time in Palo Alto and he and I drifted apart. Last I heard he got transferred to Southern California. How 'bout you? You marry or get serious with anyone while riding the circuit?"

"Nah. Too busy moving around."

"Did you know about Raylene's divorce when you came back?"

He stretched out until his shoulder rested against hers. She didn't seem to mind, so he stayed that way. "I'd heard about it. It's not why I came back, though. That just turned out to be a coincidence."

Raylene had told him it was fate.

"What would've happened if I hadn't come back?" Lucky asked.

"I would've finally gone to your mother."

It pissed him off that she would've waited until Katie was out of options. "You know how messed up that is, Tawny?"

"I can't go back and change things. If I could, I would. I am truly sorry, though." She started to get up, but he pulled her back down.

"Just sit with me for a while." When she settled back next to him, he said, "I'm worried that she won't get better and this is all the time I have with her."

Tawny tilted her head against the back of the couch as if to hold back the tears rolling down her cheeks. "We can't think that way. We just have to stay positive. If you're not a match, maybe your mom is."

He reached out and dried her face with the sleeve of his shirt. "Don't cry. I didn't mean to make you cry. How do you think it's going so far between the two of us?"

"You and Katie? I think good. She feels comfortable with you, that's for sure."

"How do you know?"

"I'm her mother, Lucky. I know these things. She talks about you a lot. Wants to know about your ranch, about what kind of animals you have. That sort of thing."

He liked that. He liked everything about Katie. Who would've thought of him with a daughter? Damn!

"Anything new?" she asked.

"This reporter wants to come up and interview me for *Sports Illustrated.* One of those stories about how an athlete changes careers after his heyday is over."

Tawny sat up straight. "Your heyday isn't over, Lucky. Is that what you think?"

"I don't know. I wrecked pretty bad in Billings. Had to be hospitalized. I'm getting to that age where it's hard to compete with the younger guys. I thought about going into announcing, but to tell you the truth I'm sick of the traveling. I won't lie, though, I'll miss the celebrity of it. I may not be Tom Brady, but I have my fair share of fans. I like being recognized and signing autographs."

She smiled at him. "I don't think that'll go away. You're a world champion, Lucky. That doesn't stop when you retire."

He shrugged. At least winning this year would make him the longest reigning world champion in the history of the PBR. If he had to go out, breaking his own record would be the only way to do it. Plus, having Raylene in the stands watching him ride would mean a lot to him. As far as he knew, she'd never seen him compete in any Professional Bull Riders events, unless she'd watched on ESPN. Back in high school, when she'd been the Plumas County rodeo queen, she'd cheered him on when he'd competed locally. But that had been small potatoes.

"I'd like Katie to come watch me compete in Vegas," he said, and hastily added, "You too."

"We'd like that."

"Yeah?" He grinned at her. The woman had always been nice to talk to. That night they'd made Katie, she'd been his salvation. Calming him after the nightmare at the Rock and River and helping him come up with a plan.

"Of course." She smiled back. "I think I'll turn in now."

"Is it okay if I look in on Katie first?"

"Just don't wake her up."

"You're bossy, you know that?"

She elbowed him in the ribs. "I am not."

He watched her collect the toothbrush and shirt and walk to the bathroom, enjoying the sway of her backside. He tried to visualize Raylene's ass instead, but found that he couldn't.

Katie's fever disappeared the next day and Tawny took her home. The girl could use a little less excitement. Between Cecilia's fussing and Lucky's constant roughhousing, Katie needed some downtime. And Tawny needed to start Clay McCreedy's boots.

"I'm bored, Mommy." Katie got a carton of orange juice out of the refrigerator and poured herself a glass.

"How about reading a book?" Tawny said, and Katie made a face. "What? You like to read."

"Can we go to my dad's ranch?"

"Not today, baby. I want you to rest and I have work to do."

Katie pouted, finished her juice, and went in search of her e-reader, another gift while she'd been in the hospital.

Tawny heard a car pull up and moved toward a window so she could see the street. Sam got out of her Mercedes convertible, carrying a basket, and made her way up Tawny's porch stairs. Before Sam could knock, Tawny opened the door. Startled, Sam jumped back, then started to laugh.

"Sorry," Tawny said. "Didn't mean to scare you. You come for your boots?"

"And to see how Katie is and deliver this." Sam held up the basket. "It's an autumn root gratin with ham, from Brady. Very fancy."

"It sounds delicious. Come on in." Tawny took the basket from Sam and took it into the kitchen. "Who's Brady?"

"He's the new chef at the Lumber Baron. Fabulous cook and very hot—if you don't mind tattoos. He's got loads of them on his arms. Maybe more elsewhere too. But I wouldn't know, being a married woman and all." Sam held out her ring finger and wiggled it, the gem beaming so bright that Tawny needed sunglasses.

No question the woman was in love. Tawny didn't know Nate Breyer well, but he was certainly good-looking and not your typical Nugget rancher or railroad worker. The man owned something like ten hotels, most of them in San Francisco.

"How's Katie?" Sam asked. "When you left the Ponderosa last night, we got word from Rhys, who got word from Jake, that you weren't taking her to the emergency room."

"No. The fever went down and it seemed like a better idea for her to rest at home. Today she's much better."

"Ah, Tawny. I'm so glad she's okay, but I'm sorry that you're going through this."

"We should hear fairly soon whether Lucky's a match for the stem cell transplant." Tawny knew she was putting a lot of faith in the transplant. Even if Lucky turned out to be a perfect match, a chance existed that it wouldn't work and that Katie would continue to get sicker. "Let's go out to the studio and get your boots."

Tawny quickly checked on Katie, who'd curled up on her bed with her nose buried in the e-reader. Once they got inside the studio, Tawny handed Sam her boots to try on.

Sam squealed. "They're stunning, Tawny. Absolutely perfect." She slipped into them and walked back and forth across the studio. "I've never worn cowboy boots before. They're so comfortable."

"That's because they're custom made to the shape of your feet and calves. It makes a big difference."

"I love them." Sam turned her legs this way and that as she examined the boots in the mirror. "I'm wearing them to our monthly sales meeting in San Francisco next week."

Tawny laughed. She couldn't see the boots going too well with Sam's wardrobe, which as far as Tawny could tell consisted of a lot of designer suits.

Sam must have read her mind because she looked up from the mirror and said, "I'll wear them with jeans and a nice blazer."

"Sounds perfect." Tawny gave Sam instructions on how to take care of the boots and included a bootjack in her package.

"I know this is a bad time with Katie and all," Sam said. "But is there any chance you would be interested in a setup?"

"You mean like a blind date?"

"Yeah. Sort of. Brady, the chef I told you about, is single. He just moved here, doesn't know a lot of people, and is a really sweet guy— and a good listener. I thought you two might hit it off."

"I don't know, Sam. Everything is up in the air right now with Katie's treatment. It just doesn't seem like a good time."

"I understand," Sam said. "But just come into the Lumber Baron one day and introduce yourself. Nate's petrified Brady will leave us if he doesn't make any friends."

"I will definitely do that and personally thank him for the casserole."

"Just make sure you call it a gratin," Sam teased. "Fancy chefs don't do casseroles."

She wrote Tawny a substantial check, which would keep her and Katie in Top Ramen for a while, and wore her boots out of the shop. No sooner had Tawny gone back into the kitchen to heat up Brady's *gratin* than Lucky showed up with an armful of grocery bags.

"There's more in my truck," he said, and went outside to fetch them.

"What are you doing?" Tawny took one of the packages out of his hands on his return flight.

"Stocking you up."

"Lucky, I don't need charity." It was one thing to send over a covered dish, a whole other to send an entire supermarket.

"Charity? I'm feeding my daughter. The way I look at it, I've got nine years to make up for." He stopped and tossed her an acid look as if to say *And that's your fault.* "From here on in, I'll be clothing her too." And then he handed her a check. She took one look at the amount and nearly gasped. "The rest is coming."

"The rest of what?" she asked.

"Nine years of child support. Where's Katie?"

"She's in her room, reading. I want her to rest, so don't go in there riling her up."

"I don't rile her up." He headed for Katie's bedroom door.

"She's fragile, Lucky. All that tossing her and spinning her . . . It's too much."

"I'm gentle," he said, dismissing her. Then he knocked on Katie's door and popped his head in the room. "Hey, kiddo."

Tawny heard Katie say hello and went into the kitchen to put away the groceries. Half of them would spoil before she and Katie could eat everything.

Katie and Lucky came into the kitchen. "Mommy, can Dad stay for dinner?"

Uh, way to put me on the spot. "Sure."

"What smells so good?" Lucky wanted to know.

"It's a vegetable and ham gratin that Sam brought over. The chef at the Lumber Baron made it."

"A what?" Lucky said.

"It's like a casserole."

"It sounds gross," Katie said. "Can we have mac and cheese?"

"No, we're having this with a big salad. Go wash up."

Katie skipped off and Lucky said, "She looks good. Less pale."

"Let's keep it that way." Tawny opened the oven and touched the top of the gratin to see if it was hot enough. It needed a few more minutes. "No roughhousing. I want her to go to school Monday."

"You think I could take her to lunch tomorrow? Just to the Ponderosa."

"Is your mother going?" Tawny only asked because she had a bad feeling.

"Nope. Raylene."

Bingo.

"I thought we talked about that, Lucky."

"Yeah, we did. I was hoping you would soften your stance on the whole Raylene issue since she and I are seeing each other."

"I made it perfectly clear that I don't care who you see. I only care who my daughter sees. Look, Lucky, Katie is vulnerable right now. Raylene can be, shall we say, insensitive, not to mention possessive. She's not going to like having to share you with a nine-year-old."

"Tawny, you're describing Raylene at fifteen. She's grown-up now."

"Is she?" Because the description of her at the Gas and Go didn't exactly make her sound mature.

"She's going through a bad divorce and acting out a little," Lucky acknowledged. "But I think this is more about you holding a grudge against her for picking on you when you were a kid. There's stuff you don't know about her, Tawny. Bad stuff. It doesn't excuse her . . . Could you just let it go?"

The woman had been ruthless. When she wasn't calling Tawny names, she was making fun of Tawny's father, calling him an "in-valid" and a "stupid Okie" because of his accent. Like many Californians, Franklin Wade's people had come here during the Dust Bowl, and he'd never quite shed the simple ways of his poor farming background. He moved slow and talked slow, but he was a good man, who'd raised a daughter alone after Tawny's mother had died.

Yet Raylene Rosser had never missed an opportunity to put him down. The really sad part of it was that no one noticed what a bully she was. They were so busy admiring her beauty on the outside that no one saw her rotten core. Just her victims.

For Lucky's sake, she hoped that Raylene would eventually grow out of her meanness. People could change. Melting down in a public place wasn't the same thing as being a bully. And who could blame her anyway? Her husband had cheated on her with her best friend and she'd had to come home with her tail between her legs.

"You can take Katie," Tawny told Lucky. "But so help me God, if Raylene even looks at Katie crossly, this'll be the last time."

"Okay, mama bear." Lucky's mouth quirked. "I think that thing you've got in the oven is done."

Shoot. Tawny grabbed the gratin just before it got too brown and put down an extra place setting for Lucky.

"Katie," she called. "Time to eat."

They dug in and even Katie admitted that the meal was good. To Tawny it was about the best thing she'd ever eaten.

"Brady made this?" Lucky asked, his mouth full.

"You know him?"

"Yeah. He'll be in charge of catering events I'm doing with the Lumber Baron at the cowboy camp. Why do you ask?"

"I just heard he was new in town. What's he like?"

"What do you mean, what's he like? He's a guy and he cooks."

"I was just curious is all. Sam asked me to introduce myself to him. She and Nate are worried he'll leave Nugget if he doesn't make friends."

"As long as he cooks like this, he'll make friends. Anyway, he's got Clay's wife. She's a cookbook author and sometimes helps out at the Lumber Baron."

"I think Sam meant single people. Maybe I'll tell Harlee and Darla to invite him to their bowling nights at the Ponderosa."

Lucky looked up from his plate. "Why? They're not single. You're the only person I know around here who's single. Is Sam trying to set you up with him?"

"Of course not." God, why had she even brought it up? "She just wants him to make friends. That's all."

"And date you," Lucky said. "Why not? He seems like a good guy."

"Mommy, why don't you date Daddy?"

Tawny shot Lucky a dirty look. "Finish your dinner, baby. Tonight's an early night."

Katie took a few more bites and asked to be excused.

"Okay, but I want you to change into your pajamas. A warm pair."

When she took off, Lucky said, "Sorry about that. I'm not used to having to watch my p's and q's."

"Well, get used to it. She hears and absorbs everything around her."

He nodded in understanding. "When the *Sports Illustrated* reporter comes up to do that profile I told you about, he'll find out about Katie. You and I have to decide how to handle that. I'd like us to be on the same page."

"You mean about you just learning about being Katie's father?"

"Yeah. Knowing the media, he's going to try to make one of us out to be the bad guy. That's why it would be good to get our story straight." He locked eyes with her. Tawny presumed it was to convey how important this was. "Something plausible."

"You mean like how you were accused of rape by Raylene and her dad, and how I was trying to protect my daughter from the nasty fallout?"

"Tawny, keep your voice down. You just got done telling me that our daughter is a sponge. And for the record, I'd prefer to go with a different story."

"I thought you might." She turned up her lips in a tight smile. "What did you have in mind? That I'm a selfish bitch who wanted Katie all to myself?"

"Works for me."

"All right," Tawny said.

"I was kidding, Tawny. What if we just tell the reporter that it's private—that Katie is sick and our focus is on getting her better and that we don't feel like the past is relevant."

Tawny laughed. "Yeah, good luck with that."

"Instead of being negative, why don't you try to help me out here?"

"First off, I'm not sure I even want him to know that Katie's sick."

Lucky all but rolled his eyes. "The whole town knows she's sick, Tawny. The reporter is planning on staying a few days. How long until he bumps into Owen or Donna?"

Lucky had a point, but still . . . Tawny wanted some privacy for her daughter. "I don't like this, Lucky."

"I don't like it either, but I committed to the story before I knew about Katie. Look at the bright side: It might drum up even more publicity for your boot business."

"I doubt that," she said, and Lord knew she had more business than she could handle. "The story is about you. Why would some reporter care about my boots, anyway?"

"Because I'll show them to him. Hell, that could be a whole story in itself. Your boots are pretty spectacular, Tawny. And I've seen a lot of boots in my time."

The compliment sent tingles up her spine. She had a fairly good idea of how special her boots were, but to hear it from Lucky . . . "What if the reporter goes nosing around about why I didn't tell you about Katie all this time?"

"I think it's a good bet he will. But unless you told someone, no one will be able to give him an answer."

"I didn't tell anyone," she said. "Are you worried about Raylene spilling the beans?"

"Not in the least." Lucky said it with such confidence that Tawny started to believe that maybe Raylene was different now. "She's sorry about that night, Tawny. She wishes she would have spoken up on my behalf and said what we were doing was consensual. But she was afraid of Ray. She was afraid he'd kill us both."

Ray could be mean, that was for sure. His temper was so legendary that when he'd approached Tawny about making him a pair of boots, she'd told him she couldn't take on any new clients until Katie was better. His face had turned redder than a Bing cherry, but what was he going to do? Tell Tawny she had to put his boots over her daughter's care? That wouldn't have gone over real well in this town. And Ray Rosser cared as much about his reputation as he did about the Rock and River Ranch.

Interesting how Raylene used to make fun of Tawny's father, when Franklin Wade was twenty times the man that Ray Rosser was. Never once had he raised his voice to Tawny, let alone his hands. Tawny had been an ugly girl, but everyone in Nugget knew that Franklin thought the sun rose and set on her.

"You look just like your ma," he used to say. Liza Wade was a true beauty and everyone in Nugget knew that too.

"I'm just glad that your mother doesn't work for him anymore," Tawny said.

"I made sure of that." Lucky got up and brought his dish to the sink.

"When's the reporter coming?"

"Few weeks."

"You know what I think we ought to do?" The idea had just come to her. "I think we should talk to Harlee Roberts. Obviously, we won't tell her what happened at the Rock and River. But she'll know how we should handle this guy."

"It's not a bad idea. The truth is, I wouldn't be opposed to telling people, given how absurd the story is. Especially now, when everyone can see that Raylene and I are together. But it would be embarrassing to Raylene and confusing for Katie."

"I agree," Tawny said. At least to the Katie part.

"You gonna introduce yourself to Brady?"

"Huh? Why are you bringing that up again?"

Lucky locked his coffee-brown eyes on hers. "No reason. Just curious."

Chapter 8

Jake sat at his desk at the police station, eating a Bun Boy burger, searching weekend getaways on the Internet.

"What do you think of this one?" he called to Connie, who came from her desk to peer over Jake's shoulder.

"Bodega Bay? I guess it's okay if you like fog and Alfred Hitchcock."

"What are you talking about? *Condé Nast Traveler* calls it one of the most scenic coastal towns in the country."

"Vegas. That's where I would take her."

Yeah, because nothing said romance like a casino full of cigarette smoke and old folks playing slot machines. "I'm not taking Cecilia to Las Vegas."

Rhys came out of his office. "What're you doing?"

"Lover boy here is trying to find a romantic getaway for him and Cecilia Rodriguez," Connie said.

"Let me see." Rhys bumped Connie out of the way so he could view Jake's computer screen. "Scroll down . . . Nah, you can do better."

"Like where?" Jake asked. "I've only got three days. And I don't want it anywhere around here."

"Wine country," Rhys said. "Something in the Napa Valley. I bet Nate could hook you up. He knows people."

"Yeah? You think that's better than the coast? What about the Sea Ranch?"

"Never been." Rhys leaned around Jake to type St. Helena into the search engine.

"I've been to the Sea Ranch," Connie said. "The road made me want to kill myself. It's like a sheer drop right into the ocean. I had to pull over to throw up. You should go to San Francisco."

"I don't want to go to San Francisco." Although he lived in Nugget now, Jake had had enough of big city noise and traffic to last him a lifetime. "What's there to do in wine country besides drink wine?"

"Good food," Rhys said. "It's pretty there. Women like it."

"That's a plus since Cecilia's not too hot on leaving her grandchild."

The bell above the station door chimed and Wyatt walked in. He stopped to take in everyone huddled around Jake's computer. "What's going on?"

"I'm looking for a place to take Cecilia for the weekend. Rhys says wine country."

"Why not Tahoe?" Wyatt wanted to know.

"Because it's thirty minutes from here," Jake said. "Too close to keep Cecilia from running home the first time Katie has a sniffle."

"Now that whole thing turned out unpredictable," Wyatt said, shaking his head. "Lucky Rodriguez. Who would've thought?"

"Why do you think Tawny kept it a secret all this time?" Connie asked. "I remember how shocked everyone was when she got pregnant. The girl was even shyer than I was."

"News flash, Connie, you were never shy." Wyatt jumped away before Connie could slug him. "Lucky was a horn dog back then, but Tawny Wade was definitely not his speed. He was always hanging around all those girls in Raylene Rosser's crowd. The popular girls."

"They're all fat now," Connie said.

"Uh, Raylene looks pretty good to me," Wyatt said.

"I'm telling Darla," Connie teased. "What about you, Rhys. Were you surprised?"

"I'm a cop. Nothing surprises me. Besides, I was six years ahead of them in school. By the time they graduated from training wheels, I was freezing my ass off on a fishing boat in Alaska."

Jake was the only one of the bunch who hadn't grown up in Nugget. Rhys had left when he was eighteen and had eventually gotten hired on at Houston PD, working his way up the ranks before coming home and making chief.

"What does Cecilia say about it?" Connie asked Jake.

"Nothing that I would tell you," he responded. Everyone in this town was a gossip vulture. "What's important here is that Katie has a great father and grandmother in her life now. What happened ten years ago is irrelevant."

"Have they gotten Lucky's test results back?" At least Rhys had better sense than to spend his time dissecting other people's love lives.

"Still waiting." Jake tapped on his computer keys. "That's why I want to get Cecilia out of here for a couple of days. To get her mind off it."

"How's Katie doing in the meantime?" Rhys sat sideways on Jake's desk.

"So-so. She's weak, tired, and often feverish. It's to be expected."

Rhys dragged his hand through his hair. "Jesus. If Emma ever got sick . . ."

"It's rough," Jake said, thinking of his own daughters. "I've got to give Tawny a lot of credit. This has been going on a long time and she somehow manages to hold herself up. At least she has help now."

"Lucky is sure enamored with the kid," Connie said. "I saw him with her at the Ponderosa yesterday. Raylene was with them. I guess they're an item now."

That's another reason Jake wanted to get Cecilia out of town. When she found out about Lucky and Raylene, she went through the roof. Jake hadn't always made the best decisions about women, but even he could tell that Raylene was a mess.

But Lucky was a grown man and Cecilia needed to accept that this was his life. And Jake had to be careful about getting in the middle. He hadn't earned that right yet. Not with Cecilia and definitely not with Lucky. The young man was still leery of Jake, and Jake couldn't blame him.

"I heard some reporter from *Sports Illustrated* is coming to town to interview him for a big spread in the magazine," Wyatt said. "Darla says Sam told her that he already booked a room at the Lumber Baron."

Jake looked at Rhys for confirmation. Rhys's wife, Maddy, owned the inn with her brother, Nate Breyer, who'd recently married Sam.

"Yep," Rhys said, and pointed at Connie and Wyatt. "Don't you two have any work to do? If you don't, I could find you some."

They scattered like roaches and Jake stifled a chuckle. "You getting any closer to filling that position?"

The department had gotten authorization—and funds—from the city to add a fourth officer. It would mean fewer weekend and graveyard shifts for the rest of them.

"Nope," Rhys said. "Believe me, I'm trying. If you've got someone in mind, let me know."

Far off the beaten track, Nugget had a hard time attracting civil servants other than park rangers. Most of the population worked in ranching, for the railroad, or owned a small business. A few made the fifty-minute trek to Reno, the nearest large city. And some got seasonal work in Glory Junction, a resort town near the ski slopes.

"I'll ask around," Jake said, but knew that most of the guys from LAPD who might be interested would be retirement age and looking for a second pension. Although Rhys wouldn't say it, Jake knew he wanted young blood, not veterans who wanted to rest on their laurels so they could live in the mountains and support their fishing and hunting hobbies.

When Jake had approached Rhys about the job two years ago, he'd almost been turned down. It had taken a lot of groveling to persuade the chief that he wouldn't be a slacker. Good thing, because this was the best job he'd ever had.

"St. Helena, huh?" Jake looked at the website Rhys had called up. "It looks like a spiffy version of Nugget."

"Not even close." Rhys made the lots-of-money sign with his fingers. "You want me to talk to Nate?"

"Sure." If he could swing a deal, why not? Cecilia deserved something special. Maybe one of those spa treatments and definitely a fancy restaurant. Let someone cook for her for a change. "Thanks for doing—" Before he could say more the door came crashing open and Ray Rosser pushed his way past Connie.

"I want to talk to you." Ray jabbed his finger at Rhys.

Jake stood up. Not that Rhys couldn't handle himself. But you take on a cop, you take on the whole department. Wyatt and Connie also moved in.

"What can I do for you, Rosser?" Rhys said.

"I want Lucky Rodriguez arrested."

"For what?"

"There's illegal activity going on at that bullshit dude ranch of his."

Rhys lifted his brows, dubious. Jake got the distinct impression that, like him, Rhys wasn't a fan of Rosser's. "What kind of illegal activity, Ray?"

"Drugs. They're dealing out of there."

"And you know this for a fact?"

"A couple of my hands were approached by a couple of his construction workers."

"Approached?" Rhys threw his hands up in the air. "You'll have to be more specific."

"Your wife's in bed with that boy, so I didn't expect much out of you. I guess I'll go to the sheriff."

Ray stomped out and the four of them watched out the window as he climbed into his truck and zoomed away. Rhys shrugged on his jacket and grabbed a set of keys to one of the police SUVs from a hook off the back wall.

"I'll come with you," Jake said, knowing full well that Rhys was headed to Lucky's.

"I don't think that's a good idea. You've got a conflict of interest with dating Cecilia."

"No more than you do, seeing as how your *wife's in bed with that boy*."

"Why did he say that?" Wyatt, not the sharpest tool in the shed, asked.

"Not literally, you idiot," Connie said. "The Lumber Baron and Lucky's cowboy camp are doing business together."

"Oh yeah, I knew that."

"All right, let's go." Rhys bounded out the door, Jake on his tail.

They made good time to the cowboy camp, where they found Lucky in a chute, straddling a bull. Four ranch hands were hanging off the fence, watching. Lucky motioned for one of the hands to open the gate and the bull came flying out into an old-style arena. Jake figured the setup had been left over from the Rolands' summer camp. They must've held amateur rodeos. There was even an announcer's booth. Both needed renovating. Some of the wood appeared rotted and the arena was missing many of its railings.

He and Rhys grabbed a seat on a set of metal bleachers—those at least seemed new—and enjoyed the show. Jake had only been to a few rodeos and it was exciting to watch Lucky stay glued to the bull's back, holding on one-handed while the animal did everything it could to buck him off. The bull had to be at least two thousand pounds.

One of the guys waved a stop watch in the air and Lucky let go of the rope, dove off the animal, and raced for the nearest fence, practically vaulting over it. The hands thought it was the funniest thing in the world, laughing and slapping each other's backs. That's when Lucky noticed him and Rhys, pulled his hat out of the dirt, and ambled over.

"That was something," Jake said.

"That's Crème Bullee. I was testing him out for the beginners."

"I hope you have good insurance," Rhys said.

Lucky grinned. "One of you want to try?"

"Yeah, we're gonna pass," Rhys said. "But we do need to talk to you. You got somewhere private we can go?"

"Sure." Lucky's forehead creased in worry and he led them to a nearby shed. "This doesn't have anything to do with Katie, does it?"

"Nothing like that," Rhys responded. "Ray Rosser came in the station today. He seems to think that some members of your crew are dealing drugs."

"Ray Rosser is full of shit." Lucky waved his hand in the air. "But you're free to search as soon as you get a warrant." He started to walk away.

"Son, come back here," Jake called to his back.

"I'm not your son," Lucky said, but he turned around to face them. "Rosser won't stop until he drives me out of town. He doesn't want me with his daughter. And you people are so ready to believe anything he says."

"Look," Rhys said, "we just want to ask you a few questions and nip any false allegations in the bud before it gets out of hand. You hear me?"

"What do you want to ask?"

"Is there even a slight chance some of your men could be dealing on the side?" Rhys shielded his eyes and gazed out over the ranch. "You've got a lot of guys coming and going. It could be happening right under your nose."

"I suppose," Lucky said. "But I'm more inclined to think that old man Rosser wants to give me a hard time."

"You got names and social security numbers for all your employees?" Rhys asked.

"In my office. You want 'em?"

"I'd like to run them—see if anyone has a sheet. After that we'll take it from there. In the meantime, keep your eyes open." Rhys watched the hands herd the bull out of the arena and into a corral.

"Yeah. All right." Lucky motioned for them to follow him to one of the other outbuildings.

They went inside, where a small metal desk took up one side of the room. The other side was piled high with boxes. Lucky thumbed through a cabinet, pulled out a file folder, and handed it to Rhys.

"Copy it and return it."

"Thanks," Rhys said. "Rosser said members of your crew had approached some of his hands. You know any of them who truck together?"

"Nope." Lucky squinted his eyes. "What I do know is that Ray Rosser is a known liar."

Jake locked eyes with Lucky and didn't like what he saw. "You let us handle this, Lucky. Don't go over to the Rock and River and borrow trouble. If he's lying, we'll find out."

Lucky stared down at his boots. "Last time that sumbitch got in my face, I left town. I'm not leaving again."

"Why'd he get in your face?" Rhys asked.

"He accused me of something I didn't do. Like he is now."

"Dealing drugs?" Rhys wanted to know.

It had been before Rhys's time, but Jake knew about the rape allegations, because Cecilia had told him. Once Lucky left town, Ray hadn't gone to the police.

"No," was all Lucky said. "If you don't mind, I've gotta get back to work."

"I appreciate this." Rhys held up the file. "I'll get it back to you in the next day or two."

As they left the office, Jake turned to Lucky. "The best thing you can do is ignore the man. Let us take care of this."

Lucky gave him a slight nod and walked them to their vehicle. As they pulled out of the driveway, Jake rolled down his window and called to Lucky. "Stay out of this."

They were almost to the highway when Jake told Rhys, "I give him ten minutes before he hauls ass over to the Rock and River Ranch. Stupid kid."

Whoo-wee, Sam hadn't been kidding. The man had loads of tattoos.

"Hello," Tawny called out, and watched the cook nearly hit his head on the top of the oven, he jumped so fast. "I'm sorry. I didn't mean to startle you."

"No problem." He straightened and Tawny could see that Sam had been right about another thing. The Lumber Baron's chef was indeed one fine specimen of a man. About six feet tall; thick, wavy brown hair; and hazel eyes.

"I just came by to bring this back"—she handed him the casserole dish—"and to thank you for the delicious gratin."

"You must be Tawny." He shut the oven door, gestured for her to take a seat at the center island, and poured her a cup of coffee. Apparently she was staying. "How's your little girl?"

"She's doing okay. Thanks for asking . . . Brady, right?"

"Yep." He came around to where she was sitting. "Nice boots. I hear you make them."

"Mm-hmm." She gazed around the kitchen. "I've never been back here before, just the public rooms. It's nice."

"Are you kidding me? It's fantastic. Best kitchen I've ever worked in. Not as big, or as high-tech, but really functional."

"Yeah, I'm not much of a cook, so I wouldn't know."

"What kind of stuff do you make?" he asked, and she laughed.

"Mac and cheese from a box, Hamburger Helper . . . like that."

He made a face. "Wow. That's terrible."

"Not the best," she admitted. "My daughter seems to like it, though."

"I guess I kind of liked it too when I was a kid. Now, not so much."

"Well, then it's a good thing you can cook."

"Anyone can cook," he said. "But not everyone can make boots like that. Let me get a look at those up close." Brady went down on his haunches to check them out.

Day of the Dead boots. A little wild, but Tawny liked them.

"Nice," he said, examining the hand-tooled, brightly colored masks that covered the shaft of each boot. "How long does it take you to do something like this?"

"These took six months, but they're pretty detailed. Most boots take five months or less, depending on the design."

"That's a lot of time."

"Everything's made by hand. So how you liking Nugget so far?"

"I like it pretty well." He got up, walked to the big industrial stove, put a slice of quiche on a plate, and slid it in front of Tawny along with a fork. It smelled too good to pass up, so she dug in. "Nice folks. A little on the gossipy side, though."

"Get used to it. It's Nugget's favorite pastime. But for the most part, people mean well."

"A couple of the ladies asked me to join their cooking group, the Baker's Dozen. I don't know. You think it's weird?"

"Why would it be weird? You like to cook, right?"

"A: They're all women. B: Most of them are old enough to be my mother. C: They spend more time talking about Clay McCreedy than they do about cooking. What is it with that guy?"

Tawny had to keep from giggling. "He was a navy fighter pilot and a war hero. But mostly they're just obsessed with him. Now that he's married, they'll probably find someone else to lust after."

"He's married to Emily," he said, and shook his head. "She's in the group. They talk about him like she's not even there."

"I know." She finished the quiche and before she could stop him, Brady put another slice on her plate. "They're funny that way. But harmless."

He leaned against the island. "Why don't you join?"

"Uh . . . I thought we went over the fact that I don't cook. Besides, I'm sort of overwhelmed these days."

"I can see that. It's gotta be tough with your daughter being so sick."

"Katie's dad and her grandmother are a big help."

"Lucky, huh?" Brady bobbed his head.

"Mm-hmm. He says you'll be doing the catering at the cowboy camp for Lumber Baron events?"

"That's the plan."

"Where's your accent from?" Tawny thought it was nice. Not like her dad's Oklahoma accent, which was more guttural but also nice. This one was lower in the throat, looser and more musical.

"South Carolina," he said. "I grew up in the sticks but cooked in Charleston. Where are you from? I hear a hint of something that's not California."

"Here. Born and raised. My father's people were from Oklahoma, so maybe that's what you're hearing. But to tell you the truth, this is a lot of the way we talk here."

"Unfortunately, my idea of a California accent is the Valley girl thing. Drove me nuts when I worked in LA."

She laughed. Brady was fun and funny and attractive . . . and not Lucky. How screwed up was that? So screwed up that when Raylene Rosser wandered into the kitchen in a pair of cut-off jean shorts, Tawny wanted to scratch her eyes out. It was October, for God's sake. In a couple of weeks they could have snow.

"Hi." Raylene scanned the room and let her eyes fall on Tawny, then summarily ignored her. "Do you know where Samantha Dunsbury-Breyer is? I'm supposed to be meeting with her."

"You check her office?" Brady asked, and Tawny had to give him credit for not gawking at Raylene's mile-long legs.

"The guy at the front desk did. He said to check back here."

"That would be Andy," Brady said, and let out a sigh. Apparently he didn't think too highly of the reservationist. "It's not like Sam to miss a meeting. Let me make a few calls."

While Brady got on the phone, Raylene stood awkwardly to the side. "How are you, Thelma? It's been a long time."

Well, knock me over with a feather. "Yes, it has. I'm good. Thanks for asking. How are you?"

"You've probably heard that I'm going through a bad divorce. Butch cheated on me."

"I'm sorry to hear that," Tawny said, and felt like a heel for being disingenuous. "Are you planning an event at the inn?"

"A few friends are coming from Denver. I wanted to book a block of rooms."

Tawny wondered why they wouldn't stay at the Rock and River. "That sounds nice."

"I met Katie yesterday." Raylene tugged down her top, which was showing a sliver of midriff. "Lucky took us to lunch. She's a nice little girl. I'm so sorry she's sick."

Uh-oh. If Raylene kept it up, Tawny might have to like her. "I appreciate it."

"Raylene?" Sam came rushing into the kitchen, carrying her jacket and briefcase. "I am so sorry. Our plane got detained on the runway in San Francisco. Fog. I tried to reach you, but your phone kept sending me to voice mail."

"I left it at Lucky's the other night," Raylene said. "That's okay. You're not that late."

"Let's go in my office and see what I've got open on that date."
On her way out she waved at Tawny and mouthed *Sorry.*

"I'll catch you on my way out," Tawny told her.

After they left, Brady said, "So that's Raylene Rosser?"

"Yep. I'm impressed. You didn't even ogle her."

He chuckled. "She looks like every other blonde chick channeling Daisy Duke in Los Angeles. Seen one, seen them all."

Refreshing, Tawny thought. "I'm guessing that you've heard a lot about her?"

"She's a mythical figure in this town. Cheerleader, homecoming queen, rodeo queen. Although to hear it from Donna Thurston, the woman has turned a little *Girls Gone Wild.* Supposedly, she made quite a scene at the Gas and Go the other night. Donna is chalking it up to the fact, and I quote, 'that her no-good husband screwed her best friend.' "

Now Raylene gets to screw Lucky. Tough life. "Yeah, poor Raylene Rosser."

"Don't like her much, huh?"

"When we were kids she wasn't the nicest—a bully, really. But everyone thought she was so wonderful—girl most likely to succeed and all that. Today she seemed decent, though. Perhaps she's changed."

"There's always that possibility," Brady said. "Why'd she call you Thelma?"

"That's my real name. I changed it for my business. You can't make cowboy boots for the stars with a name like Thelma."

Before Brady could respond, Maddy brushed into the kitchen holding Emma. She was officially back from maternity leave. Tawny knew that Cecilia had volunteered a few times to take Emma while Maddy and Rhys continued searching for a nanny or full-time babysitter.

"You guys hear the news?" she asked, her brows knitted. "Lucky just got arrested."

Chapter 9

"I can't believe you," Tawny said in a hushed voice, and Lucky knew that she wished she could scream at him. But Katie was in the next room. "After Jake tells you to stay away from Ray Rosser, what do you do? What the hell, Lucky? How long do you think it'll take before Katie hears about this at school?"

Lucky leaned back on the couch and put his foot up on his mother's coffee table. "Just relax, would you? The asshole had it coming—accusing me of being a drug dealer."

"I noticed Raylene was quick to run home—to Daddy."

"She went home to defuse the situation and to let him know that he can't come between us again."

"You're just very lucky that Jake is on your side. Otherwise this could've turned out a lot worse. And if I know Ray Rosser it's not over yet. Lucky, you need to be focusing on our daughter. You can't be a donor if you're in jail."

"Tawny, honey, sit down. All that pacing is driving me up the wall." He checked out her jeans. They were tighter than usual with white stitching up the sides. "Raylene said she saw you at the Lumber Baron, hanging out with Brady."

"I was returning his gratin dish. Don't try to change the subject." She sat next to him.

For some reason it bothered him that she got herself all duded up to meet the Lumber Baron chef. She smelled good too, like that Stetson perfume in the magazines.

"It's gonna be fine, Tawny. Hell, all I did was yell at him."

"You trespassed on his property and in front of his ranch staff called him a child abuser and a wife beater. Jesus, Lucky."

"Shush." He held his finger to his mouth. "They're in the kitchen, probably hearing every word we're saying. My ma doesn't like swearing."

"As soon as Katie and I leave, your mother is going to kill you. I'm just sad I can't watch."

"When did you get so dramatic? And bossy? You used to be so sweet—and quiet."

He saw Tawny try to contain a smile. "Will you promise to stay out of trouble?" she asked. "At least until we know whether you're a match. Then you can do whatever the hell you want. Trespass. Get in people's faces. Accuse them of horrible crimes."

"I promise." When she looked at him dubiously, he held up his hands, palms up. "I swear. It was a mistake. I shouldn't have gone over there." And Ray Rosser shouldn't have been allowed to treat his family the way he had. Not Raylene or her mother. Why either of them still lived with him was a mystery.

"I'm going home now." Tawny got up from the couch, but he pulled her down.

"Stay for dinner."

"I can't," she said. "I've got tons of work to do."

"You've gotta eat, Tawny. Ma made chile relleno. You haven't lived until you've had her chile relleno."

"Katie can stay without me. Just bring her home after dinner." She started to get up again, but he wrapped his hand around her arm.

"Just stay. Today was a crappy day. You make it better."

She stared into Lucky's face like she was trying to figure him out, and in a reconciled voice said, "Fine."

They sat for a few minutes in companionable silence. "Did you like Brady?" he finally asked.

"He's nice." She said it so neutrally that Lucky couldn't get a read on her.

"You ever remember that night we were together?"

"Yes," she said so quietly he could barely hear her. "You were drunk."

"I wasn't an asshole or anything, was I?"

"No."

"That's all? *No.*"

"What do you want me to say? We had sex behind a swing set while you cried over Raylene."

"I didn't cry," he said.

"You may as well have."

"Were you, like, into me?" Because why else would a seventeen-year-old virgin have sex with him? According to his mom, she'd had a crush on him.

"Wasn't every girl?" Her way of saying *you conceited jackass.*

"I remember you being nice." Maybe the nicest anyone besides his mother had ever been to him. "And really smart. You're the one who came up with the plan of how I should rack up enough wins riding the circuit to get noticed by the PBR. It changed my life." Lucky paused. "Were you in love with that park ranger guy?"

She seemed to be contemplating the question. "I think so."

"He should've stuck by you then."

"Like you have with Raylene?"

He let out an audible breath. "No question, she's my crack cocaine. I think the first time I saw her I fell in love with her. Even out on the road I thought about her a lot. I wanted to hate her when she married Butch, but I couldn't."

"So what's his deal?" Tawny asked.

"Butch?" Lucky shrugged. "I don't know anything about him other than he's a cheating piece of crap. And a cheap bastard who won't give Raylene her fair share."

"According to Raylene, that is."

Lucky pushed a wisp of hair that had come loose from Tawny's ponytail behind her ear. "I know you don't like her. I know things were tough for you as a kid, with your dad sick. And there she was, looking like she had everything. But you don't know what it was like for her growing up in that house. Ray Rosser treated her mother like dirt, he treated his employees even worse than dirt, and he put so much pressure on Raylene to be his showcase daughter that he broke her."

"You ever think that you might have a hero complex?" Tawny asked.

"Doesn't every guy? For the sake of Katie and me, you think you can give her a chance?"

Tawny slowly nodded her head. "She was nice today, I'll give her that. It was a little creepy."

Lucky leaned his head back and laughed. "When she wants to, she can be a real sweetheart. She liked Katie a lot."

"What do you think she'll tell Ray?"

"That we're together and there's no way he'll be able to pull us apart. If he gives her a hard time, she's planning to move in with me. I've gotta get out of that damned trailer."

"You think there's a chance Ray's telling the truth about some of your crew dealing drugs?"

"I don't know. But Ray made it sound like I'm running a drug operation from my ranch. And that's a load of crap."

"What do you think set him off?"

"I don't think it has anything to do with you or Katie, if that's what you're thinking. He's pissed about Raylene and me. Everyone in town has seen us together and it's put him over the edge."

"What about Raylene's mom?" Tawny asked.

"She's so afraid of Ray, she'll go along with anything he does or says. Ten years ago the woman was a total knockout. Now she looks like she's aged fifty years."

"Just stay away from him, okay?"

"I said I would."

"You also told Jake you would, and look how well that worked out."

The woman was a bit of a ballbuster, but Lucky liked her loyalty. Of course her top priority in this was Katie—as it should be—but Lucky got the sense that she was looking out for him too. Under different circumstances he could see himself being attracted to Tawny Wade.

After dinner, Lucky went home and got a good night's sleep. But by seven in the morning someone was pounding on his door. Raylene, he figured. Without bothering to get dressed, he marched to the front of the single-wide to let her in.

Jake pushed passed Lucky. "Ray wasn't lying."

"What are you talking about?"

"People have been coming and going all morning. I've had the place under surveillance since five, when your crew first got to work."

Lucky, a few inches shy of Jake's height, got up in his face. "You've been spying on my ranch?"

Jake stepped away to gain some distance. "I went to the mat for you yesterday—for Cecilia. Now I want to know what the hell is going on here. So cut the attitude and get dressed."

Lucky went into his bedroom and threw on a pair of jeans and a sweatshirt. When he came back out, Jake had brewed a pot of coffee.

Jake poured them both mugs and said, "It looks to me like either you're involved in something you shouldn't be or you've got a real problem on your hands."

"Why don't you start by telling me what you saw this morning?" Lucky hooked one of the dinette chairs with his foot, pulled it away from the table, and sat.

Jake joined him, but continued to scrutinize him like they were in an interrogation room. "Any of these look familiar?" Jake pulled out his phone and started showing Lucky pictures of cars, zooming in on each one's license plate.

"I don't know." Lucky shoved his hand through his hair. "There's a lot of people in the crew. I don't pay attention to what they're driving, especially not their license numbers."

"Well, if they're working for you, you're paying them too much. They were in and out of here in less than five minutes." Jake cued up another picture. "You know this guy?"

"That's my foreman, John."

"What about him?" Jake showed him another photo of a man leaning into the window of a pickup truck.

"It's difficult to tell from the picture, but it looks like Gus. He's been mending fences on the property."

"By my count, six different vehicles came up your driveway this morning, only to turn around and leave. Each time, one of these guys stuck his head in one of their windows. So either you've got yourself some Walmart greeters, or these guys are doing some quick transactions."

"Maybe the drivers were just lost and John and Gus were giving them directions."

"Six of them lost? Yeah, and I'm the tooth fairy. I plan on running these plates. But, Lucky, if you have something to do with this, now is the time to come clean."

"What are you saying, Jake? That you think I'm running a dope operation out of the cowboy camp? Why the hell would I do that?"

"You tell me. But usually it's the universal reason. Money!"

"I don't need money," Lucky said.

Jake flipped his gaze around the single-wide. "No?"

"No. And if I did, that's not the way I'd get it." Lucky got to his feet and paced the small kitchen area. "What kind of drugs do you think they're selling?"

Jake watched him for a few seconds. "There's a lot of meth up here, pot, maybe cocaine. I wasn't close enough to see if anything exchanged hands. And this"—he held up his phone—"doesn't have a strong enough zoom lens."

Lucky continued to pace. "Shit. What do I do, fire these guys just on the suspicion that they're up to no good?"

"No. You let us run a small sting operation on the ranch. We get a couple of guys pretending to be buyers."

"Right." Lucky laughed. "Because John and Gus and God knows who else won't recognize you, Rhys, or Wyatt."

"We'll use people from Plumas County Sheriff."

"Ah, crap." Lucky tilted his head back. "This is so messed up. I should've just gone with Pat Donnelly's crew."

"Why didn't you? He's the go-to guy for construction projects around here. Trustworthy as hell."

"Because these guys were cheap—and supposedly fast. What'll happen to me, to my place, if it turns out that they're dealing?"

"As long as you're not involved, nothing," Jake said. "But, Lucky, if you've got even a minor stake in this game, this won't go well for you. Your reputation in this town will be shot."

"I'm not involved, Jake. I swear to you." A thought suddenly occurred to Lucky. "What about Katie? She's supposed to come over today for a tour. I don't want her here if the place isn't safe."

"Hold off a few days. Let me run these plates and talk to Rhys. I'd like to set something up in the next week or two."

"I'd like to fire their asses," Lucky said. "I don't have time for this bullshit."

Jake stood up and put a fatherly hold on Lucky's shoulder. "If they're dealing drugs in this community, we'd like to get them. This is our best opportunity, Lucky."

"It's a good opportunity for *you*. For me, it'll be the worst kind of publicity. I'd rather just be rid of these yahoos and hire Donnelly. He'll put Colin Burke in charge and I won't have to worry about drug deals going down on my property."

"Obviously, we can't force you to employ people you don't want to employ," Jake said. "But Ray Rosser is shooting off his mouth. You suddenly fire a bunch of people and it'll look suspect, Lucky. Like maybe you had something to cover up. We take these guys down with your help and you'll look like a hero."

"I don't want to be a hero. I just want to get this damn project off the ground. I want my daughter to be able to visit without having to worry about criminal activity on my land. And if these people are dealing drugs right under my nose, who knows what else they're doing? I've got hundreds of thousands of dollars' worth of livestock on this ranch."

"Give us two weeks. I think we can take them down fast—and quietly. In the meantime, we'll watch your place twenty-four-seven."

Lucky let out a breath, unable to believe he was even considering letting the police do a sting. "So how would it work? These sheriff's deputies would pretend to be buyers?"

"The less you know about it the better. Just stick to your regular routine and let us handle it. Before you know it, it'll be over. But, Lucky," Jake said, "you can't tell anyone. One person knows and the whole operation is shot. That means definitely not Raylene. Not even Tawny."

"I won't tell them," Lucky said.

"No one. Not even your most trusted employee. It would not only blow the operation, but it could put our people in danger."

"I've got it, Jake. Unlike the rest of this town, I know how to keep my mouth shut. So what do I do? Just continue with the construction like everything is hunky-dory?"

"That's exactly what you do. At some point we might pull you in, but for now you go on like it's just another day. The last thing we want to do is arouse these guys' suspicions."

Tawny wandered into the living room, wrapped in nothing but a towel, to find Lucky lounging on her ratty recliner. She dashed back into her bedroom and yelled from the door, "A little warning next time."

She really had to talk to the man about calling first. He seemed to think that he could show up whenever he wanted to. Katie was at school, so she couldn't imagine why he was here in the first place.

"You shouldn't leave your door unlocked while you're in the shower," Lucky shouted back.

She'd come in after spending the morning in her studio and must've forgotten to fasten the deadbolt.

"What are you doing here?" She ditched the jeans laid out on her bed and hunted through her closet, landing on a short vintage dress.

"I needed to talk to you."

A few moments later she burst out of her bedroom. "Did you get the results?"

"Not yet. No, this is about something else." He eyed her dress. "You going somewhere?"

Embarrassed that she'd gone a bit overboard, she lied. "Yeah. I have a . . . a thing . . . a meeting with a prospective client."

"You in a rush?"

"No. The meeting isn't for a while. I've just been working all morning, needed a break and figured I may as well get ready. You want a cup of coffee?" She headed for the kitchen and he followed.

"Sure. Where are you meeting this client?"

"His house," she said, because it was the first thing she could think of. Clients always came to her studio.

"You know this guy?"

"Uh . . . yeah. Cream? Sugar?" She poured him a mug.

"Black's fine. How do you know him?"

"Lucky, what's with the third degree? I own a business. I know lots of people."

"Which reminds me, what's going on with those boots I want?"

Tawny fixed her own mug and took it to the table. "He doesn't want to sell 'em. In fact, he picked them up the other day." She touched her nose to see if it had grown. "What did you want to talk to me about?"

"There's a lot of construction going on at the ranch today. I think we should put off Katie's visit until things calm down. The dust and commotion are too much. I don't want her getting sick."

"That sounds smart. I'll pick her up then. She'll be disappointed, but—"

"Nah, I'll get her after school and we'll do something fun. Maybe we'll go to the Bun Boy for supper and do a little bowling next door."

"All right," Tawny said. "Just have her home early. It's a school night."

He winked at her. "Yes, ma'am. Why don't you drop by after your appointment? Bowl with us."

"What? Raylene busy?" Tawny didn't know what got into her sometimes.

"Bowling is not really Raylene's thing. She and I have plans later."

Tawny could only imagine. "I don't think it's a good idea, Lucky.

Your time with Katie should be yours." Precocious Katie was already plotting ways that they could be one big happy family together.

"Unlike you, I don't have a problem with sharing," he said, getting a little dig in. "But if you don't want to come, I understand."

"It's not that I don't want to come. I just don't want Katie getting any ideas."

"Ah," he said. "I get it. I figured she understood that Raylene and I were together."

"She's nine. That's not really how her mind works."

"I guess not," he said. "So we're not ever allowed to do stuff together because it might get her hopes up?"

"I don't know, Lucky. This is all pretty new. What does it matter anyway?"

"I just think it would be nice for us to occasionally do things together."

"Why?" she asked. *Just to drive me crazy?*

"I would think it would be good for Katie to see that we're friends. Besides, I like you."

Tawny didn't say anything. Before the silence could grow awkward, Lucky's phone rang. More like mooed. His ringtone was that of a bellowing bull. He must've changed it. Last time it had just been a plain old ring.

"Hey, babe." He got up from the table and went into the living room. Since the house was all of a thousand square feet, Tawny could still hear Lucky's side of the conversation. "Let him press charges, then . . . Don't worry, my lawyer will handle it . . . Hey, Raylene, I'm at Tawny's right now. Can we do this later?"

There was a long pause and then Tawny heard Lucky mutter a curse.

"She hung up on you, didn't she?" Tawny walked into the living room. "She's angry that you're over here. See, this is why we can't all spend time together."

Tawny had enough drama with Katie's illness; she didn't need any more. For once she just wanted a calm life.

"She's just a little jealous of you."

"What in God's name for?"

"Woman, have you looked in a mirror lately?" Lucky raked his hand through his hair. "It's like what you said: This is all pretty new. Me being a father, and you and Katie having me in your lives, Raylene didn't bargain for any of it. She didn't bargain for the fact that her husband dumped her for her best friend. I think we all need to cut her some slack. But, Tawny, the one thing I know for sure is that I want the mother of my daughter to be my friend. It's important to me. And I think it's important for Katie."

"All right," Tawny said. "So is Ray pressing charges against you for threatening him?"

"He says he is, but who really knows? The man's full of bluster."

She fixed him with a look. "Of course he'll press charges. You went on his property and you laid into him. What do you expect, Lucky?"

"It was a stupid thing to do, all right? Does that make you feel better? But I can't exactly take it back now."

"You could apologize."

"Never gonna happen."

Tawny shook her head in exasperation. "Really, Lucky, you should—"

"Someone's knocking."

She walked to the window and pulled the lace panel aside. Brady. Opening the door, she said hi and let him in. "What a nice surprise."

He handed her a basket. "Muffins for you and Katie." That's when he noticed she had company. "Oh. Hey, Lucky. This a bad time?"

"No, of course not," Tawny said. "But how did you get my address?"

"Are you kidding me? This is Nugget."

She laughed and held up the basket. "Thanks for these. Should we have some with coffee?"

"I've gotta get going," Lucky said, but she sensed that he was annoyed. "I'll get Katie home at around seven."

"Okay. Have a nice time and go easy on the junk food."

He nodded, grabbed his hat off the credenza at the front door, and stepped out.

"Shoot," Brady said. "Seems like I might've been interrupting something."

"Nothing. Actually we were arguing, so it's good that you came."

"What were you arguing about? If I'm being too nosy, feel free to tell me to mind my own business."

"Apparently, Ray Rosser is planning to press charges. I told

Lucky to just apologize, but his pride—and bullheadedness—won't let him."

"Since I'm already sticking my nose where it doesn't belong, is there something between you two?"

"You mean besides the fact that we have a daughter together?"

"Yep," he said. "Look, I'll just put it out there. I thought you and I could start hanging out. I left a weird situation in LA, like seriously effed-up weird, and I'm still gun-shy. But you seem like one of the normal ones. So if you and Lucky are a thing . . ."

"We're not," she said. "He's with Raylene."

"Really? Because I was kind of picking up a vibe a few minutes ago."

"You must've imagined it," she said. "So what happened in Los Angeles?"

"I'll tell you sometime after we've had twenty drinks." He looked at the half pot of coffee on the kitchen counter. "Caffeine doesn't count."

"You're actually planning to make me wait for this story?" she said.

"Afraid so." He reached into the basket. "Here, have a muffin."

By the time Brady left, she'd told him her life story and he'd told her nothing. A man of mystery. But a very engaging one.

Tawny went back into her studio and used the rest of the day to work on Clay McCreedy's boots. He'd chosen soft kangaroo leather and a simple design. The McCreedys, with the exception of Clay's first wife, who was now dead, didn't go in for the flashy stuff. The showiest Clay got was a medallion with two-color stitching. But both he and his late father had always liked quality.

With Hayes Carll playing in the background, she managed to make a great deal of headway. By quitting time, she realized that one of Brady's muffins was the only thing she'd eaten all day and went inside the house to scrounge up something for dinner. Halfway through a ham sandwich, she saw Lucky's Ram truck pull into the driveway and glanced at the clock. The man was punctual.

Katie ran in. "We went bowling, Mommy, and I got a strike. That's when you knock all the pins down in one try."

"Congratulations," Tawny said. "Come give Mama a kiss and then put on your pj's."

Katie dutifully kissed Tawny, then whined, "But it's only seven."

"I know, but it's a school night and you've been under the weather."
Tawny felt Katie's head. "Brush your teeth while you're at it."

Katie reluctantly complied, leaving Tawny and Lucky alone in the kitchen.

"Sounds like she had fun," Tawny said.

"Yep. When did Brady leave?"

"Uh, hours ago. Why?"

"It just seemed like he was planning on camping out."

"Camping out? We barely know each other."

"According to Raylene, you seemed pretty hot and heavy the other day at the Lumber Baron. She said you were practically making out in the kitchen."

"We weren't, but I can't see how it would be either of your business if we were."

"Yeah, you're right. It's not." He sagged into one of the kitchen chairs. "But all day it's been bugging me. And I don't know why. I guess I don't want another man in Katie's life—not so soon after I found her."

A small part of Tawny had hoped it was about her. "Perhaps you're overreacting, since Brady and I just met."

"Probably." He smiled at her so warmly that her stomach did cartwheels. "If I didn't know better, I'd think that I was jealous."

"Obviously that would be ridiculous." The sarcasm went right over his head because he nodded in agreement.

"I've only met him a few times," Lucky said. "But everyone says he's a stand-up guy. I suppose the four of us should go out sometime. Maybe if I got to know him better I wouldn't be having this odd reaction to the two of you."

When hell freezes over, Tawny thought. "Sure. Not to be rude or anything, but it's getting kind of late."

Lucky glanced at the kitchen clock on Tawny's electric stove. "I can take a hint." He started for the front door. "You're coming to dinner tomorrow night at my mother's, right?"

"I'll drop Katie off, but I'd like to use the time to catch up on my work. If we get the green light for a transplant, I'll have to take time off."

"As far as money, I've got your back now," Lucky said.

"No, you have Katie's back. I make my own way in this world. Good night, Lucky."

"You don't need to be so tough. You took care of my kid for nine years. Even though I'm pissed about it, the right thing to do is to take care of you." And for no reason at all he kissed her. Nothing that would go down in the annals of all-time great romantic kisses, just a rough peck on the lips.

And how pathetic was Tawny for knowing that she'd live off that kiss for a good long time?

Chapter 10

The following weekend Jake took Cecilia to wine country. During the romantic stay, Rhys was setting up an undercover team with the sheriff's department to take down the drug dealers at Lucky's cowboy camp.

Jake had run the license plate numbers of the vehicles he'd seen coming and going at the ranch that morning. It hadn't taken him long to figure out the backgrounds of the people on the list, leaving no doubt that Lucky's construction crew ran a lucrative side business. Probably methamphetamine, given the histories and reputations of the buyers.

But they weren't the target. Jake and Rhys wanted to go as far up the chain as possible. Meth was a scourge in these mountains, where cookers found abandoned cabins and mobile homes in desolate areas to manufacture the drug and have their minions distribute it.

At one time, while the Lumber Baron was still vacant, meth dealers commandeered the inn to store their cache of chemicals and equipment. Rhys wound up killing one of them after the man took Maddy hostage.

"What's going on?" Cecilia asked as Jake texted back and forth with Rhys, finalizing plans for the sting.

"Just police business. Nothing to worry about." He pulled her into his arms. God, the woman was beautiful. Strands of silver ran through her ebony hair. And her dark eyes . . . Jake could drown in them. Although she was slender, she had enough to hold on to. And Jake never wanted to let go.

She reached up on tiptoe to kiss him, winding her arms around his neck. "Does it have anything to do with Lucky's ranch?"

The woman was also smart as hell.

"Sweetheart, I can't talk about that. Plus, we're supposed to be on vacation."

"He's my son, Jake. I can't help but worry."

"I know. You're a wonderful mother." Perhaps a little overprotective since Lucky was a grown man. But Jake was the same way with his daughters. They'd never get too old for him to stop worrying about whether they'd remembered to lock their doors. About them driving alone at night. Or who they were dating. "But I really can't talk about it."

He started to unbutton her blouse and he could feel her intake of breath as he reached for the front clasp on her bra. Unlike the women of his past, Cecilia didn't go in for the frilly stuff. Practical, sturdy beige. But what was under it completely undid him. Round, heavy breasts that somehow had managed to defy gravity after forty-eight years.

"Want to take a shower first?" he whispered in her ear.

"That would be nice." They'd never done it in the shower before, and he had a fantasy about taking her while watching rivulets of water run down her naked body.

He tugged down her skirt and panties in one fluid motion and walked her backwards into the bathroom. Nate had gotten them the best room in the best hotel in St. Helena. His cabin could fit inside the bathroom alone. The shower was a work of beauty. Multiple shower heads and one of those hand-held faucets Jake planned to make good use of.

He turned on the water and quickly stripped off his clothes, taking the time to look at Cecilia in the mirror. The woman made him harder than concrete. These days he typically needed little blue pills for that. But not with Cecilia. She made him feel twenty-five again.

They moved under the spray and he pressed her against the tile stall, touching and kissing every inch of her. She murmured something in Spanish.

"Was that something dirty?" He nibbled on her earlobe. "I certainly hope so."

"Very," she said, and let out a throaty, sensual laugh that nearly made him come. "Maybe you should learn *español, mi amor.*"

He knew enough to get by. Almost every Anglo cop in Los Angeles did. "You should give me lessons. How about I put my hands on you and you tell me what you want me to do with them in Spanish? Let's see if I can figure it out."

She seemed to like where this was going because she moved his hands over her pubic bone and said, "*Te deseo*."

He knew what that meant. First he took her with his fingers, then with the hand-held water nozzle, turning the pressure up high, then with his mouth, and finally with the part of him that throbbed for her.

"Good?" He turned her around so she could brace herself against the wall.

"Don't stop," she moaned as he took her from behind, and then crumpled as she climaxed.

"I've got you." In a fireman's hold, Jake carried her out of the shower, laid her on the bed, spread her legs, and entered her again. "This is unbelievable," he said, the halting words coming out like breaths. "If I die from a heart attack, it will have been worth it." He pumped one more time, threw his head back and shouted her name.

Ten minutes later, with their limbs twined together like tree vines, Jake said, "I think I'm in love with you, Cecilia."

She cradled his face in her hands. "I think you're in love with being in love, Jake Stryker."

"Maybe," he admitted. "But this feels different. Like the real thing."

She laughed and kissed him. "Time will tell, *mi amor*."

"What about you?"

"I don't give my love so freely," she said, and kissed him again.

He knew she'd been hurt, left by the father of her child when Lucky was just born. So he couldn't be upset with her for being leery of a three-time loser. "Time will be good to us, Cecilia. My gut tells me so. And a cop's gut rarely steers him wrong."

"How does your gut feel about a meal?" She laid her head on his chest. "There's so much good food here and we only have another day."

"Let's do it. What're you in the mood for?" Jake swung his legs over the bed, wanting to duck back into the shower for a quick rinse.

"Italian," she said. "That place that Nate recommended."

"Italian it is."

"You go first." Cecilia nudged her head at the bathroom. "I want to call Tawny and see how Katie is. Maybe they got the results."

"On a weekend? Doubtful, sweetheart. But go ahead. I'll be right out."

When he got done with his shower, Jake put on a pair of khakis, a long-sleeved shirt, and a light jacket. St. Helena wasn't as chilly as Nugget, but still nippy in the evenings. He told Cecilia to meet him in the lobby, hoping the concierge could get them a reservation. Luckily, everyone seemed to know that they were Nate's people. Nate was clearly revered in the hospitality industry, because so far, Jake and Cecilia had been treated like royalty.

While waiting, Jake checked his messages. Looked like everything was a go for Monday. Frankly, he'd like to get Lucky off the ranch for a few days, make up a story that he was going away with Raylene or to a bull riding competition. But he knew Lucky would never go for it. The kid would demand to be there when the shit went down, making sure no harm came to his ranch or livestock. Jake couldn't blame him. If he were in Lucky's shoes, he'd do the same.

Cecilia came down in a red dress that knocked Jake's socks off. God, the woman was gorgeous.

"That new?" he asked her, having never seen her this dressed up before.

"Mm-hmm. I got it at Macy's in Reno. You like?" She twirled for him.

"Are you kidding? I love. Red's your color."

The concierge let them know that the restaurant could take them in an hour. So they strolled down Main Street, looking in the shop and gallery windows. Rhys had been right on the mark about the place being money. Lots of expensive clothing and shoe boutiques and stores that sold nothing but olive oil and crackers for prices that made Jake flinch. But Cecilia seemed to enjoy it. She liked going inside, browsing through the racks, and making conversation with the shopkeepers.

Such an elegant-looking woman, Jake was sure that the proprietors thought they had a real live one on the wire. But they never seemed to mind when Jake and Cecilia didn't buy anything.

"You talk to Tawny?" Jake asked as they passed an "artisan" chocolate shop. That was the other thing about wine country; everything was "artisan." Artisan sandwiches, artisan soaps, artisan toilet paper. The term was a little overused, if you asked him.

"No results yet," Cecilia said. "And Katie is doing fine. No fevers, thank goodness. I also talked to Lucky. He was with Raylene." On Cecilia's lips, "Raylene" may as well have been a curse word.

"What are you gonna do, Cecilia? He loves the girl."

"I don't know how I raised a blind son."

"I don't think his sight is off, just his judgment."

"Raylene may be a beautiful girl on the outside, but she's no good on the inside. I knew what went on in that house. Ray was a tyrant—a bully, quick with his hands and even harsher with his mouth. And for a time I felt sorry for Raylene. I even loved her. But she started becoming just like him, sneaky and manipulative. That night that Ray accused Lucky of attacking her and Raylene just stood there, playing the victim . . . it's unforgivable."

Jake rubbed Cecilia's back. "There's a chance she's changed. All you can do is give her a chance."

"Never," Cecilia said.

Jake knew that Ray Rosser's accusations against Lucky had crushed Cecilia to the bone. No mother wants to hear her son called a rapist. But Raylene had been a kid, and from everything Jake had heard about Rosser, probably a deeply abused kid. She'd been afraid to speak up. As a detective, Jake had seen it many times before.

"You might want to rethink that," Jake said. "Lucky loves her and you love Lucky. You don't want to alienate him."

"I want him to start thinking with his brain, not his penis. He has a daughter now. He needs to settle down with a good woman like Tawny."

"Tawny?" Jake grinned. "I thought you disliked her as much as you do Raylene."

"I'm angry with her for keeping Katie from us. But in that crazy head of hers she was protecting her daughter—and Lucky and me, too. No matter what, she's always been a good girl. A family girl, who took care of her father. And now Katie."

"You certainly know how I feel about Tawny."

"Yes. I think if you were twenty years younger, you'd be chasing after her instead of me," Cecilia teased.

"Unfortunately, when I was twenty years younger I would've been chasing after Raylene. And the moral of that story is: People change, Cecilia. They get wiser and better with age. What else did you and Lucky talk about?"

"He wanted to know what we were doing." She arched one perfectly shaped ebony brow and quirked her lips in a sly little smile.

"You tell him?" Jake winked.

* * *

"Why do you keep looking out the window every five seconds?" Raylene pulled her shirt over her head and scowled. "Bored with me already?"

"Everything isn't always about you, Raylene." Lucky pulled her hips between his legs. "Do you ever wear any underwear, woman?"

"Not when I don't have to." She sat in Lucky's lap, grabbed her phone off his nightstand, made those ridiculous kissy lips she apparently thought looked sexy, and took a selfie of the two of them on Lucky's bed.

"What are you doing with that?" He motioned at her phone.

"Posting it to Facebook. Why?"

"I have a manager and an agent who need to okay stuff like that before it goes on the Internet," he said, grabbing the phone from her and deleting the picture from her gallery.

"Why?"

"Because I'm a public personality. And this"—he waved his hand between their mostly naked selves—"isn't G-rated." The PBR didn't go for racy. Bull riding is family entertainment.

"Well, excuse me." Raylene rolled her eyes. "I wasn't aware I was bad for your oh-so-clean image. I wanted Butch to see what a hottie I'm with now." She nuzzled his neck.

Lucky pulled away. "You're posting this shit to make Butch jealous?"

"After what he and Barb did to me, why shouldn't I?"

"Raylene, sometimes I don't get you at all. Is this just a game to you?"

"Of course not. I've loved you since middle school. If you're embarrassed of me and don't want me posting stuff about us being together, I won't."

"I'm not embarrassed of you, Raylene. I just don't want to be used to torment your ex-husband . . . who, by the way, is still your husband on paper, which I'm getting damned tired of."

"At least I'm not hanging out at his house every day." She got off his lap and put on her jeans.

"If you're talking about Tawny, I was never married to her."

"You had sex with her. You made a baby with her. Am I supposed to feel better that you two were never married? At least Butch doesn't live in this state."

"There's nothing going on between Tawny and me." Although to be truthful, Tawny was a hell of a lot easier to get along with. She might be snappy at times, but she was reasonable. And sensitive. You could have a real heart-to-heart with Tawny. Raylene only liked talking about herself.

Lucky leaned back on the bed, spread the blinds open with his fingers, and peered outside.

"There you go again. What's out there that's so damned important?" Raylene demanded. "We're trying to have a conversation."

Trying was the key word. Lately, they didn't have much to talk about. Unless it was about how Butch was screwing her out of the Hawaii timeshare. Mostly she just liked to drink.

"Just keeping an eye on my ranch, because instead of being out there, pulling my share, I'm in here with you."

"Then I'll just go, Lucky. God forbid I should keep you from something important."

He grabbed her around the waist and pulled her down on top of him. "Shush. I love you, Raylene, but you're a goddamned handful."

"You used to like that about me." She pouted. "You used to like everything about me."

"And I still do. Mostly. But this Butch thing is pissing me off. Shit or get off the pot, Raylene. I'm not here so you can make your ex jealous, you hear me?"

"Will you stop going over to Tawny's all the time then?"

"No! My daughter lives there. Don't you get it? I go there to see her, not Tawny." Which was mostly true. "Anyway, you're the one who told me she was seeing Brady. I thought one night we could all go out and have dinner together. If the man's going to be spending time around my daughter, I should get to know him."

"I don't want to go out with them. I don't know Brady and I can tell Thelma doesn't like me."

"We're not going out with them so the four of us can become bosom buddies. For the sake of my daughter, I'd just like to get to know Brady. Plus, it wouldn't kill you to be pleasant to the mother of my child."

"All right," Raylene reluctantly agreed, but Lucky could tell she was put out.

"Your dad still planning on pressing charges?" Jake thought it could hurt the investigation. If John and Gus got wind that Ray was making allegations, they might shut down their operation until things cooled down.

"I don't know," she said. "I think I talked him out of it, but who can tell with Dad."

"Should I apologize?" Lucky asked, gritting his teeth at the thought of it.

"It might help," she said, but sounded doubtful. "If you did, he'd want it to be all public and everything. After all, you did accuse him of being a wife beater."

"Well, he is."

"If you could get Tawny to make him boots, he might forgive you. He doesn't like the idea that she makes them for Clay McCreedy but not him."

"Yeah, not gonna happen. Tawny has her hands full right now with Katie. We're just waiting on the results of my blood test and then we're going full speed ahead on this transplant."

"Ohhh." Raylene held up her hands. "God forbid your precious girlfriend should make my father's boots, which, by the way, he would pay a butt-load for."

Lucky shook his head. "Do you not get how sick my daughter is? Jesus, Raylene, sometimes I think you're heartless."

She reached out to touch his arm. "I'm sorry. It was wrong of me to make light of it. You may not believe this, but I'm very worried about Katie. The whole town is."

He exhaled. "I've got to get to work. You coming over tonight?"

"If you still want me to."

"Ah, baby, of course I do. Come here." He got out of bed and wrapped her in his arms, but a part of him felt like a phony, like this lovey-dovey thing they did was perfunctory.

"I love you, Lucky."

He was working the top button on her jeans when the phone rang. "Ah hell." On the floor he found his pants, dug through the pocket for his phone, and looked at the caller ID. "It's Katie's doctor."

Chapter 11

Tawny thumbed through the magazines on the table. All of them were about five months old and none of them held her interest. How could they at a time like this?

"What's taking so long?" she muttered.

"We're early." Lucky reached for her hand and threaded his fingers through hers. They were warm and strong and callused and made her feel like they were in this together. A month ago it had only been her shouldering Katie's cancer. For once she didn't feel so alone.

Lucky had gotten the call yesterday. This morning, they'd left at sunrise and made the five-hour drive to Stanford. Cecilia would get Katie after school and keep her overnight if need be.

"What exactly did Dr. Laurence tell you again?" Tawny gazed up at the clock. She could almost hear it ticking away the time.

"We've been over this five hundred times, Tawny. He said I'm a match, but they need to run a few more tests before moving forward."

"But you're a match?"

"Honey, I don't know how many different ways to tell you the same thing."

"What kind of tests?" she wanted to know. Dr. Laurence had never said there would be more tests. Just the one to see if Lucky was a match.

"That's why we're here. To find out." He squeezed her hand a little tighter. "You want me to go in search of coffee?"

"No, don't leave." She held on to his hand as if it were a lifeline.

"Okay." He gave her a reassuring smile. "Try to relax. I think this is good. They're just being really careful, which is what we want."

"You're right."

"Take some deep breaths." He put his arm around her shoulders and pulled her in close.

God, he felt solid—and safe. Someone to lean on. The only person she'd ever had like that had been her father, and he was gone.

"You smell good." Lucky sniffed her hair, clearly trying to lighten the mood. "Is that perfume?"

"Just shampoo."

"You warm enough? You seem cold." Why they always cranked up the air-conditioning in medical waiting rooms, Tawny would never know.

"It was warm when we got here, so I left my coat in the truck." October in the Bay Area was balmy compared to Nugget.

He took his denim jacket off and slipped it over her shoulders. She pulled it around her like a security blanket. It was warm from Lucky's body heat and smelled like him—aftershave, man, and the outdoors.

"Thanks. You're not cold?"

"Nah," he said, and put his arm back around her.

Eventually, Dr. Laurence came out and called them back into his office.

"I'm glad we could do this so quickly," he said. "I know it's a haul for both of you, but I think we're getting closer. Lucky is indeed a tissue match. Now we'd like to determine how many of his major HLA antigens match Katie's. Ideally, we'd like to have all six, which reduces the risk of graft rejection and serious infection."

"Doc, you lost me. What if I don't have all six of . . . whatever you called it?"

"Human leukocyte antigen. They're proteins found on the surface of most cells. We inherit some of them from our parents and pass some of them to our children. But to answer your question, sometimes we'll do the transplant with less than a six-out-of-six match."

"But it's better if there is?" Tawny asked, her stomach in knots.

"Yes." The doctor nodded.

"What's the likelihood of the six out of six?" Lucky asked.

"We're going to test you and find out."

It did not go over Tawny's head that Dr. Laurence hadn't exactly answered the question. "Lucky's mother, Katie's paternal grandmother, might work better if Lucky doesn't."

"That's certainly an option we can explore," the doctor said. "In the meantime, I'd like to send Lucky to the lab, let the techs do their thing, and we should know something later this week, or by early next week at the latest. Lucky, we'd also like you to have a physical. Given your profession, I'm guessing you'll pass with flying colors or Professional Bull Riders Inc. wouldn't let you ride. But we're not taking any chances."

The doctor scrawled something on a pad, ripped off the page, and handed it to Lucky. "I'll have Delores call the lab to let them know you're coming. It's just four floors down." Lucky had taken the original blood test at the hospital lab in Quincy, so they paid close attention.

"Will it hurt?" Tawny asked the doctor before they left.

Dr. Laurence laughed. "I don't figure much hurts this man—not from what I've seen on television." He turned to Lucky. "How much does one of those bulls weigh?"

"About two thousand pounds," Lucky said.

"Wow." Dr. Laurence shook his head. "To answer your question, Tawny, it's no different than what he did before—a simple blood test. We just want to look at the genetic markers on Lucky's white blood cells. And it's better if we do that here."

"Couldn't you look at the genetic markers from the first test?" Tawny asked.

"We did," he said. "But we want to do it again. Here."

"It seems like there is something you're not telling us." Tawny looked at the doctor sternly.

"The results we got back from Labport in Quincy were inconclusive. I know how anxious you are, but we want to do this right—dot all our i's and cross all our t's." He squeezed Tawny's shoulder. "We want to do everything we can to make Katie healthy."

They thanked him and headed for the lab, Tawny brimming with frustration. *Inconclusive*. What the hell did that mean?

"You seem to know a lot about this stuff," Lucky said to Tawny. "I like the way you grilled him."

"I've had to live it for four years. Do you think he was saying that Labport screwed up the test?"

"No. I think sometimes these tests have to be run multiple times for an accurate reading. He probably figures that since Stanford's doing the transplant, Stanford should do the tests. Makes sense." He put his arm around her again. "It'll be okay, Tawny. We'll get the test done today, grab some lunch, and be home in time to put Katie to bed. Sound good?"

"Yes," she said, resting her head against his shoulder. On one level she knew the gesture was too intimate, but she needed the contact and connection, so she left her head there, sighing deeply. "Thank you."

"We're in this together."

Lucky was in and out of the lab in less than thirty minutes, and they went to the mall across the way to eat a quick lunch in a small café he found. Tawny didn't have much of an appetite. The anticipation of meeting with Dr. Laurence had left her stomach roiling most of the night. And today it wasn't much better. She got a salad and pushed the lettuce around with her fork.

"Honey, eat!" Lucky tilted his head to look at her. "We just have to wait a little bit longer. That's all."

"I feel like I've been waiting forever. From the time she got sick I waited for the chemo results, the radiation results . . . I'm so sick of waiting." She tried to blink back the tears, but they came anyway.

Lucky leaned over the table to hand her a napkin. "Let's get out of here."

He paid their bill, found his truck, and helped her into the cab. Next thing she knew, he'd flipped back the passenger seat.

"Get some shut-eye. You're exhausted, Tawny. Everything will look better when you've gotten some sleep."

He was right. She'd tossed and turned all night, playing scenario after scenario in her head. Stretching out on the bucket seat, Tawny closed her eyes. The last thing she remembered seeing were city streets and the entrance to Highway 101.

She came awake somewhere outside of Sacramento. Randy Travis played softly on the stereo and it had begun to drizzle.

"You should try to get another hour in," Lucky said.

She put her seat upright. "I'm good. How long have we been driving?"

"About two-and-a-half hours. You snore."

"I do not."

"The hell you don't." He started imitating what sounded to Tawny like a pig.

"You're making it up."

"I'll record you next time." He gently slapped her leg. "You feel better?"

"I feel rested." Not necessarily better.

"I talked to my mom. Katie is helping her make cookies."

Tawny rubbed her eyes. "That's nice. Hey, how was her trip with Jake?"

"Good, I guess."

"What? You have a problem with them dating?"

"Not a problem. It's just strange. And Jake . . . I'm not sure about him."

"Why not? He's incredibly kind, has a good job, and for a fifty-something, he's gorgeous."

Lucky tilted down his Ray-Bans and gave her a sideways glance. "He's been married three times."

"Maybe your mom's the charm. You ever think of that?"

"I try to think of my mom and Jake Stryker, together, as little as possible. I like the guy just fine, but I don't want to see my mother get hurt. She's a good person and doesn't need some smooth-talking dude breaking her heart."

"I won't say that she can't get her heart broken, because it happens to the best of us. But I don't see anyone putting anything over on Cecilia Rodriguez."

"Amen to that." Lucky turned down the music. "You ever have your heart broken?"

Tawny sat there a beat, contemplating how to answer that. "Yes," she finally said.

"That park ranger guy?"

"I suppose he did, in a way. It wasn't so much that he broke my heart, it was more that he could've been the one. But due to circumstances, we never got to find out."

"Nah, he was an asshole."

Tawny jerked her head back. "Why would you say that? You don't even know him."

"Because he should've stuck by you. Your daughter gets leukemia and he gets himself transferred to Southern California. That ain't right."

Okay. Tawny guessed that was one way of looking at it. "How about you? Who broke your heart?" Stupid question, since she already knew the answer. But she wanted to hear him say it so she could continue to remind herself of all the reasons Lucky Rodriguez was a great big toad.

"Raylene," he said. "Not just that night at the Rock and River, but when she married Butch. They had the wedding at the ranch, and my mama spent three weeks sewing pearls on Raylene's veil. I was at a rodeo in Winnsboro, Louisiana. Nearly drank myself to death."

"I'm sorry, Lucky. But you're together now."

"Yep," was all he said.

"So besides the park ranger, anyone else break your heart?"

She considered telling the truth, but what was the point, other than to make him feel guilty? Or feed his already gargantuan ego. "Nope. The upside of having Katie at eighteen is that I haven't had time for men."

"How's Brady doing with Katie's cancer?"

"Lucky, I know Raylene made it out that Brady and I are some big item, but that time you saw him at the house was only the second time we've ever talked."

"Raylene said when she saw you the other day the two of you were all over each other."

"Give me a break. We were in the Lumber Baron kitchen. How all over each other do you think we could've been?"

"Depends on how kinky you are," Lucky said, and his lips curved up. "I think the four of us should go to dinner together. I'll call him when we get back."

"I would rather you didn't do that."

"Don't you think it would be good for the four of us to get to know each other?"

"Do you not hear me? Brady and I just met. He doesn't even know Katie."

"All right." He held his hands up. "Calm down. I won't call him."

"Steer, wouldya?"

"There you go, getting all bossy again." He grinned, showing his pearly white teeth.

The man was way too sure of himself. And too sexy for his own good. She'd always known these things about him. And certainly becoming a big-time bull riding star had contributed to that large ego of his. But she also knew he was solid as cement, like with Katie and her illness. Or like fourteen years ago when Franklin couldn't breathe and collapsed while he and Tawny shopped at the Nugget Market. She'd yelled for help and suddenly Lucky appeared. Ethel and Stu had hired him to sweep up the store on weekends. He'd been a few aisles over, dusting shelves.

He ran and got Stu, but insisted on waiting with Tawny until the paramedics came. As she stood there, fearing that her father would never get up again, Lucky had slipped his hand into hers. Tawny had never realized how much warmth and strength one hand could hold until she held Lucky's. Eventually they were surrounded by medics and Lucky was hustled out of the way. He may have become her hero in middle school, but that day she fell in love with him.

When they got home, Lucky dropped Tawny at his mother's and stayed long enough to kiss Katie goodbye. He had one stop to make before he headed to the ranch and wanted to get it over with.

He parked his truck on the square, next to the Lumber Baron, and walked across the green. A couple of the guys from the Nugget Mafia were sitting outside the barbershop and waved. He supposed they were taking advantage of what was left of the weather and the daylight. Soon it would be too cold and dark to enjoy the Nugget twilight outdoors. Donna Thurston was cleaning up the condiment bar at the Bun Boy. He waved to her too, but hoped she wouldn't yak his ear off.

He had his hand on the knob of the police department door and was just about to walk inside when a surly voice told him to keep moving.

"The Ponderosa. Get a drink at the bar."

Lucky did as he was told and grabbed a stool near the door, asking Mariah for a Jack, neat.

"Coming right up, bull-riding man." She poured the whiskey into a lowball glass and placed it on a coaster in front of him. When he'd left Nugget ten years ago. the bowling alley/saloon had been a dump. Mariah and her partner, Sophie, had really classed up the joint. "How are you doing, Lucky? How's the cowboy camp coming along?"

"Slow, but otherwise good. Thanks for asking."

"How's Katie? Heard anything yet?"

"Tawny and I went to Stanford today for more tests. Keep your fingers crossed."

"The whole town is, Lucky."

"I appreciate that, Mariah." He held the glass up in a salute, but didn't want the damn whiskey.

"Don't do that again," Jake said in a low voice as he came up behind Lucky. "The last thing we need is someone seeing you going into the police station. We don't want to give anyone the idea that it isn't business as usual."

"Have you started yet?" Lucky asked. "I haven't seen anyone out there."

"If you had, it would defeat the purpose, now wouldn't it?"

"Then you've started?"

Jake let out frustrated breath. "Not here. Not now."

"Then when? I want some answers."

"We're doing our thing. You do yours." He waved to Mariah. "How's Lilly?"

Mariah burst into a grin. Lilly was Mariah and Sophie's baby. Beautiful little girl.

"Growing every day."

"Last time I saw her was at Nate and Sam's wedding," Jake said.

"We just got the pictures back. When you have time, I'll show them to you. In the meantime, can I get you something, Detective?"

"I'm picking up a dinner order for Rhys and me."

"I'll see if Tater has it ready." Mariah walked into the back.

"Pulling a late night?" Lucky asked, cocking his brows.

"Yep." Jake proceeded to ignore him until Mariah came back with his to-go order. He reached over the bar to grab it from her. "Thanks."

"Take care, Detective," Mariah called to him. "You hungry, Lucky?"

"Nah, I've got to get back to the ranch, see if we've made any progress." He threw back the drink, pushed his stool away from the bar, and wandered outside. Yup, the days were certainly getting shorter.

At the ranch he found Raylene sitting on the hood of her truck. She looked so beautiful perched there with her blond hair blowing in the breeze.

"What are you doing?" he called to her.

"Waiting for you."

He liked having the woman of his dreams waiting for him when he got home. Lately, though, his dreams of Raylene didn't seem as sharp as they once had. Just elusive memories of a young girl who'd held his heart for so long he couldn't imagine not loving her.

"Why didn't you go inside?" He tilted his head at the trailer. "It's getting cold." And he didn't like the idea of her being out here alone. Not now that he knew what he was dealing with on the ranch.

"I don't mind it. How did it go at the doctor's?"

He made the so-so gesture with his hand. "More tests."

"I thought you were a match," she said.

"Apparently it's not that simple. We should know in a few days."

Raylene jumped off the hood and flew into his arms.

"Everything okay?" He tilted her chin up.

"I just missed you. Let's go inside."

He did a quick survey before unlocking the door to the single-wide. Everything looked quiet, but he wanted to check the livestock. "You wait in here. I want to take a quick pass through the corrals." Lucky left his phone on the kitchen counter and started to head out.

"Lucky, they're just cows," Raylene called, sounding pouty.

Those "cows," and the other rough stock he'd acquired, were worth a small fortune. "Five minutes, baby. Turn the heat on." He was surprised when she didn't put up more of a fuss.

Lucky took his truck because it was quicker. At least the crew seemed to have made some headway on the new barn where Lucky planned to keep his cutting horses. He wanted to kick himself for cheaping out and not hiring Pat Donnelly's people. Pat had contracted the job on his big barn, the one the Lumber Baron planned to use for weddings and other party events. Of course, Nate had shelled out the money on that project as part of their joint deal. And Pat's folks had done a beautiful job and had come in on schedule.

And the biggest bonus: They weren't drug dealers.

Son of a bitch! The whole thing pissed Lucky off. And Jake had sealed up tighter than a drum. Lucky had no idea the status of the investigation. At this very minute the place could be swarming with deputies, which would be fine with him. But what if it wasn't and Raylene, here alone, had seen something she shouldn't have? A man's ranch was his sanctuary. He shouldn't have to worry about his loved ones being safe.

He walked through the rows of corrals, stopping a few times to scratch heads. In a few years the offspring from these animals would be used in rodeos and PBR events across the country. The sperm alone from some of his breeding bulls would fetch top dollar. Lucky planned the tamer stock to use for the cowboy camp so the amateurs wouldn't hurt themselves.

Bernice had gotten out of her pen again to cuddle next to Crème Bullee. Apparently the ewe hadn't gotten the memo that she was a sheep. Lucky let her stay there. The two seemed to like each other.

He climbed up the fence and sat with his legs dangling, assessing all that he could see. Even back when it was the old Roland camp, he'd loved this place. As a kid he used to work summers in the barn, helping the stable guys ready the horses for the guests' trail rides. Never in those days had he imagined he'd be able to afford a ranch like this. The property even butted up to the Feather River, with some of the best fishing this side of the county.

Now, with Katie in the picture, he wanted more than a bachelor's apartment. There was a knoll not far from here with killer views of the river and mountains, and lately Lucky had been toying with the idea of building a home—a real home. For that he'd want Colin Burke doing the work. He'd seen what the man did on his own house. On Mariah and Sophie's home, too. Both were beauts.

Lucky looked up. Plenty of stars in the sky, and he could smell a cold front moving in. Not snow necessarily, but a definite drop in temperature. Bring it on. He'd always loved fall and winter in Nugget, especially the holidays. For Thanksgiving his mother did it up, and for Christmas she made her famous tamales. And even though they'd been poor as peasants, Cecilia had always managed to put lots of gifts under the tree.

This year they'd have Katie, which gave him a wave of pleasure. Lucky had never thought about having kids. Not that he was against it, but besides Raylene, he'd never met anyone who made him want to settle down. And truth be told, Raylene didn't seem much like the settling down type—at least not these days. Twice he'd asked her to move into the trailer with him and each time she'd come up with an excuse. *It's too small for the both of us,* or *I just got out of a bad marriage.* And on and on.

He couldn't say he blamed her, and a part of him was starting to think it would be a bad idea anyway. Certainly not the honeymoon he used to envision. The two of them didn't have a whole lot to say to each other, unless Raylene was complaining about Butch. Lucky expected that when she became less bitter, he and Raylene would get back into a groove again.

Then he'd spend less time confiding in Tawny.

He was thinking that he ought to call Tawny to see how Katie was feeling but couldn't find his phone. That's when he heard it. Two loud gunshots that echoed through the trees like firecrackers. He hit the dirt running.

Chapter 12

"Gus is dead?"

"Gus is dead," Jake told Lucky, feeling terrible that the kid was so shaken up. There was nothing he could've done. "Lucky, this is no longer a drug investigation."

"Jesus." Lucky mopped the sweat from his forehead and looked out over his property, now crawling with cops. "He was breathing when I found him. Just barely, but breathing."

Well, he wasn't anymore. "He took two in the gut." Jake watched a coroner's van come up the road. "Raylene get home okay?"

"Yeah. I talked to her a few minutes ago. She's freaked but home safe and sound."

"Good." He looked Lucky in the eye. "Does she know what's going on?"

"About the drugs . . . the sting?" Lucky asked, and Jake nodded. "No. All she knows is that my fence guy got shot."

"You can't stay on the property, Lucky. It's a crime scene now. Your mother is expecting you."

"You called my mother?" Lucky threw his hands up, like *WTF?*

Now that Jake thought about it, it was something you'd say to an errant teenager. *Your mother is expecting you.* "Just to tell her you're okay . . . I didn't want her worrying."

"Does she know about—"

"Absolutely not. And I hope you're still good on your word about not telling anyone. Especially now."

"You guys were supposed to be on this." Lucky laced his hands behind his head and shut his eyes. "I can't believe this is happening."

Jake would've liked to explain that there was no way that the police could've anticipated this. But he couldn't. All he could say was, "It's a mess."

"Ya think?" Lucky snapped, and Jake could understand his frustration. The shooting would not only stall his project, but it wasn't the best publicity for a new business trying to attract tourists. "How soon can I come back?"

"As soon as we're done processing the scene—probably a couple of days."

"Who will feed my animals?"

"I'll do it," Jake said, and Lucky looked at him like he was crazy. "Wyatt can help. It's either that or someone from Animal Control will do it until we let you back in."

"You have got to be kidding me!" Lucky took off his hat and mechanically shoved his hands through his hair. Jake noticed that Lucky did it whenever he was agitated.

"We can't have you traipsing around, compromising the scene. Make me a list of what needs to be done and I'll make sure your stock is cared for."

"Great!" Lucky threw up his arms.

Jake handed him a notebook and pen, and not having much of a choice, Lucky began scribbling instructions.

In his pocket, Jake felt his phone vibrate, looked at the caller ID and answered. "Everything is fine, sweetheart . . . He's right here." He handed the phone to Lucky. "Your mother wants to talk to you."

Jake heard Lucky mutter an expletive, but he took the phone and walked over to a quiet corner. Crime scene investigators from the sheriff's department had begun setting up klieg lights so they could comb the area looking for spent casings—although they were pretty sure the weapon was a revolver—footprints, and any other evidence they could find. The coroner's van sat at the ready while someone took pictures of Gus.

"Hey, Jake." Harlee came trudging up the walkway with her laptop and a camera.

"You know you're not supposed to come in here. It's a working crime scene, Harlee."

She gave a half shrug. "I was hoping you could fill me in on the details. Just a little bit." She made an inch with her fingers. "Rhys is being a dick and I want to update the website."

Jake smothered a chuckle. "Rhys is a little busy. What do you have so far?"

"Not a lot. Just that a man was shot and killed on Lucky's property about an hour ago. I don't have an ID, I don't know if anyone is in custody, and I don't know what the altercation was about."

"On background?" Jake said.

"Sure. Can I attribute it to a law enforcement source?"

"Well, that would kind of narrow it down, wouldn't it?" Since there were only three of them in the department. "How about just a source close to the case." That would include just about anyone living within a five-mile radius and would give Jake cover.

"Okay," she said, and got her notepad out.

"We don't have anyone in custody. We don't know what the altercation was about, and the victim was Gus Clamper. Common spelling. I don't know his DOB, you'll have to check his DMV file or the Registrar of Voters. But, Harlee, we haven't notified the next of kin yet, so you may want to hold off." Jake knew she wouldn't, but at least he'd made the effort.

"Why was he on the property in the first place?"

"He was fixing Lucky's fences."

"At seven at night?" She looked doubtful. Smart girl.

"A number of Lucky's workers who live a ways away are staying at the ranch in bunkhouses."

"Where is Gus from?"

"Placer County."

"Does he have a family? A record?"

"You know I can't discuss criminal history," he said.

"Jake, the courts are closed."

"The Internet is open twenty-four-seven. You're gonna have to work for this one, sweetheart."

"What about family?" she pressed.

"Dunno."

"Is Lucky a suspect?"

"Everyone's a suspect."

"Jake?" Harlee pinned him with a look. "Throw me a bone, here."

"Let's put it this way: If you were to print that Lucky is a suspect it would be journalistically irresponsible."

"That means you have someone else in mind. Who?"

"That's all I've got." Jake liked Harlee. She was just as pushy as the reporters in LA, but a hell of a lot more charming. And her husband made spectacular furniture. "Don't burn me, Harlee. Now get out of here before I have one of the deputies escort you off the property."

Later, he saw her sitting inside her fifteen-year-old Pathfinder on the other side of the yellow tape, clacking away on her laptop.

"Hey, Deep Throat. How goes it?" Rhys sidled up to Jake. "You read the story yet?"

"It's up already?" Jake looked over at Harlee again. She was still typing.

"She updates it every couple of minutes." Rhys held up his phone. "If you sign up, you get automatic mobile alerts. Did you know Gus was arrested three years ago in Placer County for breaking a bottle over a bartender's head?"

Jake smiled. "This is probably the biggest story she's had since turning that little rag around. Don't get a lot of shootings up here, unless it's some idiot hunter."

"Well, she's got shit in that story that I didn't even know."

"She's good," Jake said.

"Yeah, she's good. Hopefully we'll have this thing wrapped up in a few days," Rhys said.

Jake wasn't so sure. Gus's shooting had certainly complicated their dope case. Especially since the guy who'd killed him didn't have one thing to do with the drug investigation—at least according to Jake's witness.

On Lucky's way to his mother's house, Tawny called. "Are you okay?"

"I'm fine. Just homeless for a few days while they process the scene. How did you hear about it so soon?"

"The *Nugget Tribune*. I get alerts for breaking news."

Great, Lucky thought. Just what he needed. "I was thinking of swinging by and checking on Katie."

"She's asleep," Tawny said. "But if you want to look in on her, that would be okay."

A few minutes later, Lucky pulled up into Tawny's driveway. The light on the front porch was on. He climbed the stairs and quietly tapped on the window, not wanting to wake Katie up. It was such a tiny place that sound traveled.

Tawny opened the door in jeans and a sweater. Different from what she'd worn to the doctor's. It hardly seemed like the trip to Palo Alto had happened on the same day as the shooting.

"Hey," she said.

Lucky didn't know what possessed him, but he pulled her into a hug and held her until she molded to him. For a second he forgot himself and put his hand on her backside to press her against him. Bad idea. He felt himself getting hard and let her go. It was just the strain of the day, he told himself.

She pretended not to be flustered, but Lucky knew she was.

"Did you see the shooting?"

"No. I was out by the corrals, checking on the animals, and I heard it. Raylene was at the trailer, so I ran back. It was like everything happened in a split second."

"The article didn't say anything about Raylene being there," Tawny said, and Lucky sensed that it bothered her, but his head was so fogged he might've imagined it.

"The cops cleared the place as soon as they got there. Before Harlee showed up."

"Where was he shot?" Tawny asked, keeping her voice down so as not to wake Katie.

"Over by one of the bunkhouses. When I got there one of the crew members was trying to staunch the blood. Gus was barely breathing."

"Did any of them see what happened?"

Lucky blew out a breath. "If they did, they ain't talking to me. Jake and Rhys and a bunch of sheriff's deputies interrogated the whole lot of 'em and collected all the guns. These clowns were housing a freaking arsenal on my property."

Tawny's eyes grew wide. "Why?"

Ah hell. He'd probably said too much. "Uh, it's common with construction crews. A lot of equipment and material theft. They like to guard their stuff."

"Still," Tawny said. "Why would've someone shot the man? You think he was stealing from them?"

"I don't know. It could've been anything." He tilted his head to look at her. The sweater she wore matched her green eyes. "You got something to drink?"

"Juice, water, soda, or I could make some coffee or tea."

Lucky had been hoping for something harder. "Coffee would be good." He wouldn't be sleeping anyway.

Tawny led him into the kitchen. "Did you know him?"

"Gus? Not like we were pals, but he was my employee. We talked occasionally. He seemed like a decent enough guy." Until Lucky had learned that he was dealing dope.

"What are you planning to do?" She measured out the coffee and flipped the switch on the coffeemaker. "Will you keep the same crew on?"

"I don't know yet." He'd like to fire every last one of them, but he'd promised Jake he wouldn't. "You mind if I peek in on Katie?"

"Go ahead." She gave him a small smile, and once again Lucky was struck by what a beautiful woman she was. And easy to talk to.

He opened Katie's bedroom door. The room, decked out with a white canopy bed, frilly pink bedding, matching curtains, and pictures of horses, always gave him an unexpected rush. He had a girly girl. Although he could do without the boy-band poster on the back of her door—Katie was too young for boy bands. His chest expanded at the sight of her sleeping with her arms around a fuzzy pink stuffed animal, her pretty brown hair spread over the top of her pillow. Tawny had told him that she'd lost a lot of it during her chemo treatments. He stood there for a few moments, watching her chest move up and down under the covers, and felt an overwhelming need to hold her. His daughter.

He shut the door as quietly as possible, not wanting to wake her up. "She feeling okay?" he asked.

Tawny nodded her head. "She's had a good couple of days. Your mother's been so helpful that I've been able to work on Clay's boots."

"That's good," he said. "I guess things will get hectic when we do the transplant. I'm planning to build a house." It came out of nowhere, especially since Gus's body was probably still lying there on his property. Perhaps he just needed something normal to talk about. "I'm gonna ditch that apartment and go big. Do something like Colin and Harlee's place. If I can get him, I'll hire Colin to build it."

"Sounds nice," Tawny said.

"I'll put in a whole wing for Katie."

"A whole wing?" Her brows lifted.

"You know, a bedroom, rec room where she can have her friends, and a room with a computer where she can do her homework. I'll get her a horse, too."

"Wow. With all that, she'll never want to come home to me."

Lucky looked around Tawny's little bungalow—a crackerjack box, really—and saw her point. He didn't want it to be a competition, just wanted to provide Katie with all he could.

"Nah, you're her mother. You'll always come first."

Lucky saw Tawny's eyes well up and moved closer. "Don't cry, Tawny. I'm not trying to take her from you. Katie loves you."

She used her knuckles to wipe her eyes and tried to smile. "It's just been a crap day. That's all."

He couldn't argue with that. Instead, he poured them both cups of coffee and took them into the living room, where he patted the space next to him on the couch. "Take a load off." He grabbed a throw blanket from the back of the couch and tucked it over her lap. "It's cold in here."

"I'll turn on the heat," she said.

"I'll get it." He got up, found the thermostat, and cranked it up to sixty-eight degrees. Wondering if she left it off to save money, he said, "I owe you a child support check for the month."

"No, you don't. You already gave me money."

"We've got to work that out, Tawny. I don't think I'm paying you enough. Maybe we should talk to a lawyer about what the going rate is."

"You pay me plenty, Lucky. I don't want charity."

"Who said anything about charity? Damn, Tawny, stop trying to prove your independence all the time. I don't want to be like my old man. The guy never paid my mother a cent. I watched her kill herself to raise me like all the other kids. Same fancy tennis shoes, all the right clothes, a new winter coat every year. I'm not that man."

"I never thought you were," Tawny said. "You've been amazing. But the most important thing to me is the transplant, Lucky. That means more to me than all the money in the world."

"She's my kid. I'd give her a lung if she needed it."

"You hardly know her." Tawny held up her palms. "Which I know you think is my fault."

His mother had this saying, *la sangre llama*, blood calls to blood. It didn't matter that he hardly knew her. He could feel Katie in every cell of his body. His love for her was as instinctive as breathing. She was his and he was hers. "What's done is done," he said. "From here on in, I plan to be there every step of the way."

Tawny pulled her legs up and reclined on the couch. It was the most relaxed Lucky had ever seen her.

"Before you found out about Katie, did you want children, Lucky?"

"I didn't not want 'em," he said. "But my lifestyle wasn't real conducive for a family, though some of the guys in the PBR have them. Were people bad to you?" He knew it couldn't have been easy for her to be an eighteen-year-old unwed mother in a small town with a fair share of small-minded people.

"People were actually pretty wonderful. Those first couple of years, my dad and I didn't have two nickels to rub together, but the town pulled together, bringing me baby clothes, toys, even diapers."

"The way you are, it must've killed you," Lucky said.

"I had to swallow my pride."

"You should've hunted me down, Tawny."

"Honestly, at that time I don't think you had much more money than I did. You would've come home, done the right thing, Ray would've made your life a living hell, Cecilia would've lost her job, and our baby would've heard whispers about how her dad tried to rape Raylene Rosser."

"No one would've believed that crap. I grew up in Nugget . . . these people know me. For a tough woman, Ray Rosser sure had you running scared."

"I was a poor kid with a sick dad and a baby in my belly. Everything ran me scared."

The statement made his stomach churn. God, she must've been so alone. "Come here." He pulled her toward him and wrapped his arms around her so that her back fell against his chest, and held tight. "Not anymore, though, right?"

"Of Ray Rosser? Nope. I've got more pressing things to scare me."

He heard that. Absently, he stroked her hair and he saw her eyes close, long lashes sweeping the top of her cheekbones. For a long time they didn't say anything, and eventually she fell asleep in his arms. It felt natural having her there, cradled against him, though a bit cramped. He too nodded off, until dawn's early light came streaming through the lace curtains.

"Tawny." He jostled her. "Wake up, honey."

"Huh?" She flopped on top of him, trying to turn on her side.

Ah hell. He slipped out from beneath her, lifted her into his arms, and carried her into the bedroom. She squinted up at him as if she was having trouble getting her eyes into focus.

"Lucky?"

"Yeah. We fell asleep on the couch. I figured you wouldn't want Katie to come to the wrong conclusion."

"What time is it?" She wiggled out of his arms to look at the clock on her nightstand. "It's late."

Not by his standards. Then again, he wasn't much of a morning person, though that would have to change now that he owned a ranch.

She rotated her neck. "I can't believe we both fit on the sofa. God, I'm sore."

His brows went up, and she must've guessed what he was thinking because she swatted his arm.

"Get out of here," she said. "You can't be in here when Katie wakes up."

He'd never seen her room before and wanted a chance to look around. It wasn't decorated as well as Katie's, but it was painted nice.

"What would you call that color?" he asked her, cocking his head at the wall.

"Eggplant, I guess. Why?"

"Just curious."

"You need to go." She shooed him with her hands. "Or better yet, make us some coffee."

"Where'd you get that bossy gene? I remember your old man as mild mannered."

"Must've been my mom. Now get."

He snuck out the door, closed it quietly, and peeked in on Katie. Still sound asleep, clutching that fuzzy stuffed animal. Today he planned to take a couple of pictures of her to hang up in his trailer. He'd bought his ma a nice camera one year for Mother's Day. Maybe he'd borrow it. Speaking of his mother, he needed to call Cecilia, who was probably worried sick. His phone was on the coffee table with his wallet. Grabbing both, he went into the kitchen, measured out the coffee, poured in the water, and hit the switch. Then he direct-dialed his mother, who answered on the second ring.

"I stayed at Tawny's last night. Sorry I didn't call."

"Tawny's?" His mother sounded surprised.

"I came over to check on Katie and fell asleep on the couch." From the background noise it didn't sound like Cecilia was alone. "Jake there?"

"Yes. Would you like to talk to him?"

"Yeah, put him on." When Jake came on, Lucky asked, "Can I go home yet?"

"I told you it would be a couple of days."

"Did someone feed my stock?"

"I did." Jake's voice sounded gravelly, like he hadn't slept all night.

"Thanks. You make an arrest?"

Jake was quiet for a beat. "Someone is in custody."

Lucky was stunned. As of last night there hadn't even been a suspect. Lucky had only asked to needle Jake. "Who?"

"For right now we're keeping it quiet," Jake said, and Lucky heard the screen door close. "I've only got a second before your ma comes looking for me. I'd appreciate you not telling anyone. We don't want to tip our hat to the other investigation."

"All right," Lucky said. "But who do you have in custody?"

"I have to go." Jake clicked off, leaving Lucky in suspense.

"Who was that?" Tawny came into the kitchen in a long fitted sweater, black stretchy pants, and the obligatory cowboy boots, toweling her hair dry.

"Jake," he answered, and watched her bend over to pour a cup of coffee. The woman had a great ass. "I still can't go back to my place."

"I wouldn't think you could. You wanna take Katie to school?"

He smiled. "Yeah. I'd like that. She up?"

"Yep. She's doing her *Project Runway* thing."

"What does that mean?"

"It means she tries on everything in her closet before making a decision about what to wear for the day. We're invariably late."

"She have a lot of clothes?"

"Yep. The Marcum girls are taller than Katie. She gets all their hand-me-downs. And the Marcum girls are serious about fashion."

Lucky didn't know the Marcums. But he didn't want his daughter wearing hand-me-downs. "I'll take her over to Farm Supply later and buy her a few things."

Tawny stopped sipping her coffee. "Lucky, I know you're a big celebrity bull rider now, with lots of money to burn building big houses, paying scads of child support, and buying Katie everything under the sun. But I don't want you to. First of all, I can't keep up. Second of all, I don't want my daughter to be spoiled. Everyone, except for Raylene, wore hand-me-downs growing up in this town. It's the way we live up here. Try not to forget that."

"I'm making up for nine years. If I want to buy my daughter a few pretty things, I should be allowed to."

That's when Katie walked in the door wearing something more Raylene's style than anything a nine-year-old should be allowed to wear.

"Oh no, you don't," Tawny said, tugging down Katie's miniskirt. "You're not leaving the house wearing that. Go back and change."

Katie was momentarily startled to see Lucky in the kitchen. "Hi, Daddy."

He picked her up and gave her a big kiss. "How's my girl?"

"Good. But I want to wear this."

Lucky looked at Tawny, who shook her head and said, "Hurry up and change, Katie. Your dad's taking you to school and you barely have time for breakfast."

"Mom, everyone wears stuff like this," she whined.

"Please don't make me tell you again. Dress warm. It's getting cold."

Katie made a face, but to her credit did as her mother asked. Tawny was amazing with her, and Katie was a sweet girl. His sweet girl.

"Nice hoochie-mama hand-me-down," Lucky said, and shook his head. "I'll be getting her some Wranglers at Farm Supply."

"Good luck with that, because she won't wear them."

"There's got to be something there she likes that still covers her butt."

Tawny started to say something, only to be interrupted by Lucky's phone.

"Sorry," he said, knowing from the newly assigned ringtone that it was Raylene, and picked up. "Hey." He wandered into the living room for privacy. "You sleep okay?"

"No, I didn't. Where are you?"

"At Tawny's. I'm taking Katie to school." He left out the part that he'd stayed the night. Hey, he hadn't done anything wrong, unless you counted thinking about it.

On the other end, silence. Lucky waited for Raylene to berate him for spending too much time at Tawny's.

Instead, she said, "The police arrested my father last night. They say he killed Gus Clamper."

Chapter 13

After Lucky took Katie to school, Tawny went into her studio. Working would help clear her head and get Lucky out of it. He'd been so attentive lately that she'd started to imagine that he might have feelings for her. Then Raylene crooks her little finger and he goes tearing out of Tawny's house like his tail is on fire. Lucky had left in such a rush, he'd almost forgotten Katie.

She was attaching the heels onto Clay's boots when she heard a car pull up and figured it was probably the neighbor who sometimes used her driveway to turn around. But a short time later she heard Cecilia calling her name.

"I'm back here in the studio." Tawny went through the backyard and opened the gate. "Hi."

"Sorry to barge in on you like this, but I was in the neighborhood."

In the neighborhood, Tawny's ass. Nothing in this part of Nugget but run-down houses and the crappy little park where she and Lucky had had their rendezvous ten years ago. "You want some coffee? I'll make a pot."

"No, I'm fine," Cecilia said. But she was obviously curious, her eyes seeking out Tawny's shop.

"That's my studio. You want to see it?"

"I would love to."

Tawny led the way. It was just a garage with a bunch of equipment, wooden foot forms, leather, and boots, but Tawny was quite proud of the workshop. As a kid she used to sit out here for hours watching her father refurbish and repair clocks. Like her with the boots, he'd lined the shelves with clocks he was working on for clients and ones he'd bought at flea markets or garage sales with plans to fix and sell them. There were cuckoo clocks, mantle and table clocks, wall clocks, weather and maritime clocks, even grandfather clocks.

At one of the flea markets, he'd bought her a leather-bracelet-making kit that had never been opened. She'd sit in the corner of the studio for hours making bracelets. The first ones were crude and clumsy, but as Tawny got the knack of working with the leather she began experimenting with design, including using her paints to make flowers. Eventually she used an embossing tool to actually carve flowers into the leather. Soon, she was spending all her babysitting money online in the Tandy Leather craft shop and making purses, belts, and book covers.

And eventually boots.

Tawny had always been a good sewer and used her mom's old Singer to make curtains and placemats for the house. So that part of the process came naturally. First, Tawny tried moccasins. But growing up in cattle country, she'd always admired the fancy cowboy boots the folks up here wore for special occasions. A pair of Luccheses or Old Gringos were the Manolo Blahniks of the Sierra Nevada. Tawny used to peruse the boot aisles in Farm Supply or Sheplers in Reno for hours, studying the stitch work, toe shapes, and the overall construction. Finally, she found a well-known grizzled boot-maker in Sierraville who said he'd mentor her in exchange for her feeding his chickens.

For six months she made the trek, bringing Katie in her baby carrier, and gleaned everything she could from the guy. When he saw that Tawny had an aptitude for what he called "the fancy stuff," he hooked her up with one of the most famous boot-makers in Texas. Together, they awarded her a "scholarship" that paid for her flight, room and board in the Texas boot-maker's farmhouse, and a week of his tutelage. Again, she loaded up Katie and they went. To this day, she kept in touch with both boot-makers, who were happy to pass on their knowledge, hoping to keep the tradition alive.

Cecilia gazed around the shop, her eyes catching on the particularly colorful boots and the tables of machines and cutting tools. "You have quite a place here. I had no idea."

"It's small, but it works for me."

"You need a security alarm. This stuff is expensive."

Tawny wanted to laugh because this was Nugget, after all. Then again, someone had been murdered on Lucky's ranch last night, and two years ago a meth dealer had robbed the Nugget Market. The same dealer had held Maddy hostage at the inn until Rhys shot him. The residents were still talking about it like it was yesterday.

"I probably should," Tawny agreed.

Cecilia continued to wander around the studio. She reached for a pair of Tawny's "Reno" boots and stopped herself. "May I?"

"Of course."

She pulled them down from the shelf and admired the embellishments: rhinestones, stitched playing cards, and horseshoes. "These are beautiful."

To Tawny they seemed a little loud for Cecilia's taste, but they were flashy enough to catch plenty of attention. That's why she kept a pair in the shop.

"What size do you wear?" Tawny asked Cecilia.

"A seven and a half. Why?"

Tawny found a number of pairs in Cecilia's size, gathered them up, and brought them to the try-on bench. "Tell me how they feel on your feet."

Cecilia sat down and took off her sensible ankle boots, some sort of UGG knockoff that she'd probably gotten at the Costco in Reno. Tawny knew that whatever boots Cecilia reached for first were the ones she liked best. Human nature. Sure enough, she chose the same pair Tawny would've guessed for her. Polished black leather with a vine of red roses going down the shaft. Tawny loved those boots. They were classy with just a touch of pizzazz. Just like Cecilia.

Cecilia slipped them on. "They feel so nice," she said, marveling at the floral motif.

"Walk around," Tawny said.

Cecilia strutted across the workshop, stopping at every mirror to pull up her pants and admire them. "They'd be beautiful with a skirt."

Tawny nodded. "If you like them the best, they're yours."

A look of shock came over Cecilia's face, like maybe she'd misunderstood. "You're giving these to me?"

"Yep," Tawny said.

"I can't accept such a generous gift. This is your livelihood."

"Consider them a gift from your granddaughter ... for all the Christmases and birthdays she's missed." Tawny's eyes filled and she turned to wave the tears away. "I'm sorry I kept her from you, Cecilia. It was wrong. But at the time I was scared ... I didn't want to shake up anyone's life . . . cause trouble. My father and I had always lived without anyone paying us any mind. The idea of suddenly being thrust into controversy . . . I was petrified."

"There were a lot of rumors about what happened at the Rock and River that night," Cecilia said. "And Ray Rosser is a scary man. I ought to know after working for him for twenty years. But we would've handled it." Cecilia got up and put her arms around Tawny. "You were young and trying to do what was best for your daughter. And I'm assuming that as time went on, it became even more difficult to tell the truth. I'm not happy about it, but as a single mother I understand and I forgive you, Tawny."

Cecilia continued to hold Tawny, who sniffled and said, "Thank you. And please keep the boots. It would mean a lot to me. And to Katie."

Cecilia let go of her and looked down at her feet. "They're incredible and I'll cherish them always. Thank you." She rooted around in her purse and came up with a mini pack of tissues and handed it to Tawny, who blew her nose.

"I came here to talk to you," Cecilia said.

"Would you prefer to go inside?" Tawny hoped she'd at least washed the dishes from breakfast.

"That might be better." Cecilia picked up her ankle boots. "I'll put these in the car first."

Tawny thought it was nice that Cecilia had decided to wear the custom boots instead of her own. In the house she did a quick assessment. The place looked like it always did. Tidy, but threadbare. Cecilia's was always perfect. She met Cecilia at the front door and rushed back into the kitchen to make a fresh pot of coffee.

"Would you like some cookies?" Unfortunately, all Tawny had were store-bought brands. She wasn't a baker like Cecilia.

"I'm fine. Come sit."

Tawny sat beside Cecilia at the breakfast table. "What did you want to talk about?"

"The transplant," Cecilia said. "I think when it's over all of you should stay at my house to recuperate." She held up her hand to keep Tawny from interrupting. "I've done a lot of research on the Internet, and Katie and Lucky are going to need plenty of rest. And you, Tawny, need a break. You're tired, *mija*. Let me help you."

"My studio is here."

"And it took me less than five minutes to drive from my house," Cecilia said. "You can come and work with no distractions, knowing that Katie is being well cared for. Then you'll come back to my house . . . to a nutritious meal and a warm bed and to someone who'll watch over you for a change."

It actually sounded fantastic, but where her daughter was concerned, Tawny had trouble relinquishing control. It had been just the two of them for so long. "Katie's my responsibility."

"Of course she is. But you need family."

Cecilia and Lucky were Katie's family, not Tawny's. "It's a generous offer and I promise to think about it. But at this point we don't even know if Lucky will have all six of the HLA antigens necessary for the transplant. If he doesn't, we'll need you to be tested."

"Whatever you need. But in the meantime I want you to think about staying with me."

"I will," Tawny said. "I give you my word. Has Jake said anything about getting closer to solving the shooting from last night?"

"He's very secretive. But until they find the culprit, I don't like Lucky staying there alone."

Apparently Cecilia didn't know that Lucky had been with Raylene. "It sounds like he can't go back until they finish processing the scene."

"I was happy that he stayed here last night," Cecilia said, making Tawny wonder what exactly Lucky's mom thought was going on.

"Did Lucky tell you he saw Gus after he'd been shot? I think after a shock like that, he wanted to be close to Katie."

"I'm sure that's true," Cecilia said, and smiled. "But I've noticed that the two of you have become good friends. Maybe a little more than friends, no?"

"Cecilia, there is nothing between Lucky and me. He's . . . we just share a daughter."

"I know about Raylene, Tawny. I don't like it, but I know he thinks he loves her, and I will support my son. Even if he has his head up his behind."

Tawny laughed. "You know, I saw her the other day in the Lumber Baron and she was actually pretty nice. Perhaps she's changed and we should all give her the benefit of the doubt."

Cecilia patted Tawny on the knee. "You're a good girl. I have to go. Would you like me to take Katie after school?"

Tawny could use the extra time in her studio, so she took Cecilia up on her offer and wished her goodbye. It would be easy for her to start relying on Lucky's mother, but Tawny liked being self-sufficient. That way no one could disappoint her.

Lucky tried Jake again. The damn detective wasn't picking up his phone. Ever since he'd gotten the call from Raylene, he'd been trying to find out what the hell was going on. Why was Ray Rosser suspected of murdering Gus? As far as Lucky knew, the two men didn't even know each other. And what had Ray been doing on Lucky's property?

The worst part of it was Lucky had nowhere to go. His ranch was still knee-deep in crime scene investigators. Lucky knew because he'd driven up to the gate and had been told by some yahoo in a uniform to turn around. If he went to his mother's, he couldn't call Jake without running the risk of her hearing the conversation. And if he went to Tawny's, he'd break down and tell her about Ray. Something about Tawny loosened his lips. And last night had been bizarre. He'd wanted her, badly, even though he'd loved Raylene for nearly a lifetime. It was confusing.

He thought about trying Raylene again, but she and her mother were busy getting the old man a lawyer. To hear it from Raylene, they didn't know any more than Lucky. Just that Rhys and Jake had showed up in the wee hours of the morning, got Ray out of bed, and slapped a pair of cuffs on him. When Raylene had demanded answers, they'd shown her a warrant to search the house and left with her dad's Smith & Wesson 8-shot N-frame revolver. The question that kept going over and over in Lucky's mind was, how did Ray fit into the drug investigation?

"You want a refill on that iced tea, Lucky?" Mariah topped off his glass and stowed the pitcher in a refrigerator behind the bar. Apparently she'd taken over for the last bartender, who'd left without Lucky's noticing.

"Thanks." But he didn't touch it. If he drank any more tea, he'd have to swim out of the Ponderosa.

"They catch anyone in the shooting last night?" she asked.

He'd been getting the question all day. Earlier, Owen had talked his ear off about his theories of the case. The barber was a regular

Sherlock Holmes. So far it didn't seem like Ray's arrest had made the news yet. Harlee must be asleep at the wheel.

"Don't know," he lied. "Everything's hush-hush." At least that part of it was true.

"Crazy." Mariah shook her head. "That just doesn't happen around here."

"I definitely think it was an isolated incident." The last thing any of them needed was tourists thinking Nugget was the murder capital of Plumas County.

"Did you see anything?" She leaned against the bar in front of him.

"I heard the shots and later found Gus. He died a short time after."

"I'm sorry, Lucky. That must have been horrible."

Yeah, it wasn't exactly a picnic.

"Word is that it was a dispute over money," Mariah continued.

That was news to Lucky. But wasn't money almost always a motive for murder? How Ray fit in was the mystery. "Where did you hear that?"

"Harlee told Colin. He was over at the house to fix a leak and he told us."

The Nugget grapevine at work. "Did he know anything else?"

"That was it. I guess Rhys and Jake are still trying to unravel it."

Lucky pulled out his phone. "Hey, Mariah, do you know how to set it up so I get those instant alerts from the *Nugget Tribune*?"

She laughed. "It's kind of sick, but I think Harlee's circulation has doubled since the murder." She took his phone, played with it for a few minutes, and handed it back. "Here you go. It'll chirp when an update comes in. You can change it to vibrate if you want to."

"Thanks."

"In other news, I hear a *Sports Illustrated* reporter is coming up to interview you. He booked a room at the Lumber Baron."

"Word travels fast," Lucky said, hoping that the murder and drug investigations would be yesterday's news by the time the reporter got here. Fat chance of that.

"Exciting." Mariah was momentarily distracted when another patron sat at the bar. Lucky looked over to see who it was, anticipating another barrage of questions, but didn't recognize the man. "I've got to get back to work. Whistle if you need something."

"Will do," Lucky said.

He tried Jake again. Still no answer, so he decided to head over to the Lumber Baron, hoping someone there had heard something, since Maddy was married to the police chief. All he found was Brady working in the kitchen.

"Where is everyone?"

"Sam and Nate made a run to Gold Mountain to check on their renovations." The Breyers had bought a resort near Glory Junction. "Maddy took Emma to Reno to run errands. It's just me and Andy holding down the fort. I hear you've got your hands full at the cowboy camp. Did you know the victim?"

Here we go again. "He was fixing my fences." With 110 acres there were a lot of fences to mend. Lucky supposed he'd have to find a new fence guy.

"Sorry, man." Brady dished a hefty slice of coffee cake onto a plate and slid it over to Lucky. "I heard you found the body. That's gotta be tough."

"He was still alive when I got there. A couple of other workers got to him first and were trying to stop the blood. You hear anything about the investigation?"

"Just what I read in the *Nugget Tribune*."

"So Maddy hasn't said anything?" Lucky asked.

"Nah. I think Rhys keeps her in the dark on police matters. Like everyone else around here, she's prone to yammering." Brady kneaded a big ball of dough on the wooden cutting board. "How's Katie? I haven't seen Tawny around much."

"She and I were in the Bay Area for me to get some tests before the transplant."

Brady put the dough in a big stainless steel bowl and draped it with a towel. "So you're a match?"

"They think so. We're just waiting for a few more results."

"That's great," Brady said. "How's Tawny doing with all of it?"

"She's a champ. I've never met a woman like her in my life." Lucky noticed that Brady was looking at him funny. "What?"

"Nothing. I just thought you were with Raylene."

"I am," Lucky said, although sometimes he wondered. It wasn't intense between them, like the way it used to be. He could actually go days without thinking about her. Then again they were adults now, not love-struck teenagers. "What made you think I wasn't?"

"The way you looked when you talked about Tawny . . . like you were crazy about her."

"Nah, nothing like that. From what I hear, you two are an item."

"Oh yeah? Where did you hear that?" Brady asked, but Lucky noticed he didn't deny it.

"I'm not giving up my sources." Lucky laughed. "Any truth to the rumor?"

"Would it bother you if it were true? Because I'm getting the feeling that it would."

"I don't know where you're getting that." *Was it that obvious?*

Brady grinned. "Dude, it's all over your face."

"Look, she's the mother of my child. I'd be lying if I didn't say I was protective of her and Katie." And something more that Lucky didn't want to face up to.

"We're just friends, Lucky. But that doesn't mean it won't eventually go somewhere. Only time will tell."

The conversation came to an abrupt halt when Maddy waltzed into the kitchen. "Hey, Lucky, what brings you here?"

"I can't go back to my ranch until your husband and his pals finish up there. It's left me at loose ends."

"I'm sorry, Lucky. I heard you found the body. What an awful thing to have happened."

"Yeah." He blew out a breath. "So what do you hear?"

"You must know more than I do. Rhys doesn't tell me anything. In fact, I'm going over to the police station now to demand that he come home for dinner. My husband hasn't been home in the last twenty-four hours."

Maddy had turned out to be a dead end, and Brady had filled his head with a lot of stuff he didn't want to think about. The trip to the Lumber Baron could officially be called a bust.

Lucky looked at his watch. He had an hour before Katie got out of school and he could fulfill his promise to take her to Farm Supply to pick out a few appropriate outfits. Between the boy-band poster and that skirt she'd had on this morning, he could see his new role as father was gonna be a rough ride. The kid got to him, though. Cracked him up. She talked with so much passion that there was no question that she'd inherited his Latino side. The other day, she'd stood with her hands on her hips and told him, "Daddy, you have got to get a herd of baby llamas. They are the cutest things in the whole wide world." The crazy part was that after she'd said it, he went and ordered a few llamas for the ranch. He still didn't know what he'd do with the damn things.

Lucky decided he might as well kill the time at Tawny's. On his way over there he thought about what Brady had said and wondered how everything had gotten so complicated. He finally got to be with Raylene, but every time he saw Tawny, the magnetic pull between them became harder to ignore. Sure, he'd been attracted to lots of women. Sexy as hell women, who threw themselves at him. But Lucky knew this was different. Tawny was different. For some dang reason he just wanted to be with her all the time.

And it wasn't right. It made him feel like he was cheating on Raylene, even though he and Tawny had never done anything sexual. A man could lust in his heart, right? Ah hell, who was he kidding? He had to screw his head on straight. From the time he'd started liking girls, Raylene had been the one.

Even after she'd gone and married Butch, Lucky had never stopped thinking about her . . . loving her. So why all of sudden was Nugget's former introverted, green-eyed wallflower giving him second thoughts?

Chapter 14

Tawny, lost in her work, didn't hear Lucky come into her studio until he cleared his throat. He stood there, 100 percent pure cowboy, leaning lazily against the doorjamb, watching her work.

Since that morning, he'd changed into a fresh pair of jeans, worn and fitted in all the right places, and a plaid shirt that showed off the breadth of his chest. He must've gone to his mom's, where Tawny knew he kept a stack of spare clothes. His black hat dipped low, shading his mocha-brown eyes. And today he had on one of his rodeo belt buckles, drawing Tawny's eyes to a place she didn't want to go but went there anyway.

The man was sex in cowboy boots, and she had to force herself to look away to keep from blushing.

"Hey," Lucky said, and Tawny walked across the room to turn down the music.

"Anything new on the case since I saw you last?" she asked.

"Not a damn thing. I thought I'd hang out here until Katie's out of school." He cocked his head at the project she was working on. "Whose boots are those?"

"Clay McCreedy's." She tried to focus on what she'd been doing, but Lucky was too much of a distraction.

"You ever gonna make me a pair?"

She waved her hand around the room "There are plenty of ready-made ones to choose from."

"Nope. I want my own, like the bull riding ones you did."

"Get on the list. I might be able to fit you in, in two years." She reached for a wooden foot form in Clay's size.

Lucky came up behind her and watched over her shoulder. She

could feel his breath on her neck and she wanted to tell him to go away. Or stay. That was the problem. He made her so crazy she couldn't think rationally when he was around.

"Could you please sit down? You're making me nervous," she said.

"Why's that?" He grinned like an arrogant fool.

"Do you like people staring at you while you work?"

"As a matter of fact, I do." All right, bad example if you're a professional bull rider.

"Well, I don't. And at this point in the process I can't afford to make a mistake."

He grabbed a chair, turned it backward, and straddled it. "I like your hair that way."

Tawny had pinned it up so it wouldn't get in her way while she worked. There was nothing special about it, but she said thanks anyway.

"You still don't know when you can go back to your ranch?" she asked.

"When they finish collecting evidence. Whenever that is." He shrugged.

"What did Jake say?"

"He's not returning my calls. And that reporter is due in a couple of weeks. This is the worst possible time."

Not the best advertising, Tawny agreed. "None of this is your fault, Lucky. The reporter will understand that. All he has to do is look at Nugget's crime stats to know that what happened the other night is a fluke."

"Instead, what'll happen is he'll make it out that I run with a rough crowd. That we're all shoot-'em-up cowboys. Believe you me, I know how this works, and there was a time when I would've liked the badass image. But not when I'm trying to build a business . . . not when I have a nine-year-old daughter."

"Have him come talk to me," Tawny said. "I'll tell him that you're not like that. How you worked your way through high school, helping to support your mom. How since you found out about Katie you've stepped up. You really have been wonderful, Lucky."

"You'll talk to him for me?" He smiled at her in a way that made her toes curl. "I remember when you were too shy to talk to kids your own age, let alone a reporter."

"It took me a while to come out of my shell. That's what happens when you're the ugliest girl in town." She tried to make it sound self-deprecating, but it had been a horribly painful time for her.

"Not anymore. And for the record, you were never ugly. Obviously, I sure as hell didn't think so," he said, clearly referencing the night they'd had sex.

Your girlfriend, Raylene, sure thought so. But she kept that to herself. They'd been kids, and Tawny needed to let it go. "You were drunk and despondent over the love of your life, Raylene."

"Still, you must've turned me on. It's not like I would've done it with the first available woman."

"I think your memory's foggy. Because that's exactly what you did."

"Nope," he said. "There was something there. I'd be lying if I said I could remember what it was, but I know it was something."

"You're delusional." Tawny waved him off. "You didn't even recognize me when you got back."

"I didn't recognize you at first because you went by a different name and you'd grown up so much. But I did eventually. And, Tawny, you're just wrong about that night. There was something about you then and there's something about you now."

He looked at his watch and muttered, "Shit, I've gotta get Katie," and walked out the door.

Lucky was ready to collapse. Who knew a nine-year-old had so much stamina? Katie tore through Farm Supply trying on everything in her size, especially the stuff with lots of rhinestones and bright colors. He had himself a little rodeo queen in the making.

"What about this?" Katie came out of the dressing room wearing one of those half T-shirts that didn't cover her belly button.

Lucky leaned against one of the clothing racks and shook his head. "I don't think your mama's gonna go for it."

"She will," Katie pleaded.

"I'm not too thrilled with it, to tell you the truth." If a few months ago someone had told Lucky he'd be involved in picking out a nine-year-old girl's wardrobe, he would've died laughing. His own wardrobe was pretty sorry—just lots of jeans, Western shirts, and boots. Not even a suit in his closet. "It's a mite on the short side, Katie girl."

"This is what all the girls at my school wear." She pouted.

"I don't doubt that. But not my girl. Try on those jeans." He pointed to the red pair in her pile with sparkles on the pockets. She'd thought they were "awesome" on the hangar.

She slipped back into the dressing room and Lucky found a chair. Looked like he'd be here for a while.

"Hey, Lucky."

Lucky turned to find Clay McCreedy and his youngest son, Cody, pawing through a shelf of white Wrangler jeans. "Stocking up on 4-H uniforms?"

"Yup. At the rate Cody's sprouting up, these won't last either." Clay pushed Cody toward a dressing room and handed him a few pairs to try on.

Katie came out of her room, took one look at Cody, and turned the same color as her red pants. *Oh boy, here it starts*, Lucky told himself.

"Hi, Katie," Cody said.

Katie stammered something Lucky couldn't make out.

"Now that is a nice-looking pair of jeans," Lucky told his daughter, hoping to save her from the awkwardness she clearly felt. Only it seemed to make matters worse, because Katie disappeared back into the dressing room and shut the door. "You getting those?"

"I think so," she said, her voice barely a whisper.

Clay chuckled. "How you doing, Katie? This old bull rider taking you shopping?"

"I'm good," she said, and Lucky wondered if she would ever come out of the dressing room again.

"I'm glad I saw you here," Clay said to Lucky. "Been meaning to come over to your place after I heard what happened. Although from what I've gathered, Rhys and his boys have your place locked up until they're finished with their investigation. Damn shame. I didn't know the guy but I am real sorry. I presume it's holding you up."

"Yep," Lucky said. "It's a real mess."

"I'm sorry about that too. And this isn't about to make you any happier, but there've been a number of cattle thefts in the area. I've got at least a hundred head missing. I found a cut fence, and tire tracks from a stock trailer and an ATV. They rode in at night, rounded up what they could get, and are probably in another state by now. With the price of beef being what it is, I'm out a lot of money."

"Any idea who's doing it?"

"None. I called the California Department of Food and Agriculture. But they only have one investigator and he's jammed up. Apparently this is going on all over the state. Next, I'm going to Rhys. Be aware, though. Even though you don't have beef cattle, these yahoos probably don't know the difference. Or worse, they do, and they know your breeding stock is worth a small fortune."

Great, Lucky thought. Just what he needed. Drug runners, cattle rustlers, and murderers.

"I appreciate the heads-up," he told Clay.

Cody came out of the dressing room.

"You found one that works?" Clay asked him, and Cody shoved a pair of pants at Clay, who took them to the cash register. Why couldn't girls be that easy?

"Hey, kid, the coast is clear," Lucky called into Katie's dressing room.

Katie came out in another pair of glittery jeans. "That was so embarrassing."

He pulled her in for a hug and kissed the top of her head. "Nah, you were both trying on clothes. No big deal."

"Dad, that was Cody McCreedy!"

"He some big heartthrob over there at Nugget Elementary?"

"He's like the most popular boy in middle school. Him and Sam Shepard." Lucky knew that was Rhys's kid brother.

"Yeah, well, he's too old for you."

"He would never like me anyway," Katie said.

"He seemed to like you just fine. Knew your name and said hello."

"That's because you're famous."

"Katie, he didn't give me the time of day. Just said hello to you."

"Probably because he feels sorry for me because I have leukemia."

And that right there folded Lucky's heart in half. "Honey, that just means he cares about you. But this leukemia thing, we're gonna kick its ass. Now don't go telling your mother I used a bad word."

She giggled. "I won't. Can I get these?"

He looked the jeans over to make sure they passed the non-hoochie-mama test. "Yep. Add 'em to the stack."

Finally they left, with four pairs of pants, too many tops for Lucky to count, and a jacket that Katie couldn't live without. Tawny would accuse Lucky of spoiling her. Too freaking bad. He was her father and could spoil her if he wanted to.

"What do you say we grab a couple of burgers over at the Bun Boy?" He hoisted Katie into the cab of his truck and quickly felt her head. He'd seen Tawny do it so many times that it had become routine.

Katie, used to being fussed over, said, "I don't feel sick today."

"Good. Then let's get those burgers. Put your new jacket on, okay?" He didn't have to ask her twice. She bit the tags off and shrugged into the down fuchsia jacket faster than he could get to the square.

After supper he took Katie home and sat in the driveway, trying Jake for the umpteenth time.

Tawny tapped on his window. "You're not coming in?"

Usually she was trying to get rid of him. He unrolled his window and gaped at her a little longer than would be considered respectable. She'd taken her hair down and had changed into a dress. "You going somewhere?"

"No. Harlee is coming over later to take a picture of me for my website. The one on there is ancient. Katie wants to show me her new clothes. I didn't know if you wanted in on that."

"What's the deal with Cody McCreedy?"

She laughed. "Katie told me he was at the feed store. All the girls have crushes on him."

"She's too young to be having crushes."

"Oh, okay. I'll tell her that."

He grinned. "You making fun of me?"

"A little. Don't you remember all the girls who had crushes on you at that age?"

"No. Did you?" he prodded.

"I'm not telling." She started to walk away, then called over her shoulder, "You coming?"

Although sorely tempted, liking this flirtatious side of her, he said, "I've got to find out what's going on at my place." Especially after what Clay had told him. He didn't think anyone would be brazen enough to steal livestock right under the cops' noses. But he didn't like being away for an extended period of time. "No one from the Nugget Police Department is calling me back."

"Then what can you do?"

"Go over to the station and demand answers." Even though Jake had told him not to.

His phone rang. Lucky looked at the display. "It's Jake," he said, and answered. "Finally!"

"We're done," Jake said. "You can go home."

"Hey, I talked to Raylene . . ." Lucky couldn't say more because Tawny was listening in.

"Yeah?"

Ah, screw you, Jake. "What's going on with that?" Lucky was losing his patience.

"I'm not at liberty to say. I've got to go, Lucky."

Jake hung up and Lucky hit his phone against the dashboard.

"What happened?" Tawny asked.

"He says they're done and I can go home."

"What was that about Raylene?"

"Nothing. She wanted to know if the police wanted to talk to her . . . in case she has to leave town or something."

"Do they want to talk to her?"

"I don't know. Jake had to go." But he sure the hell planned to talk to Raylene before the night was over. She was another one not returning his calls.

Jake had had it up to here with Ray Rosser. After three hours of interrogation, the arrogant SOB Rosser had finally lawyered up. Some bigwig defense attorney was on his way. Another night of work. Another night he wouldn't spend with Cecilia.

In the last couple of months, he'd looked forward to sharing Cecilia's bed like he did his next breath. The woman had put him under her spell; he was so crazy about her. She, on the other hand, approached their relationship with the caution of a fox. Aloof and restrained. Not that she wasn't always warm and willing. Cecilia was an extremely sensual woman. But as far as committing herself heart and soul to him, she was still testing the waters. He supposed he too should be circumspect, given how many times he'd lost at love.

"I want to wring the turkey's neck," Jake said to Rhys, who'd joined him in the coffee room of the Plumas County Sheriff's Department in Quincy, just a stone's throw from the jail, where Ray was in custody. Nugget was too small to have its own.

"He's pretty full of himself," Rhys said. "His lawyer is a good guy, though. I've used him myself."

Jake pulled back in surprise. "Sounds like a story I want to hear."

"Nah. He was for my pop. Before we knew my old man had Alzheimer's, Shep was stealing stuff. Statues and crap he mistakenly thought were his. Dell's the one who figured out he had dementia." Shep, Rhys's dad, had died two summers ago.

"It'll be interesting to see how he handles Rosser."

"A prosecutor is on his way too," Rhys said. "Looks like we're in for a long night. You tell Lucky he can go home?"

"Yeah. The kid's been calling me all day. I finally got back to him a few minutes ago."

"My voice mail is full. Maddy's threatening to put me on the couch permanently and Clay—I don't know what he wants—has left four, five messages."

"Clay is Ray's neighbor. I'd call him back in case he knows something."

"I plan on it. Just want to say good night to Emma first."

Jake couldn't count how many times he'd missed tucking in his daughters when they were little. The life of a cop.

By the time Dell Webber showed up, the airless interrogation room smelled like a combination of sweat and desperation. It seemed that old Ray was starting to see that he couldn't buy his way out of this one.

Dell asked to talk to his client alone. Jake and Rhys spent the time tanking up on coffee and junk food from the vending machines. A man in a Western suit, cowboy hat, and lizard-skin boots found them in the coffee room.

"You Chief Shepard?" he asked. "I'm Deputy District Attorney George Williamson."

Rhys stuck his hand out and introduced Jake.

"I read the file, but why don't you get me up to speed on the last few hours and the status of the sting operation."

Rhys pointed out that their open drug case did not appear to be related to Gus Clamper's shooting. "My experience tells me that after the shooting, our suspected dealers will likely lay low for a while, which means our undercover guys won't have anything to buy."

"You're a former narcotics detective from Houston, right?" George said, and Rhys nodded.

For the next forty minutes Rhys and Jake detailed the evidence they had in the murder case, including an eye witness who saw Ray shoot Gus after an argument, the weapon believed to have been used, and preliminary ballistics.

"The only thing we don't have is motive," Rhys said.

Dell sauntered into the room. Like George, he wore a Stetson, giving Jake visions of the old West. Plumas County certainly wasn't LA.

"Ray is ready to make a statement," Dell said.

Not surprising, since they had him dead to rights. The three of them followed Dell into the interrogation room, where Rhys asked if it was okay to videotape the interview. Dell gave him a solemn nod and Jake rolled the camera.

"Before you boys start asking a lot of questions, I want Ray to tell you what happened." Dell gestured for Ray to start talking.

"Night before last, Gus stole a hundred and fifty head of my cattle. He and a couple of men cut the fence on the west side of my property, pulled in a stock trailer, and rounded them up with a three-wheeler. When I went to confront him about it, he denied it. When I threatened to go to the authorities, he attacked me. That's when I shot him. It was self-defense."

Jake looked at Rhys and raised his brows. Rhys nodded.

"You have any proof that the cattle were stolen?" Jake asked.

"Proof? Yeah, I used to have them and now I don't."

Dell took over. "Ray photographed the cut fence and the tire tracks. The California Department of Food and Ag will confirm that there's been a rash of cattle rustling across the state, including at Ray's neighbor, Clay McCreedy's spread. Same MO."

Jake looked at Rhys. Okay, now they had motive. Perhaps it would be an early evening after all.

"You went to confront Gus with a loaded gun?" Jake asked Ray.

"No. I went to confront Gus. I always carry a loaded gun. I have a license to carry."

Why a cattle rancher would be allowed to carry a concealed weapon was beyond Jake, but he planned to check when he got back to the office. "How did you know it was Gus who stole your cattle?"

"The same way I know the sumbitch was dealing dope. I've got—" Dell stopped Ray from saying any more.

"Ray has information, including a text from a neighbor," Dell said. "First we need to know if immunity is on the table."

"Immunity from the drug case or the murder allegation?" Rhys asked.

Dell slowly took off his hat and laid it on its crown. "Now, Chief, you know damn well Ray doesn't have anything to do with no drug ring. He's a long-standing, highly esteemed member of the community."

Who just shot a man in cold blood, Jake wanted to say.

George, who'd sat quietly in the corner up to now, said, "No immunity. But if your client has something that will help these boys with their drug case, we'd be willing to listen."

"That's mighty big of you, George." Dell leaned back in his chair. "What kind of charges are we talking about here?"

George snorted. "Sounds like first-degree murder to me. How 'bout you fellows?" He looked over at Jake and Rhys.

"The witness didn't say anything about an attack," Jake said. Actually, the worker who'd given Gus first aid hadn't said much. He'd conveniently missed the reason for the scuffle. But he'd sure been able to identify Ray, right down to his Smith & Wesson.

"The witness is probably one of the damn cattle rustlers," Ray said, and Dell held up his hand to shut his client up.

"First degree? Then I think we're done here, George." Dell put his hat back on and started to stand up.

George shrugged. "See you at the arraignment."

Ray got red in the face and started breathing hard. Jake worried that he might have a heart attack right there at the table.

"I'm not staying the night in that goddamned jail," Ray shouted.

"We'll get you a bail hearing," Dell said.

"How long will that take?" Ray demanded.

"Not until after your arraignment," George said. "We might be able to get something on the calendar for next week, but I can't promise anything."

"What if I give you some information?" Ray asked, his desperation palpable. "Could I have a bail hearing by tomorrow?"

Dell whispered something in Ray's ear, but Ray wasn't having it. "I'm not staying in that goddamn jail any longer than I have to!"

Dell sat back down. "I want it on the record that whatever my client has to say is against my advice."

Ray ignored him. "Well?" he wanted to know.

"Can't give you a bail hearing until you've been charged with a crime," George said. Ray was only under arrest. Under state law, the prosecution could hold him for forty-eight hours until it filed an actual case. "We might be willing to cut you loose for now . . . while the investigation is pending. But we'll require you to hand over your passport and the rest of your firearms. We'll also need a commitment that you'll surrender yourself to the court when we do file charges. Of course, letting you go early would depend on what you have."

"I have a hell of a lot," Ray said.

Chapter 15

"It was self-defense." Raylene kicked off her boots and sat cross-legged on Lucky's bed. "Gus stole our cattle. My guess is that he was gonna steal yours too."

"Jesus." Lucky scrubbed his hand through his hair.

If Gus was really involved with stealing Ray's and Clay's cattle, then there was a good chance that the rest of Lucky's construction crew was in on it too. Apparently these guys liked to diversify. Drugs, livestock theft, who knows what else they dabbled in? He had to fire these yahoos. Get them the hell out of Nugget and get his cowboy camp project back on track.

"What's going on with your dad, now?" he asked.

"He met with his lawyer, the prosecutor, and the cops tonight. Told them what happened. They're letting him go until they charge him . . . if they charge him."

"I'm sorry, Raylene. I hate the man's guts, but this has got to be hard on you and your ma."

"Honestly, I think my mother is happy to have him out of the house," Raylene said. "I don't want to talk about this anymore." She unbuttoned her blouse, thrusting out those lace-encased double D's, and held her arms wide open. "Come to bed."

But for the first time ever, he had absolutely no desire to sleep with her. He'd like to blame it on stress, but deep down inside he knew he was thinking about another woman. No way would he have sex with one while having feelings for the other. He just wasn't built that way.

But he couldn't tell Raylene that. After all these years of loving her, he was having enough trouble dealing with the idea that maybe she wasn't the one for him after all. For Raylene, it would be the ultimate rejection. Lucky didn't want to hurt her that way. At least not intentionally and not until he was absolutely sure. For all he knew, this sudden interest in Tawny was a passing fancy. Just a momentary infatuation.

Raylene was still dealing with her ugly divorce from Butch, and it had created a lot of tension between her and Lucky. Perhaps that accounted for his unexpected attraction to Tawny.

"I want to check on the animals—do another set of rounds," he said, hoping that it would give him enough time to come up with a legitimate excuse for why he wasn't in the mood to make love to her. Because Lucky was always in the mood.

"You just did it an hour ago," she complained.

"I've got a lot of money invested in that stock. Given what's been going on around here, a man can't be too careful." He sat on the edge of the bed and patted her thigh. "I know you're beat from everything that has happened today. I won't be offended if you don't wait up."

As it turned out, he didn't have to make up an excuse. Before he got to the door of the single-wide, Tawny called.

"Katie's got a high fever," she said. "I'm taking her to the emergency room at Plumas General."

"Wait for me," Lucky told her. "I'll drive." He grabbed his hat and wallet off the kitchen table, put on his jacket, and went back to the bedroom to find Raylene curled up in nothing but a filmy nightgown. "Katie is sick. We're taking her to the hospital."

"Why can't Tawny just do it?"

He glared at her and walked out. What kind of person says something like that?

On his way to Tawny's, he broke every speed limit and traffic law on the books. By the time he pulled into the driveway, Tawny had Katie bundled up and waiting. She bustled her into the backseat of his truck before he could turn off the ignition.

"Go," she said, and he could see lines of worry etched across her face.

"Take it easy." He put a consoling hand on her leg while he backed out onto the road. "It'll be okay."

She nodded as if she was trying to convince herself. "She was fine right after you left. I checked on her about thirty minutes ago and she was burning up. Just like that time at your mother's."

He squeezed her leg. "They'll bring down her fever at the hospital. Should we call Dr. Laurence?"

She looked at her watch. "It's late. We'll see what they say in the emergency room."

"Okay, but I'd like to light a fire under his ass for those test results." Lucky looked in his rearview. "How you doing, sweetheart?"

"I don't feel so good," Katie said.

"Hang tight," he told her, trying to sound confident. "The doctors will make you feel better."

When they got to the hospital, Lucky scooped Katie out of the backseat while Tawny grabbed a duffel he hadn't noticed when she'd first gotten in the truck. She must've seen him looking at it because she said, "In case we have to stay the night."

This clearly wasn't her first rodeo. The hell she'd been through with Katie made his insides ache. He should've been there for them.

A nurse rushed them back into a room and a doctor came in a few moments later. With all the busted bones and concussions he'd had, Lucky couldn't remember getting this kind of fast service in an emergency room. Thank goodness the medical staff was being so accommodating with Katie.

After an hour, Katie's fever was down, but she was anemic. The doctors said it was common in children who suffer from acute myeloid leukemia and wanted to keep her overnight. While they admitted her to a private room, Tawny and Lucky sat in the waiting room.

"You don't have to wait," Tawny said. "No need for both of us to be here."

He tossed her his keys. "Go home then."

She seemed startled by his reaction. "I was only trying to be considerate. I know that you've got a lot on your plate right now with the shooting and all."

"You think that's more important than my daughter?" A daughter he was just getting to know. "Why'd you call me if you didn't want my support?"

"Because you deserve to know," she said.

"That's rich coming from the woman who kept my baby from me for nine years."

"Lucky, I don't need this right now." Her hands trembled and he felt like a tool for fighting with her.

"I know, but stop being so damned independent. I'm not going anywhere. I'm in this all the way." She started to cry and he moved a few seats over so he could be next to her. "Why are you crying?"

"Because it's always been just me," she said, and wiped her nose with the back of her hand. "My mother died when I was a baby. My father died after Katie was born. I've come to accept that people don't stick."

"I stick," Lucky said. He got up, walked across the room to grab a box of tissues, and handed it to her. "Get it through your head, Tawny, I'm not going anywhere."

She blew her nose and they sat in companionable silence until Tawny fell asleep. Lucky found the nurses' station, got a blanket, and draped it around Tawny, nudging her head onto his shoulder. He watched her sleep, a jumble of emotions swirling through him. The woman was too damned independent for his liking. In this day and age he knew it was backwards, but Lucky had always been attracted to soft women who were just a little bit needy. It made him feel strong and useful and a whole bunch of other things that a shrink would probably have a ball with.

Yet Tawny's fierce independence was the very thing that fascinated him about her. She was a terrific mom, ran her own business, and wasn't reliant on anyone.

Shit! Except for the business part, it occurred to Lucky that he'd fallen for his mother, which gave him a slight shudder.

A nurse eventually came into the waiting room, waking Tawny, and told them that Katie had been settled into a room. They gathered up their stuff, Lucky taking the duffel bag from Tawny, and found their way to the fifth-floor pediatric unit. Katie was fast asleep. A nurse brought a cot into the small room and Lucky insisted Tawny take it. He, in the meantime, sprawled out as best he could in a straight-back chair.

By morning, Lucky awoke with a crick in his neck. Nothing that a few stretches wouldn't cure. He'd felt much worse after eight seconds on a bull. Someone brought in breakfast for Katie and toothbrushes for Tawny and him. They both cleaned up in the room's miniature bathroom and wandered down to the cafeteria for coffee.

"Katie's fever is gone," Tawny said. "But I'm still planning to call Dr. Laurence. Hopefully he'll have some news."

"You think they'll let her go home today?"

"That would be my guess." She took his arm. "Thank you for being here, Lucky."

And there she went again, treating him like she would a concerned and helpful neighbor. It pissed Lucky off, but he decided to let it slide. Eventually she'd get it through her thick head that he planned to be a full-fledged father to Katie.

In the cafeteria, Lucky loaded his tray with scrambled eggs, bacon, and potatoes. Tawny got a yogurt and some fruit. When they got to the cash register, she went to pay and Lucky pushed her wallet away.

"You ever think this could be the reason why you're still single?" It was a mean thing to say and Lucky wished he had bitten his tongue.

But Tawny laughed, seemingly unperturbed. "You ever think that attitude is why you only date buckle bimbos and brainless Barbie dolls?" Then her face turned red. "I didn't mean Raylene."

But they both knew she did.

"I've dated a lot of educated women," he said. Well, at least a few. "And guess what? They would've let me pay for their five-dollar breakfast."

"I'm not your date," Tawny said, finding them a table at the back of the room.

"Why not?"

"Because you have a girlfriend." She peered at him, challenge in her eyes.

"What if I didn't? Would you date a guy like me?"

"Probably not," she said. "Guys like you are heartbreak waiting to happen."

"That's a crock." He was genuinely offended. "I'm steady. Look at my track record. I've loved the same woman since before I could shave." Tawny had been the one to make him question what he'd once thought were unshakable feelings for Raylene.

"Why do you care?" she asked. "Like you said, you've got the woman you've always wanted."

That was the problem. Perhaps all this time he'd wanted the wrong woman. "Just curious about the kind of guys you're into."

"I don't have a particular type," Tawny lied. Her type was Lucky, but she didn't need to inflate his already fat self-image. He had arm-candy Raylene for that.

"Just not *my* type." He sounded ticked off, like it was a major shock for him to find out that there were women out there who didn't want to throw themselves at him. "If I wasn't hooked up with Raylene and you weren't such a hard-ass, you might be my type."

"You hardly know me." Even though she knew everything about him.

"I've known you my whole life, Tawny. We went to grade school together, remember?"

"You didn't know me. You knew of me. There's a difference. The night we were together, you hadn't even realized that I'd dropped out of high school. That's how invisible I was to you."

"You're not invisible to me now."

Of course she wasn't, she was the mother of their child. Their very sick child. "We should get back to Katie's room."

They bussed their own table and left the cafeteria. When they got to Katie's room, the doctor was waiting for them.

"Miss Katie here is being cleared for takeoff," he told them. "I talked to Dr. Laurence. Unfortunately, he doesn't have any news for you yet, but he wants you to keep Katie home, preferably in bed, and out of school for the next couple of days while we monitor the fever."

Tawny did as the doctor asked and got Katie tucked in as soon as they arrived home. Lucky went to his ranch to feed his stock and check on the progress of the construction, which was scheduled to resume today, with the assurance that he'd be back later to check on Katie. Tawny went into the kitchen to make some tea when she heard a faint knock on the door. Brady stood outside, holding a sack.

"Hi," she said, letting him in.

"I don't mean to intrude, but I heard you, Katie, and Lucky spent the night in the hospital."

Tawny let out an audible sigh. "She had a high fever, so they admitted her. But it's gone today. She's in bed now, resting." She looked at the foil package peeking out of his bag. "What do you have there?" Whatever it was, it smelled fantastic.

"Fresh bread, just out of the oven. And some peach jam I canned over the summer."

"Seriously." She sniffed the bag and tugged on his arm. "Let's go to the kitchen."

Tawny put the kettle on the stove to boil, pulled out two mugs, some plates and knives, and set them on the table. Then she unwrapped the bread, letting the yeasty aroma fill her nose.

"I can't believe you made this," she said, and held up the jar of jam to the light. "And this."

"Yeah. I don't make kick-ass cowboy boots, though."

"I'm making you a pair," she said, and cut a piece of the bread, smeared it with jam, and chewed. She closed her eyes for a second. "This is so good. What should I put on them? The boots."

That's when one of the many intricate and colorful tattoos on his forearms caught her attention. It was a knife and fork artfully crossed into an X. "That right there." She pointed. "That's what I'll put on them."

Brady looked down at his arm. "That'll work. But a loaf of bread and jam doesn't seem like a fair trade."

Tawny held up a hunk of the homemade bread. "Have you tasted this?"

Brady's lips slid up into a smile. "It's good stuff."

"Yeah, it is. Sorry, I'm being a pig. You want some?"

"Nope. Have at it." Brady pulled out two chairs, and they sat. "No word yet on the transplant?"

Katie shook her head. "We're still waiting." It seemed like so much had happened since she and Lucky had gone to Palo Alto two days ago.

"Lucky doing okay?"

"Considering someone was killed on his property . . . and Katie . . . he's been a rock."

"And his girlfriend's dad." Brady shook his head. "Man, that must suck."

"What are you talking about?" What about Raylene's dad?

"You didn't hear? Ray Rosser was arrested for the shooting. According to Owen, the dead guy stole Ray's cattle, so Ray shot him. We didn't even do shit like that in South Carolina."

"I can't believe it's the first I'm hearing of this." Maybe Lucky didn't know yet. Although Raylene had to be flipping out. Her father was an abusive bully, but the Rosser name was like gold in this part of the Sierra. Having him face a murder charge had to be a huge black eye on the whole family, especially someone like hoity-toity Raylene.

"Owen's info can be pretty sketchy, so I wouldn't take it to the bank. But from what I understand, someone definitely got arrested. You were probably at the hospital when it happened."

Oh jeez, she had to call Lucky. "Raylene's probably a mess."

Brady shrugged. "I'd imagine she would be. Given that Lucky called the guy out, I'm assuming that he and Ray Rosser are not close."

"Nope," she said, not wanting to go into the details. Hopefully, for Katie's sake, that story would never surface. "But he'll be upset for Raylene." That was the thing about Lucky. He was loyal to a fault.

"I know you said there is nothing between you two, but are you sure about that?"

"You mean because he's here all the time? That's just for Katie."

"That's not why. He came into the inn yesterday and I got the distinct impression that he was trying to figure out where you and I stand—romantically. And honestly, he seemed jealous."

Tawny felt her face heat with embarrassment. "I don't know where he got that." She did, though. Raylene.

"Raylene told him," Brady said. "She walked in on us talking that one day. I think we might've been flirting."

He smiled at her, and if she wasn't so hung up on Lucky she might've fallen for Brady right then and there. Ironic how she'd judged Lucky for holding a torch all these years for Raylene when she'd done the same thing with Lucky.

"You have a thing for him, don't you?" Brady asked,

"Who, me? No . . . of course not . . . Is it that obvious?"

"Probably just to me." And then, doing a dead-on Clint Eastwood impression, he said, "I know things about people."

She laughed. "Lucky is with Raylene. He's loved her forever."

"Maybe." Brady lifted his shoulders. "But I'm not feeling it."

Brady didn't know Lucky like she did. "Believe me, he's addicted to her. And I need to give him a heads-up about Ray."

Brady got to his feet. "I have to take off anyway. We've got a full house at the inn and I've got a wine and cheese service to prepare."

"Hey, Brady, are you ever planning to tell me your secret? I told you mine."

His eyes turned downcast, and Tawny wished she hadn't brought it up. "Someday soon," he said.

"Come over tomorrow and let me trace your feet."

His expression went from sad to confused. "Is that what passes for sexy time in Nugget?"

"For the boots," she said.

"Hell yeah. I'm not passing that up. I'll bring lunch."

"Excellent."

As soon as he left, Tawny checked in on her daughter, grabbed the phone, and dialed Lucky. "Hi. Where are you?"

"Home." She could hear a sheep bleating in the background. "Is Katie okay?"

"She's fine. But I just heard Ray Rosser was arrested for the shooting."

"I know," he said. "Raylene says it was self-defense. Gus was stealing his cattle."

"Is Raylene okay?"

"She and her mother got him a good lawyer. Raylene thinks he's getting out of jail."

"I'm sorry for her. Don't worry about Katie. Do what you need to do." *Take care of Raylene*, she thought, but she couldn't bring herself to say it.

"What I need to do is check in on my daughter," Lucky said, sounding surly.

Whatever. Tawny was just trying to be understanding. "Suit yourself."

"I plan on it."

When they got off the phone, Tawny heated Katie a bowl of soup in the microwave and cut her a slice of Brady's homemade bread. Just what the doctor ordered. Why couldn't the chef have been Tawny's antidote too? He was nice, sexy, and available. And damn, could the man cook.

"How's Katie?" Raylene came up behind Lucky as he threw a flake of hay to Bernice.

"Better." He turned and stood there for a while, just taking her in, wondering how feelings he'd held for so long could wither so abruptly. Maybe it hadn't been abrupt. Maybe it had been a long time in coming. "I wasn't expecting to see you today. I figured you'd want to be with your mom. Is Ray getting out?"

"He's home," she said. "A lot of drama, huh?"

Lucky would call it more than drama. The man was looking at a murder charge—twenty-five years to life. "It's a good thing you came." God, it killed him to have to do this. But it was the right thing to do. The only thing. "I thought we could talk."

"If it's about what I said last night . . . about Tawny taking Katie to the hospital, I'm sorry."

"Sometimes you can be real self-centered, Raylene." He didn't have any more excuses for her.

She shrugged, shamefaced. "I know."

"Let's go in the trailer." Lucky rubbed his hands together. "It's cold out here."

"Okay. I don't have a lot of time. Butch is coming. Daddy sent for him. He has it in his head that a family crisis will put me and Butch back together."

Butch. Lucky tried to summon some kind of emotion. Anger, jealousy, disappointment. All he felt was a slight hollowness, which he couldn't quite identify.

"Don't be mad, Lucky. I'm just playing along for Daddy's sake."

He put his hand at the small of her back and they walked the short distance to Lucky's single-wide. Inside, he flipped on the heat and Raylene started taking off her clothes.

"What are you doing?" Lucky said.

Either she was in complete denial about his intentions or her cluelessness was an act, because she wound her arms around his neck and began kissing and rubbing on him. Perhaps she thought she could seduce him into loving her again.

"I want you," she said in a breathy voice he'd once found sexy.

He pushed her off him. "We need to talk."

"We can talk after." She started unbuttoning his jeans and slipped her hand inside his shorts.

Disgusted, he pulled her hand out of his pants. "What the hell's the matter with you?"

She stared at his flaccid penis and said, "You appear to be the one with the problem."

"Raylene"—he rebuttoned his fly—"I said I wanted to talk, not have sex."

He rested his forehead against the wall. This woman, whom he'd loved forever . . . and now all he could do was think of someone else. It made him a little sick. "I can't be with you."

"What are you talking about?"

He didn't know how to say the words without hurting her. "Us. We can't be together."

"Of course we can. Oh, for heaven's sake, Lucky, is this about Butch?"

That was the thing. It should've been about Butch, and Raylene's obvious reluctance to let her ex go. But it wasn't. It was about Tawny.

"No. We're just not working. You're getting over a bad marriage and I have a sick daughter—"

"Basically, you're mad at me for what I said last night—and now because of Butch. Grow up, Lucky."

Damn straight he was angry over her careless attitude about his daughter. About her selfishness. Her pettiness. All the faults he thought she'd grow out of once she got away from Ray, but hadn't. "Raylene, don't interrupt—"

"Are you breaking up with me? Just spit it out."

"Yes." He didn't know any other way to soften the blow because even now he felt protective of her. Old habits . . .

"You're not breaking up with me," Raylene said like she was bored. "You're pissed about Butch. You'll get over it." She started for the door and Lucky grabbed her by the arm.

"Raylene, we're over."

She just rolled her eyes and walked away.

Good to his word, Lucky showed up a few hours later. Tawny could tell from Lucky's damp hair—he must've left his hat in the truck—that he'd recently showered. Besides newish jeans and a shiny pair of black cowboy boots, he'd put on cologne. Something spicy that made her mouth water. She wondered if he was going out later.

"How's she doing?" he asked, giving her a quick once-over.

Still in the same jeans and sweater she'd thrown on after getting home from the hospital, Tawny wished she'd changed into something nicer. "Good. She ate lunch, so at least she's got a bit of an appetite. She's sleeping now."

Lucky made his way through the living room to her bedroom, quietly opened the door, and popped his head in. Just as quietly he shut it, motioning to Tawny that they should go to the kitchen.

"You okay?" she asked him.

"Yeah. Why wouldn't I be?"

"Ray's arrest must have you shaken up."

"Not really. I couldn't care less if they locked him up and threw away the key. What's shaking me up is that Gus was stealing cattle, and I'd be willing to bet that the rest of my so-called construction crew were in on it. I'd like to fire every last one of them."

"Why don't you then?"

He huffed out a breath, clasped her shoulders, and backed her up against the counter, where they stood not even an inch apart. God, he felt good, his chest rock solid, and arms that felt strong enough to take on anything. And for the zillionth time she remembered what it had been like to be under all that strength while he moved over her. Inside of her.

"I'm not supposed to tell anyone," he said, his voice nearly a whisper. "But Jake and Rhys suspect these guys of more than cattle rustling."

"Like what?" she asked, having trouble focusing on the subject matter. All she wanted him to do was kiss her.

He pushed away from the counter and she instantly felt bereft of his body heat. Like she'd lost something enormously comforting.

"You have to promise to keep this quiet. The cops think they're dealing drugs, using my project as a front. They want to catch them in the act by going undercover. I swear, Tawny, if you let this leak, it'll screw the investigation. As it is, Ray probably ruined it. But I gave Jake my word that I wouldn't fire anyone until they rounded up the bad players."

"I won't tell anyone. But aren't you worried about the danger?"

"Not to me. But I sure as hell don't want you or Katie setting foot on the ranch until this is cleared up."

Tawny swallowed. "You should stay with your mom until this is over."

"That would look suspicious, don't you think? Not to mention that I want to keep my eye on the place. And I want these jokers off my property as soon as possible. The valuable lesson in all this is never hire cheap. I should've gone with Pat Donnelly and Colin. Man, am I kicking myself."

"When will the police be done?"

"I don't know," he said. "Jake is keeping me in the dark. And the shooting is bound to put these guys on guard. I wish I'd never made the deal with Nugget PD, but at the same time I want the message out that you can't get away with this crap in my town. Damn, Tawny, my people and business are here."

"What about Ray?"

"According to Raylene, he's home until the DA files charges."

"Is she okay?" To Tawny's surprise, Lucky merely shrugged, like he didn't really care.

"Butch is coming to be with the family," he said.

That explained to Tawny Lucky's show of apathy. "That bother you?"

"It should," he said. "But it doesn't. How messed up is that?"

She remembered her earlier conversation with Brady. *Lucky is with Raylene. He's loved her forever.*

Maybe, but I'm not feeling it.

It was messed up all right, as in messing with her head.

Chapter 16

"Is she getting back with him?" Tawny asked.

"I dunno."

"I'm sorry, Lucky. I know how you feel about her."

He didn't want to talk about Raylene with Tawny. There were other things he wanted to do with her instead. Lately his head had been so full of them that he'd been walking around half aroused much of his days. It was getting damned uncomfortable.

"You have dinner yet?" he asked her.

"No." She looked around her kitchen. A half a loaf of bread—it looked homemade—sat in a basket on the counter. "Sometimes I wish this town had pizza delivery."

"Or Chinese." He laughed. "I'll call in an order at the Ponderosa and pick it up. Something good, like steak."

"Mm. That sounds amazing." He liked the way her face went all orgasmic when she said *mm*.

He should've been grieving Raylene; instead, he felt like he had a clear conscience.

After phoning in an order for a couple of rib eyes with the works and charging it on his credit card, he found Tawny checking in on Katie again. "Mariah said she'd swing by with our food. It's on her way home. Katie okay?"

"Sound asleep and no fever."

He touched Tawny's back. "We should hear something soon."

"I hope so. I want her to be better . . . to live a normal life." Lucky heard everything Tawny wasn't saying and felt his chest clutch.

"As soon as this bullshit's over at the ranch, I plan on talking to Colin about building my house," he said, and she gave him a half smile. "Come sit on the couch. It's been a long day."

She followed him and they sat close enough so that their legs were touching. He toyed with the idea of kissing her, but the doorbell rang. A little too fast for the food, Lucky thought. On his feet, he pulled away the lace panel at the window and peered onto the porch.

"Jeez."

"Who is it?" Tawny asked, going to the door.

"Donna Thurston." Was being alone with Tawny for an hour or two too much to ask? It seemed like every time he was here, a visitor showed up.

"Be nice," she said, and opened the door. "Hi, Donna." Tawny leaned over and kissed the woman on the cheek.

In her typical pushy way, Donna came in uninvited, took one look at Lucky, and said, "You sure brought the excitement to town, didn't you?"

"Me?" he replied. "I'm not the one shooting people."

"Talk is all over town that Ray Rosser is home. Apparently the man bought his way out of this one too."

Lucky would give it to Donna. She was no one's fool. The Rossers might be Nugget royalty, but she saw right through the old man.

"They don't think he's a flight risk. Pfft," she continued, gazing at Lucky like he had answers. All he knew was that Rosser was claiming self-defense and hadn't been charged with a crime—yet.

"Do I look like the law to you, Donna?"

"You look like something, Lucky Rodriguez. But definitely not the law." She pulled him by his collar and gave him a kiss on the lips. "When did you become such a smart mouth?"

He flashed a neon grin, the same one he saved for an arena full of cheering people when he'd made it to the buzzer with a ninety-point ride.

Donna turned to Tawny. "How's Katie?"

"Much better, thank you." Tawny offered Donna a drink. A seat.

"I just came to drop this off for our girl while she's bedridden," Donna said, handing Tawny a bag of children's books and DVDs. Lucky silently chanted *hallelujah*. She'd be leaving soon.

"That's incredibly sweet of you," Tawny said. "I know Katie will enjoy these."

"By the way," Donna said, "I saw those boots you gave Cecilia. She's so proud of them. You done good, girl."

Although Donna had promised that she was just dropping Katie's stuff off, she managed to stay, talking their ears off, until Mariah appeared in the open doorway, holding a couple of plastic sacks.

"Looks like a party." Mariah handed the bags to Lucky.

"I was just leaving," Donna said, and sniffed the food. "Smells good."

"I put some chicken noodle soup in there for Katie."

"Thanks, Mariah. I appreciate you dropping it off," Lucky said.

"My pleasure. Give Katie a kiss for me."

Donna followed Mariah out. *Good, let her jaw someone else to death*, Lucky thought as he shut the door.

"Let's eat before it gets cold," he told Tawny.

She quickly stashed the soup in the fridge, set the table, and searched through a cabinet until she came up with a bottle of red wine. "A client gave this to me. It's supposed to be good."

"You don't have beer?"

"Sorry."

"Wine it is then." Lucky watched her open the bottle and pour it into two goblets. "What kind of client?"

"He's another winemaker from the Napa Valley. He wanted boots with his logo and brought me the wine as a gift. Nice, right?"

Lucky wondered if the winemaker was hoping for a gift in return. "You gave my mom a pair of boots?" When Donna had mentioned it, Lucky was surprised—not that Tawny wasn't generous, because she was, but because he hadn't realized that she and his mother were that friendly.

"She came by the studio the other day and I just happened to have a pair in her size. I'd made 'em for a trunk show I did in Glory Junction last year."

"What's a trunk show?"

"A couple of Western-wear designers were showing their merchandise, and I held a special sales event at some rich woman's vacation house. A bunch of her friends came and I sold a lot of boots."

"You could've eventually sold the pair you gave my mom, right?"

"I could've, but I wanted Cecilia to have them . . . from Katie, her granddaughter."

"That was nice of you, Tawny."

"It's no big deal."

Of course it was. Lucky knew Tawny needed the money. With Katie's various medical emergencies, she barely had time to work.

"Did Harlee take that picture of you the other night?" Lucky asked, and when Tawny seemed stumped, he said, "The one for your website."

"Wow . . . you remembered. As a matter of fact, she did. I already uploaded it, along with a few new boot pictures to the gallery."

He'd never looked at her website. People who worked for Lucky did his. "Does it get you a lot of clients?"

"It's hard to say. Most of my business is word-of-mouth, but they probably go to my website to check out me and my work. It's pretty visual."

Lucky bet that a lot of men liked what they saw.

The steak tasted good. McCreedy beef. Clay had an exclusive deal with the Ponderosa, which probably pissed Rosser off. He watched Tawny take dainty bites of hers.

"Good?" He cocked his head at her meal.

"Delicious. I can't remember the last time I had steak." That would change now that he was around.

When they finished eating, Tawny cleared their plates and loaded them into the dishwasher. "Want coffee?" she asked.

"Sure." Truth was he wanted an excuse to hang out.

While she prepared the coffeemaker, he got up and moved behind her.

"I have store-bought cookies for dessert if you're interest—"

Before she could say more, he spun her around and boxed her in against the counter. "This is what I'm interested in." Then he laid his lips on her mouth and kissed her.

Slow at first. But when she kissed him back, he moved over her with the urgency of a man who had been dreaming about this for weeks. Raiding her mouth with his tongue. She tasted so good, like red wine and heaven. And the way she clung to him made him so hard he feared he'd burst the seams in his fly. So he pressed into her more, hoping for sweet relief. His hands inched under her sweater, finding soft skin.

She pulled at his shirt, untucking it from his waist, and laid her hands against his bare abs, making him hiss in a breath. Never once did she stop kissing him. He reached higher until he found her breasts and fondled them through the thin lace of her bra. Flesh. He wanted the real deal, so he searched for the clasp, sprang those perfect globes free, and molded them with his hands. They were like peaches, and he desperately wanted a taste. Pushing up her sweater, he sucked her nipples and heard her let out a moan of pure pleasure. She brought his head back up and started kissing him again.

"Tawny," he said against her mouth, pressing deeper against her groin. "Let's take this into the bedroom."

She pulled away from him and grabbed the counter with her hands to find support. Lucky knew how she felt. Those kisses . . . her body thrumming underneath his hands . . . had made him unsteady on his feet.

"We can't do this." She tried to find her breath and unconsciously traced her puffy lips.

"Why not?" Seemed like they were doing it just fine a few seconds ago.

She glared at him. "Let's start with the fact that our daughter is in the next room and end with the fact that you're in a relationship."

He couldn't dispute the part about Katie being in the next room. Being a good influence on a nine-year-old was still pretty new to him. He was used to having sex when and wherever he wanted. For the sake of his daughter, that obviously would have to change.

"I'm no longer in a relationship," he argued.

For a split second he saw something—maybe hope—flicker in her eyes. But it came and went so fast he couldn't tell for sure.

"You're angry with Raylene because Butch is here. You'll get over it." Her meaning was clear: *No matter how bad Raylene treats you, you always come back for more.* "I won't be your get-even sex again."

He recoiled. "What the hell are you talking about? That's not what this is."

"Then what exactly is it?"

How could he explain it when he didn't understand it himself? "I'm attracted to you . . . I want you."

"Here's a little news flash from the real world. You don't always get what you want."

Why all the hostility when a few minutes earlier she'd been dry humping him with wild abandon? But he still wanted her. More now than ever before. And not because she was a challenge. He got plenty of that every time he climbed on top of a pissed-off bull, which he did regularly. He just couldn't remember a make-out session getting him as hot and bothered as it had with Tawny.

Holy freaking hell, had it been good.

"Here's a big news flash for you," he said. "I always get what I want."

He forgot about the coffee and went home to check on his stock.

"Maybe next time, you wear the boots." Jake lay in bed holding Cecilia in a haze of post-coital bliss. The woman knew how to float his boat.

She laughed. "They're beautiful, aren't they?"

"You're beautiful." But her in the boots, naked, would be so sexy it might just give him a stroke. Well worth it. "Let's move in together, Cecilia."

She flipped on her side to look at him. "You'd give up your cabin?"

"I'd keep it for the girls," he said. "But I know how much this house means to you."

"Father Thomas wouldn't like it."

For self-preservation he didn't point out that her priest wouldn't like the fact that they were getting it on like bunnies, either. Still, it hadn't stopped them. "What are you saying, you want to get married?"

"I didn't say that." She rested her head on his chest. "I'm saying I like the arrangement the way it is."

"I want more, Cecilia. I want to sleep with you every night and wake up to the same sunrise with you every morning. I want us to be a team."

"And what's to say that as soon as you have that, you won't want it anymore?" she asked.

Because he'd gotten it wrong so many goddamned times that he knew when it was finally right. "I know," he said. "Now all I have to do is convince you."

His cell rang and he reached over to the nightstand to get it. Rhys. "What've you got?"

"It appears that we're back in business," Rhys said.

"Ray's intel must've been good, then?" Evidently the cattle rancher kept some real lowlifes on his payroll.

"Looks like. I know it's Saturday, but what are you doing this afternoon?"

Jake brushed a strand of Cecilia's hair out of her face. "I guess I'm working."

"I'll bring lunch from my wife's personal chef."

"Brady." Jake laughed. "Sounds like he's working out well for the inn."

"Are you kidding? He's working out great for the whole Shepard family. Every night he sends Maddy home with dinner. I effing love the guy."

"All right. I'll see you around noon," Jake said and hung up.

"You have to go into the office?" Cecilia asked, and Jake suppressed a grin. The *office*. Like he was an insurance adjuster.

More than likely he and Rhys would drive up the mountain from Lucky's ranch and do surveillance from inside an abandoned Airstream trailer that they'd scoped out before the shooting, which smelled like rotting rodents.

"Yeah, but we have some time."

He rolled her under him and entered her slowly. She arched up, giving him better access to her breasts. Jake didn't think he'd ever get enough of this woman. But unlike their first time this morning, his strokes were leisurely and his loving thorough. Gradually, he brought her to the peak and joined her in catapulting off the edge. They lay there for a while, catching their breath. She smiled up at him, looking like a satisfied cat, then rolled out from under him.

Jake kissed her. "I want us to do that dinner thing we talked about. Your family and mine."

"When?" She traced the hairs on his chest with her finger.

"Sometime before Thanksgiving, if I can swing it. The homicide is keeping us pretty busy, though."

"I thought you closed the case. Ray confessed."

"Where'd you hear that?" He propped himself up on one elbow.

"It's all over town. What? It's not true?"

"You know I can't talk about the case, Cecilia."

"Is that the reason you're going in today?"

"Yep." It wasn't exactly a lie. He playfully slapped her on the bottom. "I'm hitting the shower. Care to join me?"

After they got dressed, Cecilia made him breakfast. Eggs with chorizo, potatoes, and biscuits. Since he'd met her, he'd put on five pounds.

"I'm worried about Lucky's business," she said, refilling his coffee cup. "He was supposed to open in summer. And now with this shooting on his property . . . *Ay Dios mio.*"

"Sweetheart, it was over cattle rustling," Jake said. "I'm no marketing genius, but it seems to me that it'll add to the place's mystique."

"Or Ray Rosser is trying to ruin Lucky. I wouldn't put it past the miserable man."

"Lucky will be fine," he said. "No word about Katie, huh?"

"Not yet." She sighed. "I thought I'd go over to Tawny's today and babysit so she can get some work done."

"What's Lucky doing?" Jake asked, trying to sound casual. He wanted him away from the ranch today in case things went down. Not likely to happen, though. Since the cattle thefts, Lucky had been extra vigilant about watching his place.

"I have no idea," Cecilia said. "Probably with Raylene."

From what Jake had heard, Raylene's ex-husband was in town. Who knew how that would play out? The whole Rosser family was a train wreck as far as Jake was concerned. And Ray definitely had it out for Lucky. He'd desperately tried to implicate Lucky in the drug case, saying Cecilia's son used the cowboy camp as a front to sell meth. And Jake got the impression Ray wasn't done yet. Something told him Ray would eventually get around to hanging the shooting on Lucky, too.

There was not one stitch of evidence to corroborate Lucky's involvement in either. Still, they couldn't completely rule him out. Not until they had a better handle on both cases. And Jake didn't want any appearance of impropriety since he was dating Lucky's mother. Any other department would've pulled his ass off the case. Too short on manpower, Nugget PD couldn't afford to cut Jake loose, especially since he happened to be the most seasoned cop on the force.

That's why he wanted Lucky as far away from this mess as possible.

By the time Jake and Rhys made it to the Airstream, the temperature had dropped a good ten degrees. Jake wished he'd brought something warmer than his lightweight camo jacket. Rhys pulled two pairs of binoculars from his truck and handed a set to Jake.

"These Steiners?"

"Yep. Got 'em a couple of nights ago, compliments of the Nugget City Council," Rhys said. "You're welcome."

Jake examined them. Built to military specs, the binoculars were real lightweight. "Nice."

Besides being a good cop, Rhys could get money from a beggar. When he first became chief, he'd gotten federal grants to buy all-wheel-drive SUVs for the department and had managed to talk the city into ponying up enough cash to trick them out with high-tech computer systems.

Jake gazed down and surveyed Lucky's property. From this vantage point they could see all the way to Nevada, but the knoll was hidden enough by trees and terrain that no one could see them. He focused the binos on the top of Lucky's single-wide and could make out the leaves that had fallen on the roof. "Damn, these are real good. Excellent magnification."

Rhys played with his for a few minutes, getting the lay of the land. "Looks like the crew is working on the southern part of the property. More corrals, if I'm not mistaken. How much stock does Lucky have?"

"I don't know the number, but he says he has more coming in next month. I'm surprised these guys are working on a Saturday."

"Lucky's cracking the whip. According to Maddy, he's way behind schedule. He and the inn have a couple of joint events booked for spring. At this rate he won't make it." Rhys put the binoculars down, rubbed his hands together, and shoved them in his jacket pockets. "It's cold."

Neither one of them wanted to go inside the Airstream.

"You do a lot of these stakeouts in LA?" Rhys asked.

"A fair amount. Did quite a bit during Desert Storm."

"You were a marine, right?"

"Semper fi." Jake sat next to a redwood, knowing that the tree trunk and his jacket would obscure him from sight. "How 'bout in Houston? You do a lot?"

Rhys grabbed the ground next to him. "I did so much surveillance when I started in narcotics, I pissed coffee for a year. Speaking of, there's a thermos in the truck."

Jake did another sweep with the binoculars, landing on a couple of shapes near Lucky's Ram Laramie. Two men, one getting out of a white Ford Escort. "You see that?"

"Yep." Rhys got up to find a better lookout. A couple of trees hampered his view. "I can't make out the plates from here. But it looks like Lucky, from the black cowboy hat."

"A lot of black cowboy hats in these parts," Jake said, and got the camera out of the truck to snap a few pictures.

Rhys tried to zoom his binos in better. "I can't get a clear line of sight. But they are definitely making an exchange of some sort. They're going inside the trailer now."

Jake continued snapping shots of them until they disappeared inside the single-wide.

Rhys scurried down the hill, hugging a line of trees, getting as close as he could to the Escort without flagging anyone's attention. When he came back up he had a number, which he called in to Connie to run through the DMV. With his cell held to his ear, Rhys scanned the area one-handed with his binoculars.

"You're sure the Escort isn't one of our guys?" Jake asked. The car seemed kind of obvious for an undercover vehicle—police departments typically used American models, mostly Fords. Although he'd heard that San Francisco PD was using Priuses. Embarrassing, if you asked him. In this case, the Plumas County Sheriff's Office was running the undercover show. Jake had no idea what vehicles they were using.

"No Escort on the roster," Rhys said. "Connie says it's a rental out of Reno. She's calling to see who rented it."

Rhys held, waiting for Connie to come back on the line. A short time later, he wrote something on his hand and asked Jake, "The name Noah Lansing ring a bell with you?" When Jake shook his head, Rhys said, "Connie's searching on Google. Who knows, maybe we'll get a hit."

Jake put down the camera and tried the binos again, aiming for the southern side of the property where the crew worked. "Looks like the fellows have company. A Toyota Tundra. That one of ours?"

"Hang on, Connie." Rhys shoved the phone in his pocket and looked through his lenses. "No Toyotas listed. The truck must've used the fire road." They would've seen it come up the driveway.

Jake grabbed up the camera again and shot a few pictures. "No way are we getting the license plate number from this distance. But it looks like something's going down."

Rhys retrieved his phone. "Connie, you there?" Pause. "No kidding."

"What?" Jake asked, and switched out the camera for the binoculars.

"Noah Lansing is a *Sports Illustrated* reporter."

But Jake's attention had already been pulled in another direction. "You see what I see?" He pointed over the horizon where four sheriff's rigs came rocketing across the fire road, lights flashing. Another two roared up Lucky's driveway with their sirens blaring.

"Cavalry's here." Rhys dashed for his truck with Jake on his heels. "Looks like our drug bust is about to make national sports news."

Chapter 17

"I can't freaking believe this." Lucky continued to pace across Tawny's kitchen floor. "He's there all of fifteen minutes when the place blows up with cops."

Tawny wanted so badly to say something that would make it better, but she had to admit that as far as first impressions go, Lucky's cowboy camp had failed miserably. Eight members of his construction crew had been arrested, hundreds of thousands of dollars' worth of methamphetamine had been seized, and the county's drug task force wasn't done yet. According to Harlee's story in the *Nugget Tribune*, search warrants were being served across the county in connection with what was being hailed as the largest drug bust in recent area history. The criminal activity at Lucky's ranch was apparently only a tiny piece of the operation, but had been the impetus—in no small part due to Jake and Rhys—that brought the whole enterprise down. All in front of Lucky's *Sports Illustrated* reporter.

"Where is he now?" Tawny asked.

"He went back to the Lumber Baron." Lucky threw his head back. "Can this get any worse?"

"Did you try to explain to him that—"

"That in less than a week a man was shot to death on my property . . . and then this?"

"Please don't bite my head off. I'm only trying to help."

Lucky gently clasped her shoulders. "I'm sorry, I'm sorry. Kiss me."

"What?" She looked at him like he was crazy.

"I just want to see if I imagined what it felt like yesterday. Come on, give me something good to hang on to."

"Fine." She gave him a friendly, you'll-get-through-this peck on the lips.

"Ah, that was bullshit." He pulled her in, held her face in both hands, and covered her mouth with his. Kissing and kissing and kissing her until she felt the floor tilt.

He lifted her off the linoleum and kept right on kissing her, exploring her mouth with his tongue as he palmed her bottom, pushing her into the great big bulge in his pants. "Since Katie's with my mom, can we go to bed?"

"No." She pulled away. "Are you insane?"

"I thought I was, but now I know this"—he gestured between them—"isn't my imagination. We've got serious chemistry, Tawny."

"Butch must still be in town." Tawny lifted her head heavenward like she was praying for patience. The man really thought she was daft. She tried to turn away, but Lucky caught her by the arm.

"I don't know where Butch is. I don't care where Butch is. This isn't about Raylene. She and I are no longer together."

Tawny looked at him. Really looked. The man was everything she'd ever wanted. Hot as all get-out. Gorgeous brown eyes, square jaw, chiseled face, broad and strong. Honorable and kind. Funny and arrogant—God, was he arrogant. Smart and responsible. And caring. For all his swagger and machismo, Lucky Rodriguez was turning out to be one of the most thoughtful men she'd ever known. A man who, under trying circumstances, had stepped up to the plate when it came to Katie.

Tawny could count on one hand the gifts life had handed her, and even those had come with a cost. A teen pregnancy, a child sick with cancer, a father who'd loved and left her too young. So why not take what Lucky was offering? Even if it was a one-time deal, which they both knew it was, she'd have the man she'd always wanted. If only for a short time.

"I don't have protection," she said.

He blinked, clearly stunned. "I've got us covered."

She walked into the bedroom and started removing her clothes.

"Whoa," he said. "Slow down. You sure you want to do this?"

She stopped to glower at him. The man was sure dense. "Obviously I do. I'm just a little nervous. It's been a while." Would he be thinking about Raylene the whole time?

"Nothing to be nervous about." He finished unbuttoning her blouse and kissed her. "Let's just fool around for a little while."

He kissed her neck, collarbone, and brushed the sides of her blouse away from her arms and kissed her shoulders. "You smell nice."

She'd put on perfume before he'd come over. Nothing expensive, just something she'd picked up at the drugstore while filling Katie's prescription.

He traced the lace of her bra. "This is pretty. New?"

"Mm-hmm." She'd splurged online at Victoria's Secret.

"For me?" he asked, and pulled down the straps.

"No." Raylene probably had one in every color.

"Liar." He tugged down the cups. "You've been feeling this between us as much as I have. God, you're beautiful."

Compared to Raylene's double D's, she must've seemed flat chested. She tried to pull the bra back up, but Lucky wouldn't let her.

"What's wrong, Tawny?"

"I don't think I'm good at this." The truth was she felt horribly insecure, like she wouldn't stack up against Lucky's other women.

"You were good at it yesterday," he said. "You just need to relax. Trust me."

Yeah, that was the problem. She trusted him about as far as she could throw him. Probably even less. "I'll try."

He chuckled. "We can stop anytime you want." Lucky took her blouse and bra all the way off and sucked her breasts.

It felt so good that she let out a moan.

"Mm," he whispered. "You taste good."

Tawny wanted his shirt off. Under his T-shirt he had on a long-sleeved thermal. She rucked both up until they were under his chin. Lucky tugged them over his head and tossed them somewhere on the floor. His chest and abs were rippled with muscle and scarred from where he'd been gored by bulls.

She kissed a scar above his right pec. "Did this hurt?"

"Can't remember," he said. "But you should probably kiss them all, just in case. I have some down here too." He undid the button fly of his jeans, exposing a pair of black boxer briefs and an impressive bulge.

She touched him there and heard him hiss in a breath. He lifted her hand off his erection and kissed the side of her neck. "Slow." He nibbled the lobe of her ear. "Katie's staying over at Grandma's, right? So we've got all night."

The thought of an entire night with Lucky Rodriguez sent a shiver up her spine. He tugged on her skirt, pulling it down past her knees, and she walked out of it.

He stared down at her panties and touched her over the lace. "You're wet for me."

He pushed her backwards onto the bed and came down on top of her, supporting his weight with his elbows. Ever so gently he brushed a few strands of hair away from her face and looked at her for what seemed like forever. First her eyes, then her lips, letting his gaze fall to her breasts and lower. Tawny felt hot liquid pool between her legs. When he was done looking, he kissed his way down her body, practically bringing her off the bed.

The man made her burn for him. "Lucky?"

"Hmm?" He slid her underwear down and worked her with his fingers, making her cry out while he showered her with more kisses. "This good?"

"Oh God, yes . . . What about you?"

His lips traveled up her throat. The stubble on his face felt rough against her skin, but oh so good. Next to her ear he said, "We'll get to me. First you."

He brought her to the apex not once, but twice, then rolled on a condom before thrusting into her. He leaned his head back, his eyes dark with desire, his neck taut with control, and pounded into her again and again until they both shouted out and let go. He lay there on top of her and she could feel his heart beating fast and hard, and thought for sure that he could hear hers, loud as a marching-band drum.

He muttered something about being heavy and rolled over to the side, taking her with him. Together they just lay there, staring into each other's eyes.

"You okay?" he asked.

She nodded, afraid that if she spoke she might cry. Because other than giving birth to Katie, she'd never experienced anything so intimate, so earth shattering, in her life.

"Better than the first time?" When she looked at him quizzically, he said, "At the park."

She gave him a small smile. "No comparison."

"I'll always be sorry that I didn't make your first time better," he said, and she was sure that if he looked close enough he could see that her eyes had filled. "But we got Katie."

"I couldn't ask for better than that," Tawny said, and Lucky wiped her tear away with his knuckle.

"We'll get her well, Tawny. I promise."

Something suddenly chirped and Lucky leaned over her to grab his phone off the floor. He hung over the side of the bed for a second, giving Tawny an excellent rear view, reading what looked like a text. Then he dropped the phone on the nightstand and headed off to the bathroom.

Going against every moral code she believed in, Tawny quickly lifted the phone and read the message Lucky had left on the screen.

Where are you? Heard about the bust today and am worried sick. Hopefully by now you're over your petty jealously about Butch. Call me. I love you. Raylene.

By the time Lucky came back into the room, Tawny had dressed. He stood in front of her in all his naked glory, a confused expression on his face. "I thought"—he nudged his head at the bed—"we could hang out a while."

"I have boots to make and I'm sure you have . . . things to do."

"It's nine o'clock at night, Tawny. You looked at my text, didn't you?"

She didn't say anything and she supposed that was confirmation enough.

"Do you see me texting her back?"

"You will, eventually. For right now you think it's over between the two of you." Clearly from Raylene's text she didn't, but that was another story. "But this thing with you guys . . . it'll never end. You'll take her back, you always do. And this thing with me and you . . . we were just scratching an itch. So go to her if you want. No hard feelings."

She somehow managed to make it to her studio with her dignity still intact. If there was any mercy in the world, Lucky would just leave. But no such luck. He followed her into the workshop.

"I'm not seeing her and I'm not sleeping with her," Lucky said while Tawny pretended to be too busy to meet his gaze. "I wouldn't do that to either of you."

He started to say more, but became distracted by a stack of drawings and measurements on her desk. Brady's name scrawled in big bold letters across the top of the pages.

"You're making him a pair of boots?" Lucky asked, and what could she do? Lie? So she nodded. "I thought you had a two-year waiting list. He's only lived here a couple of months."

Tawny didn't say anything.

"Ah," he said. "I see how this is. You scratching an itch with Brady too?"

"No. Of course not," she said, chasing after him. "Lucky, come back here and listen to me."

But he got in his truck and drove away.

Lucky should've gone home, but he figured the cops had taken over his place, searching all the outbuildings for any contraband they had missed. Besides, it had been a shit day and he wanted a drink.

Even with the big crowd at the Ponderosa, Lucky managed to slip in at the bar.

He ordered his usual—Jack neat—and tried to lose himself in the car race playing on the flat-screen above the back bar. Not much of a NASCAR fan, he found it difficult to get absorbed. He could've asked one of the bartenders to change the channel, but why bother?

His mind kept going back to him and Tawny and their lovemaking, which had been beyond anything he could've imagined. The two of them were so in sync it was scary. Except for when they weren't. Raylene. Brady. More drama than he could handle, especially with a sick daughter, his cowboy camp falling apart, and a reporter who wanted to document it all.

Boy, had Noah gotten his eyes full today. Police lights flashing and guns being drawn. Half his crew had been taken into custody and Lucky had fired the rest. What would he do for an encore?

The world finals were less than two months away and he'd hardly trained. The PBR took the summer off, and Lucky had used the time to recuperate from his wreck in Billings. At least he'd scored high enough early on to qualify and didn't have to travel to other events before Vegas. The whole point of staying home was to get his business off the ground. So far that had proven to be a giant joke.

His phone vibrated and he fished it out of his pocket. Another message from Raylene. He didn't have the wherewithal to deal with her now, so he stuffed the phone back in his jacket.

"You mind if I take this seat?" Noah grabbed the stool next to Lucky. Clearly, he didn't really care how Lucky felt about it.

Lucky motioned the bartender over. "Another and whatever he wants." Noah ordered a beer.

"According to your local news site, today's bust was the largest in recent county history," the reporter said, vibrating with excitement.

"Yep. Go big or go home," Lucky muttered.

"You didn't know people were dealing drugs off your property?"

Lucky debated getting up and walking out, but he knew it would just make matters worse. His agent wanted to hire him one of those crisis-manager types to fix this, but Lucky didn't really see how anyone could. "The police have asked me not to talk about it. I don't want to do anything that'll hurt their case."

Noah nodded. "This can't be good for your business . . . first the murder and now this."

So he knew about that too. Not that Lucky was surprised. It was just a matter of time. Someone played the Big & Rich song, "Save a Horse (Ride a Cowboy)" and a group of women sitting at one of the corner booths starting chanting the chorus.

"What are you planning to do?" Noah continued.

"Hire a new crew."

"I meant publicity-wise." He pulled out his notebook. "The fact is, Luiz Silva or Tuff Johnson are this year's favorites for the finals. After you took that bad fall from Bushwacker in Billings, people have been predicting this would be your last year. It seems to me that you've got a lot riding on this cowboy camp of yours. Are you panicking?"

"Nope." Before he could explain that the recent spate of crimes was an anomaly in Nugget, Sophie came over to hug him.

"I heard what happened today. My God, Lucky, are you okay?"

"I'm fine. Just a lot of craziness." Lucky introduced Sophie to Noah. "She and Mariah over there"—he pointed across the bar— "own the Ponderosa."

"Nice to meet you," Noah said. "Have you known Lucky a long time?"

"We've only lived here four years . . . didn't watch him grow up. But he's a hometown hero. You won't have any trouble finding people here who have known him since he was a baby." Sophie smiled, and Lucky remembered that before coming to Nugget she'd been a bigtime marketing executive in the Bay Area. She certainly talked the talk. "Just let us know if you need anything during your stay here.

Too bad you had to come at our worst time. Normally this is the safest place you could imagine. That's why we moved here."

"I may stop by when things are a little quieter and get some perspective from you about the area," Noah said.

"Absolutely." Sophie turned to Lucky. "Any word yet on Katie?"

"Not yet," he said.

"I know Mariah brought soup over. How's she feeling?"

"Okay," Lucky said. "She's with my mom tonight."

Sophie took both his hands. "Just know that she's always in our thoughts."

"Thank you, Sophie."

When she left to relieve Mariah, Noah asked, "Who's Katie?"

"My daughter."

Noah cocked his head. "Daughter?"

Lucky decided to cut to the chase. "She's nine. Due to extenuating circumstances"—that's what his agent told him to say—"I just learned about her a couple of months ago."

"What kind of extenuating circumstances?"

The man was a reporter, all right. "It's private, Noah. For my daughter's sake, her mother and I would like to keep this part of my life out of the press."

"I don't know that I can do that," Noah said. "This is a profile on you. Having a secret daughter will inevitably become part of it."

"She's not a secret and you're welcome to meet her. But we're not willing to talk about the past."

"Is she sick?" Noah wanted to know.

"She has acute myeloid leukemia and needs a stem cell transplant. We're waiting to hear if I'm a match."

"Jesus," Noah said. "I'm sorry." He sounded genuinely sympathetic, but Lucky couldn't miss the gleam in the reporter's eye. No doubt he was amped about stumbling onto this new piece of news.

Pete had warned Lucky that the reporter would go nuts for it, riffing off headlines like: CELEBRITY BULL RIDER DONATES BONE MARROW TO SAVE DAUGHTER'S LIFE. Lucky didn't want to turn his daughter's illness into a sideshow but knew he couldn't exactly keep it a secret either.

"When can I meet her?" Noah asked.

"Tomorrow. If you want, I'll take you over to my mother's."

"And your daughter's mother, what's your relationship with her like?"

An hour ago, their relationship had been X-rated. Now, he wasn't sure whether they were still talking to each other. "Good. You can meet her too. She makes custom cowboy boots. Everyone from Merle Haggard to Madison Bumgarner has bought a pair."

"Really?"

Lucky started to tell Noah more about Tawny when a woman draped herself over his back, covered his eyes with her hands, and said, "Guess who?"

As if he didn't know.

"Is this her?" Noah asked.

"Who?" Raylene dropped her hands and graced Noah with one of her rodeo-queen smiles.

"This is Raylene Rosser," Lucky told Noah. "She's—"

"You must be the *Sports Illustrated* reporter," Raylene cut in. "I'm Lucky's girlfriend."

"Rosser?" The reporter scratched his head. "Isn't that the name of the man arrested for the shooting on Lucky's property?"

"My dad," Raylene said. "It was self-defense. Gus Clamper tried to kill him."

Lucky thought they must've looked like a bunch of trailer trash to this guy. In the worst way he wanted to call it a night. The problem was, he'd either have to take Raylene home or leave her alone with Noah to yap her head off about Lucky's private affairs. Neither was an option.

He couldn't remember a time when he hadn't wanted to take Raylene home. The fact that he didn't now made him feel nostalgic and just a little bit melancholy.

Finally, it was Noah who said goodbye. Before he trudged across the square to the Lumber Baron, they made a plan to meet at Cecilia's in the morning.

As soon as Noah left, Raylene ditched the sweet rodeo-queen act. "Why didn't you call me back? I've been looking for you all day."

"A lot of shit went down today, Raylene. I've been busy."

"Busy with Tawny."

He wasn't about to lie to her. "Yeah, I went over there."

"Great," she said. "My life's falling apart and you're killing time with Thelma Wade."

His life hadn't exactly been a party these past few weeks. "What's wrong?"

"You mean besides the fact that the Rossers may as well be the Manson family around here?" Raylene had always had a flair for overstating things. *The Manson family.* "Butch is marrying the whore. She'll be living in my house, sleeping in my bed, and hanging her clothes in my closet.

"I know it pisses you off and makes you jealous when I complain about Butch," Raylene continued. "But you have to realize what this has done to my self-esteem. She was my best friend, Lucky."

"Raylene, let's go sit in my truck." He had to make her understand. And not in a bar with the jukebox blasting.

He tugged her off of Noah's stool. Cold air slapped them as they stepped outside and Raylene huddled into Lucky's side to get warm. He put his arm around her, hoping to feel those familiar stirrings of overwhelming love and lust that she'd always brought out in him. But nothing. Not even so much as that warm feeling that comes over you from being with an old friend.

With his key fob he unlocked his truck's doors, helped Raylene inside, and started the ignition so he could turn on the heat.

After a long silence, he said, "I'm sorry about your dad and I'm sorry about Butch. I care about you so much, Raylene, but I don't think we're meant to be together."

"Of course we are. You've always loved me," she said, her voice rasping. "You said even when I went to Boulder and didn't return your calls and married Butch, you still loved me."

"And I'm thinking now that maybe that wasn't so healthy. That maybe I'd built us up into something that didn't exist, because if you'd really loved me, Raylene, you wouldn't have married Butch. You wouldn't be bitter about him right now."

"So you're getting even with me for marrying Butch?"

He gently grasped her chin in his hand. "Look at me, Raylene. I want nothing but the best for you. You're important to me and I never want to hurt you, but, honey, this isn't working."

"Oh God." She rested her face in her hands and let out a shrill laugh. "You're screwing Thelma. This has nothing to do with Butch. How could I have missed it?"

Lucky pried her hands away from her face and tilted his head to make eye contact. "Raylene, be honest here. The last couple of weeks, you and I have been on separate wavelengths. And when Butch came, I told you it was over. You didn't listen."

"Because you always come back," she said, and started to sob. "You always, always come back."

"That's the problem, Raylene. I always come back and I just can't do it anymore."

She wiped her nose on her sleeve. "You will. You'll see." And before Lucky could stop her, Raylene flung the door open and ran.

He watched her jump into her truck and drive away, wondering if he should follow her to make sure she got home safely. Instead, he rested his head against the steering wheel and took a couple of deep breaths. Then he backed out of the square and went in the opposite direction.

Chapter 18

What do you wear to meet a reporter from *Sports Illustrated*? That's what Tawny wanted to know as she searched her closet. She and Lucky were apparently talking again, because he'd called to tell her about the meeting at Cecilia's and to ask her to come.

But he'd been all business, which was probably for the best. What they'd done last night had only contributed to her feelings for Lucky tenfold, and then to have Raylene text him while they were still in bed . . . well, it was a painful reminder that his heart would always belong to someone else.

Tawny finally settled on the denim dress she liked so much and a pair of favorite boots. In Katie's bedroom she found the new jeans and matching top Katie had gotten with Lucky at Farm Supply and packed them for her daughter. Tawny knew her little fashionista would want to wear something special.

On her way to Cecilia's, Tawny stopped at the Gas and Go to fill up her tank. Griffin came out.

"How goes it?" he asked in his typical jovial way. He wore a pair of low-slung cargo pants that looked exceptionally good on him. But Tawny only had eyes for Lucky. And Lucky only had eyes for Raylene.

What a mess.

"Good," she said. "How's business?"

"Can't complain. Katie doing okay?"

"So far, so good." Tawny took the nozzle off the pump, but Griffin stepped in and did it for her. "Anything new with you?" She was subtly trying to ask about Lina. Everyone knew he mooned after the police chief's sister.

"I sold another place at Sierra Heights. A family from Livermore."

"As a vacation home?" Tawny couldn't imagine buying one of Griff's big fancy houses and only using it a few weekends a year. It seemed rather extravagant.

"Yep. I don't get a lot of full-timers. I heard about the big bust at Lucky's. That must've sucked for him."

Tawny nodded. "He's trying to find a new construction company to finish the work. He's way behind schedule."

"He talk to Pat Donnelly?"

"I'm not sure."

"Everyone in this town swears by him," Griffin said. "Hey, we're doing another bowling party next weekend. You in?"

"It'll depend on Katie." Tawny would like to go, though. It would get her mind off Lucky.

Griffin finished pumping her gas and hung the hose back up. "Take it easy, Tawny." He ruffled her hair. "We're all thinking about you."

"Thanks, Griff."

She got back in her Jeep, nosed out onto Main Street, and parked in the cul-de-sac at Cecilia's. Lucky's truck was in the driveway. As always, the house smelled good, like homemade food and lemon polish.

"You hungry, *mija*?" Cecilia enveloped her in a hug. The first thing Tawny noticed was that Cecilia had on her boots.

"Hi, Mommy." Katie sat at the kitchen table eating pancakes with Lucky and a man Tawny had never seen before. She assumed he was the reporter.

Tawny held up a bag. "I brought you one of the new outfits you got with your dad."

Katie gasped, like the little drama queen she was. "Thank you."

"This is Pete, my agent," Lucky said, letting his gaze linger on Tawny's dress. Maybe she hadn't dressed up enough.

"Hi, Tawny. Nice to meet you." Pete stood up and shook Tawny's hand.

He was handsome and not what she expected from a professional bull rider's agent. No boots, no hat. He kind of reminded her of John Kennedy Jr., like he belonged on a sailboat in New England. Not that she'd ever been to New England, or even sailing, for that matter. But she'd seen pictures.

"Nice to meet you too," she said.

Cecilia refilled Pete's coffee cup and set a place for Tawny. Katie excused herself from the table to change.

"Pete surprised me and flew in this morning," Lucky said. "He's worried Noah Lansing will think we're a bunch of inbred hicks unless he coaches us on how to talk right."

Pete seemed to be trying to hold on to his patience. "That's a load of crap, Lucky. What I have is a very legitimate fear that a drug bust and murder will ruin your public image, lose you sponsors, and spoil what up until now would've been a perfect PBR legacy. You said no to the crisis manager I wanted to bring in, so here I am, Lucky, trying to do damage control and save what's left of your career."

Tawny swallowed hard, knowing that out of politeness Pete had left out Lucky's illegitimate nine-year-old daughter. His fans, country-conservative, family-values kinds of folks, could probably deal with the fact that he'd had Katie out of wedlock. But they would skewer him for not taking care of his daughter for all these years. And that was on her and only her.

"What would you like us to say?" she asked Pete, who gave her a wan smile.

"It would help Lucky a lot if you would tell the reporter that you kept Katie from him all these years."

"She's not telling him shit about that," Lucky interrupted. "It's none of his goddamn business."

"Lucky." Cecilia hushed him. "Katie is in the next room."

Pete lowered his voice, turned to address Tawny as if they were having a private conversation, and continued. "The reporter will want to know why you kept Katie a secret from Lucky. You can't tell him about the rape allegation, Tawny. You tell him that, game over. Perhaps you say something like you weren't sure that he was Katie's fath—"

Lucky jumped up from the table and grabbed Pete's collar. "What the hell is the matter with you?"

Tawny pulled Lucky off Pete. "Stop. He's trying to help you."

"By asking the mother of my daughter to tell a reporter she's a tramp?"

"That's not what he's saying, Lucky."

"The hell it isn't." Lucky launched himself at Pete again and Tawny had to get in the middle.

Cecilia stood there, slack-jawed. "*Ay Dios.*"

There was a knock on the door and everyone went stock-still. Pete looked at his watch.

"I'll get it," Cecilia finally said.

Tawny went in search of Katie, hoping that Lucky wouldn't kill Pete in her absence. Katie, oblivious to the scene in the kitchen, stood in Cecilia's master bathroom, curling her hair in the mirror.

"Look at pretty you," Tawny told her.

"Can I put on some of your makeup?"

"No." Tawny kissed Katie on the cheek. "You're too pretty for makeup. Let's go out and say hi to the reporter."

Unlike Pete, Noah Lansing wore jeans and boots. The jeans were a little too crisp and the boots hadn't been broken in yet. But he clearly tried to look the part.

"This is my daughter, Katie, and her mama, Tawny." Lucky immediately pulled them into the fold.

"Nice to meet you," Noah said, gracing Katie with a nice smile. Tawny thought he seemed pleasant enough.

Cecilia served him a plate of pancakes, and for a while they made small talk about Nugget, the brisk weather, and Lucky's ninety-point rides. Cecilia gave Noah a tour of the house, bragging about how Lucky had bought it for her. Pete nodded at Lucky, the message clear: He liked the way Cecilia handled herself.

Katie, bored with the grown-up conversation, disappeared into Cecilia's room to watch TV. Cecilia strolled back into the kitchen with Noah, who scribbled something in a notebook and grabbed the chair next to Tawny at the table.

"Lucky says you make boots. You make those?" He pointed at hers and she told him she had. "How long have you and Lucky known each other?"

"Since elementary school," Tawny said, and laughed.

"Really? So were you guys childhood sweethearts?"

"No," Tawny said. "I was super shy. Even in the fourth grade, Lucky was big man on campus."

Noah chuckled, clearly thinking the whole growing-up-in-a-small-town thing was a real hoot. "The woman I met last night . . . Lucky's girlfriend . . . Jolene, I think her name was. Did she go to school with the both of you, too?"

"Raylene," Tawny corrected, her heart sinking. Lucky hadn't even waited a full twenty-four hours after leaving Tawny's bed to run back to Raylene. Tawny tried to catch Lucky's eye, but he wouldn't even look at her. "Yep, she went to school with us too. She was Lucky's childhood sweetheart."

"No kidding?" Noah turned his attention to Lucky. "Have you been together all this time?"

Looking more uncomfortable than Tawny had ever seen him, Lucky said, "After high school, Raylene and I went our separate ways." But they were back together now.

"How did you two"—Noah shifted his hand between Tawny and Lucky—"get together?"

Tawny knew the question was intended as a tactful way for Noah to inquire about Katie. Unless Lucky was dating Giselle Bündchen, *Sports Illustrated* couldn't care less about Lucky's hometown love life.

The room went silent and finally Pete stepped in. "Noah, because of Katie we'd like to steer away from—"

"I'm okay with talking about it." Before Lucky could stop her, Tawny told Noah, "Ten years ago, before Lucky left Nugget to go on the circuit, we had a fling. I didn't know I was pregnant until after he left. It was at that point that I made the decision not to tell him. Not until Katie got sick and needed a donor for a stem cell match did I change my mind."

"Why didn't you want to tell him?" Noah asked.

"I was an eighteen-year-old girl. And although Lucky and I had known each other forever, we weren't in a relationship. My father was dying and I'd dropped out of school to take care of him. Katie was the only thing I had." She tried with difficulty to make eye contact. "I didn't want to share. And I knew that a man like Lucky would want joint custody. So I kept his paternity a secret. It was selfish and horrible and . . ."

"That's enough," Lucky told Tawny and faced off with the reporter. "You put any of that in the story and we're done. No more interview."

Pete stood up from the table. "Noah, is there a way we can work around this part of the story? Lucky and Tawny are good people . . . good parents, trying to protect their gravely ill daughter."

"Look," Noah said, getting red in the face. "I'm a sports reporter. I came here to write about a world champion bull rider making a new life for himself after the big hurrah. The drug bust, the shooting on your property . . . that can all be put in the shit-happens column. But having a nine-year-old daughter that your fans didn't know about can't just be glossed over. This isn't football, or even baseball. PBR riders have a reputation for being family men—"

"This is no one's business," Lucky cut in. "I'm a hundred-percent part of my daughter's life now. That's all people need to know."

"What about the cancer . . . the transplant . . . that off the record too?"

"No," Tawny said. If neither Lucky nor Cecilia turned out to be a perfect match, an article might help them get donors.

Lucky glared at her, but Tawny continued anyway. "As long as you're respectful of Katie."

"That won't be a problem," Noah said. "I'm not here to make problems. I just want to write an accurate story."

Noah stayed a few hours, interviewing Tawny but mostly Cecilia, Pete, and Lucky. When he left, Lucky pulled Tawny aside.

"Why'd you tell him that bullshit?"

"I was trying to help you." And a small part of what she'd told Noah was true. She hadn't wanted anyone to take her baby from her. "This is my fault and I'm trying to make up for it."

"I'm fine, Tawny. I don't care what he writes and I don't need any help."

"Pete seems to think you do."

"Pete's a pain in the ass. Let him worry about this. That's what I pay him for—not you."

Tawny shrugged. "I have to go home and work." Boot orders continued to pile up while she got more and more behind. She needed an assistant but couldn't afford to pay anyone.

"I wanted to talk to you about yesterday."

She felt her face heat, remembering how they had burned up the sheets. And afterward, how Lucky had rushed off to meet Raylene. "There's nothing to talk about."

Pete found them huddled in the living room and they immediately stopped their conversation.

"You did great, Tawny. Noah liked you, I could tell. Frankly, I think you saved this guy's bacon." Pete did one of those guy things where he punched Lucky in the arm.

"I did what I could." But now she was exhausted. Usually quiet and reserved, Tawny felt tapped out from all the reporter's questions.

"I've really got to get going." Tawny called to Katie that it was time to leave.

Cecilia came into the room. "You're not staying for lunch?"

They'd just had breakfast. Tawny gave Lucky's mother a hug. "I think we'll hear something from Katie's doctor tomorrow or Tuesday. If Lucky's a match, I need to get organized."

"I'll walk you and Katie to your Jeep," Lucky said. Tawny preferred he didn't, but protesting would only make a scene.

Katie came out of Cecilia's room with her overnight bag, and like usual, Tawny felt her head. Normal. Tawny zipped up Katie's jacket and they said their goodbyes. Lucky carried Katie's small suitcase, which had seen more hospital rooms than Tawny cared to remember. In his other arm, he effortlessly lifted Katie, who laid her head on his shoulder. It struck Tawny that it hadn't taken long for Katie and Lucky to get close. And the guilt jabbed at her.

Lucky opened the passenger side of the Jeep, fastened Katie in, and moved to Tawny's side. She tried to close the door, but he held it open.

"We're not done talking, Tawny," he said in a low voice, and looked at Katie pointedly. "I'll be in touch."

The call came at two the next day. Lucky, busy showing Pat Donnelly the ranch and the work that had yet to be finished, excused himself to find a private spot to talk. He strained to concentrate on the doctor's words, his heart in his mouth. Dr. Laurence threw out a lot of medical jargon that Lucky didn't understand. He seemed to drone on forever until Lucky finally got his answer. He hung up, took a deep breath, and squeezed the bridge of his nose.

He needed to tell Tawny. Just as he started to press her number, Pat waved him over.

"See this," Pat said. He'd climbed onto the top of one of the outbuildings and splintered off a piece of the shingle. "It's rotted. We'll have to replace the whole roof."

He came down the ladder. "The good news is, what your old crew did do, they did well. The bad news is, they didn't do much. It'll take at least five months to finish this job, and that's provided we don't have any debilitating weather." Which of course they would. It was the Sierra, where a couple of big storms were guaranteed every winter.

And here it was November and he needed the place done by April.

If Pat could pull it off, he'd pay him and his entire crew a bonus. But right now the only thing he could think about was calling Tawny.

"Pat, I want you to do it. But Katie's doctor just called and I've got to get ahold of Tawny. Can you work up some numbers in the next couple of days?"

"You got it," Pat said. "Good news?" That was the thing about Nugget. Everyone knew everyone else's business.

"I need to talk to Tawny."

"I hear ya. That little girl of yours is in our prayers." Hearing Pat say that was the very reason Lucky should've gone with the local guys in the first place. "I also want to talk to you about building a house. But I want Colin to be part of that."

"When you're ready to talk, we'll all sit down."

"Great," Lucky said, and started backing away. "Sorry, man, but I've gotta run. Take your time looking around and measuring. Whatever you need to do."

Lucky decided it would be better to tell Tawny in person. This news she shouldn't hear over the phone. Katie was at school—scheduled to go to his mom's afterward—so he and Tawny had time to discuss their next move in private. Then they'd have to tell Cecilia.

In Lucky's hurry to get to his truck he nearly collided with Noah. "Can't talk now, buddy."

"Everything okay?"

"I'll talk to you about it later," Lucky said, and clicked his key fob. They'd promised to keep the reporter in the loop about the transplant. Lucky would keep his word. But not now. Not until Tawny had time to digest all that Dr. Laurence had told him.

He found Tawny in her studio, cutting a large piece of leather while listening to her music. Most of the people around here played classic country and western, but Tawny had what Lucky liked to call college-radio music taste—a lot of stuff he'd never heard of. She hadn't seen him come in and was swaying her hips to the song blasting from a docking station jury-rigged to some electrical wiring. Apparently there weren't enough outlets for all her equipment.

He took the time to watch her and appreciate how pretty she was. Today she had on another pair of those leggings she liked to wear with a form-fitting sweater that hugged her small curves. And boots that went all the way up to her knees. Black snakeskin.

"Those yours?" His voice made her jump. "Sorry I startled you."

She turned down the music. "What?"

"You make those boots?" He pointed to her legs.

"No. My mentor made them for me."

Lucky thought they were sexy as hell. "Dr. Laurence called." He heard her take in a breath.

"What did he say?" She gripped the table.

Lucky pointed to the try-on bench. "Come over here and sit by me."

She crossed the room to the bench and they both sat. Lucky could see her hands shaking and took them both in his. It suddenly felt too warm, like she had the heat cranked up to eighty. Yet her whole body trembled.

"I'm a perfect match," he said. "All six antigens."

Of all the possible reactions, Lucky didn't expect her to break down sobbing. But that was exactly what she did.

"Don't cry, honey." Lucky kissed her face, wiping away her salty tears with his lips. "Why are you crying? I thought you would be happy."

She buried her face in his neck and shuddered. He wrapped her in his arms and held tight while she wept, her whole body shaking, until she seemed to have exhausted herself and finally went limp.

"You okay?" he asked her, not letting go, and she started crying all over again. "Tawny, honey. Talk to me."

"I'm relieved," she said, the words hitching like a hiccup. "I'm just so, so relieved."

She turned her face until her cheek pressed against his chest and he rubbed her back, trying to get some warmth into her. Even though it was stifling hot in the studio, she seemed cold.

"They want us to do a conference call so they can explain the procedure. I'll need to have a physical and start getting injections that'll help my bone marrow make and release stem cells. Then we'll go to Stanford and they'll begin harvesting—that's what they call it—and transplant my stem cells into Katie." Lucky knew none of it was a done deal. Katie's body could still reject him as a donor. But it was something.

"When do they want to do the call?" Tawny asked.

"Tomorrow."

She took in a couple of deep breaths and exhaled. "Your mom

wants us to stay with her during the recovery. I think I'll take her up on it."

"It'll be good," he said. "She'll take care of you."

Tawny pulled back slightly. Lucky tugged her back in.

"Me? I'm not having the procedure."

No, but Lucky knew that she, maybe more than anyone, needed TLC. "We'll all need some R & R, Tawny."

For once she didn't argue, and stayed cocooned in his arms. "We'll have to talk to Katie. She's a good patient, but hospitals and treatments make her anxious. The poor girl has had so many."

"We can do it here or at my mom's. Whatever you want."

"Lucky?"

"Hmm?"

"Thank you." She was quiet for a long time and he felt his shirt get damp. "It's just a relief not to have to do this all on my own."

A part of him wanted to say that she'd made that choice, but he left it alone. He was here now and that's all that mattered. "What would you think if we went out for dinner tonight—you, me, Katie, and my mom?"

"I guess word would get out that way and we wouldn't have to tell everyone," she said.

That's sort of what he was thinking. And they deserved a celebration, even if they weren't out of the woods yet.

"Call Cecilia," she said. "I'll go wash my face."

She needed a bathroom in the studio, he thought as he dug his cell out of his jacket pocket and hit speed dial, perusing the shelves while he waited for his mother to pick up. There was an empty space where the boots with the bull riders used to be. He still wanted those boots with a vengeance. On Tawny's drawing board sat the design for Brady's boots. A knife and fork. Lucky rolled his eyes.

Looking at one of the clocks on the wall, he wondered why Cecilia didn't answer. He suspected that she'd gone early to pick Katie up from school and had left her phone behind. Tawny and he would go over to the house together and tell them the news.

He continued to snoop around her studio. Clay's boots appeared to be almost done. Nice looking. Lucky wouldn't mind having a pair of those too. His phone pinged with a text. He checked the display, hoping for Cecilia. Instead it was Raylene.

I thought we could go somewhere for dinner. Talk about
what you said in the truck. It's been less than twenty-four
hours and I already miss you. Call me. Please. I love you.
Raylene

"What did your mom say?" Tawny came up alongside him and Lucky quickly stuffed the phone in his jacket.

"I couldn't reach her."

"Jake could be over there," she said.

"Yeah. Or she went over to the school."

Tawny looked at one of her dad's old clocks on the wall. "It's about that time."

"Yep," he said, and noticed that besides washing her tearstained face, she'd put on mascara. "You've got the greenest eyes I've ever seen."

The compliment seemed to unsettle her because she just stood there, not saying anything. That's when he moved in and kissed her. At first she let him, returning the kiss with the same fervor she had yesterday. And then suddenly she stopped and used both hands to push him away.

"We're not doing this again."

He decided not to push it. They'd had emotional news today and Tawny seemed more fragile than usual. But whether she wanted to admit it or not, she liked his kisses and they'd definitely be doing it again. In fact, as often as possible.

Chapter 19

Tawny spent the next several days working in her studio, desperately trying to finish as many outstanding projects as possible. They were having Thanksgiving early because they'd be in the hospital for the real holiday. She, Lucky, Katie, Cecilia, and even Jake would soon be heading to Palo Alto for the procedure. In the meantime, Lucky had passed his physical and had been trudging to a small clinic in Glory Junction to continue getting the daily injections that helped him grow stem cells. The side effects included bone pain and headaches, which made it difficult for him to train for the finals.

Tawny worried that he'd overtax himself. But in typical Lucky fashion he'd simply said, "I'll deal." They hadn't talked once about their hookup—although Tawny couldn't stop thinking about it—the *Sports Illustrated* story, or Raylene. That last part suited her fine. The thought of Lucky and Raylene together always made Tawny feel sick to her stomach.

On a good note, Pat Donnelly had agreed to take over construction at Lucky's ranch. The crew would have to work double time to complete what was left of refurbishing the outbuildings, dormitories, and the lodge in time for Lucky's first event—a spring barn wedding organized by the Lumber Baron, which included three days of cowboy camp activities. They also had more corrals to build for Lucky's livestock.

So far the weather had held. But around here that could change in the blink of an eye. Katie continued to go to school while Tawny and Cecilia monitored her regularly for fevers.

Tawny spent the next hour putting the finishing touches on Clay's boots. If she worked a few extra hours tonight there was a chance she could finish them before they left for the Bay Area. In her free time—

like she had any—she tried to work on Brady's pair. Those were just for fun and she enjoyed executing a design that was 100 percent her own. No input from the customer.

Since Lucky had come into the picture, money hadn't been an issue. The man paid her an enormous amount of child support and had given her nine years of back pay, which Tawny had immediately deposited into a fund for Katie's college education.

Tawny wanted her daughter to have every educational opportunity. If Tawny had her way, Katie would be the first Wade or Rodriguez to go to college.

As she found her rhythm, letting her work take her away, she didn't hear Noah's approach until he banged on the door.

"Hi," she said, surprised to see him. They'd never discussed him coming over and Tawny had never given him her address. Although it wouldn't have been difficult for a reporter to find her. "I wanted to see your boots," he said. "People said you have seconds and samples for sale."

"Sure." Tawny waved at the shelves. "You looking for anything in particular?"

"No." He looked down at the boots he wore. "I guess something like these."

They were your typical store-bought variety. When he got a load of the price of hers, he was bound to have sticker shock. She got his size and directed him to a few shelves.

"Feel free to play and try on anything you want." She pointed to the try-on bench.

Instead, he walked around her studio, taking in her equipment and some of her works in progress.

"What is this?" He examined her sketches for Brady's boots.

"That's just something I'm working on for fun."

"Fork and knife, huh?"

"They're for a chef friend of mine . . . Brady at the Lumber Baron."

"I know Brady." Of course he did. Noah had become a full-time resident at the bed and breakfast. He must have a hefty expense account. "Nice. You make boots for Lucky?"

"Nope. Ariat is one of his sponsors," Tawny said.

"Still, I would imagine that a champion bull rider would have at least one custom pair in his closet."

"Ariat might do his custom. I don't know."

"Lucky says you've made boots for all kinds of famous people." Noah continued to wander around, poking into everything. He seemed genuinely interested, so she didn't mind.

"Some," she said. "A lot for people who have trouble fitting into conventional boots."

"I never thought of that. What? Are their feet too big?"

"Not necessarily too big, but they have a misshapen toe or an odd arch or larger calves than the typical boot will accommodate. A lot of ranchers around here do it for comfort. They want a boot they can literally sleep in."

"You sound like a good story yourself." Noah laughed.

"The *Nugget Tribune* did a nice piece on me, but I'm friends with the reporter."

He perused the shelves with boots his size and pulled a few pairs down. "What's wrong with these?" He pointed to a chocolate-brown pair made of kangaroo leather.

"They're not seconds, if that's what you mean." She cruised the shelves until she found a boot with an S drawn in the inside of the shaft and showed it to him so he could distinguish the seconds from the rest. "These"—Tawny picked up the kangaroo pair—"were a custom job for a man who got into some financial trouble and couldn't afford to pay for them."

"In other words, you got stiffed."

She laughed. "I got a nice deposit, but yeah, I got stiffed."

He flashed her a grin. "You're very different from Raylene Rosser."

She didn't exactly know how to take that. Most men, including Lucky, went gaga for Raylene.

"Let me ask you something," he said. "Is she a reliable source?"

Tawny flinched at the unexpected question, wondering what the reporter was getting at. "What do you mean?"

Noah sucked in a breath. "I don't think it comes as any surprise to you that I'm interviewing half the town for this story about Lucky. Owen, that barber guy, seems straight up. But sometimes I get the idea that he pretends to know more than he does. Donna Thurston, the woman who owns the Bun Boy, has a definite flair for exaggeration. Clay McCreedy, who seems like he'd be a credible interview, won't give me the time of day. I've heard through the grapevine that his wife has had bad experiences with the press—something about a missing child. Nothing I'm interested in for the purpose of Lucky's story, unless it has something to do with him, which I'm pretty sure it doesn't."

He sat on the bench and started to take off his boots. "So far, you seem to be the most reliable of the people I've talked to. Cecilia is wonderful, but she's the guy's mother. And Raylene . . . yeah, I don't know how to read her."

"I can't help you there," Tawny said. When it came to Raylene, Tawny had a hard time being objective.

"That's the thing," Noah said. "I think you can. I get the feeling you don't like her. Not because of anything you've said or done. It could just be that I'm picking up a rivalry between you two over Lucky. I don't know what it is, but my reporter Spidey-sense says you don't like her and that there may be a good reason for it."

He slipped into her boots and struggled to pull them all the way on.

"You must have a high arch," she said.

"You're not going to play, are you?"

"No," was all she said.

"Did Lucky force himself on Raylene when they were teenagers?"

Tawny jerked back. Apparently the cat was out of the bag. She was woefully inexperienced with dealing with the press or anything having to do with a celebrity athlete. Left up to Tawny, she would tell Noah the truth and believe that the truth would prevail. However, Pete's voice floated into the back of her head, telling her how naïve that probably was.

Talk about the rape allegations and *game over*, he'd said.

"You need to talk to Lucky or Pete about that." Hearing herself say it, she knew the statement made Lucky sound guilty.

"Did he ever force himself on you? Because he wouldn't be the first athlete to think no meant yes."

"Never!" she said because she couldn't control herself. "Any relations Lucky and I have had"—a mere two—"have been completely consensual."

"But Raylene could've had a different experience, right?"

She pinched her eyes closed out of frustration, knowing that she was about to fall into his trap. "All I'm willing to say is that you shouldn't trust anything Ray Rosser says. The man is suspected of murder, for goodness' sake."

"He's not my source on this," Noah said.

She looked closely at him. Was he saying that Raylene was the source? Because that didn't make any sense. Why would she try to make her boyfriend look like a rapist? What would that say about her being with a guy like that? "Well, then who is your source?"

"Raylene," he said. "I don't hesitate to tell you that because everything she's said has been on the record. At first she only intimated it and then did a complete retraction. But she's been regularly texting and calling me, and each time her allegations get more unwavering."

"Excuse my ignorance, but what does *on the record* mean?" Tawny was in way over her head. She needed to stop talking and politely ask the reporter to leave. But she couldn't help herself.

"It simply means that everything she's said I can attribute to her."

"So she's accusing Lucky of raping her?"

He nodded his head. "Yep. And I can't lionize the guy in a story—telling the world how he's donating his stem cells to his daughter, how he bought his mother a house, and is the greatest sports hero since Derek Jeter—for the world's premiere sports magazine, and ignore these allegations. I'm not that kind of reporter."

"Did you ask Raylene why she would continue to see a man who supposedly raped her?"

"I don't believe she's seeing him anymore."

"What?" She needed to call Lucky, but she was like a child drawn to the flame.

"I wanted to come to you before I approached Lucky."

"You need to talk to him . . . Raylene is a liar." She wanted to tell him about what a self-centered, mean girl Raylene had been growing up. How she would do anything to save her own hide, but stopped herself.

"She says he forced her the night before he left town. That her father caught him and threatened to press charges, but she begged him not to."

"That's not what happened," Tawny said.

"So you know about that night?"

"Yes. But you should talk to Lucky or Pete."

"Just talk to me on background," he said.

"What's that?"

"It means you help me make sense of her allegations and I don't attribute any of it to you in the story."

She didn't know if she could trust him. At the same time, though, she didn't want Lucky, the best man she knew, to be ruined because of a crazy, selfish woman. And she desperately didn't want Raylene's bogus allegations to come back to Katie or to hurt Cecilia. "You swear?"

"I swear."

"If in fact she's no longer with Lucky, I don't know why." Except that Lucky had told Tawny that they were no longer together and she hadn't believed him. But if they had indeed broken up, why had Lucky met with Raylene the night he'd been with Tawny?

"What I can tell you is that he didn't rape her ten years ago—or ever," Tawny continued. "Raylene and Lucky were sexually active since her freshman year. Everyone in high school knew it. And I suspect that Raylene was sexually active with other boys besides Lucky, but obviously I can't say for sure. That night, however, Ray caught them in the act, went ballistic, and accused Lucky of . . . god-awful things. Ray is known to be mean, racist, classist, and abusive. Not to mention that he shoots people he thinks are responsible for stealing his cattle. No judge, no jury, just boom." Tawny wanted Noah to understand exactly what kind of man Ray Rosser was. "In Ray's mind, no way would his darling daughter have consensual sex with the Mexican housekeeper's son. I suspect that Raylene was so scared of Ray that she went along with whatever he said to save herself.

"Why she's telling you this now, I have no idea," Tawny continued. "I will tell you that she's vindictive, incredibly self-absorbed, and like her dad, mean as a snake."

"And perhaps a woman scorned," Noah said.

"I don't know," she said. "A few days ago Lucky told me they were no longer together—that her ex was back in town. But you said you'd met her the other night with Lucky, so I assumed they were back on. It's like that with them—breakup and makeup."

"I can't ignore her allegations, but after what you've told me I'm apt to be more skeptical."

"It would be a terrible injustice to Lucky to write about it. He's never been one of those types of guys who think they are entitled to whatever they want. He and his mom worked hard for everything they earned, and Cecilia raised him to respect women."

"I'll be honest with you," Noah said. "After Raylene's allegations,

I'd wondered if maybe Lucky had done something similar to you and that's why you waited until Katie needed a transplant to tell him about his daughter."

"Now that you know the story, I can tell you the truth. I didn't tell him about Katie because I was afraid he'd come rushing back and Ray would make trouble for him. I didn't want my daughter to have that as a legacy."

"Are you in love with Lucky?"

Tawny blinked. "Why would you ask me that?"

"A woman who loves a man would go to a lot of trouble to protect him."

"I could never love a man who could force a woman into doing something she didn't want to do."

Noah smiled. "You didn't really answer the question, but I get your gist. Thanks for being so candid with me. And, Tawny, this conversation goes no further."

"What do you want me to do?" Jake came up behind Cecilia as she was chopping onions, and put his arms around her.

"Why don't you set up the bar?" She wiped her eyes with her forearms.

"I helped make the pies," Katie called from the kitchen table, where she folded cloth napkins.

"Well, then I'll be sure to have an extra piece," Jake said, and looked at his watch, wondering what was taking his daughters so long. Only three could make it for dinner, but the other two were coming for the weekend.

And he was anxious. He wanted his girls to like Cecilia and for Cecilia to like his girls.

Cecilia looked out the window. "The weather is good. They'll be here soon, Jake. Stop worrying." The woman could read his mind.

Lucky came through the door, carrying three bottles of wine and a bouquet of flowers. "Noah's behind me."

"You invited the reporter?" Jake said.

Lucky hitched his shoulders. "He didn't have anywhere else to go and thought it would be good color for his story."

"I think it was generous of you to invite him," Cecilia chimed in. "Where's Tawny?"

"She's not here yet?" Lucky looked at Katie, who'd stayed the night to help Cecilia with the preparations, leaving Jake to stay at his cabin.

"I forgot, Grandma. She called while you were in the shower. She's trying to finish Mr. McCreedy's boots, but will be here soon. She's bringing a salad and wine."

"Thank you, Katie."

Lucky kissed his daughter and asked what he could do to pitch in.

Jake laughed. "Men are relegated to setting up the bar."

"I'll set up the bar," Lucky said.

"One of you, then, should build a fire. I want it to be nice when Jake's girls get here." Cecilia slid her diced onions into a sizzling frying pan.

A few minutes later Noah showed up and was put on glass duty, which consisted of him inspecting each piece of stemware for spots. Cecilia was pulling out all the stops. Jake had just gotten the fire going when he heard a car pull in. Up on his feet, he opened the front door.

"What took you so long?" he said, going outside to wrap all three girls in a bear hug.

"There was a lot of traffic," his eldest, Sarah, said.

"Come in and meet everyone."

The girls grabbed some packages out of the trunk. It looked like they too had brought wine, a box of chocolates, and flowers. Jake's heart warmed with pride.

Tara, Jake's sixteen-year-old, whispered in his ear, "What are we supposed to call her?"

"Cecilia," he said, and winked. "You'll like her. You'll like everyone."

"Is the rodeo dude coming?" Janny asked.

"Yep. And his nine-year-old daughter, Katie, and Katie's mother, Tawny. There's also a reporter from *Sports Illustrated*."

"Get out," Janny said. "How come?"

"He's doing an article on Lucky."

They seemed duly impressed. When they got to the front door, Cecilia was waiting with her arms open.

"Welcome." She hugged each of Jake's daughters. "You had such a long drive."

"Thank you for having us," Sarah said.

"I've been looking forward to meeting you. Jake talks about you so much." Cecilia pulled Lucky into the circle. "This is my son, Lucky. And my granddaughter, Katie. That's Noah." He waved from the bar. "And Tawny should be here soon. Come in, get warm by the fire, and Lucky will make you a drink. Katie, you take Tara into the kitchen and show her what kind of soft drinks we have."

"What would you like us to do with these?" Sarah held up the bag of wine and candy.

Cecilia told Katie and Tara to take it to the kitchen. Janny asked for a vase and said she'd arrange the flowers. And again Jake couldn't have been prouder.

"I'll call Tawny," Lucky said. "See what's holding her up."

Not for the first time, Jake wondered if there was something going on between those two. It was as if Raylene had fallen off the planet, which Jake knew would make Cecilia happy. Although rumor had it that Tawny was seeing the new Lumber Baron chef.

Lucky didn't have to call because Tawny showed up a few minutes later, lugging a giant wooden bowl from her Jeep.

"Need some help?" Jake asked.

"There's wine and soda and cider still in the car," she said. "And cranberry sauce. It's the kind in a can, though."

Jake didn't say anything but knew Cecilia wouldn't use it. He brought it in anyway, along with the rest of the stuff. Lucky came into the kitchen and greeted Tawny with a big smile on his face. Yep, something was definitely going on between those two.

"What took you so long?" Lucky asked her.

"I wanted to deliver Clay's boots. One less thing to do before Monday."

Jake knew she was nervous about the transplant. He couldn't blame her. "Come meet my daughters."

He introduced his daughters to Tawny and left them to get acquainted with each other. Katie seemed to have adopted Tara. Noah, who claimed to have put himself through college working as a bartender, took over making the drinks. Jake suspected he just wanted something to keep him busy, being the outsider.

As awkward as it could've been, everyone seemed to be getting along and enjoying themselves.

"They're beautiful girls, Jake." Cecilia came up alongside him. "And so polite."

"Their mothers did a good job," he said. "I'm proud of the women they've become."

"I'm sorry Erika and Jillian couldn't make it for dinner."

"You'll meet them this weekend."

"How is it that you didn't have one boy?" Cecilia gazed across the room at Lucky, who was talking to Tara and Katie.

"Beats the hell out of me. But I wouldn't trade one of them." He wrapped his arm around her.

"Lucky said he'll take them riding tomorrow. Katie is over the moon."

"You think Tawny will be okay with Katie getting on the back of a horse before Monday?"

"Lucky will take her on the horse with him. It'll be fine."

"How you holding up?" Jake asked, knowing that between getting the news that Lucky was a match for Katie's transplant and preparing for this dinner, Cecilia hadn't had a moment to breathe.

"I'm happy to have all of us together." She kissed Jake, surprising the stuffing out of him. Behind closed doors, Cecilia was a passionate woman. In public, she tended to be more reserved. But the kiss pleased him enormously.

He nuzzled her ear and whispered, "Marry me."

She swatted him away, but this time he noticed that she didn't out and out say no. There was hope yet. He just had to break through the woman's resolve.

Cecilia and Tawny worked companionably in the kitchen to put appetizers out. Jake was heartened to see that the two women had formed a nice camaraderie. He caught them laughing with his daughters in the kitchen.

"What's so funny?"

"Janny has been telling us her dating travails," Cecilia said.

"That's my cue to leave." The last thing Jake wanted to hear were stories about his daughter's crazy love life. Last time she'd brought home a guy, Jake had wanted to shoot him for lazing on the deck while Janny waited on him hand and foot. Thank the good Lord, she'd dumped him over the summer.

In the living room, Lucky and Noah planted themselves on the couch. It seemed like a safe enough place for Jake too. So he plopped down beside them.

"If you're not training, how are you preparing for the finals?" Noah asked Lucky.

"I'm watching a lot of video. As soon as they take me off the meds, I'll be fine. The procedure itself is done outpatient, so I'll have the beginning of December to train."

Noah nodded. "You planning on watching video this weekend? If so, I'd like to join you."

"Sure. That's not a problem. Tomorrow I'm taking the ladies riding, though."

"Do you have an extra horse for me?" Noah asked.

Lucky gave him a cool perusal. "You ride?"

"Not great. But I can hold on."

"How 'bout you, Jake? You want to come?" Lucky asked.

"I've got to work tomorrow." And no way in hell was he climbing onto the back of a horse.

Noah turned to Jake. "That drug bust must've been something for a town this size."

"I won't say that we don't occasionally have our problems. But the scope of this was large even by big-city standards."

"And the cattle rustling?" Noah grinned when he said it. Jake got it. The term cattle rustling seemed so *Lonesome Dove*. But even now it was a big problem in California. So much so that the state had passed laws with stricter penalties for people convicted of stealing livestock.

"Looks like we nipped that in the bud when we took out the drug ring."

"They were for sure connected, huh?"

"Looks like," Jake said, not wanting to go into the details. It was still a pending investigation.

"Where does that leave Ray Rosser?" Noah asked.

"It'll depend on whether the evidence points to self-defense."

"That'll be kind of tough, since he was trespassing on my property, looking for a fight," Lucky said.

"You don't like him much, do you?" Noah asked.

"That's an understatement." Lucky got up. "I want to see if they need help in the kitchen."

Once Lucky left the room, Noah said, "No love lost between those two, huh?"

"Nope," Jake said.

"Were you around ten years ago when Ray Rosser leveled the sexual assault accusation against Lucky?" Noah watched Jake closely.

"I was not." Although Cecilia had told Jake everything about that night at the Rock and River Ranch. "But Ray Rosser isn't a man to be trusted." The Plumas County DA agreed with him on that one. As soon as George had his evidence, he planned to charge the SOB.

Jake sincerely hoped that Lucky got as far away as possible from Raylene. Troubled women had once been Jake's specialty, and Raylene reeked of trouble.

Cecilia came into the living room. "We're having snacks in the kitchen. You're missing out."

The men dutifully followed her. Jake's daughters had made themselves at home, lounging on stools at the center island and eating from the elaborate spread Cecilia and Tawny had put out. Katie sat on Lucky's lap, sharing a plate of appetizers. Tawny rinsed a few stray dishes and loaded them into the dishwasher. Wine glasses got refilled while conversation and laughter flooded the room.

Cecilia's eyes found Jake's from across the kitchen and her lips curved up. Her face positively glowed, telling Jake that everything she'd ever wanted was right here in this room. Family and friends and hopefully a man she could always love and depend on.

Jake wanted to be that man . . . was that man. Now all he had to do was persuade Cecilia of that.

Chapter 20

Lucky didn't know why she continued to text him. Couldn't Raylene take a hint? Hell, it had been more than a hint. He'd flat out told her they were over. Not just in his trailer and truck, but several times after. He'd texted her that they were done, left it on her voice mail, and told her to her face when she showed up at his single-wide at two in the morning, drunk off her ass. What did he have to do? Hire a skywriter?

Raylene was so relentless and desperate that she was telling tales. Lucky knew that she'd given Noah a twisted version of what happened at the Rock and River Ranch ten years ago. He knew that she was using the story to manipulate him. And he knew that she'd try to ruin him if she couldn't get him back.

He'd always known that she was spoiled and even vindictive when she didn't get what she wanted. But this was a side of her he'd never seen before. Or maybe he'd been too blindly in love with her to notice just how vicious she could be. The woman was nothing like the one he'd pined for all those years. Maybe she'd never been that woman. Maybe he'd let himself create her out of a youth's fantasy.

"What's wrong?" Tawny asked as Lucky slipped his phone back inside his pocket.

"Nothing."

She gazed around the Four Seasons suite he'd gotten them. "This is amazing, Lucky. Was it terribly expensive?"

He didn't care how expensive it was. These next few weeks would be tough on everyone, and he wanted them to at least have a little luxury at the end of the day. "Nah. You guys brought your swimsuits, right?" He'd been fantasizing about seeing Tawny in a bikini since the moment he told her about the heated indoor pool.

"I did," Katie said. She'd found the minibar and was poring through the candy section.

"Hey," Tawny told her. "Close that up. A Snickers bar is fifteen dollars."

Lucky would give it to her; she wasn't one of those women who liked to spend his money. Jake wouldn't spend Lucky's money either; Lucky had tried to pay for Jake and Cecilia's room, but Jake wouldn't have it.

Tomorrow doctors would start harvesting Lucky's stem cells. Depending on how many they got, that could take a few days. But today they were free to do whatever they wanted.

"You want to go over to that mall?" Lucky hated shopping, but he figured his clotheshorse daughter and Tawny would like Bloomingdale's and the other big department stores they didn't have in Nugget or even Reno. "Or we could go swimming."

"Mall now, swimming later," Katie shouted.

Tawny looked at Lucky and shook her head.

Lucky grinned back. "Mom and Jake are doing their own thing, so let's get a move on."

They wandered the Stanford Shopping Center. Katie loved looking in the windows and stores. Tawny pretended not to be that interested, but Lucky saw her green eyes light up every time she saw something she liked. Pretty clothes that she probably couldn't afford. He'd buy her whatever she wanted, but Tawny was the type to get offended. She couldn't stop him from buying his kid stuff, though. That was his right as a parent.

At the food court they stopped to get some lunch. Katie ran off to get a pretzel, giving Lucky and Tawny time to talk alone, which they hadn't done since Lucky got the news about the transplant.

"How you holding up?" Lucky reached for her hand and before he knew it, he and Tawny had threaded their fingers together.

"I'm nervous, but hanging in."

"Cowgirl tough." He kissed her cheek.

Every time he was around her now, he hankered to kiss her. Not like this, but like the way they'd kissed the evening they'd made love. He still didn't know whether she was seeing Brady or what he was getting himself into. The whole thing was pretty crazy, given that until recently it had always been Raylene.

"How about you?" she asked him.

"It sounds fairly straightforward. Just praying to the man up there that it works."

"The man up there?" She cocked one eyebrow. "You mean the woman up there?"

"Yeah," he said. "Ain't touching this one. You want something else to eat?" In his opinion she hadn't been eating too well. Even at their pre-Thanksgiving dinner he saw her pushing food around on her plate. Nerves would do that to you.

"I'm good. When Katie gets back I'll have a bite of her pretzel." They both gazed over at the long line where Katie waited.

Lucky whistled to catch his daughter's attention and held up two fingers. She nodded back in understanding.

"God, I love that kid," he said. "She's got a natural talent with horses. You should've seen her riding the other day, like she was born in the saddle. As soon as this ordeal is over, I'm getting her a horse of her own."

"She's too young," Tawny said, and he knew she was just being protective. "How were Jake's daughters?"

"Good. The youngest one, Tara, she's had a lot of lessons. Rides English, though. Janny—that chick is fearless. I'd worry about her if I were Jake. Sarah's a nice lady. She's in law school. I didn't get much time with the other two—Erika and Jillian. But they seemed nice enough."

"Cecilia liked them and they seemed to like her. But five step-daughters and three ex-wives . . . whoo! That's a lot to take on."

"Who says anything about my ma taking that on?"

Tawny glared at him. "Lucky, where have you been? Your mother is nuts about Jake and he is besotted with your mother. What do you think that dinner was about?"

"Giving thanks, eating until I popped a button on my jeans, and making new friends."

"Yeah," she said. "You keep thinking that."

"What do you think it was?"

"They wanted their two families to get to know each other before taking their relationship to the next level." She took off his cowboy hat and smacked him across the head with it. "Are you dense? Why do you think Jake's here, spending what is probably a week's salary on that luxurious hotel we're staying in?"

He'd been so caught up in his own problems these last few

weeks that he hadn't really given his mother and Jake a lot of thought. "You don't think they're serious enough to get married, do you?"

"Would it bother you?"

"Jake isn't exactly good husband material, given that his last three marriages ended in divorce. I don't want my mother burned, and he has the capability to burn her bad."

"She's awfully happy, though." Tawny stopped talking when Katie came loping back, and grabbed one of the pretzels from her hand. Katie gave Lucky the change and sat down next to him to eat.

"How long until he makes her unhappy? That's the question."

"Who?" Katie wanted to know. "Who's making who unhappy?"

"No one," Lucky said, and looked over Katie's head to smile at Tawny. "Give me a bite of that." He took a piece of Katie's pretzel and dipped it in her mustard.

After they finished eating they continued to wander around the outdoor mall, which Tawny seemed to know as well as she did the square in Nugget. It was a beautiful day, much warmer than home. There didn't seem to be anything that Katie didn't want to see, and how could he not indulge her?

"You've been here a lot, haven't you?" he asked.

"When we stayed at the Ronald McDonald House and Katie was feeling up to it, we used to come here and walk around." He couldn't help but respect Tawny's perseverance and courage. She was cowgirl tough, all right.

They strolled into Nordstrom and Tawny stopped to admire a coat.

"Try it on, Mommy."

Tawny took a quick look at the price tag and motioned for them to keep walking.

"Don't you want to at least try it?" Katie asked.

"Another time," she said.

They continued to the kids' section. Lucky found a bench and plopped down while Katie proceeded to look at every rack and display. Tawny shrugged at him apologetically.

"I've got to find a men's room," he told her.

It took a while to figure out how to get back to that coat, but he suspected he wouldn't be missed. At least not for a while. He found a sales lady, had her wrap it up, and made a beeline for his truck, where he stashed the package behind the backseat in his crew cab, and returned to the store. Like he thought, Tawny and Katie had barely noticed he was gone.

"What do you have there?" he asked Tawny, who was holding a couple of garments in her hand.

"She wants to wear a dress on the day of the transplant." She looked at him like *Don't ask.*

"Pick one," Tawny told Katie.

"But I like them both," Katie said.

Lucky was ready to scoop up the two dresses, throw them at a cashier, and pay so they could finally get out of here. But Tawny's body language told him if he did that he wouldn't live very long.

"You get one. Choose, or you don't get any." Tawny held both up.

Katie started to pout. Lucky suspected she was milking this transplant for everything she could. And who could blame her? Except Tawny was trying to raise her right, teach her the value of a buck, when all he wanted to do was spoil her.

Katie stuck out her bottom lip and looked right past Tawny to Lucky. "Daddy, can I have both?"

Lucky didn't have to see Tawny's expression to know how angry that had made her. "You heard your mom. Pick one. You've got five minutes or we're out of here."

He glanced over at Tawny, who gave a slight nod. As if to say *Good, we're on the same page.* Katie deliberated for what seemed to Lucky like hours. It was a goddamn dress. How long could it take to choose?

"I'd go with the pink one," he said, hoping to expedite the process. The lights in the store made him bleary-eyed. The air was stuffy. Plus, he sincerely liked the pink dress for his little girl. The other one seemed a little grown-up for a nine-year-old, not that he was any kind of an expert. Until now his full experience with dresses had been the fastest way to get them off.

"All right," Katie said. "I'll take the pink one."

"Good choice." Tawny kissed the top of Katie's head. "Now stop being a brat."

They went up to the cash register and Tawny and Lucky pulled out their wallets at the same time.

"I've got it," Lucky said.

Tawny glowered at him. "No. I'm buying the dress for *my* daughter."

Not wanting to make a scene, Lucky refrained from mentioning that Katie also happened to be *his* daughter, and shoved the wallet back in his pants. He really wished the woman was less independent and less controlling. He didn't find it the least bit attractive.

That's when he felt his phone vibrate and looked at the display. Another text from Raylene. Suddenly, independent women seemed more appealing. Everyone in Nugget knew that he and Tawny were in Palo Alto for Katie's transplant. Did Raylene not get the memo, or was she so selfish that she didn't care?

While Tawny finished the transaction, Lucky stood off in a corner and read the text.

Call me, or I'm telling Noah the whole story.
Raylene

Lucky didn't know what the whole story entailed. Raylene had already filled Noah's head with so much bullshit, Lucky couldn't imagine her having any lies left to tell. Because he wanted the transplant to go smoothly and didn't know what Raylene was capable of, he sent her a quick text back.

Can't call now. In the Bay Area for Katie's transplant. Will contact you when I get home.
Lucky

Tawny and Katie came up alongside him and he put the phone away. "We done now?"

"We're done," Katie said, and Lucky tickled her.

By the time they got back to the hotel, Lucky was ready for a nap. The meds were doing a number on him. But Katie wanted to swim.

"I can take her," Tawny said. She'd noticed how sluggish he'd been, which bothered him. He didn't like being listless and he didn't like anyone knowing that he wasn't in top form.

"Nah. I've been looking forward to this." Looking forward to seeing Tawny in a bathing suit.

They went into their private rooms to change. Lucky looked at his phone again to make sure Raylene wasn't still haranguing him. No texts, thank goodness. He put on his trunks, a pair of cowboy boots, and shrugged into the hotel's complimentary robe.

Except for the cowboy boots, the girls had done the same.

"You're not wearing those, are you?" Katie asked, wrinkling her nose.

Lucky laughed. "You don't like the look?" He opened the robe to give them a full view of his getup.

Tawny eyed his Hawaiian-patterned trunks with the cowboy boots and let out a laugh. Then her eyes moved up to his chest and lingered there. Lucky saw her lick her lips. Time to close the robe before she witnessed just how much he liked her looking at him.

"You ready to go?"

"Really, Daddy, you can't wear those." Katie pointed to the boots.

"Why not?" He enjoyed teasing her. "World champion bull riders can dang well wear their boots anywhere they want."

Tawny pealed with laughter. It was nice to see the worry lines gone from her face. He had other ways of smoothing those lines, but this was a G-rated trip.

"Let's go," he said, and for effect grabbed his Stetson off the fancy-pants table sculpture he'd been using as a hat rest and put it on his head, which sent Tawny into hysterics.

"Seriously, Daddy, you look like a freak." But even Katie was laughing now.

Lucky viewed himself in the full-length mirror. "Y'think?" Before Katie could answer, he grabbed her and hung her upside down over his shoulder. "I'll change then, just for you."

Back in his bedroom, he pried off the boots and slid his feet into a pair of flip-flops. On their way out of the suite, Lucky perched his hat back on the sculpture. The pool was empty. Lucky assumed the hotel guests, mostly business travelers, didn't have time to swim in the middle of a weekday. Katie wasted no time diving in. Tawny was more tentative, dipping her toes first, then sitting on the edge and dangling her legs in the water.

She still had the robe on. Lucky took his off and waded in up to his waist, walking over to the side where Tawny sat.

"You coming in?" he asked her.

"I'm not much of a swimmer." For a minute they watched Katie shoot up and down the lap lane like a fish. Whoa, the girl could swim. He'd have to put in a pool.

"Watch me do the backstroke, Daddy."

Lucky watched, wearing a big grin. "You're pretty amazing there, Katie girl." He turned to Tawny. "Where did she learn that?"

"I got her lessons at the community pool as soon as she was old enough to walk. You hear so much about children drowning."

It struck him that Tawny hadn't been much more than a child herself when Katie had been old enough to walk. Yet she'd had the forethought to get Katie swimming lessons. When Katie had become sick, Tawny got her the best medical care in Northern California—maybe even the country. The woman was a force to be reckoned with.

"You never learned?" he asked her.

"I can paddle around, stay afloat, but I don't like getting my face wet."

He caught sight of the empty spa. "We can sit in the hot tub while Katie swims."

"You don't want to do a few laps?"

"Not particularly." The truth was his bones were sore from the meds. He hoped the hot water would soothe him. A lot of times after PBR events, he and the other bull riders would get in their hotel's hot tub to relieve the aches and pains.

"All right." Tawny got up and met him at the spa. It was right next to the pool, so they could still keep a close eye on Katie. She crouched down and tested the water. "Hot."

"Good," he said. There must've been pain in his face because she stuck her hand out for him.

"I'm fine. Just a little achy from the drugs. This'll help. Come sit with me."

She slowly took off the robe and Lucky could tell she was shy about him seeing her in a modest one piece. During sex, they'd been too busy taking their fill of each other to get self-conscious. But the woman had to know how beautiful she was. Not the same kind of voluptuous as Raylene, but her petite curves were sexy as hell. Long legs, a tiny waist, and in his opinion, perfect breasts. Just enough to fill his hands. And every bit of her was real. The part that he couldn't get enough of, though, was her face. Those green eyes and plump pink lips.

Tawny went in up to her knees and then got out. "I've got to get used to it."

Fine by him. He got in, sat near one of the jets, and blatantly took her in from head to toe.

"What?" she scolded, clearly embarrassed.

"You're pretty. I like looking at you."

That got her in the spa, hiding under the bubbly water, as far away from him as possible. "Don't say things like that."

"Why not?"

"Because it won't work with me and because it makes you sound smarmy."

"I'm just being honest. Anyone can see that you're a beautiful woman. Brady obviously thinks so. Pete. Noah too."

She splashed him with water. "What are you talking about?"

"You tell me. Are you and Brady together?"

"No. I already told you that."

"Then why are you making him boots?"

"Not that it's your business, but the man is constantly bringing me and Katie food he prepares. I wanted to do something nice for him in return."

Not buying it, he just stared at her.

"What did Pete and Noah say about me?"

"Why should I tell you? It'll only give you a big head." He could tell how badly she wanted to know, and laughed. "They think you're hot."

"They do not. You're such a liar." She splashed him again.

He wiped water from his eye. "Next time you do that, you won't like the consequences."

She splashed him again and he leaned over and pulled her into his lap. Despite the water temperature, Lucky felt his trunks grow tight. Oddly enough, she didn't try to move away. He wrapped his arms around her and checked the pool to make sure Katie was okay. Too busy doing handstands under the water, Katie didn't pay them any attention.

"I'm not a liar. That's what they told me. Why? You interested?"

"Of course not," she said.

"Damn straight. You're only interested in me."

"Don't flatter yourself, buddy boy. What? Raylene dump you again?"

Lucky tightened his grip because he didn't want Tawny to squirm away. "Raylene and I are over. That's all you need to know."

Tawny chewed on her lip, seeming to be contemplating something. "She told Noah that you forced her at the Rock and River that night."

"I don't care what she says."

"I told Noah the truth."

"I know," Lucky said.

She reeled back. "Did Noah tell you that?"

"No. He said reliable sources disputed the allegations. I knew you were the reliable source."

"How?"

"Because you're reliable." He kissed the back of her neck, then the side of her throat, until he turned her around and kissed her full on the mouth.

"Not with Katie," she said against his lips, but she didn't seem like she'd be stopping anytime soon.

"I want you," he told her. "Tonight. I'll ask my mom and Jake to take Katie to dinner and a movie."

"Don't do that." She pulled free. "I don't want them to think there is something going on between the two of us. Because there isn't."

"I don't know what it is, Tawny. But there is definitely something going on."

Lucky heard Katie get out of the pool and he gently moved Tawny off his lap. "You ready to go back to the room?" he called to Katie.

"You think Grandma and Jake are back?"

"I think there's a good chance of it, yeah." He tugged Tawny up, got out, and handed her a towel.

"Wrap yourself up," Tawny told Katie, and cinched the girl's robe tie. "I don't want you catching a chill."

"You neither," Lucky said, and purposely stared at Tawny's nipples through her wet swimsuit. While handing her the hotel robe, Lucky let his hand graze over her breasts. He heard her sudden intake of breath and threw her a wicked grin.

They walked through the lobby of the hotel to the elevators, and through the hallway to their suite. Lucky wanted to take a shower, wash off the chlorine, then hand wash Tawny. Unfortunately, that wasn't going to happen. At least not now.

But later, anything was possible.

Chapter 21

Tawny put on a dress that she saved for special occasions. Not that going out to dinner the night before Lucky got a catheter stuck in his chest was a special occasion, but she thought she should look appropriate for a nice dinner out.

The five of them had a reservation at a restaurant Tawny had never heard of but came highly recommended. A little part of her—if she wanted to be honest, a big part of her—had hoped that she and Lucky would stay in. His idea, not hers. He'd either been talking a big game or he'd chickened out. Either way, it was for the best since Lucky couldn't seem to stop checking his text messages every five minutes.

Raylene, of course. He was probably hoping she'd beg his forgiveness and they could live happily ever after.

"You ready to go?" Lucky broke into her thoughts as he popped his head into her room while she put on her mascara. "We're supposed to meet Ma and Jake in the lobby in five minutes."

"Yep." She called to Katie. "Let's go, Miss Fashion Queen."

Katie came out of the bathroom wearing her new dress.

"I thought that was your transplant outfit," Lucky said, his lips curving up into a half smile that made Tawny's stomach flutter.

"I want to wear it tonight too." Katie patted down the folds, getting out any wrinkles.

"Well, you look beautiful. I've got a good-looking family." Lucky pulled Katie under his arm and took a picture of them with his camera phone.

"I want that picture," Katie said.

"I'll make a print of it. Come on, Tawny. Let's get one of the three of us."

She felt like the odd person out, but it would be petty to resist. Lucky posed Katie between the two of them and snapped another photo. A thought, too horrible to contemplate, shot through her mind. *If the transplant didn't work, these could be the last . . .* She wouldn't let herself think that way.

Lucky must've felt Tawny tense because he asked, "Are you okay?"

"Just cold."

"Well, then I've got just the thing," he said, and left Tawny's room only to return with a Nordstrom bag.

"What's this?"

"Open it, Mommy."

Tawny caught Katie's eye, but her daughter seemed to be as much in the dark as Tawny. Opening the bag, Tawny pulled out the tissue paper and found the green wool coat she'd admired during their trip to the mall.

She examined the coat, then Lucky, with a combination of wonder and annoyance. Did he think she couldn't afford her own clothes? "Why did you buy me this?"

"Because it matches your eyes. Put it on and let's skedaddle."

At home she wore an old down jacket that kept her warm but was about as attractive as the dead chickens that had been plucked for the filling. This coat was elegant and really did match her eyes, but the price tag was way too extravagant.

"You shouldn't have gotten me this." But even as she said it, she itched to feel the cashmere next to her skin.

"Try it on." Lucky lifted it with one finger and draped the coat over her shoulders.

Tawny slipped her arms into the sleeves, pulled the belt around and tied a perfect square knot. Nothing had ever felt more deluxe. She kept petting the wool.

Katie pushed her toward the full-length mirror. "It's beautiful, Mommy."

Tawny turned this way and that. "It is gorgeous."

"Good," Lucky said. "Now can we please go before we lose our reservation and Jake puts out an APB for us?"

Katie dashed to the door while Tawny started to take the coat off.

"What are you doing?" Lucky asked.

"I can't keep this. It's too expensive and I'm not your . . ."

"What?" Lucky said. "You're not my what?"

"Girlfriend."

"No, you're not," he said. "I bought it for you because you're under a lot of stress and I thought you could use something to cheer you up. It's a small token. So put the damn thing back on and let's go."

Tawny shrugged into the coat again and cinched the belt. When they got to the lobby, Cecilia and Jake were dressed up too. Cecilia gave Katie a big kiss and praised her new dress.

"And look at you, Tawny. What a beautiful coat."

"Lucky got it for me," Tawny said, feeling self-conscious. The last thing she wanted was for Cecilia to think that Tawny was taking advantage of her son's money.

"Good for him." Cecilia gave Lucky a hug and turned back to Tawny. "You deserve someone giving you something pretty for a change." And that's when Tawny realized that Cecilia was wearing the boots. It seemed to Tawny that Cecilia wore them every chance she got. A true compliment.

Jake ushered them out the door and they squeezed into Lucky's crew cab. They found the restaurant and after ten minutes of searching for parking, they were shown to their table on the patio. The outdoor heaters made it more than comfortable and the twinkly lights strung through the trees added a warm ambiance. Romantic.

Lucky sat next to Tawny and Katie sat next to Lucky. Her daughter couldn't seem to get enough of the man. Jake ordered champagne for the table and got a mocktail for Katie, who glowed with excitement at being included with the grown-ups.

When the food came, their chatter ceased and everyone ate. Tawny couldn't have asked for a lovelier evening. Being enveloped in such warm company had taken her mind off tomorrow. Although the actual transplant wouldn't happen for a few days, she'd be back in a hospital bright and early. Fighting for Katie's life.

Tawny felt Lucky's hand on her leg. At first he squeezed her knee as if he knew where her thoughts had gone and wanted to reassure her. *Everything will be fine. We've got this covered.*

Then his hand started to boldly roam up her thigh, and higher, until he reached the edge of her panties. Within seconds he was in, stroking her with his finger. She moved her leg to nudge him with her knee, but that only gave him better access. The man had to be insane. Here, in a restaurant, with his family? She pinched him under the table, which only made him touch her more . . . and she was wet . . . and throbbing. Dear God, in another second she would go off like the champagne cork.

The check came, saving her the embarrassment. Lucky stopped fondling her so he could reach for his wallet.

"I've got it," Jake said, and handed his credit card to the waiter too fast for Lucky to argue.

"Thanks, Jake," chorused the voices around the table.

"Cecilia and I were thinking of taking in a movie. Anyone want to join us?" Jake asked, and Tawny knew this was Lucky's doing.

"I want to." Katie practically bounced out of her chair, then looked at Tawny for permission.

Tawny in turn looked at Jake and Cecilia.

"Of course," Cecilia said.

"I'd like to turn in early if it's all the same to you," Lucky said. "And Tawny could use some rest—a little alone time."

Alone time. Ha. What a liar.

"That sounds wise," Jake said, signing the bill and rising.

"Why don't you drop us off at the hotel and take the truck," Lucky suggested.

A short time later she and Lucky were making their way through the revolving door of the Four Seasons, into the lobby.

"You're crazy," she told him as the elevator door opened and they stepped in.

An elderly couple tried to follow them, but Lucky slapped the button, letting the door close on them. He pushed her up against the wall and slid his hand up her dress.

"Where were we?" He pulled the leg of her panties to the side and began stroking her again. She could barely stay standing, it felt so good. "You like this?"

"Let's wait until we get to our room."

"You didn't answer me." He kissed the side of her neck and nuzzled her ear, taking tiny nips.

"Oh God, yes." She groaned. "Someone will see us, though."

He tugged the bottom of her dress down but moved his hands over her breasts, pressing the thick ridge in his pants against her. She went up on tiptoes so she could feel him where it counted the most.

When the door opened, he all but dragged her out, muttered a curse when he couldn't get the key card to immediately work, and pulled her across the threshold.

"By my estimate we have three hours, give or take some." He pulled off her new coat, then tugged her dress over her head when all he had to do was untie the belt. But she couldn't breathe, let alone talk. "I want to make the best out of every single, solitary second. You with me?"

He unhooked the front clasp of her bra, slid the straps down her shoulders, weighed her breasts in his hands, and leaned down to take them in his mouth. Stopping, he looked up. "Well? You with me?"

"Yes," she said, and started tugging at his clothes. Thank goodness for Western shirts and snaps. "Bed."

"You got it." He lifted her like a bride, carried her to his room, and laid her on the bed just long enough to shuck off his shirt, pants, and shorts. Standing over her, his erection jutting out, only one word came to Tawny's mind. Perfection.

Lucky Rodriguez was flawlessly made. Not too tall for a five-foot-four woman, and a body built of muscle and steel. Without knowing what possessed her, she got off the bed and down on her knees and took him in her mouth. Never before had she been this brazen, but she wanted him like this—a little at her mercy. She was rewarded with a loud moan of pleasure.

"Ah, Tawny, you're killing me. Stop, baby."

He tugged her up, pushed down her underwear, sat on his haunches and returned the favor. The difference was she didn't stop him until he took her over the edge while screaming his name.

"Oh yeah," he said. "Good?"

Her legs shook so badly, her heart pumping a million miles a minute, that all she could do was nod. Lucky got off the floor and backed her against the bed until she fell onto the mattress. He followed, continuing to touch every inch of her with his hands and lips and the part of him she wanted inside of her.

"I can't wait anymore," she said. "Please tell me you brought condoms."

"Right here." He climbed over her and pawed through his suitcase until he found a box still sealed in plastic, which he ripped open with his teeth, scooping out a handful of foil packets.

She watched Lucky roll the condom down the length of him before coming to the end of the bed. He spread her legs wide, entering her a little at a time, letting Tawny get accustomed to his size. But she didn't want that. Instead, she wrapped her legs around his waist, demanding that he go deeper. He reached under her bottom and pumped hard and fast.

The pleasure of it drove her to the brink.

"Holy hell, you feel good," he said, his muscles straining. "At this rate I won't make it to the buzzer."

He flipped over so that Tawny was on top and sat her up so he could fondle her breasts. "Let's try this a while."

She moved on top of him, liking how she could control the pace.

"Jesus," he said, gazing up at her. "I can't get enough of looking at you."

He outlined her breasts with the tips of his fingers. Reaching up, he pushed back the hair that curtained her face. "Ride me, baby."

She rocked into him faster, planting her hands on his thighs, arching her back. He clasped her hips with his big hands and met her stroke for stroke, grunting his appreciation when he wasn't laving her breasts with his mouth.

"You getting close?" he asked in a rough voice, using his fingers to bring her higher.

Incoherent, Tawny said something unintelligible, but the answer was yes. God, was she close. Lucky moved her onto her back and took over until he raced them both across the finish line. He lay sprawled on top of her, taking in deep breaths. Although he was heavy, she liked having his weight on top of her, and pressed her breasts against his slightly furred chest.

He kissed her over and over again. "Am I crushing you?"

Before she could answer, he lifted off and moved to the other side of her, slinging his arm over his eyes to block the light. Tawny hadn't noticed it before, but the overhead fixture was turned on. He gazed at the bedside clock, reached up, and dimmed the switch.

A few seconds later, Tawny felt Lucky's hands roaming over her stomach and between her legs.

"Looks like we've got two and a half hours left," he whispered in her ear. "How do you want to spend it?"

* * *

At nine o'clock the next morning, Dr. Laurence and his team stuck a plastic tube in Lucky's chest and used it to suck out his blood. The blood was then cycled through a machine that separated his stem cells from other blood cells. The doctors kept what Katie needed and gave Lucky back the rest. It took four hours. Other than the discomfort of the catheter, the procedure was fairly painless. Boring as hell, though.

Tawny had come with him and tried to keep up a steady stream of conversation. But with medical staff constantly coming and going, they couldn't talk about anything of substance, like the incredible sex they'd had the night before.

It had been fast and furious and wild and exciting and . . . something else that Lucky couldn't quite define. Whatever it was, it was deeper than he wanted it to feel. What was that saying? Jumping from the frying pan into the fire. From Raylene, a woman he thought he knew but didn't, to Tawny, a woman he'd initially thought was a schemer, but turned out to be . . . everything.

"You all right?" Tawny asked for the twentieth time since they'd arrived.

"I'm fine. How 'bout you? All the blood making you queasy?" He had to admit that watching blood circulate through a clear tube all morning wasn't for the faint of heart.

"It doesn't bother me," she said. "Does it hurt? They say you'll probably have to do it two or three more times before they do the transplant."

"Nah. But I'm glad my mom and Jake stayed with Katie. This might scare her."

"With everything she's been through, you'd be surprised. No sense, though, in having her sit through this."

Lucky sat through it two more times before Katie got her infusion. That day turned out to be the most emotional of his life. They'd decided to celebrate it like a birthday party—the first day of Katie's new, healthy life. God willing. Tawny decorated the room with balloons, Cecilia and Jake brought a cake, and Katie wore her pink dress and a tiara that said "Birthday Princess."

Lucky had a hard time watching the catheter inserted into his daughter's small chest. For weeks Katie would be under close medical supervision. And even then they wouldn't know whether the transplant took. The doctors said it could take as long as a year for blood counts to become normal and her immune system to work right.

As he watched a nurse attach one of the packets of his stem cells to Katie's IV, Lucky felt profoundly responsible. This all came down to him. Could he save his little girl?

Dr. Laurence came in the room as the infusion started. "How's everyone doing?"

"Good," Katie said, and smiled so brightly from her hospital bed that it made Lucky tear up. The kid had been through so much and still acted like a trooper.

"Would you like a piece of cake, Dr. Laurence?" Cecilia asked. His mother would feed the world if she could.

"No, thanks," he said. "I just grabbed breakfast."

"How you doing, Lucky?" The doctor gave him an appraising look.

"A little sore, like muscle cramps. I'm sure it'll go away soon."

"I'll have the nurse give you some calcium supplements," Laurence said.

"All right." Lucky nodded. "I'll be going into training mode, so I'm guessing the calcium will be good for that too."

"Training mode?" Laurence looked at him quizzically. "What do bull riders do for that?"

"Cardio, strength training, like any other athlete."

"I suggest you wait a few weeks," the doctor said. "Your body needs time to recover from the meds and the procedure itself."

"Afraid I don't have the time," Lucky responded. "The world finals are right before Christmas."

"Lucky," Dr. Laurence said, "it's inadvisable that you climb onto the back of a bull this soon."

"Why?" Lucky asked while everyone in the room went silent. The general consensus was that it was inadvisable to get on the back of a bull, period.

"You'll be weak and your body won't function the way you're used to it functioning. Bull riding is dangerous enough without having thoroughly healed from a rigorous medical procedure like this. Look, I can't stop you, but I strongly urge you to sit this one out."

Sit this one out? This would be his last hurrah. After the spill he'd taken in Billings, he'd been fortunate to qualify at all. Since his place had become crime central, he needed the good publicity of a win to get his cowboy camp back on track. If he dropped out of the finals, he wouldn't have the legacy—longest reigning champ in PBR history—that he wanted. Needed.

"Thanks, Doc. I'll think about it."

Tawny sent him a dark look, and if it wasn't for the fact that no one wanted to upset Katie, his mother would've been all over him too. But this was something he had to do. He'd just tough it out like he always did. What was the worst that could happen to him?

Chapter 22

It felt like forever since Tawny had slept in her own bed. They'd spent three weeks in Palo Alto and now she and Katie bunked at Cecilia's house.

So far there had been no complications. Dr. Laurence worried about infection, and for that reason had kept Katie on antibiotics. Her red- and white-cell and platelet numbers were down, but that was par for the course. They continued to watch for pneumonia and kidney and liver malfunctions. But the biggest worry of all was whether Katie's new cells would attack her body instead of getting her better. That's why she had to be monitored closely. Once a week they had to return to Stanford for checkups. Clay, who owned several planes, had volunteered to take them back and forth so Katie wouldn't have to withstand the long travel time in a car. Normally, Tawny wouldn't accept such a generous offer. But in this case she did it for Katie.

Against the doctor's wishes, Lucky had started a rigorous exercise program. Back at the Four Seasons he'd spent two to three hours a day in the gym on the elliptical, treadmill, and weights. A bull rider needed a lot of upper-body strength.

But the workouts seemed to be doing more harm than good. He was exhausted, and Tawny was convinced that he was anemic. A bull rider friend of his had suggested that he try yoga and Pilates. At first he'd resisted.

"No self-respecting cowboy does chick exercises," he'd said.

Then he found out that half the guys in the PBR were adding "chick" exercises to their workout regimes. That and martial arts. Lucky had hired Pam, owner of the Nugget yoga and dance studio, to train him. And while the program she'd mapped out for him was demanding, it seemed to be less taxing than his old plan.

Besides changing his workouts, they'd stopped having sex. His stamina for that was just fine, but they obviously couldn't continue under Cecilia's roof.

On the nights Katie had been in the hospital recovering from the transplant, Tawny and Lucky had stayed in the suite in the same bed, making love. She'd like to think that it had been a way for her to work off the stress of the transplant and find a modicum of comfort while constantly worrying over Katie's health. But she'd be lying. The truth was, Tawny was falling deeper and deeper in love with Lucky.

Unfortunately, he was the ultimate cowboy, never talking about his feelings for her—if he even had any—or where the two of them might be headed relationship-wise. All she knew was that he liked sleeping with her.

And there was no guarantee that Lucky had completely gotten over Raylene. He might've gone cold turkey for now. But for Lucky she was a hard habit to break. And Raylene wouldn't let him go that easily. Tawny suspected that she still texted him. His phone would ping, he'd look at it, shake his head, and tuck the cell away in his pocket. Then again, for all Tawny knew, it was someone else from his bevy of buckle beauties.

She tried not to get jealous, since she had no hold on him.

Noah frequently came to the house. The transplant had become a big part of his story, especially the fact that the doctor had told Lucky not to ride and he planned to do it anyway. Today, he'd come by as she was leaving for her studio.

For much of the morning she tried to get caught up on orders. Around two, she heard a noise and went to investigate. Lucky stood up against the backyard fence, trying to catch his breath.

"What's wrong?" she asked, fearing that it was more than the rigorous exercise routine. "Were you over at your mom's? Is it Katie?"

Lucky held up his hand. "No, nothing like that. I saw Raylene today."

Her heart stopped. Looked like today was the day Lucky fell off the wagon. Deep down inside, Tawny knew it was coming. "Oh," was all she said.

"Can we go in the house or the studio?"

She led him into the studio. It was closer and she wanted to get this over with.

Lucky gazed at her cutting table, where she'd been tracing a knife and fork out of leather. "Brady's boots, huh?"

"Yep." Ever since they'd gotten back, Brady had been bringing dishes to Cecilia's house.

"I thought you were backed up on your paying jobs."

Not that it was any of his concern, but she tilted her head at the project and said, "This is what I do when I'm taking a break. So you and Raylene are back together?" She shoved her hands in the back pockets of her jeans because they had started to tremble.

"Can I have a drink of water?" The truth was, Lucky didn't look so good. Pale.

"I'll get it for you. Sit." She wheeled her work chair his way and pushed his shoulders down until he sat. "I'll be right back."

Tawny went inside the house and filled a tall glass with ice and water and grabbed a bottle of ibuprofen on her way out. He'd been popping the pills like they were mints. The man was crazy to attempt riding in the finals. All she had to do was look at him to know that he shouldn't be exerting himself this way.

"Here." She handed him the glass and watched him down the water in a few big gulps. "You want more?"

"I'm good." He put the glass on her table. "She's beyond pissed at me."

Clearly he meant Raylene. "Why, because you left her to take care of your daughter?" Tawny couldn't control the contempt in her voice.

"Because she knows I'm sleeping with you."

Tawny let out a sour laugh. "I can imagine. Me being ugly Thelma Wade. Why are you sleeping with me, anyway? Convenience?"

Anger flashed in his eyes. "There's nothing about you that's convenient, Tawny."

He motioned to the bench next to him. "Sit down for second." And she knew it was coming. Lucky was back with Raylene.

"Ray and Raylene are telling the police, and anyone who will listen, that I lured Ray to my ranch so that Gus Clamper could kill him—that it was a murder-for-hire until Ray got the drop on Gus. They claim they have proof."

Tawny gasped. "My God. What proof could they possibly have?"

"I have no idea, but Ray's a wily coyote. I wouldn't put anything past the sumbitch."

"But not Raylene?" Tawny huffed.

"Raylene isn't smart enough to fabricate evidence. She just goes along with whatever Ray tells her." *Like ten years ago*, but Tawny didn't say it. "I'll weather this, but I don't want it upsetting Katie . . . or my mom."

"How will you weather something like this? If he really can show proof, you could be in a lot of trouble, Lucky."

He looked at her funny. "You're not buying into this murder-for-hire bullshit, are you?"

"Of course not. But you yourself said Ray is wily, not to mention that he has a lot of influence in these parts."

"I'm not exactly a nobody."

She supposed that was true, but it didn't stop her from being scared for him. "How does Raylene feed into this?"

"She's blabbing it all over town, including to Noah."

Tawny blew out a breath. "Oh boy. Have you talked to Jake?"

"No. It's awkward, given his situation with my mother."

"What about Rhys?"

"Nah. I think I'll talk to Clay first."

"Why Clay? He's not in law enforcement."

"No, but he's Rhys's best friend. Besides, he knows me. He knows I wouldn't do anything like that and he knows Ray Rosser and what a hothead he is, especially when it comes to his cattle. I trust the guy."

"Okay." Tawny didn't think talking to Clay could hurt. The McCreedys had even more influence in these mountains than the Rossers. "You want me to come with you?"

He tilted his head sideways and looked at her, a little smile playing on his lips. "I've got it, but thanks."

"Whatever." All she'd wanted to do was stand up for him. "Just trying to be a friend."

"Is that what we are, Tawny? Friends?"

She purposely didn't answer. "What'll you do about the finals?"

"What I always intended to do. Win." He gave her a quick peck on the cheek and headed for the door. "Don't work too hard." He let his gaze drift back to the pieces of Brady's boots. "I'll see you tonight."

Not if he got arrested.

As soon as she heard Lucky pull away in his truck, Tawny put on her new coat, got in her Jeep, and drove to the police station. If he wouldn't talk to Jake, she would. At the square she found parking right in front of the department's old-timey stucco building and heard the bells jingle when she opened the door.

Connie sat at the front of the office, wearing a cordless headset. "Hey, Tawny. How's that little girl of yours?"

"She's doing well. Thanks for asking. Is Jake around?"

"He's in the chief's office. I'll get him for you." Connie got up and walked to the back of the room.

Tawny had only been in the station a couple of times. There was a big map of Nugget on the wall and an FBI fugitive poster. The rest of the office was bland—just messy desks and an alcove with a refrigerator, sink, and coffeemaker.

A few seconds later, Jake, followed by Rhys, came out of a small glass office and waved to her.

Rhys gave her a warm smile. "How's Katie making out? I think Maddy went by Cecilia's today."

"So far, really well. Better than we expected. I must've missed Maddy while I was at my studio." He nodded, clearly curious about why she was here.

"Jake, you have a few minutes?" She wanted to talk to him in private. It was bad enough she'd gone behind Lucky's back. She didn't want to announce the Rossers' allegations to the entire police department.

"For you I do," Jake said, and took her hand. "Let's go into the conference room."

Jake led her into a room with a long table and a few chairs. She sat and Jake grabbed a chair across from her. "To what do I owe the pleasure?"

Tawny frowned. "Ray and Raylene are telling everyone that Lucky lured Ray to his ranch on the day of the shooting. They're saying that Lucky hired Gus to kill Ray."

"I know," Jake said.

Tawny waited for him to say more and when he didn't, she added, "They're telling everyone they have proof. How could they, when Lucky didn't do that?"

"Are you sure?" Jake asked, and she flinched.

"Of course I am. Lucky would never do anything like that. You're not saying that you believe them, Jake?"

"As a cop I have to keep an open mind," Jake said. "I'm also in a compromised position here."

"Because of Cecilia, you mean?"

"Yes. Officially, I can't talk about the case with you, unless of course you have some pertinent information." He waited with his arms crossed.

"No . . . only that I know he didn't do it and he needs your help."

Jake sighed. "You hire a lawyer for this kind of help, Tawny. You should tell him that."

"He actually needs a lawyer? The Rossers are lying, Jake."

"And a good attorney will help him sort that out."

"Do you know what kind of evidence they have against Lucky?"

Jake didn't answer. Just sat there with his arms still folded.

"My God, you do," she said, realizing this was even worse than she thought. "And you think it's damning."

"Have him call his agent," Jake said. "Pete will know a good lawyer. Ray's already got the best one here."

Tawny couldn't believe her ears. "Does Cecilia know?"

Again, Jake didn't answer. The man had suddenly closed up tighter than Raylene's jeans. In Palo Alto, they'd been like a family. Now he was all business. This would kill Cecilia. Tawny needed to tell her before she heard it from someone else. Then Tawny would call Pete.

"Thanks for your help, Detective." She got to her feet, tucked her chair in, and left.

By the time she got to Cecilia's, Lucky was already there. From the pall over the kitchen, Tawny could tell that he'd told his mother. The two of them were sitting at the breakfast nook table, Cecilia clutching a cup of tea.

"Jake called," Cecilia said. "Don't be upset with him, *mija*."

Tawny didn't know how she could say that. Was love that blind that Cecilia couldn't see that her boyfriend wouldn't help her son when he desperately needed help? And then Tawny thought about it. Lucky had been so blinded by love that all these years he'd believed the best of Raylene.

Was it like that for her too? But there was no part of her that believed Lucky could be capable of murder, no matter how she felt about him.

"We need to call Pete," she said. "Have him recommend a good lawyer."

"I called him," Lucky said in a soft voice, presumably so Katie wouldn't hear. "He and some hotshot San Francisco lawyer are flying up tomorrow morning."

Tawny got up and walked to the room she and Katie shared. Inside, she checked on her daughter, who lay in the bed fast asleep. The transplant had left her fatigued, one of the side effects.

"She okay?" Lucky asked when Tawny returned to the kitchen.

"Yes. But I don't want her to know about this. She's become so attached to you . . . The news will upset her." Thank goodness Katie wasn't in school, where she'd hear the gossip sure as day.

"I'll make this go away, Tawny. I promise." Lucky got up and took her in his arms right in front of his mother. "It's all going to be okay."

She didn't know how he could make those assurances. What if it wasn't okay? "Jake knows what evidence they have."

"A text message from my phone to Ray's," Lucky said.

It just kept getting worse. Almost too afraid to ask, Tawny said, "What does it say?"

"That I knew that Gus had stolen his cattle and that we should confront him together."

"Did you send it?" she demanded.

"Of course not."

"Then how do you even know about the text?"

"Clay told me. Ray has been telling everyone."

"So he obviously made it up if you didn't text him," Tawny insisted, looking from Lucky to Cecilia. Cecilia had tears in her eyes.

Lucky pulled out a chair for her. "Sit down, honey." He waited for her to take a place at the table and said, "The text exists. I didn't send it, but it's on his phone from my phone."

"If you didn't, then someone else did," she said. "Who had access to your phone?"

"Half the construction crew," he said. "The question is, what motive would they have had to set me up like that?"

"Maybe they weren't trying to set you up," Tawny said. "Maybe they were just trying to get Ray to come to your property so they could ambush him."

Lucky smiled. "You missed your calling as a detective."

"This isn't funny, Lucky. Here's another thing I don't get. The shooting was weeks ago. Why are these allegations against you suddenly surfacing now?"

"Clay says Ray has been holding out on the police, hoping that his information on the drug ring might've bought him immunity. But rumor is that the DA is just days away from charging him with killing Gus. That's why he started spewing this crap about a murder-for-hire scheme."

Tawny turned to Cecilia. "You doing okay?" This had to break her heart. It was like ten years ago when Ray had thrown the fake rape allegations in her face.

"We will get through it," Cecilia said, acting brave. Tawny had to wonder how this would affect Cecilia and Jake's relationship.

Lucky got to his feet.

"Where are you going?" Tawny asked him.

"First to check on Katie, then to meet Raylene."

Both Tawny and Cecilia tried to stop him, but what was the point? No matter what that woman did, Lucky always forgave her. Or made up ridiculous excuses for her. *She was scared. She's misunderstood. You don't know what it was like growing up in that home.*

Why would now be any different? Just the thought of Lucky with Raylene made her chest ache and her throat tighten.

"This is between you and my dad, Lucky. I don't have anything to do with it," Raylene said.

She'd agreed to meet him at the high school rodeo arena—neutral ground. And a place that held so many memories for Lucky that they all came rushing back, transporting him to a time when just a smile from Raylene had made him giddy.

He used to sit on top of the bull shoot and watch her race her horse around the barrels, her cherry-red cowboy hat blowing off her head and her blond ponytail flying in the wind. Man, she'd been something.

"It's a load of crap," he said. "Just like the last time your father accused me of something. This time I thought you'd do better, Raylene. This time I actually thought you'd stand up for me."

"Why? So you and Thelma Wade and your love child could ride off into the sunset?"

"Ah, for Christ's sake, is that what this is about? You're jealous so you go around telling half the town and a journalist that I lured Ray to my ranch and hired someone to kill him?"

"It's just the truth," she said, the gleam in her eyes so mean that Lucky hardly recognized her. "I saw the text message you sent."

"Someone else sent that text because it sure the hell wasn't me. I hated your father for coming between us and making me leave my home. But if it wasn't for Ray, I wouldn't be who I am today. So I've got no motive, Raylene."

"Sure you do. Get rid of my dad, marry me, and get his property." She smiled so coldly that Lucky got the chills just looking at her.

Had she always been this awful, or had Butch made her bitter? Clearly Raylene's scenario was the motive Ray had presented to the cops.

"There was a time I wanted nothing more than to marry you." He'd lain awake at night so full of want for her that his body burned with it. "Now I wouldn't marry you for every piece of land in Nugget."

"Poor Thelma and Katie," she mocked. "What will they do when you fry?"

Lucky had to control his anger and gave her a long look. "What happened to you, Raylene? What the hell happened?" He put his face in hands. "God, how I used to love you."

"Used to. Past tense." Her voice hitched. "All I've got is my family now."

She backed away, got in her truck, and Lucky watched her taillights disappear. He walked over to the calf pens and searched the wooden fence. It took some time until he found it. The old corrals were weathered and chipped, but under the green peeling paint was the heart he'd carved into the wood with his penknife more than a decade ago. Inside the heart he'd scrawled "LR and RR Forever."

He considered using his Swiss Army knife to scratch out the letters. But what would be the point? The wooden fence didn't have much life left. Soon it would be history—just like him and Raylene.

He got in his own truck and halfway to his mom's he got a call. No ID. "Hello."

"Meet me at the Airstream trailer on the hill above your property."

Lucky hung a U-turn, took the road to his ranch, made a right at the fork, and motored up the hill. It had gotten dark, and with little moonlight to guide the way, he took the bumpy trail slow. He didn't even know who owned the land or even how many acres it was, only that the hill had been annexed from his ranch years ago. From the looks of the trailer, it had been there since biblical times. One day he planned to look up the property records and make an offer on the place. The private plateau had fantastic views. The perfect spot for a big house.

When he got to the top, he parked near the Airstream. There were no other cars, so he checked his phone for texts. He didn't like going too long without checking in on Katie. There was only an email from Pete confirming his and the lawyer's flight.

Lucky jerked his head up when someone rapped on his window, and he opened the door. "You scared the shit out of me. Where's your truck?"

"I didn't want anyone to see me, so I parked a borrowed car behind a couple of trees at the bottom of the hill and hiked up."

Lucky had a feeling he knew whose car. He got out of the truck.

"You got a lawyer coming tomorrow?"

"Yep," Lucky said.

"Good."

"Why? You planning to arrest me, Jake?"

"I'm planning to arrest the person who sent that text." He looked at Lucky hard, as if he wanted to make sure he understood. Lucky nodded.

"Let's go through it together." Jake sat on the ground with his back against the Airstream and Lucky joined him. "The time stamp on the text was 6:12. The 911 call at 6:50."

Lucky had already done this over and over in his head. For the life of him all he could remember was having his phone on him when he'd left Jake at the Ponderosa. He'd used it, after all, to call 911 after the shooting. "Yeah?"

"That leaves you thirty-eight minutes to account for," Jake said. "All we need to figure out is who had access to your phone at 6:12. You do that by counting backwards."

"Believe you me, Jake, I've tried over and over again."

"Okay, then we'll work forward. What time did you leave me at the Ponderosa?"

"I wasn't looking at a clock." Lucky wanted to bang his head against the Airstream.

"Was it still light outside?"

"Yeah," Lucky said, sitting up straighter. "But just barely. I remember Owen and the rest of the Mafia sitting outside and thinking to myself that they were taking advantage of the light before the days got shorter."

"Good. Was it light when you got back to your ranch?"

Lucky thought about it. "Enough so that I could make out Raylene sitting on the hood of her truck. But dim enough so that I wondered why the motion lights I'd recently installed on the single-wide hadn't gone on. I was worried about Raylene sitting there because of the drug dealing."

Jake got out his phone and Lucky asked what he was doing.

"Searching to see what time it started getting dark that day." Jake tinkered on his phone awhile. "Around 5:53, according to the sunrise and sunset calendar, which means you were already home when the text went out. What did you do after you saw Raylene?"

"I went to check on the livestock," Lucky said.

"Do you remember having your phone with you?"

"Yeah, I must've, because otherwise I couldn't have called 911."

"Where were you when you heard the shots?"

Lucky tried to play it back in his head, but that whole evening had become a blur. All he could remember was walking around the corrals, doing a head count. "Bernice."

"Who's Bernice?" Jake got excited.

"My sheep. She got in the pen with Crème Bullee. I remember that because I decided that I'd let her stay with the bull. That's when I heard the shots."

"What did you do next?"

Lucky raised his arms. "I guess I must've called 911."

"From Crème Bullee's pen?"

"I remember running back to the trailer, worried about Raylene. I don't know if I called before I started running or while I was running." He thought about it for a while. "Then again, I drove to the corrals, so that doesn't make sense."

"Do you remember if your phone was in your truck?" Jake's frustration was palpable.

Lucky pinched the bridge of his nose. "Wait a minute." He got to his feet and started to pace. "I remember wanting to call Tawny to check on Katie when I was at the corrals and couldn't find my phone. So yeah, I must've left it in the truck. But I don't remember calling 911 from the truck. Truthfully, I feel like I ran the whole way back to the single-wide. And then at some point I went over to where the guys were bunking and found Gus."

"Did you have your phone with you then?" Jake asked.

"Yes. I distinctly remember having my phone because I called Connie to see what the hell was taking the ambulance so long." Lucky started searching his call history. "Here it is. See?"

Jake noted the time stamp. "That was 7:10. Your truck wasn't at the bunkhouse where we found Gus. Otherwise we would've processed it. So either you drove home from the corrals and walked to Gus's, or you left your truck at the corrals and did everything on foot, which doesn't explain how you got your phone back. Let me ask you this: Could you see your truck at all times?"

"Ah jeez, Jake, I can't remember. I was paying attention to my animals."

"Lucky, I'm just gonna put it out there: Could Raylene have had your phone?" Jake watched him, and it occurred to Lucky that the detective had been set on this theory for some time. He confirmed it when he said, "She certainly had opportunity and … well, this wouldn't be the first time she let you be the fall guy, would it?"

Clearly he was referencing what had happened ten years ago. It surprised Lucky that his mother had told Jake. Except for Lucky telling Tawny, he and his mother had kept what happened at the Rock and River that night under wraps. Once Lucky left town, Ray had never said another word about the incident.

"No way," he said. "She was a scared kid back then. This is completely different."

"Okay." Jake held his hands up in surrender and got to his feet. "Let's walk through it again. As soon as you got back to the ranch, you went to check on the animals?"

"Right after I talked to Raylene."

"Did she come with you? Because you said you went back to the trailer after you heard the gunshots to make sure she was okay."

"Right," Lucky said. "She waited for me in the trailer. I remember that because she complained about me leaving."

"So you went inside the trailer before you checked on the animals?"

Lucky shut his eyes, trying hard to recall whether he had. "Yeah,

yeah. Like I said, I was concerned about Raylene being alone. I'm the one who unlocked the door—so I must've gone in."

"How long do you estimate you were in the trailer before checking the animals?"

"Not long. Probably just a few minutes. I vaguely remember putting my stuff on the kitchen counter and—"

"What stuff?"

"Crap from my pockets. My keys, my . . . phone." He jerked his head up to look at Jake. "I called 911 from the trailer. The phone was on the counter where I left it."

"Alone with Raylene."

"Ah, Jake, no way." Lucky leaned his head back. "Jesus. Why?"

Lucky kicked a rock and headed for his truck.

"Where are you going?" Jake called to him.

"Where do you think I'm going?"

Jake ran after him and grabbed him by the back of his jacket. "No, Lucky. The last time you went to the Rock and River for a confrontation, you riled Ray, you embarrassed him, and he wanted to make you pay." Jake tilted his head at Lucky's phone. "What do you think that text was about? Not only did Ray build himself quite a nice self-defense case, but he dragged you into taking the fall. I want you to confront Raylene, but I want you to do it wearing a wire."

"I just want to talk to her, Jake. I just want to know why."

Jake shook his head. "Not without a wire, son. This is your life on the line."

"All right." Lucky still couldn't believe Raylene would do this to him—she was spoiled, self-centered, narcissistic, even vindictive, but this was pure evil. "We'll do it your way. I have to call to check on Katie."

"Don't say anything about Raylene," Jake said, and began punching in numbers on his cell phone. "Not until we wrap this up."

"Yeah, all right."

Lucky sat in his truck while he called his mother's house. After about the fifth ring, Tawny answered.

"Everything okay?" he asked.

"We're fine. You with Raylene?" Her voice sounded accusatory . . . and hurt.

"Not at the moment. I'll be a while and wanted to make sure Katie was all right."

"She ate dinner, which is a good sign. Are you . . . Never mind."

"Good night, Tawny." He ended the call. If he'd stayed on any longer he would've told her.

"Let's go," Jake said, and hopped into Lucky's passenger seat so he could fetch Cecilia's car from the bottom of the hill.

Two hours later Lucky sat in his truck at Nugget High's rodeo arena again and waited for Raylene. He'd told her that he wanted a reconciliation. That he loved her. It's what Jake and Rhys had told him to say after they'd hooked him up to a recording device.

Raylene apparently bought it, because she'd agreed to meet him. He felt like a first-class sleazebag. First off, he didn't like lying. And there was no way in hell he'd love someone like Raylene ever again.

Truthfully, it had been over between them ever since Tawny had reentered his life. An image of Tawny hugging Katie suddenly filtered through his memory and shook him like a bucking bull. Tawny in her studio, making those beautiful boots. In the Four Seasons hot tub, afraid to get all the way in. Setting the table with his mother on the night of their early Thanksgiving celebration. All he could see was Tawny.

He heard a car drive up and without moving his lips said, "She's here."

Raylene got out of her truck and Lucky noted that she'd definitely dressed for making up. Black leather dress and red cowboy boots. There was a time when the outfit would've turned him on.

He leaned over his console, opened his passenger door, and waved her in.

"It's cold." She shivered, and he nearly said *just like your heart.*

"I know you sent the text, Raylene."

"Is this why you called me out here in the middle of the night?" She started to get out, but he stopped her.

"Why'd you do it, Raylene? Why'd you set me up?"

"I don't know what you're talking about." She refused to look at him, but she wasn't trying to leave.

"The phone was in the kitchen when the text was sent. It's time stamped. I have an alibi at that time. One of my ranch hands was out by the corrals when I got there. I didn't have my phone on me, so I asked to borrow his . . . to check on Katie. He's ready to go to the police. So cut the shit, Raylene, and tell me why you did it."

"You're crazy, you know that?" Raylene spat out the words, but Lucky could tell she was nervous.

"Get out of my truck." He reached over and pushed open the door. "You heard me, get out. I'm going to the police. Planting evidence . . . you'll go to prison, Raylene."

"He made me do it," she blurted, and started to cry big crocodile tears.

"Who?" Jake wanted as much on the recording as possible.

"My dad. He said you wouldn't get in trouble. That Gus was a cattle rustler and that Clay McCreedy would back you and my dad. He wanted to show the police the text right away to help him with his defense, but I threatened to tell the truth. Then, later . . . I told him he could."

"Why?" Lucky asked.

"Because you didn't love me anymore." She started sobbing. For real this time, and Lucky found a stack of napkins in the glove box and shoved them at her. "You picked Tawny over me."

"Raylene, do you hear what you're saying? Murder-for-hire is a capital crime. You'd see me executed for something I didn't do because I'm with someone else?"

"No." She blew her nose. "I wouldn't have let it get that far. I just wanted you to feel the pain I was feeling."

"Jesus." Lucky hit his hands on the steering wheel. "When you married Butch, I went on a month-long bender. I was getting up on bulls when I couldn't even see straight. But I never would've hurt you. Ever."

"I know," she said and choked on a sob. "That's why it hurt so bad. Because no one ever loved me like you did. Not my mother. Not my father. Not Butch. No one." Her face was covered in mascara and snot. Lucky pushed some more napkins at her. "I'll go to the police, Lucky. I'll tell them the truth."

That wouldn't be necessary. "You shouldn't have let it get this far. What? Did Ray panic after he shot Gus and call you to tell you to steal my phone and send the text?"

She started blubbering all over again. "He sent me over to your house to do it." He could barely understand her, she cried so hard.

"Huh?"

"He sent me to you. He was angry at you for calling him an abusive father and husband. And livid about Gus taking his cattle. All day he paced and shouted how no one messed with Ray Rosser, yelling, 'Not Gus. And not that bastard, Lucky Rodriguez.' Then you made it easy by leaving me and your phone alone in the kitchen."

Lucky took a while to process that, then very softly said, "You were a vision sitting there on the hood of your truck that night. Looking as beautiful as I'd ever seen you. I knew we were over—we had nothing to say to each other anymore—but even then I loved you." Lucky tilted his head against the backrest and shut his eyes. "Get out of my truck."

"Lucky, please—"

"If you're not out of my truck in two seconds, I'll physically remove you."

She opened the door and put one foot on the running board. "I'll go to the police right now and tell them the truth. I swear."

"Get out!" He slammed his door shut, ripped off the wire the police had carefully taped to his chest, and floored it back to his ranch.

Chapter 23

"What's happened?" Cecilia asked the minute Jake walked in the door and found her and Tawny sitting at the kitchen table.

Jake felt like he hadn't slept in days, but was at the same time exhilarated. Not since Los Angeles had he done hardcore police work like this. And while he wouldn't like it to become a habit, it had revved his engine.

"You want coffee?" Cecilia got up and poured him a cup. The woman was always one step ahead of him.

He took off his jacket and plopped down next to Tawny. The house was nice and toasty and as usual the kitchen smelled good—like home cooking. Cecilia stuck a plate in the microwave and handed him his coffee. Even at midnight the woman looked fresh as a daisy.

"Come sit, sweetheart."

"I will." The microwave dinged and she set a plate of lasagna in front of him. "Tell us while you eat."

"Raylene confessed," he said. "She sent the text."

Cecilia and Tawny cried out at the same time, and Jake proceeded to tell them about Lucky's meeting with Raylene at the rodeo arena, and how, unbeknownst to Raylene, he had worn a wire. Jake kept his and Lucky's rendezvous at the Airstream trailer to himself. For a cop, the meeting had been highly unethical.

"After we got her on tape, she came to the police station and spilled her guts," he told them.

"Oh God," Tawny said. "Poor Lucky. This must have killed him." She got up from the table.

"Where are you going?" Cecilia called to her as she gathered up her coat and purse.

"To Lucky's. You'll watch Katie for me, right?"

"Of course. But it's late, Tawny. Talk to him in the morning. You shouldn't be out on the road this time of night."

"I'll be fine."

Cecilia started to protest, but Jake covered her hand with his. He got up, walked Tawny to her Jeep, waited until she drove away, and came back to the kitchen.

"I told you that girl was no good." Cecilia prepared Jake a second helping, though he hadn't finished the first. He supposed she needed to keep busy. "Why would she do such a horrible thing?"

"Ray asked her to, and the girl's under his thumb. I also suspect she felt deserted by Lucky—hell hath no fury . . ."

"And because she has a screw loose," Cecilia added.

Jake couldn't argue with her there. "The important thing is Lucky is in the clear. It's over, Cecilia."

She brought him the rest of the lasagna and he pulled her down into his lap. "Lucky will be fine."

"I told him to watch out for that woman. He never listens to me."

Jake kissed her softly on the cheek and reminded her, like he always did, that Lucky was a grown man.

"You helped him, didn't you?"

He shook his head. "Nope. Lucky had suspicions about Raylene and asked for the wire. I did my job like any other cop."

"Jake, I know my son. He never would've handled it that way. He would've taken the blame for Raylene, just like he did ten years ago."

"But he didn't, Cecilia. He made no excuses for her this time."

"What will happen to Raylene? Will she go to jail?"

"That'll be up to the DA. Right now, George's main focus is on convicting Ray."

"*Ay Dios*, what a night." Cecilia cupped Jake's face in her hands. "You're tired. You've worked so hard. Why don't you stay?"

"With you? Or in the guest room?"

"The girls are here, Jake. You know how I feel about that."

"I do." Cecilia Rodriguez was a proper lady. "How's Katie feeling?"

Cecilia made the sign of the cross. "She's doing better every day. And every day I pray she pulls through this. *Pobre niña*, she's just a baby." She rested her head against Jake's shoulder. "I don't think I ever told you how much I appreciated you staying with us in Palo Alto . . . for everything."

"I wish I could've stayed the whole time, but the department is small. It's difficult to take more than a few days. We may have a line, though, on someone to fill a slot for a fourth officer."

"Really?" Cecilia's eyes lit up. Jake loved how she took an interest in his job and how she'd never given him a hard time about his long and strange hours. "Where's he from?"

"She. She's someone I knew from LAPD. A young woman I'd worked with in the homicide division."

"Why would she want to leave such a big department?"

"She had some problems there and needs a change. Anyway, it's not a done deal yet. Rhys still has to interview her and she'll have to decide whether Nugget is the right place for her."

"Should I be jealous of this young woman?" Cecilia asked, half teasing. She knew his past. He had never kept anything from her.

"Ah, Cecilia. Since you, no one will ever have my heart again."

She laughed and let her eyes fall to his lap. "What about the rest of you?"

"Sweetheart, I'm a one-woman man now. All of me."

Cecilia fell quiet and looked into his eyes. "In that case, if your offer still holds, yes. I will marry you, Jake Stryker."

He couldn't believe his ears, having been rebuffed by her so many times. "Did I hear you right?"

She teared up and nodded.

"Cecilia"—he clasped both her hands—"you won't be sorry. I'll make you happy until the end of time."

"You've already made me happy. *Te amo*, Jake."

When Tawny went to Lucky's trailer she found him doing push-ups. There he was in a pair of boxers on the ratty carpet, trying to kill himself with exercise.

"Go home," he said. "Our daughter needs you."

"Katie's fine and Cecilia is with her. Lucky, Jake told us."

"Then you know I'm in the clear. So go home. I've got world finals to train for. And, Tawny, next time, knock."

"I did."

He got up, grabbed a towel off the ugly plaid sofa, and wiped the sweat off his chest.

"For what it's worth, Raylene went to the police and told them everything," she said.

"They already had it on tape." Lucky scowled.

"She didn't know that."

"Who knows what she knew. She's a liar."

"The DA is charging Ray with murder."

"I don't give a shit," he said. "Now if it's all the same to you, I'd like to take a shower . . . and be alone."

She didn't scare that easily. In the kitchen she made a pot of decaf and found a carton of milk in the refrigerator. She fixed two cups, put them on the coffee table, and waited. The water finally shut off and Lucky walked out of the bathroom with nothing but a towel wrapped around his waist. He hadn't shaved and a layer of scruff covered his face.

"Still here, huh?"

"I came to tell you something and then I'll leave."

He went into his bedroom and reappeared a short time later in a worn pair of Levi's that he hadn't bothered to button all the way up and an old Reno rodeo T-shirt.

She motioned at the coffee. He took a mug and sat in the recliner across from her.

"Despite what she did, Raylene loved you, Lucky. She always has." She paused, wanting to do this right. "But Raylene is screwed up. For God's sake, look at her parents. Her father is a brute and her mother may as well be in a coma. You've always known this about her. But you loved her anyway, because you're a good man—"

"You done?" He rested his head against the back of the chair, defeated. "Raylene played me . . . makes me wonder whether the entire time we were kids she was just using me. You knew all along what kind of person she was. What does that say about me?"

"That you see the good in people. And that you wanted to save Raylene. But some people can't be saved."

"Yeah. I guess it makes me as screwed up as she is."

"I don't think you're screwed up, Lucky. I think you're the best man I know." She wanted to hug him, but something about his body language said he wouldn't appreciate the gesture. Not right now. "Katie is blessed to have you as a father."

He stared up at the ceiling, looking sadder than she'd ever seen him. "I had Pete hunt down your messages. I don't know how his tech people did it, but they recovered your ten-year-old emails. They'd gone into my spam filter. They couldn't find the voice mails, though. By the time you'd left them, I'd changed cell providers."

Lucky shut his eyes. "I'm sorry, Tawny. More sorry than you'll ever know." He got to his feet, went into the kitchen, and poured himself a glass of water. "You want one?"

"No." She watched him drain the glass and come back to his chair. He sat hunched over with his forearms on his thighs, his body just a few inches from her.

"I need to put my head on straight—focus on the finals." He exhaled. "You mind if we slow things down . . . take a break?"

It's not like they'd been moving at warp speed. They hadn't even been sleeping together. "No, I don't mind," she said, realizing that this was his tactful way of breaking it off with her. "I understand how it is." But she didn't.

Halfway to Cecilia's, Tawny had to pull over to the side of the road. She felt nauseous. Raylene. It was always Raylene.

The next morning, Katie ate a full bowl of cereal and an entire muffin, compliments of Brady. Tawny didn't think she'd eaten that much for breakfast in the last five years. And her color looked good.

"Mrs. DeLeo brought you a stack of schoolwork, if you're feeling up to it." Katie had missed so much school that Tawny wouldn't be surprised if this time her daughter got held back a year. In the scheme of things, a small price to pay.

"Daddy said he's picking me up after he's done with yoga and taking me to the ranch."

"Oh?" Tawny looked at Cecilia, who shrugged. "This is the first I've heard of it."

"He called this morning," Katie said. "Can I go?"

"Of course. What are you guys planning to do?"

"I don't know," Katie said. "He wants to show me around so I can help him pick out a spot for his new house."

"I want you to bundle up. It's cold." Tawny thought it might even snow. She'd prefer Katie stay home today and rest, but it wasn't worth a fight with Lucky.

At the sound of an engine, Katie looked outside the kitchen window. "He's here."

"Go get dressed," Tawny told her. "Warm clothes."

Katie took her bowl to the sink and ran off. Cecilia greeted Lucky at the door. He looked like crap. Tawny wouldn't be surprised if he'd been up all night.

"Hi," she said. His idea of a greeting was to bob his head.

"You want breakfast?" Cecilia asked him.

"Nope. On a diet." Lucky didn't have an ounce of flab on him. But Tawny assumed being lighter would give him an advantage at the finals. "Where's Katie?"

"She's getting dressed," Tawny said. "Don't keep her out too long. She needs to stay warm and dry."

"I won't," was all he said.

Cecilia reached up and held his chin. "We're all sorry about what Raylene did. It was a terrible thing."

"You always had her number, Ma." He walked over to the coffeemaker, got a cup, and filled it.

"How is the training going?" Cecilia asked.

"Not good. I'm out of shape and my bones still ache from the drugs."

"I'm sorry, Lucky," Tawny said, knowing how much the finals meant to him.

"You don't have anything to be sorry for. Katie's getting better. That's all I care about."

Still, Tawny understood how much he wanted to win.

"Is there anything we can do to help?" Cecilia stuck a protein bar in his jacket pocket.

"No. Clay's coming over later. I thought I'd take one of the horses around the arena."

Tawny knew that he'd ride bareback and hands-free. She'd seen rodeo bull riders train that way before. It was nothing close to riding a bucking bull, but it helped cowboys find their center of gravity. Staying on a bull required a good deal of core strength. That's why Lucky had been spending an hour a day standing on top of a twelve-pound medicine ball.

"You want me to pick up Katie?" Tawny asked.

"No. I thought she'd want to watch." She probably would, but

Tawny didn't want her out for too long. "Just make sure she doesn't push it, please."

"Tawny, have a little faith."

She had to stop being such a control freak. But Katie's recovery was fragile so soon after the transplant.

"I'll go see what's taking our girl so long." Cecilia left Tawny alone with Lucky.

"You talk to Jake today?" Tawny asked him, wondering whether Raylene would be charged with a crime.

"Nope."

"You cancel with Pete and that attorney?"

"Yep."

She let out an aggravated sigh. "I know you're hurt. But despite me keeping Katie from you all those years, I'm not Raylene. I'll never be Raylene." No, she wouldn't be. Because Raylene had been the one Lucky loved. Never Tawny.

"If I thought you were anything like Raylene, I'd fight for full custody of Katie." He cocked his hip against the kitchen counter and they stood silent until their daughter wandered in. "How's my girl?"

"I ate a whole bowl of cereal and a muffin," Katie said with pride.

"You're getting your appetite back. That's great." He lifted her in the air. "You ready to go?"

"Yep."

Tawny got Katie's jacket and hat from the mudroom. "Put this on, baby. Where's your scarf?"

"I'll get it." Katie trotted off toward the bedroom they were sharing, and Tawny went to follow.

"Tawny," Lucky called to her. "I'll take good care of her."

She had no doubt that he would. Lucky might not have a lot of experience with fatherhood, but he'd taken to it like he'd been with Katie from day one.

On her way to the studio, Tawny let the tears flow until her sobs turned to spasms. She loved him, but he would never love her. Even without Raylene in the picture.

The day passed in a haze. Despite her misery, she finished a pair of boots she'd been toiling over for six months. The client, a musician, had chosen a design of a guitar being engulfed in garish red flames, and Tawny could never work up the enthusiasm to finish them. Finally she packed them in a box and sent off an email to the boots' owner that his order was on its way. Tawny was en route to the post office when Cecilia called.

"Jake and I are on our way to Lucky's," she said. "We thought he could use a pep rally and wanted to see if you'd like to join us."

"I'm in the middle of a project that I need to finish before Vegas." If Katie's doctor signed off, they were all going to watch Lucky compete. Under the circumstances, Tawny would've begged off. But she wasn't ready for Katie to travel without her. Not this soon after the transplant.

"Oh." Cecilia sounded disappointed. "He could really use the support."

Tawny supposed she could go just long enough to pick up Katie. It was already three. Katie should have a nap. "All right. I'll meet you there."

She finished shipping her package, crossed town, and got on the highway—the shortest route to Lucky's ranch. At the top of his driveway there must've been more than a dozen trucks and cars parked. She figured the vehicles belonged to Pat Donnelly's crew and found a spot for her Jeep. As she walked to the arena, she noticed that a good crowd had filled the metal bleachers. Harlee stood on one of the arena railings, taking pictures. Above, in the announcer's box, Noah watched the activity from up high. Griffin Parks sat in the front row with Owen and the rest of the Nugget Mafia. Clay McCreedy was in the ring with Lucky while his two sons and Katie sat on top of the bucking shoots. Even the police chief and Nate Breyer had turned out.

"Why is everyone here?" Tawny asked Harlee, who was loading pictures onto the *Nugget Tribune*'s website from her phone.

Harlee shrugged. "As soon as I started live blogging and posting photos of Lucky, they began showing up." She gazed up at the grandstand, which continued to fill. "Darla's on her way. She just had to close the barbershop. My guess is the only one who won't be here is Raylene Rosser. What a biotch."

"So you heard about that, huh?" Stupid question since there wasn't anything Harlee didn't hear. "It's been rough for Lucky."

"As far as I'm concerned, Raylene did him a big favor." Harlee pretended to shudder. "Even her best friend, Hannah, denounced her in my article."

Lucky's construction crew had stopped to take a break, and workers slowly filtered into the stands. Donna and her husband, Trevor, set up barbecues by the arena and unloaded bags of hamburger patties and buns. It appeared that Lucky's training was turning into a late-afternoon party.

Colin came up behind Harlee and Tawny. "Is he riding a bull yet?"

"Not yet," Harlee said. "I don't think that's in today's program. Lucky said it was too risky this close to the finals."

Thank goodness, Tawny thought to herself and watched as Lucky loped around the arena on the back of a horse, his arms held out to his sides. The only things controlling the mare were his knees. As he went past her he nodded.

Justin, Clay's eldest, helped Katie scramble down from the bucking shoot so she could run over to say hi.

"How you feeling, baby?" Tawny was heartened to see that Katie was still bundled up. She even had on a pair of mittens. Where those had come from, Tawny had no idea.

"Good. I've been sitting with Cody and Justin."

"I saw that. Did your dad feed you?"

"Soup in his trailer. And we picked out a spot for his house." She pointed up a hill that was too high to see anything. "He says he has to buy it first."

Tawny looked at Colin, who she assumed had been in on the house talks.

"It's property that doesn't belong to him," Colin said. "But if he can buy it, the views will be fantastic. He wants to do something like our house." He smiled at Harlee. The man was clearly smitten with his wife.

"Sounds beautiful." Tawny had only been to Colin and Harlee's once, but the place was gorgeous. Colin had built it with his brother-in-law.

Talk of Lucky's plans for a house depressed her. How long until he started his own family there?

People had started lining up for Donna and Trevor's burgers. Tawny told Harlee and Colin that she wanted to get Katie something to eat and she and her daughter headed over to the barbecues.

"My goodness, Donna. You guys went all out."

Donna handed Katie and Tawny plates with burgers and chips. "We saw Harlee's blog, heard Owen and the Mafia were headed over, figured it was just a matter of time before the whole town showed up, and decided to make a fiesta out of it." Donna bent over to whisper in Tawny's ear. "I never did like those Rossers. They were always snooty, if you ask me."

It seemed that the impromptu party wasn't just about celebrating the local celebrity bull rider. The town wanted to stick it to the Rossers. Nugget didn't mind infighting—in fact, it thrived on it—but the townsfolk drew the line when the battle got as vicious as false murder accusations. And Lucky was their hero—a resident who had made a big name for himself but never forgotten where he came from.

"Well, here's the man of the hour," Donna said, and Tawny turned around to find Lucky striding their way.

Over his jeans and plaid shirt, he had on suede chaps and a down vest with the PBR logo. Tawny's stomach fluttered. He tossed Katie a big grin and gave Tawny a once-over but didn't say anything.

A couple of kids surrounded him to ask for autographs, and Katie left her half-eaten burger with Tawny to go stand by him. He absently put his arm around Katie, and the sight of them together made Tawny's eyes brim with tears. She couldn't help but grab for her phone and snap a picture.

"I want a copy of that." Cecilia came up behind Tawny. "I hope you don't have plans tonight."

"I don't," Tawny said too quickly, and wished she'd made up something. In a short time, she'd become too attached to the illusion of family.

"Good." Cecilia hugged her. "Be home at around six. We have a lot to celebrate . . . and Jake has something to tell everyone."

From the corner of her eye, Tawny caught Lucky watching them. She made her way through the small crowd that had come to wish Lucky well in the finals. "You have a minute?"

Lucky nodded, excused himself from the group, and in a defensive voice said, "Katie's fine. I've taken good care of her."

"I know. Where did you get the mittens?"

"I had to stop off at Farm Supply for some feed. I got her wool socks too."

Right then and there she wanted to tell him how much she loved him. How she had always loved him. "I plan to move Katie and me back home tomorrow. Tonight, though, your mother and Jake are holding some sort of celebration at the house. Cecilia wants me there. Is that a problem for you?"

"You're the mother of my daughter. Wherever Katie is, you're always welcome."

Except for his heart. "All right." She started to walk away.

"You're still coming to Vegas, right?"

"As long as Katie's doctor says it's okay." They had an appointment in two days.

"Hang on a sec." He caught up with her. "Why are you moving out of my mom's?"

"I wasn't planning to stay there forever, just until Katie felt better." They both watched Katie horsing around with a group of kids. Cody McCreedy laughed at something she said. "Soon, God willing, she'll go back to school. It's time for us to be normal again."

He nodded. "I'm working with Colin on my house."

"He told me. You're planning to buy more property?"

"Ten acres on the top of the hill. It'll be private from the cowboy camp. Clay knows the owners. I'm just waiting to hear if they've accepted my offer."

"I'm sure it'll be lovely. And, Lucky, I am truly sorry about Raylene."

He must've sensed her thoughts because he blurted, "The house was never meant for Raylene and me. Even before she set me up, even before I'd broken up with her, I'd fallen out of love with her . . . It was when I started spending time with you."

Lucky walked away, leaving Tawny to puzzle over the meaning of that statement. *It was when I started spending time with you.*

Chapter 24

"You panicking?" Rhys asked Jake.

They'd come back to the station after watching Lucky and eating a few burgers, compliments of the Thurstons. A few loose ends still needed to be tied up on the Rosser case. The DA had given Raylene immunity in exchange for becoming a prosecution witness. If Ray decided to take the case to trial, Raylene would have to testify that her father had coerced her into making Lucky the fall guy. Jake doubted it would come to that. More than likely Ray would plead out in exchange for whatever deal he could get.

"Nah, I've been down this road before," Jake said, but he was nervous as hell.

"You guys doing a big dinner?"

"You know Cecilia. She says she's going simple, but I'd be willing to guess that at the last minute she'll put together a feast. My daughters are flying into Reno." Jake looked at the time. "In fact the shuttle service should be dropping them off anytime. I better get moving."

"Good luck."

"Thanks." Jake grabbed his jacket and scarf and headed out.

His daughters were already at Cecilia's by the time Jake got there. He found them in the kitchen, helping Cecilia with the meal. The five of them jumped him with hugs and kisses. Cecilia stood back, her smile so bright it lit up the room. God, he loved her.

"Where's your brood?" Jake asked.

"Lucky is on his way. Tawny and Katie are in the other room getting ready. They're going home tomorrow." Cecilia frowned.

"Birds gotta fly, sweetheart."

"I just so enjoyed having them."

"Katie will come over after school and on weekends. They just live down the street."

"You're right." Cecilia kissed Jake.

"You still haven't told them?" Jake's girls, who were busy setting the table, had known the minute he'd asked them to drop whatever they were doing and make the last-minute trip to Nugget.

"No," Cecilia said. "With everything . . . well, it's been difficult. I'm sure they have an inkling."

Lucky came through the back door and blinked a few times when he saw all of Jake's daughters. "I wasn't expecting a full house. Wow. Good to see you all."

More hugs were exchanged, and Jake got the impression that Lucky didn't have a clue. He wondered how Cecilia's son would take the news, not that it would change anything.

At the sound of her father, Katie burst into the kitchen. "You're finally here."

"You got your pink dress on," Lucky said, and scooped Katie up into his arms. "Where's your mama?"

"I'm here," Tawny said, and immediately dove into helping with getting the food on the table.

They sat to eat and everyone began talking at once. The girls all wanted to know about the finals. None of them knew much about bull riding, yet they'd gotten caught up in the excitement. Lucky said he'd reserve a box if they wanted to come.

"What's Noah doing?" Tawny asked.

"He said he'd be spending the night organizing his story," Lucky said. "He's got no shortage of material, that's for sure."

Jake sincerely hoped that the reporter stuck to the positive stuff and left the Rossers out of the piece. "Looks like Pat is making good headway on the ranch. I had a look around while we were out there today, and things are shaping up."

"If the weather holds, he thinks they can finish by spring and start on the house," Lucky said.

He talked awhile about his plans for a two-story log cabin up on the hill where Jake and Rhys had spent hours doing surveillance. Jake could certainly attest to the view. A person could see clear to the Nevada desert from there.

As they came toward the end of the meal, Jake cleared his throat and got to his feet. "I have an announcement to make."

A hush fell over the room.

"It's been a tough couple of months. We feel blessed to have Katie here at the table, looking hale and hearty." Jake reached out and mussed Katie's hair. "And I know I can speak for all of us when I say thank goodness that Lucky's problems are behind us. Next week, in Las Vegas, we'll be rooting for you." Jake tipped his wineglass toward Lucky. "No matter what happens, though, you'll always be a world champion."

Everyone at the table applauded.

"I'm not finished yet." Jake chuckled. "In other news, Cecilia and I have decided to make us official. We're getting married."

Everyone erupted in hoots and hollers. Across the table, Jake made eye contact with Lucky, who gave an affirmative nod and grinned. Sarah and Janny tapped their glasses with their forks. That was Jake's cue to kiss Cecilia. Happy to oblige, he pulled her out of her seat and gave her a sloppy smooch. Lucky was next to get to his feet.

"Whoa," he said, and cast his eyes at Tawny. "I guess I should've seen this coming—actually, someone told me it was. Still, you've surprised the hell out of me and I'm a little lost for words. All I've ever wanted for my mama was happiness, and, Jake, you make her happy. Here's to the both of you." He held his glass up and clinked it with the person's next to him until everyone had a chance to do the same.

Jake saw Tawny smile at Lucky in what he presumed was *I told you so*. After the toast everyone started shouting questions in unison. "Have you set a date?" "Where will the wedding be?" "Is there a ring?"

Cecilia held up her finger and let her diamond wink under the chandelier light. "We were hoping to do it on Valentine's Day in Lucky's barn." It was the only finished building on the property thanks to Nate and Samantha Breyer, who'd seen to the renovations themselves because they'd held their own reception there.

"Nothing fancy," Cecilia continued. "We just want all our friends and family."

Jake hadn't thought it possible that he would be standing at the head of Cecilia's dining room table, planning a lifetime with her.

Tomorrow, an announcement would run in the *Nugget Tribune*. But tonight, they'd savor their future with just family.

And this time, Jake would get it right.

*   *   *

Clay flew them into the Palo Alto Airport and they took a cab to Dr. Laurence's office. It was just one of Katie's post-transplant checkups, yet each one filled Tawny with dread. Doctors had warned her that the infusion was not a sure thing. Any number of problems could still occur: fever, vomiting, and complete loss of appetite. The key was whether her bone marrow would go back to producing healthy blood cells.

Katie still had the catheter in her chest, where it would remain for months. Today, the big question would be whether Katie was healthy enough to travel to Las Vegas to watch Lucky in the finals.

"You okay?" Lucky asked Tawny as they shuffled into the doctor's waiting room. Although he'd been keeping his distance, he could read her like a book. These appointments were hell on her, and he made sure to be as attentive as possible. He was a caring person. But Tawny would be a fool to think it was anything more than Lucky just being sensitive.

"Yep," she answered, not wanting Katie, who viewed these weekly visits as an opportunity to fly in Clay's private plane and eat in a nice restaurant, to see how nervous she was. But when Katie found a quiet corner away from them to thumb through a kid's magazine, Tawny squeezed Lucky's hand for moral support. He'd made it clear that she shouldn't become dependent on him, but today she gave herself a pass. She needed the boost.

"You nervous about next week?" she asked, trying to focus on something other than doctors and cancer.

"Nope. Whatever happens, happens. We should probably talk about Christmas soon."

"What about Christmas?" She had always made as much as she could out of the holiday. But with Katie sick, Tawny had never gone all out with a big tree or elaborate dinner. They weren't religious, so no church. Just a few presents for Katie.

Lucky shrugged. "Like what gifts you're getting her so we don't duplicate. My mom wants us for Christmas Eve, Christmas morning, and Christmas dinner. I wanted to make sure that was okay with you . . . that you didn't have your own traditions."

Tawny didn't know who "us" was and didn't want to be the fifth wheel at the Rodriguezes. "Let's talk about it later, okay?"

"Sure," Lucky said. "No pressure."

A nurse eventually called them back to an exam room and Dr. Laurence asked the usual questions and took the usual tests, including Katie's temperature and a sample of blood to check on her numbers.

"So you want to take her to Vegas, huh?" Dr. Laurence knew Lucky desperately wanted his daughter at the finals. "Of course, I'll have to wait for the results of this." He held Katie's vial of blood and let out a breath. "The problem with crowded places is the chance of infection."

"We'll have a box at the Thomas and Mack Center," Lucky said.

"You want to go, Katie?" Dr. Laurence listened to her chest with a stethoscope.

"More than anything in the world," she said with a breathlessness that made Tawny laugh.

"You'll take her back to the hotel room right after Lucky's rides?" Dr. Laurence was aware that it was a five-day event.

"Yes," Tawny said. "We'll limit her audience time as much as possible."

"No strolling around the casinos either. Stick to room service. There's so much cigarette smoke in those places I don't know how people stand it. And keep her warm. It's cold in the desert this time of year."

The finals were usually held in October, but for some reason had been moved to December this year. The competition was scheduled to follow the National Finals Rodeo, which was also held at the Thomas and Mack Center.

"I will do all of the above," Tawny promised.

"I'm very pleased with Katie's recovery," the doctor said. "Her cell counts have been steadily rising and her immunity functions seem to be rebounding. She's really made an astounding bounce back. In my experience, when a patient is this robust after a blood stem cell transplant . . . well, it's too soon to say for sure, but fingers crossed, we may have licked the leukemia."

Tawny heard the cry before she realized that it had come from her. Her eyes welled up and everyone turned to look at her. "Excuse me." She rushed out of the exam room, found the bathroom, sat on the toilet seat, and broke down.

"Hey," Lucky called through the door, and she let him in.

"Sorry. It's just . . . emotional."

"I get it." He brushed her hair away from her face and held her.

"You should go back to Katie so she won't worry."

"I will in a minute." He just continued to hold her, rubbing little circles on her back, while she let out four years of the worst fear a mother could carry.

"I've never heard Dr. Laurence sound this optimistic before," she said between sobs. "It's not that he was the voice of doom, but to say we may have licked the cancer . . . it's just the best news." And she started to bawl all over again.

"It's good, Tawny. Katie's getting better because of you. You saved her."

Tawny pushed out of his arms. "No, Lucky. It was your stem cells. You saved her. My God, if it hadn't been for you . . ." She wept so hard her whole body shook from it.

"Shush." He pulled her against him and rocked her like a baby until she stopped crying. Then he dried her eyes with his hands. "Let's get our daughter and go home."

A week later they flew to Las Vegas—this time on a commercial flight, first class. Lucky thought it would be better for Katie. Cecilia sat next to Tawny, looking at bridal magazines.

Cecilia sighed. "These dresses are made for twenty-year-olds."

"You could pull off any of them," Tawny said. "What are you doing for shoes? Because I'd love to make you a pair of wedding boots."

Cecilia squealed with delight. "I would love that. Do you have time, though?"

"I'll make time." Tawny was nearly finished with Brady's boots. "But pick out your dress first so we know the style."

Cecilia put her hand on Tawny's arm. "Your time will be here soon. You'll see, Lucky will come around."

"It's not like that with us, Cecilia."

Cecilia made a face. "*Mija*, who are you trying to fool? My son hasn't been the same since you came into his life."

At McCarran International, they caught a shuttle to their hotel. This time Lucky had gotten them separate rooms, not a suite. Tawny unpacked her and Katie's suitcases and was considering taking a bath when there was a knock. She opened the door to find Noah standing in the hallway.

"Hi," she said. "When did you get here?"

"A few hours ago. I had to check in at the press room. Your friend Harlee's down there, by the way." Lucky had worked it out so that the *Nugget Tribune* would get a press credential. If the whole town couldn't come to the Professional Bull Riders Built Ford Tough World Finals, then by golly, Harlee would bring it to them.

"The next few days will be crazy for me," Noah said. "Besides working on Lucky's piece, the magazine has me doing live coverage of the event for its website. So I just wanted to tell you what a pleasure it was meeting you and thank you for letting me intrude on your family during a particularly trying time."

"You're welcome." She couldn't help asking, "Do you think you'll put the whole Rosser ordeal in the story?"

"I don't want to commit to anything, Tawny. Stories have minds of their own and I don't know where this one will take me. What I do know is that the transplant and the cowboy camp will take center stage."

"Thanks for being honest." Tawny said her goodbyes and went back inside.

She had just enough time to bathe and get her and Katie dressed before dinner and the opening ceremonies. Another knock came and she was tempted to ignore it. Instead, she looked through the peephole, saw it was Lucky, and opened the door.

"Aren't you supposed to be getting ready?"

"I'm ready," he said, and came in.

Katie held up her outfit. "What do you think?"

Lucky gave her a thumbs-up and told her to hurry and get dressed. At this rate there was no bath in Tawny's future.

"I've got to skip dinner," he said. "They're doing a press thing and a bunch of other garbage I've got to attend."

"I understand," Tawny said. "Go do your thing. We'll be in the box watching you."

"Okay." He started to go, but stopped to say, "Thanks for coming. It means a lot to me."

"Of course." Tawny didn't know what else to say. *Why can't you love me the way you loved Raylene?*

That night, after all the pomp and circumstance—more fireworks than the Fourth of July—Lucky managed to cover his bull for eight seconds, but his score put him in fourth place. Not exactly a confidence booster for a man who was already flagging. He tried to stay upbeat even though he'd lost a lot of that signature Lucky swagger.

The next night wasn't much better, though he'd made it to the bell. By the fifth night, despite mediocre scores, he'd succeeded in making it to the sixth and final round. The playing field had been whittled down from thirty-five riders to fifteen. Lucky was somewhere in the middle. But if he could pull off a magical score in this round, and some of the other top riders got bucked off, he still had a shot at winning it all—the Built Ford Tough event and the world championship. The latter was based on the rider's score from the entire season.

Before the night's competition started, Lucky came to Tawny's room. "Where's Katie?"

"Your mom and Jake took her over to the arena to beat the crowds." Tawny could feel the tension ebbing through his entire body. He wanted to win and he wanted it badly. "Come in for a second, I have something for you."

She handed him a box and watched him pop off the lid. For a few seconds he just stared at the boots inside, a mixture of pleasure and confusion lighting his face. Then he gingerly removed one for a closer inspection, like he couldn't believe it was the same boot from her studio.

"I thought you made these for someone else."

She shrugged, embarrassed. "I made them for you after you won your first National Finals Rodeo."

"That was seven years ago." Before he'd started riding for the PBR. He cocked his head in question. "I don't understand. Why did you say they belonged to someone else?"

She evaded the question. "I thought maybe they'd bring you luck tonight."

"How did you even know my size?" He kept looking at the boots like they were a puzzle to him.

"You gave the ones you wore for your NFR championship to Cecilia to donate to the annual Nugget High Rodeo Team fund-raiser. I bought them."

He scrubbed his hand through his hair, still looking confused. "Why?"

"So I'd know your size."

"I mean, why did you go to so much trouble to make me boots

when I didn't even return your emails? Then when I saw the boots and said I wanted them, you lied. It doesn't make sense."

Nothing about my feelings for you makes sense. "I'd originally planned to send them to you anonymously. A gift to an old friend. If you don't want them—"

"Hell yeah, I want them." He pried off his old boots. "I wanted them the minute I saw them. I still don't get why you told me they were for someone else." Lucky shook his head in bafflement, put them on, walked across the floor a few times, and did a couple of squats. "They feel great. But—" He stopped when he saw the bedside clock. "Shit. I've gotta run. You have a ride to Thomas and Mack, right?" He started backing out of the room. The opening ceremony was in less than twenty minutes.

"I'll take the shuttle over," she said.

"I'll see you there, then." He looked down at his feet with that mystified expression still on his face. "And, Tawny, thanks for the boots."

The boots were nothing. She gave lots of people boots. But as he jogged down the hall to catch the elevator, she wondered if she'd given away too much of herself.

Chapter 25

Lucky kept looking down at his feet. Tawny bewildered him. Why would she go to so much trouble to make him a pair of boots and then keep them from him? Even more bizarre was why she'd made them in the first place.

A gift to an old friend, she'd said.

They might've known each other their whole lives, but they weren't exactly what Lucky would've called friends. Except for that night in the park, they'd barely said two words to each other. His mother had said Tawny used to follow him around like a lamb when they were kids, but Lucky had no recollection of it.

The only real memory he had of Tawny all those years ago was that one night. She'd been his shoulder to cry on and had been the one to suggest riding the rodeo circuit so he could someday make it into the PBR. And in thanks, he'd knocked her up and had forgotten her existence altogether.

Yet she'd still made him the boots. Went to the trouble of buying his old ones at a charity auction to get the size right.

Lucky made it into the arena just in time to have his name called out for the introductions and to announce which bull he'd drafted. Tonight he chose Whole Lotta Shaking. He'd wanted Moocho Dinero, a bull so rank that only a few had managed to ride him. The kind of bull that if he didn't kill you, would win you high scores. But Luiz, the Brazilian rider in first place, had drafted Moocho.

Riders were scored based on their form, their position on the bull, and how much they spurred during their eight-second ride. The ranker the bull, the higher the score. Lucky had ridden Whole Lotta Shaking before, and while he was a spinner, he was no match for Moocho Dinero.

And Lucky would need the best ride of his life to win.

Although he'd hoped to make history tonight, he supposed he should be happy for getting as far as he had. The first five rounds, he'd left the arena feeling dead on his feet. The only thing keeping him going was Tawny. He wanted to win it for her, since the PBR had been her idea in the first place. A dream that had changed his life.

A few times during the week, while dropping down into the chute, he'd glance at her front-row box and wait for her to look his way. Her lips would curve up and her face would flush . . . And that was all the encouragement he needed.

Tonight, he was at the bottom of the lineup, so he stood by the back pens with a few other cowboys, stretching. Squats for the hamstrings and quads. Every so often he'd move closer to the chutes to check out the scoreboard and gaze over at the Rodriguez box. Tawny had finally gotten there. Her hair was down and she wore a pretty red sweater. God, she was beautiful. Katie sat next to her, watching the spectacle.

"Nice boots," Tuff Johnson said. He was in third place and could easily take the competition. All he needed was for Luiz to get bucked off and the cowboy in second place to get a so-so score.

"Thanks. My girl made them." Lucky didn't know why he'd said that. Tawny wasn't his girl.

"No kidding." Tuff lifted Lucky's pant leg to get a better look at the design. "You see these?" he called to Clint Rafter, one of the event's announcers.

"Nice," Clint said. "Where'd you get 'em?"

"My girl, Tawny Wade, professional boot-maker, Nugget, California." He knew Clint would talk about the boots during Lucky's ride. Like every other sport, the announcers were always hungry for personal nuggets to add color to their commentary. Good. This was definitely the crowd for drumming up publicity. Tawny deserved it. Her boots were works of art.

Lucky glanced over at the box again. Tawny was laughing at something Jake said. He liked when she laughed. She caught him watching her and gave a little wave. He crooked his finger at her to come over to where he was standing. She motioned that she didn't have a pass. He crooked his finger again.

She made it as far as security. Lucky stepped in and told the arena staff that she was with him.

"What's wrong?" she asked.

"Nothing. I just wanted to know what you were laughing about."

"You called me over here to ask me what I was laughing about?"

"And to see you." He grinned. "Why'd you make me the boots, Tawny? Did you make them for the same reason you're making Brady boots?"

She absently straightened the collar of his protective vest. "No. On yours I put a ridge on the heels for your spurs."

"That's not what I meant, and you know it."

"Don't you need to bounce up and down or something?" A lot of riders warmed up that way just before they climbed into the chute.

The chute boss waved Lucky over. "Gotta go," Lucky said.

"Lucky—" Tawny started, then seemed to reconsider what she wanted to say. "Just don't kill yourself." She headed back to the box and Lucky headed to his chute.

There were only four of them left. Six of the fifteen had been buck-offs and one had been disqualified for touching the bull with his arm during the ride. The other two had scored in the eighties, still leaving the field wide open.

Luiz was up next. He tossed his bull rope to the gate man, who threaded it underneath Moocho Dinero's chest. Luiz mounted the bull and nodded his head. The bull went charging out of the gate as the crowd roared and the music blared. Lucky watched, holding his breath. His instincts told him that Luiz would cover his bull the full eight seconds, and so far it was a hell of a ride.

He gazed over at the Rodriguez box and even from a distance could see Tawny frowning. The buzzer went off and Luiz dismounted as fast as he could while the bullfighters distracted Moocho. Lucky stared up at the board. A score of 89.5 flashed, and Lucky's stomach dropped.

Tuff was up next. His scores had been the best in the first four rounds, but suffered when he got bucked off in the fifth and freight-trained—run over—by the bull, landing in the emergency room with a broken jaw. Lucky could tell he was hurting.

"Good luck, Tuff," Lucky called to the cowboy as he mounted up.

The gate opened and the crowd went crazy. Everyone loved an under-dog. His bull started spinning and then changed directions. That's when Tuff went down the well, hanging over the side of the bull. The bullfight-ers sped out, fearing that Tuff would get tangled up in the bull rope, dragged, and trampled. But Tuff managed to free himself and got as far away from that rank son-of-a-gun as fast as he could. No score for Tuff. But the crowd cheered him anyway.

The fourth-place cowboy was instantly disqualified for a slap. His free hand—not the one used to hold on to the bull rope—grazed the side of the animal. That left Lucky.

He looked up at the board again, did a few quick calculations in his head: 95.5. That's what he needed to win it all. To make history. It was pretty much like needing a miracle.

Lucky handed his bull rope to the gate man while the stock contractor adjusted Whole Lotta Shaking's flank strap. He climbed into the chute and put on his glove. After his wreck in Billings, Lucky had vowed to wear a helmet and face mask. But not tonight, he decided. He didn't want the extra weight. Still woozy from the transfusion, he didn't want anything encumbering his vision either.

From the chute he could see Katie standing at the railing for a bird's-eye view; and Tawny, who probably didn't want to block the people behind her, straining from her seat to see him better. He looked down at his boots as he mounted up and gripped the bull rope.

"For luck," he said out loud and nodded to the gate man to let 'er rip.

Whole Lotta Shaking leapt out of the gate, spinning, bucking, and jumping. The bull shook Lucky so hard that he didn't know if he'd temporarily blacked out. That's when everything started to move in slow motion. Even as the bull violently bucked in one direction, then briskly switched to another, Lucky felt like he was floating on air. And then it struck him like a bull's-eye. He loved Tawny. He loved everything about her.

The way she fretted over Katie . . . over him. Hell, even her damned independence had started to grow on him. The woman took care of business . . . the people she loved. But did she love him?

In the hazy background, he heard music blaring and splinters of Clint's commentary. It was like being underwater and grabbing bits and pieces of a conversation each time he came up for air. "Custom made . . . Tawny Wade . . . Nugget, California . . . Lucky's hometown."

He tried to find her in the crowd, but Whole Lotta Shaking kept changing course. He looked down at his boots and saw himself spurring the bull. Until that moment he couldn't recall doing it. It was like he was on a cloud.

Somewhere in the distance he heard a buzzer go off, saw people come to their feet, and watched as their hands went up in the air. The fog cleared, and Lucky used his free hand to release his riding hand from the rope, then flung himself off, as far away from the bull as he could get.

Every spectator in the Thomas and Mack Center was standing, watching the instant replay on the Jumbotron. The cheers were so loud he could barely hear himself think. All he wanted to do was find Tawny. He would've missed his score if the crowd hadn't sent up a roar of approval. Ninety-seven flashed on the board.

Before Lucky could get to Tawny, he got caught up in a swell of cowboys dumping water over his head. A few of them hoisted him up on their shoulders and carried him around to thunderous applause.

Someone from the PBR brought Katie, his mom, and Jake into the arena, but he didn't see Tawny anywhere. Amid all the hoopla he couldn't ask where she was. Cameras flashed in his eyes, reporters stuck microphones in his face, while officials presented him with his belt buckle and world champion cup. He'd done this three times before, knew the routine, but somehow it seemed overwhelming. Like he'd lost something critical.

"Where's Tawny?" he managed to whisper in his mother's ear.

She pointed to the box where a lone figure, with tickertape in her hair, stood cheering. "She wouldn't come down with us. Said she wasn't family. With everything happening so fast, I didn't have time to drag her."

He tried to pull away to get to her, but a group of reporters swarmed him. He nudged his mother to take Katie back to the room. "I don't want her to get sick."

An hour later he fended off a straggling TV reporter and made a quick getaway. When he got back to the hotel he found everyone in his mother's room. "What are you all doing in here?" he asked, worried that maybe Katie had had a relapse.

Jake popped a bottle of champagne and everyone shouted congratulations. Katie threw herself at him.

"I'm so glad you won, Daddy." He kissed her on the top of her head.

"Where's your big trophy?" Cecilia asked.

"Pete got it for me, along with my check." A million bucks.

Jake passed around glasses of champagne and everyone toasted

Lucky. Tawny smiled but stood in the background, acting like the proverbial outsider.

Lucky drained his bubbly and grabbed Tawny's hand. "You mind if I borrow her for a minute?"

Before anyone could answer, he pushed Tawny out the door, made a beeline for his room, jabbed the card key in the door, and corralled her.

"What's going—?"

Before she could finish, he smothered her mouth with a kiss. "Why'd you make me the boots?"

"Seriously?" She tried to pull away, but he boxed her in against the wall. "I make lots of people boots."

"Do you keep them for seven years?"

"Oh, for God's sake, I had a silly crush on you. Big whoop."

"How 'bout now, Tawny? Do you have a crush on me now?" He didn't wait for her to answer. "Why didn't you come into the arena with everyone?"

"I didn't belong. It was for family. And I kept thinking that maybe a part of you wished Raylene was there."

"No, Tawny. Ever since you pushed your way into my trailer, it's only been you. I'm in love with you."

She jerked her head up. "Did that bull gore your brains and make you crazy?"

"Crazy in love with you." His lips curved up. "So I guess I owe that bull."

She had tears in her eyes. "I thought you couldn't forgive me for keeping Katie from you."

"Can you forgive me for never contacting you after that night? For never making sure you were all right? Because if you can, so can I."

A funny sound came out of her throat and he wrapped his arms around her. "Do you have something you want to tell me?"

"I love you, Lucky." It was a whisper.

"I can't hear you." He held her out from him so that he could look into her green eyes when she said it.

"I love you, Lucky."

Epilogue

"Not again," Lucky said. "You've read it ten times. I can practically recite the damn article."

"But it's so good." Tawny had been so nervous about the *Sports Illustrated* story that she couldn't believe how well it had turned out. Everyone in Nugget was talking about the piece. "I love this picture of you on Whole Lotta Shaking."

"Noah said he could get us a copy. I'll frame it for you. Now put the magazine away and come back to bed." It wasn't even seven yet and she was getting ready for the day.

Lucky had moved in with Tawny and Katie while their house was being built. They'd closed escrow on the hilltop property two weeks ago and had gotten rid of the rusted Airstream trailer. Once the city signed off on their architectural plans, Pat and Colin would break ground. Lucky had included a separate building for Tawny's new studio, which would not only have its own bathroom and kitchenette, but a small shop where she could sell sample boots and various other leather items to the cowboy-camp guests.

The outbuildings and dormitories were almost finished. And Pat and his crew had added a warren of corrals and barns. Soon, they'd start fixing up the old arena. Barring any unforeseeable obstacles, Lucky's cowboy camp would be ready to open by spring. Many of his PBR sponsors wanted in on the action, offering to hook Lucky up with gear if he'd continue to promote their equipment.

"Come on." Lucky held his arms out.

"I can't," Tawny said. "I have to finish your mother's boots. The wedding will be here before you know it."

"What about our wedding?"

"What about it? I don't recall a certain cowboy proposing."

"Propose?" His mouth slid up. "Ah, come on. We have a nine-year-old, I want more kids, and no one could love you better than I do. So it's implied. We're getting hitched. Just pick a day."

"Implied?" Tawny looked down her nose at him. "I don't think so."

He winked. "You want me to get down on one knee?"

"Yes. And a ring would be good too. And flowers. And maybe some candy."

He laughed, but she knew he already had a plan. Harlee had let it slip that Lucky had put down a deposit on the Ponderosa for a big surprise engagement party. Well, it was no longer a surprise. But she could pretend.

"Come on," Lucky said. "We finally get a little time to ourselves."

Dr. Laurence had given Katie the thumbs-up to go back to school. Her recent tests showed that her blood counts were increasing and the doctors said her prognosis was fantastic. In fact, Dr. Laurence continued to marvel at her recovery. Still, Tawny and Lucky watched Katie like a hawk. Tawny didn't think she would ever stop feeling her daughter's head or looking for bruises or other signs that the leukemia was back. That was just being a parent.

"I have to make boots!" Tawny said. "You may be temporarily retired, but I still have a job."

"There might be a ring under here." He lifted the blanket ever so slightly and she dove into the bed, giggling like a schoolgirl.

The last month since the world finals had been the best of her life. The entire town had welcomed Lucky home with a parade and pancake breakfast at the community center. Then they'd celebrated Christmas with the biggest tree Tawny had ever seen and an obscene amount of presents.

Even news about the shooting and drug raid—there had been no more cattle thefts in the county—had died down. The Rossers put their ranch on the market to pay for Ray's legal bills. According to Owen, he was getting Gloria Allred to defend him. Tawny highly doubted it, but it was a good story anyway. The word on Raylene was that she'd gone back to Butch, who'd been dumped by her best friend. Sort of predictable, Tawny thought. Before leaving, Raylene met with Lucky one last time and apologized for what she'd done to him—now and ten years ago. She did seem sincerely sorry. And Lucky seemed totally immune to her.

Cecilia had included Tawny in all the wedding plans and Jake's daughters had come up a couple of times to help. Having a big extended family was like a dream come true.

"You find anything yet?" Lucky asked, holding her hands and gliding them under the covers and down his chest. "I suggest you really feel around down there. Use both hands, now."

Tawny pretended to play along, running her fingers through his chest hair. As she worked her way down, she felt something velvety and enticing.

"Help yourself," he said, a playful smile on his lips.

She pulled out a box, flipped the lid open, saw the diamond, and shrieked in delight.

Please turn the page for an exciting sneak peek of
Stacy Finz's newest Nugget romance
BORROWING TROUBLE
coming in February 2016!

Chapter 1

Sloane McBride didn't know what to make of Chief Shepard. He was young for the top cop of a police department—somewhere in his thirties if she had to guess. Good looking and cocky. Not a good mixture for a boss in her experience.

The good-looking ones tended to have roaming hands and the cocky ones tended to be spineless.

Of course she'd been jaded by her experience at LAPD. Not by the work. She'd loved being a homicide investigator in the gritty city. Her father and brothers liked to tease her that Los Angeles—filled with palm trees, swimming pools and movie stars—was amateur night compared to the South Side of Chicago. But she'd seen the devil in the City of Angels.

This place, Nugget, was nothing like it. Serene as the surrounding Sierra Nevada mountains. The place even had one of those old-time burger drive throughs and the citizens actually knew their neighbors. It was the epitome of Small Town, USA. Although a few months ago, there'd been a murder and a drug bust that rivaled some of the gangland slayings down south. So maybe she could do good work here.

"We're a team." The chief continued spewing platitudes about the department, trying to sell her on the job. She knew her former LAPD co-worker, Jake Stryker, had told Rhys Shepard about her difficulties in Los Angeles. The chief had offered her the job anyway. "We've got each other's backs here."

Yeah, yeah. That's the way it was supposed to be at LAPD. What a joke.

The dispatcher—Sloane thought her name was Connie—lightly tapped on the glass door, then barged in. "Maddy is on the phone. She said you're not answering your cell."

The chief immediately picked up his line. "Everything okay? . . . Sure, sugar, that'll work. But I'm in the middle of an interview right now. Can I call you back?" He smiled over something she said and hung up. "Sorry about that. My wife."

Connie still loitered in the chief's office, checking Sloane over. "You taking the job? It would be good to get some estrogen in this place."

The chief shot the dispatcher a look.

"What? I'm just saying." The dispatcher turned to Sloane. "When you're done in here come find me. I'll give you the real skinny."

After Connie left, shutting the door behind her, Chief Shepard apologized. "We're a little loose around here. But we're a good department. Before I came back from Houston the town contracted with the Plumas County Sheriff out of Quincy. That's more than a half-hour away. Folks here are real appreciative to have us."

The man didn't have to push so hard. So far, this was Sloane's best option since the larger departments around the state wouldn't touch her with a ten-foot pole. The good-old boy's network at LAPD had made sure of that. But here she had Jake advocating for her, and if she had to guess, Nugget PD was hard-up for officer candidates. The rural railroad town, four hours north of San Francisco, was way off the beaten path. It wouldn't have appealed to Sloane if she didn't need the job so badly.

At least it was a pretty place—lots of trees, rivers and lakes—and since she'd originally come from Chicago, the cold and snow didn't scare her. She'd make the best of it until the heat was off her and she could find something better.

"How is the rental market around here?" she asked.

Chief Shepard lifted his shoulders. "Not the best, I'm afraid. A lot of rental cabins that aren't really fit for year-round living. There are lots of homes for sale in Sierra Heights, our only gated community. But they'll run you close to a mil. Griffin Parks, the seller, might be willing to rent you one, but we're talking big bucks. I own a duplex on Donner Road. One of the apartments is vacant. I don't know how you'd feel about me being your boss and your landlord. But it's cheap and clean. I'll give you the key and directions. You could drive up and have a look at it. If you're not interested, you could swing by Sierra Heights. See if you can make a deal."

A half hour later she chugged up a craggy road in her Rav4. Good thing it was four-wheel drive. Although people she'd talked to said the winter so far had been mild, the place typically got sixty inches of snow a year. And it was only January.

She hadn't wanted to offend Chief Shepard so she'd agreed to look at his duplex. But after what she'd gone through in LA, Sloane didn't want her private life overlapping with her professional one. She'd just make an excuse why the apartment wouldn't work and try to find something else.

At the top of the hill she nosed down the driveway, parked on a well-maintained pad next to an old van, and got out to take a look around. The duplex was nothing fancy from the outside, just a single-level rectangular box made of wood shingles with two apartment doors and a nice front porch. On one side sat a pine-log rocking chair and a matching swing. Cozy. The view included downtown Nugget, which up close wasn't much, but from this height looked like a Christmas card with the snowy Sierra mountain range looming in the background. She had to admit that it was way more picturesque than the glimpse of the bougainvillea-covered cinder-block wall she got from her Echo Park apartment window. Lots of pine trees and a river on the other side of the railroad tracks.

In her jacket pocket she found the key and climbed the porch stairs. One of the doors creaked open and a man came outside.

"You Sloane McBride?"

She took a step back. The man had startled her for a second.

"Rhys said you were coming over to look at the place." He stifled a yawn, and from his smooshed hair she got the impression that he'd been taking a nap.

"I'm Sloane. You must be Brady." The chief had mentioned the tenant, something about him being a chef at the hotel where Sloane was staying. Given that he wore a pair of baggy black-and-white-striped pants and a chef's jacket, Sloane thought this had to be him.

"You don't smoke, do you?" he asked. "The duplex shares the same ventilation system."

She blinked up at him. "No." And she wasn't taking the place, so it didn't matter.

"Good. I've got to get back to work." He headed to the van and opened the door.

"Hang on a sec," she called and jogged over to him. "Have you lived in Nugget long?"

"Since summer. Why?"

He had about six inches on her so she had to look up. "I'm just trying to get a feel for the place."

He gazed at his watch. "I've got about fifteen minutes. What do you want to know?"

She shrugged. "Anything you can tell me."

He smiled and she noticed he was nice looking. Really nice looking. Brown hair, hazel eyes, and a day's worth of stubble on his chin. She hadn't missed his Southern accent, either. She was a sucker for a Southern accent. Between him and the chief, she had to wonder what the rest of the guys in Nugget looked like.

"Good people," he said. "But gossipy as all get out. Great skiing a half-hour from here in Glory Junction. If you like to hike, there's a ton of trails. Great fishing and hunting, too. Lucky Rodriguez will hook you up with a horse over at his cowboy camp if you like to ride. It's a great way to see the countryside." He nudged his square jaw at her. "What are you into?"

"I like to run." And until she'd gotten promoted to the robbery-homicide division, she'd like to dance. Salsa. "Go to the gym."

"No gym here. But there's a yoga studio on the square. And you can run anywhere. It's safe as long as you don't mess with the wildlife. A couple of the women in town organize bowling parties over at the Ponderosa. It's probably slower paced than what you're used to, but it's a welcoming little town. So, you taking the job?"

"Yeah, I'm pretty sure I am."

"LAPD, huh?"

"Uh-huh. How'd you know?"

He chuckled. "Everyone here knows everything about everybody. What they don't know, they make up."

She waited for him to ask her why she'd left the department, but he didn't. Maybe the whole town knew already.

"I've got a wine and cheese service in thirty minutes. You renting the place?" He cocked his head at the apartment next to his."

"I haven't looked inside yet." She wasn't about to tell him the truth. "I was hoping for something a little closer to town."

"You can walk from here," he said, and started getting inside his van. "I'm over at the Lumber Baron Inn if you have any more questions."

She waved goodbye, then let herself inside the apartment to have a look around. It wasn't much, but it was roomier than what she'd had in LA. It had a decent sized living room and the bedroom would easily fit her queen bed. The bathroom was right off the kitchen. A funky location. She assumed the layout was what people called a railroad apartment because it resembled a passenger train car. It made sense, given that this was a railroad town. The chief hadn't been lying when he'd said the place was clean. More like spotless.

After Donner Road she headed to the subdivision called Sierra Heights. For a gated community the security sucked. She got right past the empty guard kiosk and zipped around, looking at the mammoth houses, their elaborate decks and giant yards. The chief had been correct in assuming that this place was too rich for her blood. Gorgeous, though. If she had the money, she'd make this her hood.

On Main Street she found a real estate office and popped inside. A woman named Carole said she had a couple of rentals Sloane could look at, but her hopes deflated after the house tour. The first stunk like a dog kennel and gave Sloane the creeps. Lots of chain-link fence and gaudy statuary in the yard, including one of those boy-peeing fountains. The second was a cabin that hadn't been winterized. The third would've been perfect. It was right in town with a sweet little rose garden backyard, but it was also for sale. The owner would only rent it on the condition that it be made available for showings. No go. Not only didn't Sloane want the inconvenience, but she didn't want to have to move again in a few months.

Disappointed, she drove back to the Lumber Baron. If only she'd found an apartment or a house half as comfortable as her room at the inn. The bed-and-breakfast was pretty spectacular with its period architecture and elegant furnishings. Sloane hadn't realized that the chief's wife owned the place until he'd mentioned it during their interview. Last night, when she'd gotten in, there was only the young guy, Andy, manning the desk. And this morning she'd rushed out to meet Jake for breakfast at the Ponderosa, the kooky Western restaurant/bar/bowling alley across from the inn on the town square.

When she walked into the lobby she nearly collided with Brady, who looked to be on his way out. The man had changed into jeans and a long-sleeved waffle knit shirt—and was seriously buff. Not like a gym rat, but like a guy who spent a lot of time outdoors. Mile-wide chest, big pecs, flat stomach and muscular arms.

"You staying here?" he asked by way of a greeting.

"Yeah. I checked in last night. Is that hamburger place any good? I was thinking of grabbing something before it closes and bringing it up to my room."

"It's good," he said. "Or if you want to be around people you can go to the Ponderosa for happy hour. The food's good there, too."

She wondered where he was off to since other than bowling there didn't seem to be anything to do. Unless he was headed to the Ponderosa's happy hour or to meet a girlfriend.

"Okay. Thanks."

"Chicken-fried steak and eggs for breakfast," he said, grabbing a down jacket from a closet behind the check-in counter and slinging it over his shoulder. "Catch you later."

"You must be Sloane." A dead ringer for the beautiful woman in the wedding picture on the chief's desk came into the lobby. "I'm Maddy, Rhys's wife."

"Nice to meet you."

"You taking the job?" Whoa, people around here didn't beat around the bush.

"I'm gonna sleep on it, but probably . . . yeah."

Before Sloane knew what was happening, Maddy enveloped her in a hug. "You don't know how happy that makes me." Sloane didn't usually get this kind of reception from the wives of other cops. "It'll just be nice to have a fourth person on deck, you know what I mean?"

Yeah, they need someone to work graveyard and holidays.

"Sure," she said, and tried to pry herself loose from Maddy's embrace. The woman was stronger than she looked.

"Rhys said you might be taking the apartment on Donner Road. That used to be my apartment. It's where Rhys and I fell in love."

"Really?" A little TMI, but sweet just the same. For whatever reason it made her feel better about Shepard. She didn't know why he'd left such a bad taste in her mouth in the first place. The chief had seemed completely professional—even decent.

Then again, they all did until you broke the code of silence. That's when the people who you thought had your back left you to fend for yourself while the world blew up.

"It's a great apartment," Sloane said. "Conveniently located, clean, spacious. But to be completely honest, I feel a little weird about having my boss as a landlord."

Maddy nodded. "Rhys feels weird about it too. We decided that if you take the apartment that we'd have my brother, Nate, act as the go-between. Nate and I co-own the Lumber Baron."

"How would that work?" Sloane asked, thinking that this might be a more comfortable solution.

"You would just have all your dealings concerning the apartment—rent, deposit, repairs—with Nate or my sister-in-law, Samantha. Rhys and I would stay out of the picture."

That seemed better—less company townish. "I'll let Chief Shepard know what I decide tomorrow, then."

"Great. And, Sloane, I do think you'll really like it here. I know you're from Los Angeles and a small town like this can be a culture shock, but it's a wonderful place. People look out for one another. I came from San Francisco and never thought I'd get used to the slow pace of small-town living. What I found was that the big city had been pretty darn alienating. And of course I'm biased, but I think my husband is a wonderful boss."

Sloane laughed. Jake had said the same thing and she respected his opinion. The man had been a cop while Sloane was still a toddler. And unlike her, he'd survived the snake pit.

"It'll take some getting used to but I'm up for the challenge." She wanted to stay positive.

"And Brady will be a great neighbor. If you're lucky, he'll cook for you."

Sloane thought if he was that good of a cook he wouldn't be stuck in the sticks, working at a bed-and-breakfast instead of running his own restaurant. But she kept that to herself.

"He seems nice." And hopefully quiet, since they'd be living right on top of each other and her hours were bound to be odd as the new hire.

"Very," Maddy said. "We're crazy about him."

Sloane bet most of the female population was, anyway. After a little more small talk with Maddy, she made her way across the square to the hamburger place. It was called the Bun Boy, which cracked her up. There were walk-up and drive-through windows, but no indoor seating. Just a smattering of picnic tables on a swath of lawn, under a few big trees. Nice in summer, but way too cold this time of year. She got her food to go and took it up to her room. She probably should've gone to the Ponderosa for happy hour to get more acquainted with the town, but between her interview with the chief and all the new people she'd met today, she was talked out. Nugget was a chatty place.

She ate at the writer's desk while flipping through the channels on the flat screen. Nugget at least had cable. The food was better than expected, she thought while wolfing down a large order of seasoned curly fries. In LA, she and her girlfriends liked dining at all the trendy bistros and cafés. Sloane didn't consider herself a foodie by any stretch. Not like her friends who read the *Times* restaurant reviews religiously and traded names of hot new chefs like little boys did baseball cards. Sloane couldn't name one famous cook unless it was Paula Deen or Gordon Ramsay. But she enjoyed eating and experiencing new cuisines and flavors. Everyone in her family cooked except her. Her mother was an avid baker and her father and three brothers worked in a firehouse, where kitchen duty was as much a part of the job as putting out blazes.

She could've gone home to Chicago—her father had actually insisted on it when he found out what had happened on the job. "No one messes with a McBride," he'd said. But Sloane preferred to stand on her own two feet. So Jake's suggestion that she come here seemed like the winning option. Still, she had to wonder whether she was making a huge mistake. Having never lived in a small town, it would take a lot of adjustment. *Like what kind of place doesn't have a gym?*

The room phone rang, making Sloane jump. In LA, she'd had to change all her personal numbers. Not that that had helped. The problem with cops was that they could always find you.

With trepidation she picked up. "Hello."

"How'd it go?" Jake's reassuring voice came across the other end.

She took a deep breath. "Good. I'm planning to take it."

"Wise decision," he said. "It'll help get your confidence back. It's good work, Sloane. People here are appreciative of what we do. You'll be welcomed with open arms."

She thought about Maddy and bit back a laugh. "The chief has a vacant apartment. What do you think about me taking it?"

"The place up on Donner Road? It's perfect."

She told him how the chief's brother-in-law would act as landlord to prevent any awkwardness.

"That'll work," Jake said. "But, Sloane, Rhys is a fair guy. You don't have to worry about him."

"He certainly seems to be in a rush to get me here. Is there something you guys aren't telling me?"

"Nah. He liked you from the phone interview—likes your résumé, too. Most of the candidates we get up here are retirees. Rhys wants young blood."

"Looks like a lot of cowboys up here going by all the hats and boots in the Ponderosa this morning. Will I have trouble with the town accepting a female cop?"

Jake laughed. "These are ranching people, not Neanderthals. You'll do just fine."

"I'm meeting Connie for lunch tomorrow. What's her story?"

"She grew up here, started up the department with Rhys, and is a coffee snob—her sister lives in Seattle. She's an excellent dispatcher, has a smart mouth, and we love her to death. I'm glad you're having lunch with her. She knows where all the bodies are buried. What are your plans for dinner tomorrow?"

"I haven't thought that far ahead," Sloane said.

"Cecilia and I would like to have you over. She's a marvelous cook and desperately wants to meet you."

Sloane accepted the invitation and Jake gave her directions to his house before signing off. Instead of going straight to bed, Sloane decided to take a soak in her slipper tub. Since she'd never bathed in one, the charming clawfoot had called to her the first time she'd seen it. Everything about the inn did. It was just so warm and inviting.

On her way to the bathroom she swiped her cell off the bed and checked emails. The first one was from her parents who wanted to know how the trip had gone. All three of her brothers had left texts, demanding the scoop on Nugget.

But it was the last message, marked urgent, that chilled her to the bone and convinced her that the faster she got out of LA, the better.

"Sloane McBride, you can't hide. We're coming to get you."

Printed in the United States
by Baker & Taylor Publisher Services